D1741960

Please Return To:

RAGE OF THE INNOCENT

Frederick E Smith

Novels by the same author:

OF MASKS AND MINDS
LAWS BE THEIR ENEMY
LYDIA TRENDENNIS
THE SIN AND THE SINNERS
THE GROTTO OF TIBERIUS
THE DEVIL BEHIND ME
THE STORM KNIGHT
WATERLOO
THE WIDER SEA OF LOVE
THE WAR GOD
A KILLING FOR THE HAWKS (American Literary
Award)
THE TORMENTED
THE OBSESSION

Novels in the same series:

633 SQUADRON
633 SQUADRON: OPERATION RHINE MAIDEN
633 SQUADRON: OPERATION CRUCIBLE
633 SQUADRON: OPERATION VALKYRIE
633 SQUADRON: OPERATION COBRA
633 SQUADRON: OPERATION TITAN

SAFFRON'S WAR
SAFFRON'S ARMY

THE PERSUADERS: BOOKS I, II, and III.

RAGE OF THE INNOCENT

A novel by
Frederick E Smith

PIATKUS

Copyright © Frederick E Smith 1986

First published in Great Britain in 1986
by Judy Piatkus (Publishers) Limited
of 5 Windmill Street, London W1

British Library Cataloguing in Publication Data

Smith, Frederick E (Frederick Escreet)
  Rage of the innocent.
  I. Title
  823'.914[F]   PR6069.M482

ISBN 0 86188 538 4

Typeset by Phoenix Photosetting, Chatham
Printed in Great Britain by Mackays of Chatham Ltd

To my Mother and Father.

Members of the bravest and most enduring generation this country has known.

The author wishes to acknowledge his debt to the following autobiographies and works of reference:

My mother's autobiography.

The Way We Were 1900–1914	James McMillan (William Kimber)
History of the 1st World War	Purnell
In the Cannon's Mouth	P. J. Campbell (Hamish Hamilton)
With a Machine Gun to Cambrai	George Coppard (Imperial War Museum)
Machine Gunner 1914–1918	C. E. Crutchley (Bailey Bros and Swinfen)
The Face of Battle	John Keegan (Penguin Books)
The Western Front 1914–1918	John Terraince (Hutchinson)
The War Illustrated	(Amalgamated Press)
The 1st Hundred Thousand	Ian Hay (William Blackwoods and Sons)

PART 1

Chapter 1

The boy, half-hidden in the hedge, was sitting very still. Even when a fly landed on his forehead, he did not stir. Only his eyes moved. They were playing back and forth across a field of young corn that lay like a sunlit lake before him.

The fly moved down to his nose. He grimaced and the insect flew away. The hum of summer pervaded the silence. With the sun a glowing cauldron above and the tall trees motionless, time seemed as hushed and expectant as the boy himself.

A lark with a seed in its mouth swooped down and disappeared into a nearby tuft of grass. At the same moment a ripple showed on the silken surface of the corn. As the ripple moved towards the hedge, the boy held his breath.

It was a young weasel that appeared a few seconds later, its nose twitching for any scent of danger. Taking courage, it moved out of the corn and began rummaging for rodents in the grass beneath the hedge. Watching it, the boy took in its red-brown fur and its caution. It searched about for a half-minute, then suddenly turned and dived back into the corn.

The boy heard the reason a moment later: the neigh of

a horse and the rumble of cartwheels in the lane behind him. Relaxing he settled back again to his vigil.

He had come from the city two days ago. It had been market day there and the main road he had taken to the railway station had been alive. Barrel organs had been hammering out the latest tunes, horses and buggies had clattered past, dray horses had heaved and dragged along carts laden with sacks or barrels.

The pavements were equally crowded. Women in ankle-length skirts were everywhere. Some, in the height of fashion, paused elegantly to gaze into shop windows. Others, dowdy and careworn, shouted shrilly at their gaggles of excited children. Men in stove-pipe trousers strolled among them, some lifting their bowler hats, others pausing to pass the time of day. Few if any noticed the sweating workmen in collarless shirts and tattered waistcoats who humped their wares into shops and warehouses. The summer air was heavy with noise, bustle, and the smell of sweat and manure.

With time to spare before his train left, the boy paused outside a confectioner's shop. The shelves were full of dummy samples of the sweets within, bars of chocolate, bottles of boiled sweets, and tins of toffees. As the boy's eyes settled on a display of whipped cream walnuts, the morning sun reflected his image from the glass.

Harry Miles was a boy of fourteen years with a thin but wiry body. His shirt and shorts, although clean, were worn and frayed. His features were both intelligent and sensitive, with a well-shaped mouth and nose topped by a mass of curly black hair. It was a face full of the wonder and promise of life and yet there was a solemnity about the boy's brown eyes that suggested he was already aware of its mendacity.

He showed no envy as he stared into the window. Envy had played no part in Harry Miles' upbringing. As

4

he turned away, the sound of martial music caught his attention. Behind him a policeman was holding up the traffic. The reason became clear a few seconds later when a military band swung out on the main road. It was followed by a section of soldiers, smart in their red-striped trousers and round black hats.

Men, women and children crowded to the pavement edge as they swung past. A cheer rose and ran along the road. The Boer War was still fresh in memory and the local regiment had played their part in it. In reply the band began playing *Boys of the Old Brigade*.

The boy stood watching, his young eyes glowing at the spectacle. Then, as the music began to fade and he picked up his suitcase again, a voice sounded at his elbow. 'Hello, Harry, lad. Where are you off to?'

The speaker was a man in his forties, tall and lean with a somewhat melancholy face. Harry recognised him as the owner of the small pharmacist shop at the corner of his street. 'Hello, Mr Jackson. I'm going to my grandpa's. At Burton Stather.'

'How long for, lad?'

'A week, Mr Jackson. I've a week there every year.'

'Aye, I've heard your mother say. You like it there, don't you?'

The boy's face shone. 'Oh, yes. I wish we lived in the country.'

'When did you break off school, lad?'

'Last Friday. But I'm not going back. I begin my apprenticeship in September.'

'What're you going to do until then?'

'Look for a job. Will you keep an eye open for me, Mr Jackson?'

'Aye, 'course I will, lad. If I hear of anything I'll tell your mother. What time's your train?'

'Eleven o'clock,' the boy told him.

5

The man pulled out a huge silver watch from his waistcoat pocket. 'Twenty-five minutes to. You'd best get moving, hadn't you?'

Harry nodded and picked up his suitcase again. Jackson hesitated, then fished into his trouser pocket. 'Here, lad. Take this.'

The boy gaped at the coin he was offered. 'It's a threepenny bit, Mr Jackson.'

'I know that, lad. Buy yourself some sweets with it.'

Harry's excitement turned into doubt. 'My mum says no one should take money they don't earn.'

Knowing the boy's mother, Jackson could believe it. A small thin figure with the complexion of an ailing woman, she nevertheless had the sweetest smile he had ever seen. A woman who had lost her breadwinner three years ago and yet with sacrifice and a deep religious faith had managed to turn out a son like this. He ruffled the boy's curly hair. 'If that's worrying you, lad, you can always come round and sweep out my shop when you come home. Now off you go and have a good holiday.'

The cart creaked past the boy's hiding place, low country voices were heard, then the sounds died away. The hum of high summer returned, a hypnotic note that made Harry think of the organ his Grandma Agnes sometimes played in the village chapel.

A bee swept along the hedge, searching the dog roses for nectar. It was followed by a second lark that fluttered down and sank into the grass. As it dabbed down with its beak, the boy imagined he could hear the hungry cries of its fledglings.

Fascinated, he wanted to move closer but was afraid of disturbing the parent lark. Thirty seconds later the nurturing bird flew away, to be replaced almost immediately by its mate.

The sun moved imperceptibly across the sky. Lapping the shadow of the hedge, the sunlight moved from the boy's boots to his bare legs. It took the sound of a human voice, distant but shrill, to break the spell.

Voices could now be heard advancing along the lane, one a man's baritone, the other a boy's. As they drew level with the nest, the lark in attendance took alarm and began climbing into the cloudless sky, trilling its decoy song as it went.

Harry's eyes followed it. Its song, washing down, brought him a pleasure he could not define. As he shaded his eyes to watch it, there was a sharp report from the far side of the hedge.

Instantly the trilling ceased. The bird, vibrantly alive at one moment, became a shapeless bundle of feathers that plummeted down into the cornfield. The man gave a laugh. 'Well done, Master Michael. I thought you were wasting your shot on that one.'

The boy's reply was full of self-deprecating pride. 'It wasn't too bad a shot, was it, Burgess? I think it was further away than the pigeon.'

'Aye, it was. And it was on the wing too. You're coming on well, lad. In no time at all you'll be as good a shot as your father.'

'Do you think I will, Burgess?'

'I know it, lad. Just keep on practising and you'll show 'em all up when the season starts.'

The shot had momentarily stunned Harry Miles. Then, jumping to his feet, he ran to the gate and climbed over it.

The man and the boy were twenty yards down the lane. The man, wearing gamekeeper's clothes, was in his middle forties and burly of build. The boy, carrying a shotgun, was dark-haired, good-looking, and well-dressed.

Harry ran towards them. 'What did you shoot that lark for? It wasn't doing you any harm.'

The boy, about his own age, stared at him, then laughed. 'Who are you?'

'I'm Harry Miles. Why did you shoot that lark? Didn't you know it was feeding its young.'

The other boy was taking in his bare legs and scuffed boots. He turned with a laugh to the gamekeeper. 'What's he talking about? Who is he?'

Burgess was grinning. 'He's the grandson of old Leason. One of your father's tenant farmers.' He turned to the distressed Harry. 'You want to watch your tongue, lad. Don't you know who you're talking to?'

The needless killing had brought the boy near to tears. 'I don't care who he is. He oughtn't to go about shooting birds like that. Why didn't you stop him?'

Burgess's grin turned into a frown. 'Don't start getting cheeky, lad, or you'll end up with a thick ear. Master Michael's father is Sir Henry Chadwick. He owns all the land round here, so his son can shoot whatever he pleases. Anyway, what were you doing in that field? Don't you know it's private property?'

'It doesn't give him the right to kill things for fun.' Harry cried. 'It was cruel and stupid.'

Burgess's face darkened. 'All right, lad, that's enough. Run off now before I give you a hiding for your cheek.'

At the far side of the hedge the second lark had returned and was singing its alarm song almost above the lane, Occupied with Burgess, Harry did not notice Michael grin and lift his shotgun. The report that rang out made Harry start and turn. He was just in time to see the lark, which had not been killed instantly, fluttering

8

and spiralling down into the hedge.

Michael Chadwick's laugh was mocking. 'It's your fault, Miles. I wouldn't have shot it if you hadn't interfered.'

With a cry of distress, Harry ran forward and tried to take the shotgun from the boy. In their struggle the two of them lost their footing and as they hit the ground the shotgun struck Michael across the face, bringing a gasp of pain from him.

The grin left Burgess' face as he saw the two boys rolling over in the dusty lane. Cursing, he seized them and dragged them apart. As he twisted Harry's arms behind the boy's back, Michael pulled out a linen handkerchief and held it to his nose. As he lowered it, soaked in blood, he gazed in disbelief at Burgess. 'Look what the little beast has done! I think he's broken my nose.'

Apprehensive at the condition of his ward, Burgess tightened his grip on the struggling Harry. 'Why don't you punch him back, Master Michael? It's what he deserves.'

The boy dabbed again at his streaming nose. Then, with a cry of outrage, he ran forward and struck at Harry's face. As he was about to strike again Harry kicked out and caught him on the shin with a boot. Crying with frustration the boy snatched up his gun and aimed it at Harry.

Burgess' voice immediately changed. 'Hold it, lad! You don't point a gun at anybody, even if it's empty. Put it down.'

Michael's good-looking face was disfigured by blood and fury. 'I won't. It'd serve the little brute right if I shot him.'

The gamekeeper released Harry and walked towards the boy with outstretched hand. 'Now do as I say, lad. Give me the gun.'

9

Michael backed away, still pointing the gun at Harry. 'No. I want him arrested, Burgess. He struck me without reason. That's assault, isn't it?'

'Lad, you don't want the police dragged into this. It's not worth it.'

The boy's voice turned threatening. 'If you won't take him to the police, I shall go myself.'

'But lad, you'd only get your father into trouble. At your age you're not supposed to be out in public with a shotgun.'

Michael showed contempt. 'Do you think they'd dare to take action against my father?'

'I don't know about that, but it would embarrass him. And for that he'd blame us both. Give me the gun, Master Michael. It's for the best, believe me.'

For a long moment it seemed the boy would not obey. Then he shoved the gun at the gamekeeper and turned on Harry who, ignoring his own bleeding nose, was searching in the hedge for the wounded bird. 'You're not getting away with this, Harry Miles. I'm going to tell my father to see old Leason. He should never allow ruffians like you on the estate.'

Harry turned sharply. 'It's not my grandfather's fault! He doesn't even know I'm over here.'

Sensing the boy's Achilles' heel, Michael laughed. 'You should have thought about that before you began hitting people, shouldn't you?'

Harry was showing distress again. 'You can't get him into trouble It wouldn't be fair.'

There was triumph in Michael's laugh now. 'I'll bet you ten to one my father will be round today. See if I'm not right.'

Before Harry could protest further, the gamekeeper caught Michael's arm and led him away. Harry watched them for a moment, then resumed his search for the bird. Three minutes later, scratched by thorns, he found the small creature crumpled and still in the fork of a hawthorn branch. Wiping tears and blood from his face, the boy made his slow way back along the lane to his grandparents' cottage.

Chapter 2

Agnes Leason paused by the boy's chair, peered down at his face, and gave a tut-tut of concern. 'Let me put some steak on that eye, lad. It's going to look bad tomorrow if we don't.'

Harry lowered the book he was reading. 'It's all right, Gran'ma. It is, honestly.'

An impatient voice came from the far side of the fireplace where, in spite of the warmth of the summer evening, a fire was burning. 'Leave him be, Agnes. You're fussing too much.'

The woman, in her fifties, glanced round with equal impatience. 'You're forgetting the lad goes back home in a couple of days. We don't want Polly to think we haven't been looking after him, do we?'

The man seated by the fireplace gave a grunt. Ten years older than his wife, he had a churchwarden pipe in his mouth and a pair of steel-rimmed glasses perched on the end of his nose. His clothes, a tattered waistcoat and a pair of corduroy trousers tied by string at the ankles, were those of a farmworker. Removing his pipe and lowering the newspaper he was reading, he turned with some scorn on the woman.

'Polly's not daft. She knows you can't stop young lads

12

from fighting.'

'It's all right you talking. You haven't taken a proper look at the lad. And you know how Polly feels about fighting.'

Muttering something beneath his breath, Bill Leason rose and went over to the boy. Finding the evening light inadequate, he brought over a paraffin lamp and peered down again. His laugh was a mixture of amusement and derision. 'You're fussing about nothing, you silly old fool. The swelling will go down in a couple of days and then all he'll have is a shiner. Every lad gets one sooner or later. . . I'd dozens when I was his age.'

With the confidence of a long relationship behind her, Agnes sniffed scornfully. 'Aye, I know all about you and the trouble-maker you were. Your mother told me often enough. But Harry's different. Aren't you lad?'

Bill Leason's glance returned to the embarrassed boy. Although it contained affection, some element in it suggested the man was not displeased by the boy's condition. 'Tek no notice of her, Harry. She's a silly woman: she can't understand how young lads are.' He paused, then grinned. 'How was the other lad when you finished, Sir Henry's son?'

'I don't know,' Harry muttered.

'Had he a nose bleed?'

'Yes. He said it was broken.'

'Naw, that'd just be his imagination.'

'I don't know,' Harry muttered. 'The shotgun seemed to hit him when we both fell down.' His grandfather's expression brought his fears to the surface again. 'It can't cause you any trouble, can it?'

Leason avoided his wife's eyes. 'No, course it can't, lad. Squire Chadwick's a fair man. He knows men aren't responsible for the things lads do. And from all you've told us it was a fair fight.' Placing the oil lamp back on the table, he walked to his chair and picked up his pipe. Finding it had gone out, he struck a match and held it to the bowl. His words came just as the boy was relaxing. 'The only thing he might feel is that it was a bit of a daft thing to fight about.'

The boy stared at him. 'But he killed those larks for nothing. All they were doing was feeding their young.'

Bill Leason puffed out smoke. 'They were still only birds, lad. You forget you're in the country. If folks hit one another everytime someone killed a wild creature, we'd be fighting all the time.'

Realising he was being criticised, however mildly, the boy showed distress. Seeing it, Agnes intervened quickly. 'Your Grandpa isn't blaming you, lad. He knows you've still to learn country ways. But I'd steer clear of that Michael Chadwick in the future, if I were you. They say he's a mean and spiteful lad. Only don't tell anyone we've said so.'

At that moment there was a clatter of hooves on the cobbled lane outside. As they stopped outside the cottage Agnes put a hand to her throat. Reading her mind, Leason laid his pipe on the hearth and walked to the door. Before opening it, he glanced at Harry. 'Stay in here, lad, while I see who it is.'

Running to the window, the boy watched him walk across the small cobbled yard and open the gate. A moment later a horse and rider entered. As Leason re-latched the gate, a hushed voice sounded at Harry's elbow. 'I thought so. It's the squire. Are you sure that's all that happened, Harry? You didn't do anything else to the lad, did you?'

Harry, whose bruised face was as pale as Agnes' by this time, shook his head. 'No. Only what I told you.'

Outside the two men were talking while the squire tethered his horse to an apple tree. He was a tall man

14

with a stomach that his tight-fitting jodhpurs were having difficulty in containing. Nodding at Leason's question, he followed the farmer to the cottage.

They entered the kitchen a few seconds later. Leason glanced at the nervous Agnes. 'Sir Henry, Mam. He wants a word with the lad.'

The woman bobbed her head at the squire. The lamp-light showed him to be a man in his late forties with ruddy, confident features. He raised his riding crop to Agnes, then turned his eyes on the boy standing alongside her. 'Is this the lad?'

The farmer nodded. 'Aye. He comes here most years on his holidays.'

'How old is he?'

'Fourteen, sir. He left school this year an' he's waiting to start his apprenticeship.

'What as? A pugilist?'

Leason was unsure whether to smile or not. 'No, sir. A carpenter.'

The squire took a couple of steps towards the boy. His voice contained a mixture of amusement and censure. 'So you're the lad who struck my son today. Do you know where I had to take him this afternoon?'

The pale-faced boy shook his head. 'No, sir.'

'You fractured his nose, lad. His mother made me take him to hospital. He says you started the fight. Why?'

The boy's words came out breathlessly. 'He shot two larks, sir. They weren't doing anyone any harm. They were feeding their young.'

Sir Henry gave Leason a quizzical glance. 'Does he always go around striking people who carry shotguns and shoot birds?'

'No, sir. He's not caused any trouble before. But his mother says he can't bear to see things killed. I've tried

15

to tell him how it is in the country but he can't get used to it.'

'He didn't have any cause to shoot them,' the boy muttered. 'And anyway I didn't do anything until he shot the second one. That was after I told him to stop.'

The squire nodded. 'That sounds a bit like my lad. He doesn't like being told what to do. Not even by me. Just the same, boy, you can't go round hitting people in the face and putting them in hospital. My boy said you hit him without warning. Is that true?'

'No, sir. I only fought him after he'd shot the second bird. And it was the gun that broke his nose when we fell.'

Sir Henry moved forward and examined the boy's swollen face. He showed satisfaction as he stood back. 'It looks as if my lad gave as much as he got. Only he said you kicked him when you were fighting. Is that true?'

'No, it isn't.'

'He's got a damn great bruise on his shin, lad. How did he get that? Come on, I want the truth. Did you kick him or not?' When Harry still did not answer, his voice rose angrily. 'Are you defying me, lad? I'm asking you a question. Answer me!'

At that the boy's face lifted. 'Yes, I did kick him, sir. But only because he hit me when the man was holding my arms.'

There was a gasp of shock from Leason. Sir Henry showed disbelief. 'What did you say?'

The boy's face was pale but he did not flinch. 'He hit me when my arms were held. That's why I kicked him.'

Purple patches appeared in the man's cheeks. He was breathing hard when he turned to Leason. 'Does he often tell lies like this?'

The farmer was showing dismay. 'No, sir. He's always been as honest as the day's long.'

16

The squire glanced back at the boy, then jerked his riding crop at the door. 'Come outside! I want a word with you!' With a nod at Agnes, he walked into the yard.

Leason turned to the boy. 'Is that the truth? Did he hold your arms?'

Harry blinked back his tears. 'Yes, 'course he did.'

William laid a hand on his trembling shoulders. 'Then it's all right, lad. I'll come outside with you.'

They found the squire standing alongside his horse. His heavy frown settled on the pale-faced Harry. 'Now you listen to me, boy. I came here tonight only because my wife threw a fit when my son returned home and she insisted I found out what had happened. As far as I'm concerned, a son of mine has to look after himself and if he gets his nose bloodied in a fight, that's his own stupid fault. But what you've said changes everything. You're as good as accusing him of being a coward and I'm not letting that idea spread round the estate. I want the two of you to have a fair fight to settle this thing once and for all. Are you willing to do that?'

Leason broke in before the boy could answer. 'He's not a scrapper, sir. His mother's a good Chapel woman: she's never allowed him to fight.'

'Then it's about time he took some notice of her, isn't it?' Sir Henry said dryly. 'But that's beside the point. No one's going around saying my son's a coward. I want a fair fight and I want nothing said about this entire affair until the fight's over. I'm holding you to that, Leason. You, your wife, and this lad here are to keep it to yourselves. Do I make myself clear?'

The farmer sighed and inclined his head. 'Aye, all right, sir.'

Giving a terse nod, Sir Henry swung onto his saddle and pointed with his riding crop at the gate. 'All right, boy. Open the gate.'

Harry moved to obey, then halted. He received a stare. 'Didn't you hear me? Open the gate!'

Although Harry looked close to tears, he did not move. Sir Henry stared at Leason. 'What's the matter with the lad? Is he deaf or just daft?'

The boy turned and muttered something to Leason. The farmer had never looked more embarrassed when he glanced back at the squire. 'It's not that, sir. It's something he promised his father. He thinks you ought to say please.'

Sir Henry's jaw dropped. 'What!'

'It was his father, Squire. He used to tell the lad that every man has the right to good manners.'

The squire's face was a study. 'What was his father? One of those damned Socialists?'

'I don't know, Squire. He was a quiet man when he came here and never said much. But I think he had his own ideas on some things.'

'Own ideas?' Sir Henry's eyes turned on the pale Harry. 'Now I see where this one gets 'em from. You've some odd characters in your family, Leason.'

'His mother's my family, Squire. Not his dad.' Then, ashamed of his protest, Leason went on quickly: 'All the same I always found him a fair and likeable man.'

'Likeable? Raising trouble and discontent? The fellow was a damned Socialist, I tell you.' Sir Henry turned his eyes back on the boy. 'And you obviously take after him, boy. I ought to put this riding crop around your shoulders but I've every reason to think my boy'll teach you manners when the two of you meet.' His voice turned richly sarcastic. 'Now open that gate – please!'

Without a word Harry ran forward and drew it open. Sir Henry spurred his horse through it, then reined back. 'You'll be hearing from me. you little scoundrel, as soon as my son's fit to fight. And if you say anything about this or refuse to meet him, I'll make it hot for you and anyone who houses you.'

Glancing at Leason, who had winced at the threat, the man spurred his horse again and galloped away.

Chapter 3

The young girl was peering eagerly from the window down the long garden that ran behind the house. She was a girl of quick, vibrant movements with bright blue eyes and golden hair that hung down to her waist. At intervals she would glance round impatiently at a gilt clock that stood on the sitting room mantelpiece.

Her mother was sitting sewing in an armchair. In her middle thirties Ethel Hardcastle was a somewhat prim figure with thick brown hair piled up on her well-proportioned head and held in position by whalebone combs. The effect was enhanced by the high collared blouse she was wearing and the precise movements of her hands as she embroidered a pillow case. A slim woman of medium height, she was handsome rather than beautiful and the image she offered to the world was that of a calm, well-ordered personality.

Ethel's only other child, Connie, was sitting at a piano practising a simple melody. Two years older than her sister, Mary, she was heavier of build and lacked her quick-silver movements. Her hair was the same shade as her mother's and although she was not unattractive, she wore an air of discontent that sat badly on the shoulders of a sixteen-year-old girl.

At the moment her attention was more on her sister at the window than on the piano keys and every now and then a discord would marr her performance. The wince her mother made on her third mistake hinted that the composed image Ethel liked to present to the world might hide a more highly-strung personality. Lowering her embroidery, she turned to the pianist.

'Connie, what on earth are you doing? Miss Walton's going to have a fit if you play that way next week.'

Connie ceased playing and glanced resentfully at her sister. 'It's Mary. I can't play with her bobbing up and down like that. It puts me off.'

Ethel turned to the younger girl. As with Connie, something in her voice suggested disapproval that went deeper than her complaint. 'She's right, Mary. Anyone would think the Mayor was visiting us. Your father never gets home before six o'clock, so sit down and stop fidgeting.'

The girl opened her mouth to reply, then dropped instead into a chair and picked up a book. Ethel glanced back at Connie. 'Now try to concentrate. You're supposed to have that piece perfect by Tuesday.'

The uncertain music commenced again. It was interrupted half a minute later by the sound of a door closing. With a cry of excitement, Mary jumped out of her chair and with hair and long dress flying, ran out into the rear quarters of the house. As Connie stopped playing again, her excited voice could be heard, answered by the deeper voice of a man.

The girl burst back into the room a minute later, followed by a man in his middle forties. The girl's bright, intelligent face was full of excitement. 'Dad says Mr Barlow *is* leaving. And I can have his job. Isn't that wonderful?'

Ethel Hardcastle stiffened. Across the room there was

the jangle of piano keys, then Connie's complaining voice. 'It's not fair. Why should she get an easy job like that when I have to work in that awful dress shop? It's not fair. Is it, Mother?'

William Hardcastle turned to the tearful girl. He was well over six feet tall, with the kind of girth that Victorians and Edwardians liked to call well-built. His hair was dark with greying streaks and he sported a large walrus-type moustache. With his high winged collar and double-breasted broadcloth suit, he was a man of considerable presence. His voice, Northcountry in accent like the rest of his family, contained a mixture of irritation, reproach and patience.

'Don't talk silly, Connie. Mary's going to work just as hard as you. Harder, more likely, because I don't keep shop hours like Mrs Gibson does.'

The girl gave a sob. 'It's not fair. Mother doesn't think it is either. Do you, Mother?'

Ethel, who had risen to her feet, showed some annoyance at the girl's remark. 'Don't talk to your father that way, Connie. Go upstairs and start getting changed for dinner. I'll call you when it's ready.'

The girl stared at her, then, bursting into tears, she turned and ran from the room. Ethel's eyes moved to Mary. 'You too. I've laid your dress out on the bed. Off you go.'

Afraid what persuasion her mother might use in her absence the younger girl glanced at her father for reassurance. Patting her shoulder he gave her a gentle push. 'Do as your mother says. We've plenty of time to talk about the job later.'

Reluctantly the girl left the room and closed the door behind her. Avoiding Ethel's eye, William walked over to a large mahogany cabinet. 'Like a sherry before dinner, Ethel?'

'No, thank you, William.' Ethel watched him pour himself a large whisky. Her eyes followed him to a chair into which he lowered his eighteen stone with a sigh of relief. 'Do you think you should drink like that, William? You know what Armstrong said.'

William half drained his glass before replying. 'Yes, I know what Armstrong said, Ethel. How long will dinner be?'

'At least half an hour, I'm afraid. I haven't got Molly tonight.'

'Why not?'

'She asked for the afternoon off. Her brother was getting married.'

William took another sip of whisky. 'I didn't know she had a brother.'

'Oh, yes. She comes from quite a large family.' Seeing William was not going to make it easy for her, Ethel drew closer. 'William, do you think you're doing the right thing in giving Mary Mr Barlow's job? She's only fourteen. Still only a child.'

Although expecting the complaint, William frowned. 'I know her age, Ethel. And I'm not taking her away from school. She'll still go to Mrs Harris every morning, like Connie did.'

'That's not the point. I don't think it's right for her to be mixing with workmen every afternoon. Goodness knows what she'll pick up.'

William had pulled a pipe from his jacket and was packing it. 'She's known most of my men for years. Both girls have. Why should she pick up things now?'

'It's different when she's working alongside them. You know it is. Men like that don't care what they say.'

'She won't be working alongside them, Ethel. All she'll do is take their stock and tally cards. Most of the time she'll be in my office working on the accounts.'

'I still think it's wrong for an impressionable young girl to mix with tradesmen and labourers. We've given both girls an expensive education these last three years and I don't think we should throw it away.'

William pretended to fumble in his pocket, then glanced up. 'You wouldn't fetch me a box of matches, would you, love? I must have left mine in the office.'

Biting her lip, Ethel turned and walked into the kitchen. Although for some time she had decided to fight William over his plans for Mary, she was all too aware how he disliked interference in his business affairs. To some extent she had found her excuse by arguing the children were as much her responsibility as his. At the same time she was handicapped emotionally, for after seventeen years of marriage Ethel was still deeply in love with her husband.

However Ethel had a will of her own and views that had been moulded and cast by her personality and her background. She was the daughter of Arthur Basset, a successful lawyer, and Doris Jones, an elementary school teacher who, in the fecundity of the age, had produced two boys and seven daughters. Ethel had been the last girl arrival and by that time other things than her mother's health had been nearing exhaustion. Swains were becoming in short supply as well as her father's ability to provide dowries for them and when, almost out of the blue, the handsome young William Hardcastle, first heir to the lucrative Hardcastle druggist business, had asked for Ethel's hand, glasses had secretely clinked in the Basset household.

It was an engagement that had brought special joy to both Ethel and her mother. In the pecking order of the day lawyers came well before elementary school teachers and in the society in which the Basset family moved, not one of Doris' daughters had been left un-

24

aware that her mother had married above her station. Ethel, who had had a special relationship with her mother, had been more sensitive to the issue than her sisters, and the condescensions and innuendoes aimed at Doris had hurt her deeply.

William, then, highly prized for his parents' money and station, had arrived like some medieval knight to drive off the dragon of class insecurity. In Castle Bountiful, Ethel had been able to forget her inhibitions and enjoy in full the birth of Connie, her first child.

Then in quick succession three blows had fallen. First Doris's health had collapsed in a massive nervous breakdown which had led to permanent confinement in a mental home. (At this time Ethel had discovered, to her secret concern, that an aunt of her mother's had suffered the same fate.)

The second blow had fallen during Mary's birth. Complications had set in, an operation had been necessary, and on regaining consciousness, Ethel had learned she could have no more children. Knowing how desperately William desired a son, and loving him as she did, Ethel had found this a cruel blow and without her knowledge it had turned her heart against Mary.

The third blow had come when William had had a bitter quarrel with his father. To this day Ethel did not know the cause but its effects had been dire, sweeping William and his family from Castle Bountiful into the harsh world of the proletariat.

The result of all this misfortune had been a return of Ethel's old insecurity. Reduced to working class conditions while William fought tooth and nail to establish a druggist business of his own, Ethel had been poorer than at any time of her life and she had reacted by isolating herself from her neighbours. The ridicule this posture had earned her had only served to feed her class consciousness and she had demanded any sacrifice from William and herself so that their daughters should receive a modicum of private education.

With William thrustful and ambitious, her banishment into the lower regions of society had not been of too long a duration but it had left its mark on Ethel and Connie. It had marked Mary too but in a different way. Perhaps because of her age or perhaps because of her different temperament, she had emerged with a sympathy towards the working class. It was a sympathy laced with condescension – because of the girl's age and environment it could hardly have been otherwise. Nevertheless it was a difference and one that was already beginning to take effect between the girl and her mother and sister.

There was another, perhaps more dangerous, time bomb in the Hardcastle household. From the time William had achieved his ambition to own his own warehouse and set up his name outside it, Mary had shown signs of inheriting his business acumen. Ethel, although she had supported William in every other way during his years of struggle, had learned to her dismay that she lacked this sense: her use to William lay in her domestic roles of housekeeper and mistress. Nor was Connie, who took after her in temperament, any different. But Mary had inherited her father's characteristics and William, denied a male heir, had consciously or unconsciously turned to her as a surrogate son. Ignoring her young years he had encouraged her to learn everything about his trade and to his delight Mary had shown herself willing. As a result, although unaware of it, Ethel was growing more and more jealous of her fourteen-year-old daughter.

Back in the sitting room William, unable to light his pipe because of his subterfuge, was now waiting impatiently for Ethel's return with matches. He could hear her talking to someone in the back garden but not the text of the conversation. As he pressed a finger down on the unlit tobacco, his thoughts switched back to Connie's tantrum and Ethel's complaint. He had expected something of the kind once he had established Barlow was leaving and he gave the post to Mary, but the scene had been no more welcome for that.

It was a pity, he thought, that Ethel could not stop making her occasional forays into his business affairs for in bed she was a devoted and ardent lover, a quality William valued highly. Surely by this time she ought to have realised her limitations. He wondered if she would have made such an issue out of it if Connie had not shown such jealousy. Connie had virtually accused him of favouritism but how could a man help such decisions when one child took an intelligent interest in his business and the other showed interest only in clothes and new hair styles?

Moreover, in Ethel's case, wasn't it a matter of the pan calling the kettle grimy? At least in pocket money and gifts he had always treated the girls equally while Ethel had always sided with Connie both with her favours and in the girl's quarrels with Mary.

In many ways William was a man of his time, a man totally confident of his decisions, the undisputed head of his household and his business. He was also a relentless churchgoer while at the same time enjoying the pleasures of the flesh, which included twice-weekly visits to a young working-class girl at the other side of town. Like the rest of his generation, William found nothing untoward in pursuing this extra marital activity while at the same time warning his daughters of their fate if either of them ever stepped off the path of sexual righteousness.

Nevertheless, on Edwardian standards he was a kind and just man – his workmen respected him and his womenfolk loved him – and it was disturbing him to know that Connie felt he was acting unfairly towards her.

His eyes wandered round the sitting room while he waited for Ethel to return. Taking stock of his acquisitions since his days of hardship was an unconscious habit of William's when he had problems, and in a less confident man would have been seen as a need for reassurance.

To his right was the Steinbeck piano bought especially for his daughters to practise on. By the fireplace was a small but comprehensive organ which William always played on Sundays. But the object on which his eyes rested with the most pride was a magnificent sideboard that ran along the wall behind his armchair. Carved with legendary Greek figures, possessing five guilded mirrors, it had cost William no less than fifty pounds when a nearby country estate had come under the hammer. It was a piece of furniture loved by Mary as well as himself. As a small child she had found fascination in the Greek figurettes and William had already determined to leave it to her in his will.

He was about to pour himself another whisky when the voices outside ceased and footsteps were heard retreating down the path. A moment later Ethel entered the room and handed him a box of matches.

'Who was it?' William asked as he lit his pipe.

'Mrs Ellis from next door. She wanted to know if we'd seen the dog at number forty-one. You know, the house at the far end of the lane.'

'Dog?'

'Yes. The Wilkinsons. They've just moved in and brought this huge Labrador with them. Mrs Ellis says it's quite fierce and frightened her little son this morning.'

William knew they were both talking to postpone the

next chapter of their argument. 'What does she want us to do?'

Ethel hesitated. 'I think she'd like us all to get up a petition if it causes any more trouble.'

'It's early days to think about that. Let's first make certain the dog is dangerous. That son of hers is a nervous little lad.'

In the brief silence that followed, the sound of quarrelling voices could be heard upstairs. They gave Ethel the excuse she needed. 'It's causing such trouble between the girls. Have you ever asked Mr Barlow if he'll stay on? If you offered him a few more shillings a week he might change his mind.'

William shook his head. 'He's moving out of town, Ethel. In any case I couldn't pay him any more for a job like that. Clerks are two a penny these days.'

'But you do have another vacancy, don't you? I heard you say the other day you wanted a handyman.'

'I want a lad to do odd jobs, yes. But what's that to do with Barlow?'

'I heard him say he'd a son leaving school this year. If you offered him a job, that might change Mr Barlow's mind.'

William made an impatient exclamation. 'Ethel, Barlow's a tally clerk and part-time accountant. He's not going to be satisfied for his son to be a glorified stable boy. In any case I think I might already have a boy for that.'

Ethel took a deep breath. 'Then let me help.'

William stared at her' 'What did you say?'

Although she was unaware of it, there was defiance in Ethel's voice. 'Let me help you. The girls can take over more of the housework and I can come over for at least a couple of hours in the mornings and afternoons. More if necessary.'

William knew he must not laugh. 'Ethel, you know it wouldn't work.'

Small red spots appeared in Ethel's pale cheeks. 'Why not?'

'It just wouldn't, that's all. You know it wouldn't.'

Ethel's lips tightened. 'You don't think I could do it, do you?'

William frowned heavily. 'I didn't say that.'

'No, but it's what you're thinking. You don't think I can do the work but you believe our fourteen year-old daughter can. Have you thought what an insult that is?'

William's temper broke. 'Now listen, Ethel. I don't have to explain what I do to you or anybody else. I'm giving the job to Mary and that's the end of it. Now will you please see to the dinner. I'm hungry and I'm sure the girls are too.'

Very stiff and erect, Ethel stood gazing at him with a pale accusing face. Then, turning abruptly, she made her way to the kitchen. Unseen by William her eyes began flooding with tears.

Left alone, William reached out for the evening newspaper, stared at it for a moment, then hurled it aside. Seeing his glass was empty, he rose and crossed over to the mahogany cabinet.

His thoughts were resentful as he refilled the glass. Why couldn't the confounded woman know her limitations and leave the business side of things to him? She took too much after her mother, a touchy, interfering woman in William's opinion, with the same insecurity and prejudices. The same wilful temper too, that in the end had brought her humiliation and tragedy.

Not wanting to think about that, William changed his mood. In other ways Ethel was good to him. She had given him magnificent support after his quarrel with his father, even if she had acted like some great lady when they'd been forced to live in a tenement house in the Hessle Road area. And didn't all men have problems with females and wouldn't those problems fade away when the girls grew older and their sibling jealousies disappeared?

Drawing comfort from the thought, William drained his glass, only to find his mood changed again. He was forty-six with a bad heart and at least three stone overweight. If Ethel had given him a son, this problem would never have arisen. As she hadn't, how could she blame him for teaching one of the girls how to run his business? He had nearly killed himself creating it. Was he supposed to let it fall into uncaring hands after his death?

If William had needed justification for his decision, he found it in that thought. At that moment, with the ignorance of women that was endemic to men of his generation, it could be safely said that William had no idea what strife and sorrow his decision that day would bring to his family and those who became linked with it. Instead, comforted by drink and convinced of the justice of his cause, William returned to his chair and waited to be called to dinner.

Chapter 4

Harry Miles climbed on to the footbridge that crossed the railway assembly yard and started across it. Beyond the road a tumble of huddled houses, narrow streets, and factory chimneys reached out to a skyline of dock cranes and anchored ships. The air was full of soot, the clang of metal, and the heavy panting of engines.

The boy noticed one of the engines making its way towards the bridge, jetting up smoke and dragging three wagons behind it. Lowering his suitcase, he waited until grey smoke billowed around him and hid the bleak view from sight. As the last wreath of smoke drifted away he picked up his suitcase and moved on. He had performed the act as long as he could remember and yet if anyone had asked Harry why, he would have been unable to tell them.

He crossed a road, passed by a small chemist shop, and turned down a long narrow street. The rows of houses had no front gardens: their front doors opened out on the uneven pavements. Here and there women wearing aprons stood in doorways chatting. Children on their school holidays were scampering about everywhere, some chasing wooden hoops which they steered with sticks, others whipping tops which occasionally catapulted away to threaten nearby windows. Half a dozen raggedly-dressed boys were dribbling an old tennis ball along the street. As Harry drew level with them, one detached himself and ran up to him. 'You just got back, Harry?' he panted. When Harry nodded, the boy went on: 'Are you goin' to have a game with us before supper?'

With his ragged clothes, skinny build, and hollow face that always seemed smudged with dirt, Gareth Evans looked the archetypal street urchin whereas in fact he had a lively and inquisitive intelligence. He was an orphan in all but name, his father having died five years ago and his mother having run off with a commercial traveller shortly afterwards. At first he had been looked after by his grandmother, who had lived with the family, then, after her death, by his sister who was eight years older. With his intelligence and interests matching Harry's own, the two of them had been close friends since the beginning of their school days.

Before Harry could answer, Gareth noticed his bruised face and whistled. 'What's been happening, boyo? You've not been fightin', have you?'

With the confrontation with his mother only minutes away, Harry was in no mood for questions. 'I'll come out if I can,' he muttered. 'It depends if I've anything to do at home.'

Gareth was grinning. 'Fightin', eh? It'll be bread and water for you, boyo.'

Frowning, Harry hurried on down the noisy street. He found his mother kneeling on the pavement outside No. 102. Keeping the front step of the hovels scrubbed and stoned was one of the few ways a woman could let the world know she kept a clean and respectable house and rain or shine, sick or well, Polly Miles seldom failed to attend to hers.

With a cart rumbling past, she failed to hear the boy approaching until he was almost at her side. A small woman with faded brown hair, hardship and ill health had prematurely aged her and yet traces of the beauty that had once bewitched Arthur Miles were still visible in her features, large, patient eyes and a shapely mouth that gave such an extraordinary sweetness to her smile.

She noticed Harry as she turned to wring out the cloth in the pail of water beside her. Her cry of welcome died when she noticed his swollen face. A hand rose to her side. 'Lad, what's happened?'

Worried about her health, it was a moment the boy had been dreading. Feeling certain that his grandparents would write home, he had known there was no way to keep the wider truth from her. 'It's nothing, Mum. Please don't make a fuss.'

Shock made the woman lean on him for a moment as she climbed to her feet. Recovering, she examined him anxiously. 'Was it an accident? Were you knocked down?'

To hide his shame, Harry picked up the pail. 'Let's go inside, Mum. I'll tell you in there.'

She followed him into the tiny living room. To delay his ordeal a little longer, Harry took the pail into the kitchen and poured its contents down the cracked sink. As his mother followed him, distress made the boy's voice impatient. 'Can't you wait a minute, Mum? It's nothing to fuss about.'

Shaking her head, Polly turned and sank into one of the frayed armchairs. A country girl, Polly Leason had married Arthur Miles, a Sheffield-born carpenter, when she was twenty-three, and in the following years had had five pregnancies. The first had produced Elsie, who was now nineteen, the second two had ended in miscarriages, the fourth had produced a baby girl who had died in its first year, and the fifth had resulted in Harry, her only boy.

Polly's poor health had not been her only problem. Although Arthur had been a quietly-spoken man, he had been ahead of his time with his Socialist views. Unlike Polly, who was a devout Methodist, he had not been a religious man but Polly had been perceptive enough to recognise that his ideals were nearer to Christian concepts than the ways if not the pretentions of Edwardian society that so punctiliously attended church or chapel attired in its Sunday best. As a result, although she had brought up her two children to be devout chapel-goers, she had found no problem in standing aside when Arthur had occasionally passed on his ideas to their children.

Her problem had been the secular one of survival, for Arthur had paid a heavy price for his egalitarianism. With employer after employer declaring they wanted no trouble-making Socialist in their workforce, Arthur had eventually been forced to work for a builder who had paid rock bottom wages and ignored every safety precaution in the statute book, and they were few enough at that time.

With Polly having to count every penny, the family had struggled on until the inevitable had happened and Arthur had fallen thirty feet from an unsecured scaffold. He had lain unconscious for a week and then died without recognising her. Two days later Polly had received a five pound note and a short letter of regret from his employer.

From that moment every day had been a fight for survival for Polly. Terrified that her two children might be taken away from her, she had taken on any task her small frame could perform. By charing and washing clothes, by nursing old people and running errands, she had somehow managed to feed and clothe her children until their schooling was over. Elsie had brought relief if not security to Polly with her wages but now another crisis was looming. The girl had fallen in love and wanted to marry. Without her wage, Polly was wondering how she could afford to let Harry take an apprenticeship.

Polly had a further worry although she had never discussed it with her children. For the last year the pain in her right side had been growing worse. She could not afford to see a doctor, nor did she dare to visit one in case he broke the news she feared. Polly could only pray to the God in whom she still miraculously believed that she could hold on until her second and last child could fend for himself.

Harry returned to the living room, noticeably avoiding his mother's eyes. As he picked up his suitcase to carry it upstairs, her worried voice checked him. 'It was a fight, wasn't it, Harry? Sit down and tell me what happened.'

All the way back in the train, the boy had been wondering how much he could tell his mother without breaking his promise. Obeying her, he dropped into the other armchair. 'It's nothing to get upset about,' he muttered. 'I just had an argument with a boy who was shooting birds.'

'You mean one of the country boys?'

Feeling that was no lie, Harry jerked his head. 'Yes. He was shooting them for fun.'

Knowing the boy's love of animals, Polly's voice softened in spite of herself. 'You still shouldn't have fought him, love. You know what the Scriptures say. You'd every right to talk to him but not to hit him.'

'I did talk to him,' Harry muttered. 'And all he did was shoot another.'

'Who was the boy? Do you know his name?'

Unused to deceiving his mother, the boy was feeling hot and cold. 'I promised not to say.' Knowing it had to come out sooner or later, he took a deep breath. 'Mum, I have to go back to Burton Stather. Not yet. But in two or three weeks.'

Polly turned pale and her hand rose to her side. 'What are you saying? That you're being taken to court?'

'No, Mum. It's nothing like that. I've just got to go back, that's all. Only for a day.'

'But what for, lad? Why won't you tell me?'

'I can't,' Harry muttered. 'I promised. But it's nothing serious. It isn't, honestly.'

'Is that the truth, Harry?'

'Yes. Cross my heart. The only thing is I'll have to get money for the train fare. But that should be all right if I can get a job until my apprenticeship starts in September.'

Polly, knowing how truthful the boy was, was beginning to relax. Realising he was bound by his promise she made no further attempt to question him. 'That's something I had to tell you. I went into Mr Jackson's shop for some sweet nitre yesterday and he told me Mr Hardcastle, the druggist on Ellerby Road, is looking for a lad. So Mr Jackson asked the traveller to mention your name.'

The boy was on his feet immediately. 'I'll go now, Mum. It's only three o'clock.'

'I think you should in case he gets someone else.' Polly Miles sighed. 'Only I haven't the tram fare to give you, love.'

'That's all right, Mum. I can still get there before they close.'

With an effort Polly rose from her chair. 'You can't go like that,' she said. 'Wash your hands and face and clean your shoes while I find you a clean shirt.'

37

Five minutes later the boy was ready. At the front door Polly eyed his face with concern. 'I don't know what Mr Hardcastle will make of those bruises. I hope he doesn't think you're a little hooligan who's always fighting.'

Impatient to go, Harry shook his head. 'Don't worry, Mum. It'll be all right.'

Polly, who only that morning had prayed the boy would get the job so that she could buy Elsie a wedding present, shook her finger at him. 'No fibs now, love. If he wants to know what happened, tell him the truth.'

The boy sighed. 'Yes, all right, Mum. I'd better go now or I might be late.'

Polly stood a moment watching the slight young figure running down the street. Then, closing the door, she entered the kitchen where three large pails of boiled clothes were standing on the stone floor. Alongside them was a wringer with a dolly tub attached. Dropping half a dozen garments into the tub, Polly began turning the large handle that agitated the wash. The work was hard and she was forced to pause every few minutes to regain her breath.

When she considered the garments ready, she fed them through the rollers of the wringer to squeeze out the last of the dirty water. She then scrubbed the garments on a washboard and ran them through blue water. Finally she fed them through the rollers again, dipped them in a fine starch, and carried them out into the tiny yard behind the house where she hung them out to dry.

Returning to the kitchen, she dropped more clothes into the dolly tub and then repeated the process. By the time the full load of washing was hanging out to dry, her face was pinched and the pain in her side insistent but she knew that a few more days of security had been won for her family. Dropping into a chair, edging round her body to ease the pain, Polly waited for her son to return.

Chapter 5

The houses at the surburban end of Ellerby Road, although semi-detached, were large and well-kept, with high attics and lace-covered windows. No. 57, Harry's objective, had its number proclaimed in shining brass both on its front gate and on its imposing oak door which also contained a brass bell handle. Hesitating a moment, Harry pulled it.

With no money for his tram fare and with William Hardcastle's warehouse at the far side of the city, the boy had been forced to run until he was breathless, walk until he recovered, then run again. He had made swift progress this way but it had done nothing for his appearance. As he heard the bell tinkling inside the large house, he tucked in his sweat-stained shirt and tried to polish his dusty boots on his socks.

Ethel Hardcastle answered the bell. She was wearing a green velvet, high-waisted dress with a whalebone collar. Although her dress, full below the waist because of its under petticoats and skirt, reached to the floor, the boy could see the peep of smart, buttoned shoes as she stepped forward.

'Yes, boy. What do you want?'

'I'm Harry Miles. I've come about the job.'

39

'Job? What job?'

Harry explained. Ethel took in his bruised face and sweat-stained clothes without relish. 'Are you sure Mr Hardcastle said he would see you?'

'Yes, Mrs. At least that's what Mr Jackson told my mum.'

Ethel walked out to the front gate and pointed down the road. 'Go down that side street and you'll find a lane on your left. It'll lead you to a large warehouse. Ask there for Mr Hardcastle.'

Harry touched his cap and hurried away. He found the fenced lane ran at the back of the main road houses. As he passed a wooden gate that led into the long back garden of No. 57, the sudden snarling of a dog caught his attention. A slight bend in the lane hid his view but as he hurried round it, he saw a large black Labrador had a girl trapped against the fence. Breaking into a run, he halted near the dog and held out his hand. 'Hello, boy. What's the matter? Come over here and tell me.'

The dog turned its head and snarled. Coaxing and soothing with his voice, Harry drew nearer. 'It's all right, boy. No one's going to hurt you.'

With the boy showing no fear, the dog was looking puzzled. Ceasing to bark, it took a few steps forward and cautiously sniffed Harry's outstretched hand. Giving it a few seconds, Harry stroked its shoulder and then began rubbing its chest. 'That's it, boy. It's all right now.' He glanced up at the girl. 'Who's it belong to?'

The girl, who was looking shaken, pointed at a nearby gate that was swinging open. 'That's where it came from. They must have left the gate open.'

With the dog placid now, Harry led it by the collar into the garden and latched the gate. 'Have you had any trouble with it before?'

'No. The people who own it only moved in a few

weeks ago. It's always barked at us when we've gone past but until now it's always been kept in the garden.'

Harry glanced back at the Labrador that was now whining behind the gate. 'It looks neglected. It makes dogs bad-tempered, just as it does people.'

Recovering from her fright, the girl was now smoothing her dress. 'Thanks for helping me. It was very brave of you.'

The boy shrugged. 'Dogs don't bite people unless they've been trained to or unless you're scared of them. Hardly any animals do. They're more scared of us than we are of them.'

The girl was taking in his appearance now. 'How have you learned things like that?'

'My grandad in the country taught me. He knows a lot about animals.'

'Do you live in the country?'

'No. I wish I did.' Harry, until a year ago oblivious of girls, was thinking how beautiful she was with her white skin, long golden hair and shining blue eyes. Suddenly feeling tongue-tied, he glanced down the lane where, behind a wide gate, he could see a two-storied warehouse and a sign proclaiming THE HARDCASTLE DRUGGIST COMPANY. 'I'll have to go now,' he muttered. 'I have to see Mr Hardcastle.'

The girl gave a start. 'Mr Hardcastle?'

'Yes. I'm goin' about a job. Do you know him?' When the girl nodded: 'What's he like?'

The girl's eyes twinkled. 'Oh, he's ever so big and bad-tempered. I wouldn't work for him if I were you.'

Harry grimaced. 'I have to if he'll take me on. My mum needs the money.' He started forward. 'I'll have to go. It's gettin' late.'

To his surprise the girl turned with him. 'I'll show you to his office.' At his expression, she laughed. 'I work for him too. I'm one of his daughters, Mary Hardcastle.'

Harry frowned. 'Why didn't you tell me?'

'You didn't ask me, did you? I didn't know you were the boy looking for the job.'

The boy realised she was right. 'Did you mean it about him being bad-tempered?'

The girl laughed as she swung open the gate. ''Course I didn't. Dad's got a temper but he doesn't lose it unless someone's disobedient.'

Harry gazed around the yard as the girl re-latched the gate. Facing the warehouse was a stable and a couple of large sheds. Beyond them was a huge pile of empty wooden crates. A long low building lay across the far end of the yard. As the boy watched, a man wearing an apron emerged from it, threw an empty box on the pile, and disappeared into the building again.

'What do you do?' Harry asked as the girl led him to a door in the warehouse.

The pride in the girl's voice could not be missed. 'I stocktake and do Dad's accounts.'

Harry was suitably impressed. 'What accounts?'

'I work out the invoices and statements. To send to customers so they know what they owe us.'

They were now inside the warehouse. Carboys packed in straw stood everywhere and huge vats lined the walls. The fascinated boy pointed at the vats. 'What's in those?'

'Piccalilli,' Mary told him. 'Or red cabbage and pickled onions. Dad makes condiments and sells them to the shops.'

Down the warehouse a brawny man wearing a hessian sack around his trousers was uncorking a carboy. Another man wearing stained blue overalls was talking to him. Both gazed curiously at Harry as the girl led him towards a flight of wooden steps. 'The one in overalls is

Mr Brown,' Mary said. 'He's the foreman and the one you'll work under if you get the job.'

'What's he like?' Harry asked.

'A bit grumpy but he's all right.' Mary's eyes were on the boy's bruised face. With the curiosity of the well-brought-up young lady about the goings-on in the forbidden world of the working class, she had wanted to ask the cause since learning that he was seeking the vacant job but until now had not found the courage. 'What happened to your eye and cheek? Have you had a fight?'

Without Harry realising it, his voice took on a hostile note. 'It's nothing. Just a few bruises, that's all.'

The girl's voice was hushed with excitement. 'Do you often have fights where you live?'

''Course we don't. I don't anyway. My mum thinks it's wrong to fight.' Before Mary could answer, Harry turned to the closed door at the top of the stairs. 'Is this where your dad is?'

Realising she was to learn no more, Mary nodded. 'I'd better find out how busy he is first. Wait here a minute.'

The girl slipped through the door and closed it behind her. A moment later Harry heard her eager young voice talking to someone inside. Re-appearing, she gave him a smile. 'It's all right. Dad says he'll see you now.'

The large room the boy entered was part office and part workroom. William Hardcastle, a formidable figure to the boy with his huge build, walrus moustache, and broadcloth suit, was seated at a desk alongside a window that overlooked the warehouse yard. Behind him were four wooden filing cabinets. A second smaller desk and empty chair stood at the opposite side of the room. The surrounding walls were covered with shelves carrying bottles and boxes of all sizes, shapes, and colours.

To Harry at that moment, William and his desk seemed larger than life. The druggist's deep voice, with its middle class Yorkshire accent, added to the over-powering impression. 'Come on in, lad! I want to take a good look at you.'

Harry advanced to the desk. Beneath his bushy, black eyebrows, William's eyes travelled over his wiry body. 'My daughter says you're Harry Miles. The lad Mr Jackson recommended. Is that right?'

'Yes, sir.'

William's eyes returned to his bruised face. 'You've been fighting, haven't you, lad? Do you fight very often?'

Harry swallowed. 'No, sir. Hardly ever.'

'I hope not, lad. We've a reputation to keep in the neighbourhood. Mr Jackson told my traveller you want a job until your apprenticeship starts. When is that?'

'September, sir. The fifteenth.'

'So you could work for me for ten weeks?'

'Yes, sir.' Before William could speak again: 'I'll work hard, sir. My mum needs the money.'

William frowned. 'Your mother's a widow, isn't she, lad?'

'Yes, sir. My dad died three years ago.'

William appraised his wiry body again. 'Do you think you could take care of our horse? Groom her, feed her, clean out her stall and the rest?'

Harry's face brightened. 'Yes, sir. I like handling animals.'

For the first time William smiled. 'So my daughter says. She's told me how you handled the dog in the lane.' He turned to Mary whose bright, young eyes had been moving anxiously from one to the other as the interview progressed. 'What do you think, lass? Shall we give him a try?'

The girl's eager voice left no doubt of her wishes. 'Yes, Dad. Please.'

William turned back to the relieved boy. 'You'll have to be here at seven o'clock every morning to get Prinny ready for the day's deliveries. And you'll have to stay on until the deliveries are over so you can rub her down and bed her for the night. In between our foreman, Mr Brown, and my wife will find you jobs to do. I can pay you seven shillings a week and give you a midday meal. Do you think that'll suit your mother?'

The boy's eyes shone. 'Yes, sir. I know it will. When can I start?'

'Tomorrow morning. But you'd better first take a look round the place and meet Mr Brown.' William turned to his daughter. 'Show him around, will you, lass?'

Mary, who was looking as delighted as the boy himself, led him outside and closed the door. 'There. I thought you'd get it. Are you pleased?'

The boy gave an eager nod. 'You helped me by telling him about the dog,' he said.

The girl laughed and ran down the steps. 'It was true, wasn't it? You did help me.'

'It wasn't anything. It wouldn't have bitten you.'

'You didn't know that at the time. I think it was very brave of you.'

They emerged into the yard. A gust of wind blew out the girl's golden hair like a fan. Once again the boy could not understand the emotions he felt. They crossed the yard to the large shed that housed the stable and the delivery rully when it was not in use. Mary wrinkled her nose. 'It smells, doesn't it? That's because we're short-staffed at the moment.'

Harry shook his head. 'It's a good smell. It makes me think of the country. How old is your horse?'

'Prinny? She's five. We only got her last year.' The girl led him down the yard to the long low shed at the end. 'We keep the volatile drugs in here.'

Harry peered inside curiously as Mary opened the door. The air was pungent with the smell of ammonia. 'What are volatile drugs?'

'Drugs that give off fumes. We're not to go in here. It's supposed to be dangerous.'

They walked back along the yard. 'Have you any sisters or brothers?' the boy asked.

'A sister. Connie. She's two years older than me.'

'Does she play with you?'

'Only when we have musical evenings. Dad plays his organ, Mum the violin, and sometimes Connie and I play duets on the piano.'

The boy looked awed. 'You've got a piano and an organ? Your dad must have barrelfuls of money.'

'Don't be silly. Lots of people round here have organs and pianos. People don't think girls are educated until they can play a musical instrument.'

They found the foreman in a middle room of the warehouse. He had donned gloves and a leather apron and was syphoning liquid from a carboy into a large vat. As steam boiled from the neck of the carboy, he waved the girl back. 'Keep out of here, Miss Mary. It's sulphuric acid I'm pouring.'

The girl retreated with Harry back into the doorway. 'Dad told me to introduce Harry to you. He's starting with us tomorrow.'

The nod the foreman gave the boy was not unfriendly. 'I'm to find work for him, am I? All right, lad, I'll go over things wi' you in the mornin'. Now get outside, both of you, or you'll end up wi' sore throats.'

Mary turned to the boy as they withdrew into the yard. 'That's all for now. I can't show you the horse and delivery cart 'cause they won't be back for another hour or two. But they'll be here when you come in the morning and Mr Brown will show you what to do.'

Harry glanced back at the lane where trees half hid the row of large houses from sight. 'What about your mum? Didn't your dad say I'll be doing some work for her too?'

Mary shook her head. 'You can meet her another day. She'll be busy getting dinner ready now.'

The boy explained how he had called at the house earlier on. 'She was wearing a green dress. Was that your mum?'

'Yes. Did she say anything to you?'

'What about?'

Mary hesitated. 'About your appearance. The bruises on your face?'

'No. She didn't say anything. Why?'

The girl looked uncomfortable. 'Mum's got a thing about neighbours. I think it's because our warehouse is so near to their houses, even though it was here before they were built. So she's particular how everyone looks and behaves, especially our workmen.'

Harry looked suddenly anxious. 'She won't try to change your dad's mind, will she? About taking me on?'

Mary hesitated, then her face cleared. 'It wouldn't matter if she did. Dad doesn't let anyone change his mind once he's made it up.'

Once again the breeze stirred the girl's hair and once again Harry felt tongue-tied. 'I'd better get back,' he muttered. 'Mum will want to know if I've got the job.'

The girl walked along the lane with him as far as the gate of No. 57. There she paused. There was a shyness in her voice now. 'So we'll see you tomorrow?'

The boy nodded. 'Seven o'clock.'

She laughed. 'We don't come until eight.'

'Eight o'clock then,' he said. He opened his mouth to say more and backed away instead. 'Cheers, then.'

'Cheerio,' she said.

He began running down the lane. Turning at the end

47

he saw she was still standing at the gate. Hesitating, he gave a wave and saw her wave back before she opened the gate and disappeared into the garden.

A wave of happiness washed over the boy. Turning on his heels he ran up the street towards the main road, skipping and dancing as he went.

Chapter 6

Lucinda Chadwick was arranging flowers in one of the large frontal windows of The Grange when she heard the unusual sound of a petrol engine. Drawing aside the fine lace curtain, she saw a large, carriage-like contraption entering the pebbled forecourt. Emitting blue smoke, it halted with a series of explosions below the steps of the main entrance.

She made an exclamation of impatience as she let the curtain fall back into place. In another mood Lucinda would have conceded that it was better for her that Henry wasted his money on mechanical novelties than on the well-fleshed females favoured by most of his peers. But today she was not in a charitable mood as the dark line between her elegant eyebrows hinted, and in such moods Lucinda Chadwick could be a formidable figure. Since hearing about the affair between Michael and the Leason boy, she had decided Henry's decision was absurd and it was her intention to tell him so at her first opportunity.

She was a tall, slender woman with a long aristocratic face. Her hobby of flower arrangements had been born during her last two years at finishing school in Switzerland. Although seven years younger than her husband she possessed none of his robust health and after the birth of Michael, their first child, she had borne no more children in spite of Henry's lusty attentions. With Henry showing concern about this single link in his lineage chain, she had been sent to specialist after specialist, but though all had made encouraging noises and all had charged exorbitant fees, Michael still remained the sole heir to Henry's title and estate. Although Henry had never openly blamed her, it was no comfort to Lucinda that his younger brother's wife had produced a whole basketful of babies.

She heard Henry's footsteps on the marble floor of the hall and his voice calling for her. 'I'm in here,' she said. 'In the morning room.'

He entered the room a few seconds later, his face alight with enthusiasm. 'Come and see my horseless carriage. I've driven it all the way from the village.'

In Lucinda's mood it was not easy to smile. 'I've already seen it. Have you bought it?'

'Not yet but I think I will. Everyone believes they're the coming thing.'

'You mean that rascal Arthur Wright, who has the agency, thinks they are. How can they take the place of horses when they're so unreliable?' Without being aware of it Lucinda adopted the tone of a mother chastising a child. 'The idea's quite ridiculous.'

Somewhat predictably Sir Henry's enthusiasm died. 'They'll soon get more reliable, particularly when more and more people start to buy them.'

Lucinda shrugged impatiently. 'If you want one, that's your business. But don't expect me to ride in it. I'm not a lover of oil and grease and unreliability.'

Frowning at her waspishness, Sir Henry glanced round the room. 'Where's Michael?'

'He went riding with those two friends of his. They left about thirty minutes ago.'

The squire gave a start. 'What horse did he take?'

Lucinda shrugged her slim shoulders. 'Shamrock, I think. At least I heard him tell Roberts to saddle her up.'

'Damn it, I told him I wanted that horse resting. Roberts thinks she's got a strained tendon.' When Lucinda showed her disinterest by re-arranging a flower in one of the vases, Sir Henry gazed at her resentfully. 'It doesn't concern you when he disobeys me, does it?'

It was the precise cue Lucinda needed. 'If you want the truth it doesn't surprise me. The boy looks up to you and all you do is find fault with him. Can't you understand that's the reason he sometimes get his own back by disobeying you?'

Sir Henry swore. 'The reason he disobeys me is because he's a wilful little devil who's been spoilt to death. I thought they'd teach him discipline at this damned expensive school of his but if anything he's become more arrogant since going there. Don't you realise that one day he's going to take over this house and estate? If he hasn't learnt any responsibility by then, God help the staff and tenants.'

Lucinda's voice was cold with sarcasm. 'So now it's the staff and tenants you're thinking about?'

Sir Henry was making a massive effort to keep his temper. 'No, damn it. It's everything. I want a son who behaves well towards his underlings and shows the responsibility of his position. Is that too much to ask?'

Lucinda's laugh was mocking. 'And you're teaching him these qualities by making him fight this young hooligan who broke his nose last month. You think that's the right way to handle him?'

Sir Henry nodded grimly. 'I thought we'd eventually come round to that. That's why you've been so damned moody these last few days, isn't it?'

'Are you surprised? What possible purpose can it

serve to make Michael have this fight?'

'I've told you that at least a dozen times. No one, and particularly my tenants, is going to believe a son of mine is a coward.'

'But you've already got Leason's word he won't say anything. And who's going to believe a fourteen year-old nobody if the boy talks about it?'

The squire scowled. 'There's more to it than that. And don't tell me you haven't guessed it.'

Although Lucinda tried to hide it, uneasiness sounded in her scornful voice. 'Guessed what?'

Sir Henry walked to a cupboard and poured himself a brandy before turning to her. 'Hasn't it ever occurred to you that the Leason boy might be telling the truth?'

Lucinda gave a start, then her aristocratic face set. 'Are you saying we should take the word of a young hooligan before the word of our own son?'

The squire half drained his glass before answering her. 'Our son doesn't have a monopoly on the truth. Leason says this lad was brought up by his mother to be truthful. After meeting him, I'm inclined to believe it.'

Lucinda was breathing hard now. 'You believe him even though he broke Michael's nose without reason? I don't believe I'm hearing this, Henry.'

Sir Henry frowned and shook his head. 'You'd have to meet the lad to understand. For one thing Leason tells me he's deeply religious and believes it's wrong to fight. But with that he has some sort of pride. Do you know what he said when I told him to open Leason's gate? He told me to say please.'

Lucinda was gazing at him as if his mind were suddenly suspect. 'And you believe a boy like that? A cheeky little whelp who mocks his betters?'

'No, Lucinda. It wasn't like that. He wasn't cheeky. In fact he was almost apologetic. He just seemed to believe

I should say please. And afterwards I realised he was right.'

Lucinda gave an exclamation of disgust. 'I've never heard such nonsense in my life. The boy seems to have bewitched you. Have you forgotten Burgess saw everything that happened? He says the boy's story is a pack of lies.'

'Burgess? Do you think he's going to tell me my son behaved badly? Look, Lucinda, I know well enough Michael's not a coward. God knows, if anything he's too reckless. But I'm not so happy about his morals. I think he can be a ruthless little devil when his temper's up.'

'So what will this fight prove?'

'It'll prove to everyone who's heard about this affair that Michael's not a coward and didn't need Burgess's help. That's important to me and it's also important to Michael. Don't forget he wants this fight too.'

Lucinda's lip curled. 'Which of our friends is likely to think Michael's a coward? They all think just the opposite. It'll make us a laughing stock. I think you're drinking too much brandy, Henry, and it's affecting your judgements.'

The purple that flooded into the squire's cheeks warned her she had gone too far. 'Damn it, woman, that's enough! Michael's fighting the boy when his face is better and that's the end of it. I don't want this mentioned again, do you understand?'

When Lucinda made no reply, Sir Henry strode to the door and turned. 'There's one thing you haven't taken into account. If you took the trouble to study Michael's curriculum, you'd see that he gets boxing lessons at school three times a week. And unlike the rest of his studies, his marks for boxing are excellent. Does that mean anything to you?'

Across the room Lucinda had started, then turned

pale. Sir Henry's voice became richly sarcastic. 'I see you're getting the picture. If Michael told us the truth, why did he come out worse in the argument?'

Mary did not see the boy until she was halfway up the garden: a large apple tree hid him from sight. He was standing on a box washing the back windows of No. 57 and did not notice her until she was a few yards away. 'Hello, Harry. Are you working for Mother this morning?'

His face lit up on seeing her. 'Yes. Mr Brown told me to come over as soon as I'd cleaned out the stable.'

She paused alongside him. 'How are you getting on with Mr Brown?'

He shrugged. 'He's all right.'

'He's not working you too hard, is he?'

The boy showed contempt. 'No. I worked twice as hard on my holidays last year.'

'What were you doing?'

The boy wrung out his washleather in the pail beside him. 'I got a job on the docks. They work you to death there.'

Mary was examining his face. 'Your eye's nearly better. It looked awful when you first came. Has it stopped hurting?'

Harry climbed back on the box. 'It never did hurt much. I told you so.'

'It still looked awful. Would you like a cup of tea?'

Harry hesitated. 'If you're going to make one.'

At that moment the rear door opened and Ethel appeared. Her eyes showed faint disapproval as they moved from Harry to the girl alongside him. 'What are you doing here?' she asked Mary.

'Mrs Harris sent us home. She wasn't feeling well. Can I make a cup of tea, Mum?'

'Didn't you have one with Mrs Harris?'

'Yes, but Harry hasn't had one this morning. Can I make one for him?'

Ethel hesitated, then nodded. 'Yes, all right. But don't hold up his work. I want all the windows clean before Mrs Armitage comes this afternoon.'

Mrs Armitage was the wife of the local vicar and consequently held in high esteem by Ethel. As her mother withdrew, Mary glanced up at Harry who, taking Ethel's hint, was in full industry on the windows again. 'I'll go and put the kettle on now. I won't be long.'

She emerged from the house five minutes later with a mug of tea and two buttered scones. As Harry, who had moved on to the kitchen windows, reached down for the mug, she drew back. 'You can't have your tea and work at the same time. Mother didn't mean that. Sit down and drink it properly.'

The boy hesitated, then sat down on the box. Mary's eyes widened at the rapid disappearance of the scones. 'You're hungry,' she accused. 'Didn't you have any breakfast this morning?'

The boy was immediately on the defensive. ''Course I did,' he muttered.

'What did you have?'

He frowned and picked up the mug of tea. 'I'd enough.'

'I don't believe you. You're hungry; I can see you are.' Before Harry could reply, the girl turned and ran indoors to her mother who was sewing in the living room. 'Mum, Harry's hungry. Can I make him a sandwich?'

Ethel frowned and glanced at the gilt clock on the mantelpiece. 'It'll be lunch time in ninety minutes. Can't he wait until then?'

'But you should see how he ate those scones. I think

55

his mother's too poor to feed him properly.'

'Don't be silly, child. All young boys are hungry. They'd eat all day if you let them.'

'But, Mum, his mother's a widow and has to work all hours to keep the family together.'

Ethel laid down her sewing. 'How do you know so much about him? Have you been talking to him behind our backs?'

'No, of course I haven't. In any case, he never talks about himself. Mr Price, our traveller, told me.'

'How does Mr Price come into this?'

'He heard about Harry when he called on Mr Jackson, the chemist, for his order. Mr Jackson says Harry's mother is the hardest working woman he's ever known.'

Ethel's frown deepened. 'Why are you so interested in the boy?'

The girl's tone changed. 'I'm not interested in him. He's just nice, that's all. Everyone likes him.'

'All the same, I don't want you to get so friendly with him. It's not fitting for a young lady.'

Mary showed defiance for the first time. 'You don't like him because he's poor, do you?'

Ethel gave a start. 'What's that?'

'You don't like him because he's poor. You've never liked poor people since we were poor ourselves.'

Red spots appeared in Ethel's cheeks. 'We were poor for a very different reason, young lady. And your father and I soon took care of that by working hard. The working classes don't make the effort to help themselves. That's the big difference.'

The girl was close to tears now. 'That's not true of Harry's mother or Harry either. Harry's father's dead. That's the difference.'

Ethel's face set. 'I shall have a talk with your father when he comes home, young lady. You're getting these ideas from the boy and I'm not going to have it. Go and make him that sandwich and then get upstairs to your room. I don't want to hear any more of your nonsense this morning.'

Opening the kitchen door, Connie paused and stared. 'What are you doing?'

Mary, who was about to slip a piece of cheese into a carrier bag, flushed with guilt. 'Nothing.'

Moving closer, Connie jerked the bag away from her sister and saw it contained half a loaf of bread and rashers of bacon. She gazed at Mary accusingly. 'This is for Harry Miles, isn't it?'

Mary pulled herself together. 'What if it is?'

'Have you asked Mother's permission?'

Mary bit her lip. 'No.'

'Then you're stealing it, aren't you?'

'Don't be silly. Of course I'm not.'

'Yes, you are. Mother has to buy it and you're taking it without her permission. That's stealing.'

Mary realised her only hope was to draw on her sister's compassion. 'Harry isn't getting enough to eat, Con. His mother's been ill for the last two weeks and hasn't been able to work. She's going hungry herself to give Harry what she can.'

'Is that what Harry tells you?'

'No. I've been round to see Mrs Miles. She's had the flu or something and been really ill.' Seeing Connie's expression, Mary realised the mistake she had made. 'You won't tell Mother, will you?'

'Of course I'll tell Mother. I'll have to. You know you should never go into that part of town on your own.'

'But I wasn't on my own, Con. I asked Harry to take me. He didn't want to but I made the excuse I wanted to call on Mr Jackson about an order. You'd like his mum, Con. She's ever so sweet and nice.'

'Does she know you're taking this food without Mother's permission?'

'Of course she doesn't. She thinks Mum sends it. She wanted to write and thank Mum until I stopped her.'

'Didn't that make her suspicious?'

'No. I told her that Mother didn't want Dad to know.' At Connie's expression she went on: 'I know I've been telling lies, Con, but it can't be wrong to help people, can it? Don't tell Mum, please. All she'll do is blame Harry, and he's never asked for anything.'

Connie pushed the bag back at her. 'You've got to tell her yourself. Otherwise she'll find out and then you'll be in trouble.'

'But why should she find out? I'm not taking much. Only enough for Harry's breakfasts.'

'Don't be stupid. Of course she'll find out. Only the other morning I heard her grumbling to Molly that she didn't know where the eggs are going. If you don't tell her, she'll believe Molly's the thief and that'll get her the sack. You don't want that, do you?'

Mary gave a start. 'I hadn't thought about Molly.'

'No, of course you hadn't. All you can think about these days is Harry.'

The younger girl sighed. 'Then I suppose I will have to stop. But it doesn't seem right when his mother's so poor.'

'You'll do more than stop,' Connie told her. 'You'll tell Mother what you've been doing.'

Mary flinched. 'But why? She'll only take it out on Harry.'

'You'll tell her because she's already suspicious of Molly,' Connie said. 'You can't leave her under suspicion like that.'

The unhappy girl realised she had no choice. 'All right. I'll tell her tomorrow.'

'No, you won't. You'll tell her after Dad's gone back to work this afternoon. Otherwise I'll tell her myself.'

Chapter 7

Ethel barely allowed William the chance to pour himself a whisky before she unburdened herself. 'As soon as I saw that boy, Harry, I knew it was a mistake to take him on. Do you know what Mary admitted to me today?'

Groaning inwardly, William turned. 'What did she admit?'

Ethel told him about the theft of food. William looked astonished. 'Why on earth would she do that?'

'It's obvious enough. The boy's spun her a yarn to gain her sympathy. It's hardly a new trick.'

William frowned. 'I don't mean that. I want to know why she didn't ask you for the food in the first place.'

Suddenly realising that tale-telling carried its own penalties, Ethel switched her attack. 'It hasn't stopped there. She's been round to see the boy's mother who's supposed to have been sick for the last couple of weeks. Imagine it, going there without saying a word to us.'

'Where is she now?' William asked. 'Upstairs?'

'No. She threw a tantrum and went off to see Aunt Selina. But she should be home soon.'

William took his whisky over to a chair and sank into it. He sat silent for a moment, then turned to Ethel. 'I don't like the sound of this, Ethel. If she's been so worried about the boy's welfare, why hasn't she told us? Doesn't she have any faith that we'd help him?'

Ethel was quick to see the trend of the question. 'I expect the boy asked her not to. He would if he was stringing her along, wouldn't he?'

William's frown deepened. 'Are you saying he's got some kind of influence over her?'

'Yes, I think he has. After all, they're the same age and I know she likes him.'

'All right,' William said. 'I'll have a word with her when she gets home. I certainly want to know why she didn't confide in us.'

Ethel's tone changed. 'I don't think you should blame her. After all, she's at an impressionable age. It's the boy you should talk to.'

William stared at her. 'But you've just told me she's been stealing from you. Are you saying now we should let that pass?'

'She didn't see it as stealing, William. The boy's influenced her. You know what a tender-hearted girl she is.'

William had never expected his younger daughter to receive such support from her mother. 'Then what do you want me to do?'

'Get rid of the boy. After all, he'll be leaving in six weeks in any case. Get rid of him before he worms his way into her affections any more. She's in her puberty, William. It could be dangerous.'

Frowning, William pulled out his pipe, fished in a pocket for his tobacco pouch, then gave up the attempt and turned his eyes back to Ethel. 'Have you stopped to think it could all be true and the woman might have been sick? After all, Mary's never lied to us before.'

'That's exactly why I'm worried Harry might be influencing her.' When William shook his head, Ethel went on: 'In any case it would have been easy enough for

61

the woman to pop into bed while Mary was there. We all know the kind of tricks these people get up to.'

'Do we?' William asked.

Ethel flushed. 'You might not but I do.' When William fell silent she went on: 'You could see the kind of boy Harry was when he first came round here.'

William nodded. 'That set you against him, didn't it?'

'Are you surprised? Decent boys don't go around looking like miniature pugilists.'

'Ethel, how often have I to tell you that the fight might not have been his fault? Someone might have attacked the lad. Or he might have been defending somebody.'

'Then why wouldn't he tell us?' Ethel challenged. 'Is that the way an innocent boy behaves?'

William was silent for a moment, then sighed. 'I can't tell my workmen what to do in their private lives, Ethel. All I can ask of them is that they behave well here. And I haven't a single complaint against this boy.'

'Not when he's the cause of Mary stealing from me? You don't think that's a cause for complaint?'

William's expression gave warning that his patience was wearing thin. 'If you want my opinion, all this is a storm in a teacup. All that's worrying me is why Mary didn't feel able to ask us to help. That's something I intend to find out when she returns home.'

Ethel was standing very erect and stiff. 'You're not going to do anything about Harry?'

'Not if he's innocent and didn't know Mary was taking the food without our permission. How can I?'

'It doesn't worry you that he's influencing Mary into these bad habits?'

'Only if I find out that he is. My bet is the boy believes we've given Mary permission to help his mother. 'I've always found him an independent little begger.'

Her petticoats rustling, Ethel turned stiffly away.

'Then there's nothing more to say, is there?'

Inwardly cursing, William picked up his glass and heaved his bulk out of the armchair. His voice checked Ethel in the doorway. 'Ethel, I know all this comes from my giving Mary a job in the warehouse. One way or another you were bound to find something to complain about. Am I not right?'

Ethel was pale to the lips. 'No. It's nothing to do with that. You're not being fair.'

In his mid forties William was beginning to believe the truism that dripping water eats away the hardest stone. 'I'll go this far with you, Ethel. If I find out the boy is influencing Mary or if he gets into trouble in any other way, then I'll get rid of him. Does that satisfy you?'

Ethel's stiff voice gave no indication of triumph. 'You must do as you wish, William. As you've told us often enough, you are the master in your own house.'

With that the hall door closed and Ethel had gone. This time William's curse could be heard across the room. In God's name, what had he done to deserve a household of squabbling, illogical women? Why in the name of hell couldn't they keep to their knitting and leave his affairs to him? Noticing again that his glass was empty, William started with determination across the room and snatched up the bottle of whisky.

Ethel caught sight of Mary as she entered the warehouse yard. The girl was at its far end and as Ethel watched her she disappeared behind the huge pile of empty crates. Curious, Ethel waited and when the girl did not reappear, followed her. As she reached the crates, she heard children's voices and laughter. Setting her lips, Ethel found a gap between the boxes and edged her way through it.

She found Mary and Harry sitting on two crates that had been pulled from the main pile. Both were holding mugs of tea and Mary had a plate of scones on her lap. With Ethel pausing to watch, it was not until Mary held out the plate to Harry that the girl noticed her mother.

'What are you two doing hiding here?' Ethel snapped.

Mary's look of surprise turned into dismay at her mother's tone. 'We're not hiding, Mum. We're having our morning tea.'

'Morning tea? Hiding out of sight behind these boxes? Why can't you have tea with your father in his office?'

'Workmen aren't allowed in there,' the girl told her. 'And Dad doesn't think it fair on the workmen to have a girl around during their morning break. So this is the only place there is.'

Ethel gave Harry a hostile glance. 'You mean it's the only place you can meet him, don't you? Does your father know about this?'

To her surprise Mary nodded. 'Yes, of course he does.'

'How long has it been going on?' Ethel demanded.

'Only when Harry's working over here.'

'I shall have a talk with your father,' Ethel said grimly. She turned to Harry who was looking as distressed as Mary. 'If you're not teaching my daughter to do one deceitful thing, it's another. Don't you ever persuade her to see you in private again. Do you hear me?'

Tears were beginning to flood the girl's eyes. 'He didn't persuade me. I suggested it myself. Why are you being so horrible, Mother? We weren't doing anything wrong.'

Ethel was breathing hard as she glanced back at Harry. 'Leave your tea there and get back to work! At once! Go on.'

The boy touched his cap and with a dismayed look at

Mary hurried away. Ethel swung back to the girl. 'Haven't you learned yet that nice girls don't meet workmen in secret? I don't know what's coming over you, girl.'

Mary was sobbing bitterly now. 'I don't know what you're talking about. I was only giving him a scone.'

Ethel pushed her through the gap. 'Don't argue with me, girl, and don't you ever let me catch you here with him again.'

Chapter 8

Sir Henry reached down and handed the pale-faced boy a pair of boxing gloves. 'Have you worn gloves before?' When Harry shook his head: 'Then you've never done any boxing?'

'No, sir,' the boy muttered.

The squire frowned. 'But you are still willing to fight my son?'

Nervousness allowed Harry only to swallow and jerk his head. The squire glanced up at Bill Leason who was standing behind the stool on which the boy was sitting. 'Are you sure you can manage this, Leason? I can send one of my nephews over if you like. He'll see the boy's properly looked after.'

Leason shook his head. 'With respect, Squire, I think he'd prefer me at a time like this. I'll take proper care of him.'

Sir Henry gazed into the farmer's weatherbeaten face but it was expressionless. Giving a curt nod, he crossed the lawn to another stool where Michael was sitting. Burgess was kneeling alongside the boy with a pail and sponge beside him. With high privet hedges enclosing the private lawn, the only other onlookers were standing in a small curious group behind Burgess. One, a man in his early fifties, was Sir Henry's brother-in-law, James Vernon, a barrister. The two younger men talking to him in low tones were Vernon's sons. One was carrying a small bell and at a nod from Sir Henry he rang it to draw the attention of the two combatants.

The squire drew both boys into the centre of the lawn. With the two of them now close together, it was seen that Michael stood a good two inches taller than Harry, a fact that did not go unnoticed by the onlookers. Michael, clearly confident of the outcome of the fight and with only a slight discoloration remaining around his eyes, was grinning at the smaller boy in anticipation.

After making certain Harry's gloves were tied on properly, Sir Henry gave the boys their final instructions. To Harry, who had a feeling of unreality, they seemed to reach him through a thick blanket.

'You'll hit only above the waist and you'll separate the moment I tell you to. If either of you is knocked down, you'll have ten seconds to climb back on your feet or the other boy will be declared the winner. This doesn't mean you can lie down the moment you are hurt, however. I shall expect you both to continue fighting until you can no longer stand. After the fight, whoever wins, I shall expect you both to shake hands and bear no malice to one another in the future. Is all that understood?'

When both boys nodded, Sir Henry glanced at their seconds. 'Then go to your corners now and wait for the bell. When it sounds, come out with your hands up and start to box.'

The boys obeyed. Bill Leason laid a hand on Harry's thin shoulder and discovered the boy was trembling. He leaned down in concern. 'Are you feeling all right, lad?'

'Yes,' Harry muttered.

'You're quite sure?'

This time the boy sounded angry. 'Yes, I'm all right.'

The bell sounded a few seconds later. Dreading the encounter as he had been dreading it for weeks, Harry rose slowly from his stool and took a few steps across the lawn. In contrast Michael had left his corner like a sprinter from his blocks and was throwing punches at him almost before he had time to lift his gloves. Reeling from the attack, Harry dropped his arms and a blow to the chin sent him toppling down to the lawn.

Half-stunned he heard the squire saying something to him but could not make out his words. As his eyes cleared he saw Michael grinning down, challenging him to rise. A moment later Sir Henry tapped his shoulder. 'Come on, lad! You can do better than that.'

Taking a deep breath, the boy rose on one knee, then straightened. Immediately he had to face a new barrage of blows. A blow to the temple made his head swim, another to the stomach made him gasp for breath. Instinctively he struck out and for a moment the barrage ceased. Then it began again, sending him reeling first one way and then the other as he tried desperately to defend himself.

The three-minute round seemed an eternity to Harry. But somehow he kept his feet and at last found himself slumped on his stool with Bill Leason bathing his face with a cold sponge. 'How do you feel, lad? You've had enough, haven't you?'

The boy wanted to sob that he had. The fight had no purpose for him and he knew he was afraid. But Harry Miles knew nothing about the pedigree of resistance in his stock that stretched back to the Saxon fyrds at Hastings and the Norseman at York. He only knew that his body and speech seemed to have taken on a will of their own. 'No,' he muttered. 'Leave me be.'

'But lad, you're no match for him.'

Harry drew an arm across his bloodied, tear-stained

68

face. 'Let me be,' he muttered again.

Across the lawn the young man with the bell was talking in low tones to the squire. 'He knows nothing about boxing, Uncle. It's hardly a fair fight.'

Sir Henry frowned. 'He's not much of a match, I agree. But I'll have to let it go on a bit longer.'

The man nodded and rang the bell again. Full of confidence, Michael advanced on the unsteady boy. His voice was pitched too low to reach his father. 'Come on, you little coward. Make a decent fight of it.'

A glove smacked into Harry's right eye and another into his bleeding mouth. He swung out desperately and felt his fist contact some part of his tormentor's body. Through the rushing of blood in his ears he heard a cheer from the sidelines.

He quickly paid for his success. A heavy blow, smashing through his guard, caught him full in the face. As stars burst before his eyes, he heard Michael's vengeful voice. 'You little swine. 'I'll teach you who your betters are.'

Harry did not feel the next blow that hit him but found the coolness of the grass against his cheek again. Above him, Sir Henry waved Michael back. 'That's enough. Go back to your corner.'

Michael showed his disappointment. 'He's not badly hurt, Father. He's just shamming.'

Waving him away, the squire bent over Harry. 'What's it to be, boy? It's no shame if you stop now.'

A cry followed from Bill Leason. 'That's enough, lad. You've done your best. Let's go home now.'

Sir Harry laid a hand on the boy's trembling shoulder. 'Come on. Let me help you up.'

Harry was to remember little of what followed and what he could remember seemed the action of a stranger. He pushed the squire's hand away. 'No. I want to go on.'

'I don't think you should, boy. You've taken quite a beating.'

The stranger's voice came again, through swollen lips. 'I want to go on. I've a right to, haven't I?'

'But lad, you can hardly stand.'

With an effort the boy rose to his knees and then to his feet. 'I want to go on,' he muttered.

Sir Henry hesitated, then stood back. 'Very well, boy. You've earned the right. Just a little longer.'

Showing delight at his father's nod, Michael ran forward and measured the swaying boy. But before he could strike, Harry summoned up the last of his strength and to a delighted cheer from the onlookers, threw a flurry of blows at the surprised Michael.

It was a gesture of defiance that could last no longer than the boy's failing strength. As he paused and fought for air, Michael took his revenge. Blows, accompanied by Michael's taunting voice, crashed into his face and thudded into his body. With his arms too heavy to lift, he was defenceless. Before Sir Henry could intervene, a blow caught him full on the jaw and he collapsed like a puppet whose strings had broken.

For two or three seconds the boy did not move. Then, crying something Sir Henry could not catch, he caught hold of the squire's legs in his effort to rise. There was both astonishment and respect in the man's voice. 'No, lad. You've done more than enough. Leason! Come over here and give me a hand with this brave lad of yours.'

There was a cry of disappointment from Michael who was still standing alongside his father. 'I didn't hit him that hard, Father. He's shamming again. Let him get up and take his punishment.'

Sir Henry swung round on his son. His low voice drove the triumph from his face. 'One more word out of you and by God you'll regret it. Go over to your corner and

70

wait there. I've things to say to you.'

Crestfallen and sullen now, Michael walked back to Burgess while Sir Henry and Leason helped Harry back to his stool. Lowering him gently down, the squire peered into his face. 'How are you feeling now, boy?'

Reaction was bringing tears down the boy's swollen cheeks. 'All right,' he muttered.

'That was a brave fight you put up. One of the bravest I've seen.' Sir Henry glanced round at Leason. 'I'm sorry I had to arrange it. But I couldn't leave things as they were, could I?'

The farmer made no comment as he picked up the sponge and began gently washing the boy's face.

Sir Henry frowned. 'You can't deny it was a fair fight, Leason.'

Leason's wrinkled blue eyes fixed on him for a moment before returning to the boy. 'I'd like to get him home, Squire. He needs to get to bed.'

Frowning again, Sir Henry peered at the boy's face. 'Perhaps he ought to see a doctor. We'll take him to The Grange and I'll send for one.'

The sobbing boy muttered something to Leason, who turned to the squire. 'He doesn't want a doctor, sir. He just wants to go home.'

Hesitating a moment, the squire reached into a pocket and slipped something into Leason's hand. 'If his mother wants to call one in, give her this.' He turned back to Harry. 'You're still going to keep your promise, lad? To say nothing about this to anyone?'

'He'll have to tell his mother,' Leason said. 'He can't go home in that state without telling her something.'

'Can she be trusted?'

'She's our daughter, sir. She won't give you away.'

Giving the farmer a look, Sir Henry stood back. 'Very well. Stay here, the two of you, and I'll send my horse

71

and buggy to drive you home.' His eyes moved back to Harry. 'I'll tell you this, boy. The next time we meet I'll be careful to say please before I ask anything of you. You're a brave, brave lad.'

With that he turned and crossed the lawn. Reaching the apprehensive Michael who was standing alongside his stool he glanced at Burgess. 'Go and tell Taylor to run Leason and his grandson home. Tell him to show them courtesy. Is that understood?'

Burgess touched his cap and hurried away. Seeing his brother and nephews had disappeared, the squire waited until Burgess was out of earshot, then swung round on Michael. 'Now, boy, I want the truth. You lied to me about what happened, didn't you?'

Although the boy did not reply, his sullen expression was an answer in itself. Sir Henry nodded grimly. 'There's a vindictive streak in you, boy, and today it's shamed me as well as you, and by God no one does that twice.' With his personal code violated, the incensed squire allowed himself to say things that in the years ahead were to have profound effects on the innocent boy he was defending. 'You showed it when you taunted that lad and disgusted your own cousins. The truth is, if he'd had half your advantages, he'd have knocked your head off. Clean yourself up and then go to your room and stay there! I don't want to see you for the rest of the day.'

Across the lawn, Leason was watching the squire and from his expression the farmer guessed what was being said. As Sir Henry turned and strode angrily towards the house and Michael stood gazing at Harry, Leason's voice was troubled. 'You've made a good friend of the squire, lad, but a bad enemy of that son of his. Although he's a headstrong and vindictive boy, they say he's always looked up to his father and he's not going to forgive you for what happened this afternoon. We've got to make sure you don't cross paths with him again.'

Harry was feeling too sick and dizzy to speak. In the distance there was a clip-clop of hooves as a buggy made its way down the drive towards them. Remembering, Leason fished in his waistcoat pocket. His low whistle made the pale-faced boy look up at him. 'It's a five pound note, lad. At least it'll be a godsend for your mother.'

Ethel met William at the door. 'Have you seen Harry today?'

William sighed. 'Yes, I've seen him.'

'What have you done? Dismissed him?'

William made for the whisky cabinet. Ethel followed him. 'You promised me, William. You said if he got into trouble again you would get rid of him. Have you spoken to him?'

'Yes, of course I have.'

'What did he say?'

William sloshed whisky into a glass. 'He wouldn't say anything. He muttered something about he couldn't help it and he'd made a promise not to talk. That was all.'

'And you believed him?'

William paused, then took a sip of whisky. 'Oddly enough I did.'

'You believed him? A boy gets his face battered like that then promises not to tell. Could his mother be doing it?'

'A frail little woman like that? In any case I asked him. He said she'd never laid a hand on him in his life.'

'Then who else would he keep silence for? She hasn't a man living with her, has she?'

William gave her a look. 'She's a devout Methodist.

73

It's nothing to do with his family. I'm certain of it.'

'Then it has to be something he's ashamed of. Or why would he risk his job by not telling you?'

William dropped heavily into his armchair and took another sip of whisky before answering her. 'Do you know why I believe the boy?'

'No, I don't.'

'Because all he had to do was make up a story that made him seem the innocent party. If he's a liar why didn't he do that?'

In spite of herself Ethel's voice was hardening. 'I'm not concerned whether he's a liar or not. I'm concerned about Mary. We don't know anything about the boy except that he's always getting into trouble and yet Mary's obviously infatuated by him. Can't you see how dangerous it is? Mary'll soon be a young woman.'

William sighed. 'So what do you want me to do?'

'I want you to keep your promise to me, William. Dismiss him before we both regret it.'

William lifted his glass again, saw it was empty and frowned. Followed by Ethel's eyes, he heaved himself up and returned to the cabinet. A full thirty seconds passed before he turned to the waiting Ethel. 'You know how this is going to upset Mary?'

'Of course I do. That's all the more reason he should go.'

William sighed. 'All right, Ethel, I'll keep my promise. I'll give the boy his notice tomorrow.'

PART 2

Chapter 9

Six years slipped past. In Britain they were years of paradox. Everywhere there was still sweated labour. Fewer than twenty per cent of workers were organised into unions and unions themselves could win few concessions from venial and unsympathetic employers. At least a quarter of the population lived on wages so pitiful that a shilling a week could mean the difference between life and death to a family.

Even for those in work life could be dangerous, for industrial legislation was minimal. In 1904 alone a thousand people were killed in workshops, over twelve hundred in the mines, and over four hundred on the railroads.

Yet, and here was the paradox, these same workers were beginning to see light on the horizon. Science, so long the province of the few, was beginning to have an impact on the masses. More and more people could claim they had seen an automobile. Bicycles, once a luxury of the rich, were becoming cheap enough for even factory workers to escape on them from the fog-ridden cities to the leafy lanes of the countryside. There were even exciting rumours that over in America two men had flown in a powered machine. Miracles seemed to be happening everywhere and with the Boer War won and the future of the British Empire ensured, science would surely flourish and pour out its achievements for all to enjoy.

It was true that, as always, there were a few clouds as well as sunlight on the horizon. Germany was recognised as an increasing threat to Empire Trade and her naval rearmament and her great Zeppelins were being brandished by a belligerent German Press to impress and intimidate their great rival. But there are few races less hysterical than the British and with the Boer War victory tucked beneath his belt the man-in-the-street lost little sleep over distant mutterings from 'Little Willie's' Germany.

Instead he read about science's new miracles (from his master's newspaper if he could not afford the halfpenny for one himself) and began to believe in the Millenium. The Press said it was coming and the politicians promised it – if the public would be patient a little longer. Even Polly Miles, who by 1910 knew that her days were numbered, began to hope that one day her children would live to walk with shining heads into the new Utopia.

The young man entered the shop on the corner just as Mary Hardcastle was thanking the chemist, Mr Jackson, for his order. As she turned, she almost collided with him. 'I'm sorry. I didn't see you . . .'

His eager voice interrupted her. 'You're Mary, aren't you? Mary Hardcastle.'

With the summer sun streaming through the window his face was in shadow. 'I'm sorry. Do I know you?'

'I'm Harry. Harry Miles. Don't you remember? I worked a few weeks for your father back in 1904.'

Her face lit up. 'Of course. Harry! How are you?'

'I'm fine. What are you doing here? Do you still work for your father?'

'Yes. One of our travellers is off sick and I'm standing in for him. Mr Price, the old man. Do you remember him?'

He nodded as his eyes travelled over her. She was wearing a cream blouse and a long beige skirt. Although her hat was wide brimmed it could not hide the long blonde hair that hung down to her waist. 'How are your family?' he asked. 'Your mum and dad and Connie?'

'They're fine,' she told him. 'What about your mother and sister?'

His tone changed. 'Mother's not well. She's in hospital at the moment. I came to pick up some drugs for her.'

'I'm sorry,' she said. 'What about your sister?'

He stood on one side for a customer to reach the counter. 'She moved to Leeds with her husband. I don't see much of them these days.'

With the sun no longer at his back, she could now take in his appearance. Although he was now a young man, there were many resemblances to the boy she had known. His black hair was still curly and his wide-set brown eyes held the same odd solemnity. The shapely mouth that he had inherited from his mother also drew her eyes. The differences were in his jaw and cheeks where the softer contours of a child had given way to the leaner features of a man. In height she estimated him about average, three inches taller than herself, and he had retained the wiry build of his younger days. He was wearing a somewhat threadbare shirt and with his sleeves rolled up she could see a small but livid scar on his right forearm. He still looked poor, she thought, and yet, just as in his childhood days, something in his bearing and gentle manner set him apart from other young men of his kind.

She knew she could not meet him this way and then say goodbye. 'Harry, why don't you get your mother's drugs and then have tea with me? We must have a hundred things to tell one another.' When he hesitated, she misunderstood the reason. 'Or don't you have the time?'

He gave her a wry smile. 'Time's not my problem. The firm I worked for went bankrupt last week.'

Her eyes twinkled at him. 'Then there isn't a problem. Dad always stands me meals when I'm out travelling for him and he won't begrudge us tea and scones when he hears who I've met. Come on. I want to hear everything you've been doing these last six years.'

'How do you like your tea?' she asked.

He shrugged. 'Anyway. As it comes.'

She poured in milk, then handed him the cup and saucer. 'Help yourself to sugar and take what you want to eat.'

He motioned at the ham sandwich that she had ordered along with buttered scones. 'Why did you order that? Do I still look hungry?'

His tone disturbed her until she remembered the way he had always turned defensive when offered help or sympathy. 'You look thin,' she said. 'But you don't have to eat it if you don't want to.'

He frowned for a moment, then took the sandwich. Feeling that a small victory had been won, she said the first thing that came into her head. 'How long has your mother been in hospital?'

'Two weeks,' he muttered.

'What's wrong with her, Harry? Do you know?'

Only a slight twitch of one eye betrayed his pain. 'They say she has a growth. They're going to operate at the weekend.'

Without thinking, she reached out and put a hand on his arm. 'Oh, Harry, I am sorry. Your mother is such a lovely person.'

He frowned but she felt that in another dimension he was crying his heart out. Before she could offer more sympathy, he glanced at her hand then said quietly. 'I see you're not married yet. Or even engaged.'

She blushed. 'No. But Connie is. She married a dentist and lives in Middlesbrough now.'

'And you're still working for your dad?' When she nodded, he went on: 'I liked your dad. Is he keeping well?'

'Not too bad. But he's hopelessly overweight. The doctors keep telling him to lose some but you know Dad: he loves his food too much.'

Their laugh was a relief to them both. She was thinking how much his speech had improved during the years that had passed. Curious, she said: 'Did you finish your apprenticeship?'

'Yes. A year ago.'

'So you're a qualified carpenter now?'

He gave another wry smile. 'Yes. For all the good it does me now that Willcots' have gone bust.'

'But surely now you're qualified you shouldn't have much trouble getting another job?'

His glance made her blush. 'I'm sorry. I know I don't know much about these things. Is work that hard to find?'

His reply told her she was already forgiven. 'I've been thinking I might try for something different. I've been studying at night classes for the last five years with that old friend of mine, Gareth Evans.'

She had the feeling the years were rolling back to the days when they had shared their childhood secrets together. 'Night classes? Who runs them?'

'Our chapel. And my father's old Socialist Club. Members give their time free.'

'That's wonderful. What subjects have you taken?'

He grinned at her. 'First how to speak properly. My dad used to say that in England it's far more important to speak well than to know anything. He said the public schools have known that for centuries. Dad never got the chance but I felt I owed it to him to give it a try.'

She knew for certain now that her childhood instincts that he was no ordinary boy were vindicated. Suddenly the buzz of voices around them and the clatter of plates faded as she listened to him. 'My other subjects were social history, English literature and Zoology.' His sensitive lips gave a grimace. 'I know I ought to have kept to fewer subjects if I was to better myself but I think I've got a butterfly mind.'

She knew it was the reverse: an intelligent, under-nourished mind hungry for knowledge of any kind. She felt a lump rise in her throat. 'I think that's wonderful, Harry. It puts me to shame. I haven't tried to learn a thing since I left school.'

'You didn't need to,' he said. 'You went to a good school.'

Her dimple appeared as she lightened the mood. 'I'll bet they couldn't teach you much about country life on the Zoology course, though. I was very impressed that day you told me how to handle dogs.'

As he laughed with her, her expression suddenly changed. 'I hate what happened, Harry. You know that, don't you?'

He nodded. 'It wasn't your fault. Or your dad's. Your mother didn't like me, that was all.'

She was in no mood to defend her mother. 'She's a social climber, Harry. She's terrified of losing face with her neighbours.'

He grinned wryly. 'I suppose I did look like a young thug when I came for the job. No wonder she didn't want us to be friends.'

'It wasn't just that,' she said. 'She's a snob and she was afraid Connie and I might find out a few truths about the world. She still is, if it comes to that.'

He toyed with his cup for a moment before asking his question. 'Does that mean she still keeps an eye on your friends? Men friends, I mean?'

She felt it was a question within a question and wondered for a moment how to answer it. When she did, she found herself blushing again. 'I don't have any men friends. At least not friends the way you mean.'

She imagined she saw relief in his eyes although his voice teased her. 'I'd forgotten. Nice middle-class girls have to be watched and chaperoned, don't they? It's a bit different where I live although some parents try their best.'

She knew he was thinking of his mother again. 'I'm sure they do. My parents have always been strict. Even Dad keeps a watchful eye on me.'

When he made no reply, she held out the last scone to him. 'Have it, please. I've had more than enough.'

He shrugged but accepted it, convincing her it was the first meal he had eaten that day. 'I hope you're getting enough to eat while your mother's in hospital?'

'I manage all right,' he said. 'Sometimes one of the neighbours cooks for me.'

She poured him another cup of tea. As she reached over the table to hand it to him she noticed for the first time that there was a pipe protruding from his shirt pocket. 'Do you want to smoke?' she asked. 'If you do, I don't mind.'

He fished into his trouser pocket and pulled out an old tobacco pouch. She could see it contained little tobacco and noticed that he only half filled the pipe. As he applied a match, the question that had plagued her for years was suddenly too pressing to bear. 'Harry, why wouldn't you tell us what happened? Who made you promise not to? It's puzzled and worried me ever since.'

Smoke hid his expression for a moment. When he did not answer, she went on quickly: 'If it's something you still can't talk about, I'll understand. But it seemed such a shame Dad had to get rid of you like that.' She laughed to hide her embarrassment. 'I know that I cried about it for days.'

She saw his eyes were examining her through the smoke. Removing the pipe, he gave a wry grin. 'I did make a bit of a mystery about it, didn't I? But I'd no choice. I'd made a promise and also I couldn't risk getting my grandparents into trouble. It began when I was on holiday with them.'

He told her the story from beginning to end. When he finished her eyes were large and distressed. 'Then none of it was your fault at all?'

He shrugged. 'At the time I didn't think so. Looking back on it now, I probably made more fuss about the larks than I should have done.'

'I don't think so. Harry, I'm sorry. It's awful you got the sack for something you couldn't help.'

He laughed. 'Don't look so upset. It was six years ago. In any case, it wasn't your fault.'

She bit her lip. 'No, it was Mother who jumped to conclusions, as she usually does. Dad didn't want to do it, you know. He always liked you.'

'I'm sure he didn't. Your father was always a fair man.'

'Are your grandparents still alive?' she asked. When he nodded: 'Do you still visit them?'

'Sometimes. But not as often as I did.'

'Why? Are you still afraid it might get them into trouble?'

She did not miss his slight hesitation. 'No, not really. Michael's probably forgotten all about it. In any case he'll be at university now.'

'Then why don't you go more often?'

His sensitive mouth quirked in amusement. 'I've had a living to earn these last six years.'

'Of course.' An idea had come to her while they were talking. Novel and exciting, it burst from her before she had time to weigh up the consequence. 'Harry, how would you like to work for us again?'

He gave a start. 'You're not serious?'

'I am. Mr Price is only a couple of years off retirement and he's always off sick. If Dad could get a good replacement, I think he'd be quite happy to let him go on pension.'

He gave a laugh. 'Me? A traveller? I don't know the first thing about it.'

Her eagerness was growing. 'That's no problem. I could teach you in a few days.'

His expression changed as he stared at her. 'You don't have to do this, you know. You don't owe me anything.'

'Who said anything about that? You'd be an asset to us.' When he shook his head, she went on: 'For one thing you'd save me having to go out everytime Mr Price falls ill.'

'You've forgotten about your mother. She can't stand the sight of me.'

'That was when you were a boy and she thought you were always fighting. It'll be entirely different now.'

'Are you sure of that?'

She was not sure at all but would not allow the doubt to dim the brightness of the idea. 'What would it matter anyway? You'd be working for Dad, not for her. Let me ask him, please, Harry.'

He glanced down at his pipe which was growing cold in

his hand. As she waited for his answer, a midday siren from the docks could be heard through the chatter of voices around them. As a second one followed in its wake, he stirred and glanced back at her. 'Are you sure about this?'

It was only then she realised that she had been holding her breath. 'Yes, of course I'm sure.' The affirmation had barely left her lips before she regretted it. With her mother certain to object, was her father likely to risk a family quarrel for an inexperienced young man he had only known for a few weeks six years ago? Her smile was as much reassurance for herself as for him. 'Dad does take some notice of my opinions these days. I'm sure it would work out for all of us.'

A full ten seconds passed before he took a deep breath and shrugged. 'I suppose I haven't very much to lose. All right. Talk to your father and see what he says.'

Even she, with her feminine instincts giving her odd and disturbing signals, had no idea it was a moment that would change the entire pattern of their lives. Instead her eyes shone with pleasure. 'That's marvellous, Harry. 'I'll talk to Dad the moment I get back.'

Chapter 10

Ethel, erect in her chair, was pale with two red spots high on her cheekbones. 'I think you've both gone out of your minds.'

William, seated at the head of the dinner table, frowned. 'Why? Price can't help it but he can't put in a full day's work any longer. We need young blood to get us new business. After talking to Harry, I think he might be just the man I'm looking for.'

Ethell glanced at Mary before turning her accusing eyes on William again. 'You've let Mary talk you into this, haven't you? Have you stopped to think what our customers are going to say when a young hooligan like that walks in to represent us? At least Mr Price is a gentleman.'

Mary, pale herself, broke in before William could answer. 'You haven't listened to a word we've said, have you, Mother? Harry's become a well-spoken young man. He's also intelligent and has a nice personality.'

Ethel gave a sniff of contempt. 'I would hardly expect you to say anything else, would I?'

'What do you mean by that?'

'I haven't forgotten how the two of you used to behave, even if you have.'

Mary stiffened. 'What do you mean by that?'

'Don't tell me you don't remember how you used to meet behind our backs.'

Ignoring the frantic gestures from William, Mary leapt to her feet. 'You've no right to suggest such things. We were only children who liked talking to one another. If we didn't talk in front of you, it was because you wouldn't let us.'

'That's your story, young lady. I've got my own.'

'I'm sure you have,' Mary said. 'You've that sort of mind. You always had.'

Lips compressed, Ethel turned to William. 'Are you going to allow your daughter to speak this way to me, William?'

Before William could reply, Mary ran to the door. 'Why must you always spoil everything? You got Harry the sack six years ago when all he was doing was protecting his grandparents. Why can't you think well of people for a change?'

The door slammed and the girl could be heard running upstairs. William glanced back at Ethel's set face. 'She's right, you know, Ethel. We were unfair to the lad. Why won't you see him and talk to him? You'd find out what a presentable young man he's become.'

'I won't see him because I don't believe you can make a silk purse out of a sow's ear. People of that class don't change, William. When will you learn that?'

'But we know now the boy was only keeping a promise. He was behaving well, not badly.'

Ethel's voice was disdainful. 'How can you be so sure of that? Why can't he be lying now?'

'How can he? He knows I've only to check with his mother or his grandparents.'

'What proof would that be? People of that kind have no scruples. If he's angling for the job, all he has to do is tip them off.'

'But he isn't angling for the job. Mary said it was difficult to make him agree.'

'And you believe that?'

'Yes, I do. I believe my own daughter. And so should you.'

William's criticism made Ethel flinch for a moment. 'Can't you see I'm only doing this for Mary's sake? Six years ago she was infatuated with the boy. Why shouldn't the same thing happen again?'

'For heaven's sake, Ethel, they were only fourteen years old then. They've grown-up now.'

'Doesn't that make it more serious. Are you prepared to take the risk?'

Breathing hard, William leaned forward. 'What risk, Ethel? Tell me.'

Ethel remained defiant. 'You know perfectly well what I mean?'

'No, I don't. Are you saying they might have an affair?'

Ethel steadied herself. 'Yes. I think it's quite possible.'

William's face turned thunderblack. 'Now you listen to me, Ethel. We've brought up our daughters to be respectable girls and that's what they've been so far. Why should you think Mary will change now?'

'I've told you why. I believe she's still infatuated by him. Otherwise why would she want him back here? I know my daughters, William. Remember I'm their mother.'

William's voice rose. 'Since when has Mary done anything behind our backs? Tell me.'

'I didn't say she had. I said it might happen if you take on Harry Miles.'

'Why? Because you once found the two of them talking among those damned crates six years ago?

What's the matter with you, Ethel? Is Mary right about you?'

Ethel looked as if he had struck her. 'That's a dreadful thing to say. But then Mary's always right, isn't she? Even when she insults me.'

Incensed, William was shouting now. 'What do you think you're doing to Mary? You're making her sound like a trollop.'

Ethel gave a sob. 'This is all because of that wretched boy. And he isn't even working for us yet.'

William had been caught by such tactics before. 'Damn it, woman, I won't have you meddling in my business affairs. I've told you a hundred times before.' With his temper at flashpoint William was never to know whether his decision to take on Harry was based on merit or the desire to punish Ethel. 'I like the lad and I'm going to give him Price's job. Now stop talking about him.'

Although trembling, Ethel made one last try. 'Even in spite of how I feel about him and Mary?'

William's huge fist, crashing down on the table, made tea cups dance on their saucers. 'Yes, damn it, even if he seduces every woman down the road. I'm taking him on, do you hear? And that's the end of it.'

With a sob, Ethel grabbed up her skirts and ran out into the kitchen. Breathing hard, William dropped back in his chair. Then, cursing, he rose and made for the whisky bottle.

In spite of the coke stove, William's office was cold that January evening. Snow rimmed the window, and a few flakes illuminated by the gas light inside, were seen brushing against the glass. Seated at her own desk against the opposite wall, Mary, although wearing fur

90

lined boots and a thick cardigan, was finding it difficult to hold the pen in her chilled hand.

The round-faced clock on the wall was showing ten minutes past six when William sat back from his desk, yawned, and stretched himself. Pulling out his large silver watch from his waistcoat to check the time, he glanced at Mary. 'I think that's enough for the day, lass. Did you say Harry isn't coming back tonight?'

Mary nodded. 'He's been working at the other side of town today. To save him an extra journey, I told him to bring in his orders in the morning.'

Nodding his approval, William heaved his bulk from his chair, stretched again, then crossed over to the coke stove. Pulling open its door, he began raking its contents.

Mary sat watching him. A sudden draught from the window brought a flicker from the gas mantle. She waited until the light steadied before making her announcement. 'Dad, I'll be going out tonight.'

William paused in his raking to glance at the frosted window. 'You've picked a rum night, love. Where are you going? Mabel's place?'

Mabel was a girl of similar age to Mary who lived nearby. Since her parents had moved house three years ago, she and Mary had been good friends. Wishing she had the nerve or the dishonesty to lie to her father, Mary felt her pulse quicken as she shook her head. 'No, Dad. I'm seeing Harry. He asked me if I'd go to the Picture Playhouse with him. You don't mind, do you?'

There was a sudden silence as William ceased raking the stove. 'Harry's asked you?'

'Yes. He's asked me before and I can't go on saying no.' Seeing William's expression, she went on hurriedly: 'It'll be all right, Dad. The film ends at ten. I'll be home by ten-thirty.'

William's heavy face was showing concern. 'I don't know about this, lass. I don't like the Playhouse to begin with. They say a lot of funny people go there.'

'No, Dad, that's just talk. Harry says they're mostly people like ourselves. In any case the film's *Joan of Arc*. And I'll have Harry to look after me.'

William frowned. 'I'm not just thinking about the other people, lass. I'm thinking about Harry. Will he behave himself?'

The girl stared at him, then flushed. 'Harry? Good heavens, of course he will.'

'How do you know? You haven't been out with him before, have you?'

'No. I'd have told you. This is the first time.'

'Then how do you know he'll behave himself.'

The girl hesitated. 'Because he's Harry, that's why. He's always gentle and nice to me.'

William cleared his throat to hide his embarrassment. 'Does this mean you're fond of him? Going out with him, I mean.'

Her blush deepened. 'I like him, yes.'

'I don't mean just like him, lass. Is it more than that?'

Her eyes fell. 'Yes, dad, it's more. I can't help it.'

Forgetting about the open door of the stove, William dropped heavily into his chair. 'You know what your mother's going to say, don't you? She'll say I told you so and want me to get rid of him.'

Mary showed instant alarm. 'You wouldn't do that, would you? You've always said what a good worker he is.'

'He is but that won't carry any weight with your mother. She'll say it's a disgrace for you to get over-friendly with a workman.'

'But, Dad, Harry's better than any of us these days. I don't know a tenth of the things he knows.'

'It's not what he knows, love. Not to your mother. It's where he comes from.'

Mary's voice turned bitter. 'And where does he come from? His mother was the sweetest woman I'd ever met. It's tragic she died so young.'

'I know all that, lass. But your mother has this thing about class. She can't help it so we mustn't be too harsh on her.'

The girl was close to tears. 'So what are you saying? That I can't go out with him?'

William's frown betrayed his inner conflict. 'Where did you arrange to meet him?'

'Outside the Playhouse at eight o'clock. I can't just leave him waiting there, Dad. It'll hurt him terribly.'

William's voice turned gruff. 'You ought to have asked me first, lass. You always have in the past.'

'I know but I was afraid you'd speak to Mother and she'd stop me. Let me go just this once, Dad. We won't do anything wrong, I promise. And if Mother finds out he's taken care of me, perhaps she won't mind so much another time.'

While William had his doubts about that, he always found if difficult to disappoint his favourite daughter. 'Isn't there a film showing in St Peter's Temperance Hall tonight?'

Mary looked puzzled. 'Is there?'

'Yes. I noticed it in last night's paper.' William, who was paying his twice-weekly call on his girlfriend that same evening, cleared his throat before continuing: 'If you promise me that you and Harry will behave yourselves and you'll be home no later than ten-thirty, then perhaps I could tell your mother I'm dropping you off there to meet Mabel.' In his effort to justify himself. William looked for a moment like a shamefaced schoolboy. 'It won't be a complete fib. The tram does stop outside the Hall.'

Mary's eyes shone at him. 'You mean you won't mention Harry?'

At that moment a gust of wind down the chimney sent acrid coke fumes belching across the office. Rising, William swung the door shut before making his gruff reply. 'Not tonight. Mind you, she'll have to be told if this goes on.'

With a cry of joy, Mary ran across to him and buried her face in his waistcoat. 'Oh, Dad, you're such a good sport. Why can't Mum be more like you.'

Clearly moved, William bent down and kissed the girl's golden hair. 'I like you to be happy, lass. But be sure you know what you're doing, Promise?'

She reached up and kissed him. 'I promise. Don't worry.'

Giving her a last affectionate hug, he reached up and turned off the gas light and the two of them left the office together.

Chapter 11

Ethel's voice was bitter. 'So you're going to allow it, are you?'

'Ethel, the girl's nearly twenty-two. She's a woman now. What right have I to interfere?'

'You've every right. You clothe her and give her board. You let her work with you. And on top of that she respects and obeys you. If you wanted to, you could stop her even seeing the man, much less getting herself engaged to him.'

'But what would be the point? They're in love.'

'Love,' Ethel said contemptuously. 'The girl's too young to know what love is.'

It was not unknown for William to be tactless when irritated or frustrated, as he proved now. 'Have you thought that we might lose her if we start interfering? Don't you remember what it's like to be in love?'

Ethel went very pale. 'No, William. I haven't forgotten. But there are all kinds of ways of showing love. If we care about Mary's welfare, we ought to make certain the man she marries is worthy of her.'

'And you're saying Harry isn't? Even though he's increased our business by thirty per cent in the two years he's been with us?'

'I'm not talking about his work. I'm talking about his background. Do you know what his father was?'

'Yes. A labourer. There's no sin in that, is there?'

'He was more than a labourer. He was a Socialist preaching all that poison about class equality. That's why he could never keep a job. Do you think his son is any different?'

William frowned. 'If he isn't, he's never talked Socialism to me. Or to any of the other workmen for that matter.'

'He's talked about it to Mary,' Ethel declared. 'I can tell by the things she says these days.'

William gave an impatient shrug. 'He's a young man. He'll grow out of all that rubbish when he gets older and has children.'

'What if he doesn't? What if he drags Mary down to his level? Do you know he goes out drinking at nights?'

'You mean he goes to a pub once or twice a week with an old school friend. What do you expect a single young man to do? Sit at home like an old woman? In any case all that'll stop once he and Mary can go around together.' When Ethel shook her head stiffly, William frowned. 'Ethel, you've got to stop attacking the boy like this. If things go well, he'll be our son-in-law in October.'

Ethel's bitterness grew. 'So you've agreed a date for their wedding too?'

'Yes, I have. And I don't want you spoiling it with tight lips and a sour face.'

Ethel tossed her head. 'You're assuming I'll be there, then?'

William's voice turned grim. 'You'll be there, Ethel. Make no mistake about that.'

The depth of Ethel's feelings could be measured by her defiance. 'You might be able to make a horse go to water, William, but you can't make it drink. Do you realise the laughing stock we'll be to all our friends when our daughter goes down the aisle with one of your workmen?'

William took a deep breath. 'My God, you're a snob, Ethel. You really are.'

Ethel's pallor deepened. 'Now you're being profane. You'd never have talked to me this way before that wretched man came into our lives.'

William cursed again. 'I suppose the lad's to blame for that fire in Hawthorne Avenue last week? And for the Irish wanting Home Rule? There's no logic in your prejudice, Ethel. Harry hasn't done one thing in his life to harm you.'

The sudden blaze in Ethel's eyes made William stare at her. 'Done nothing to harm me, William? How blind you can be sometimes!'

The young couple were standing arm in arm on the riverbank. Before them a dragonfly was hovering above the water. With its slender body iridescent in the sunlight, it looked like some exotic Eastern sapphire. Then, as an insect dimpled the water a few yards away, it vanished towards it in a flash of speed and colour.

The couple turned and drifted along the riverbank. Harry was bare-headed and carrying his jacket over his left shoulder. His shirt sleeves were rolled back and his right arm was now around Mary's waist. She was wearing a long white dress which brushed the summer grass and released its pollen. She had removed her wide-brimmed hat and every now and then fanned her face with it. Her long hair hung in golden tresses over Harry's bare arm.

They were whispering the words of lovers and every now and then their bodies would lean together. Each time it happened shyness would make the girl look round but she could see no one in the surrounding meadows.

They reached a clump of trees and here Harry paused and laid his jacket on the grass. For a moment the girl resisted his pleading. Then, with his hands gently urging her, she sank down beside him.

He pressed close to her. The touch of his body brought her sensations that had no name but gave promise of pleasure too exquisite to bear. Brought up to fear and to reject sex before marriage, she restrained his eagerness and made him lie back. As she ran a finger along his lips, she smiled down at him. 'You've got your mother's mouth. Do you know that?'

In reply he raised his hands to her face and kissed her. She responded for a moment, then sank down beside him. As they lay with hands intertwined, a chaffinch landed on a bush and eyed them solemnly. It darted away as the girl stretched herself. 'Oh, I love coming to your grandparents. Do you think we can come again before the summer's over?'

'It depends on your dad,' he said. 'Whether he'll give us another long weekend. The old people won't mind. They like you.'

'Do they? Really?'

'Yes. I heard them talking. They think I've made a good choice.'

She laughed with him. For a moment they lay listening to the drowsy hum of summer. Then her hand reached out for his. 'Do you know the date, Harry? It's just eleven weeks to our wedding.'

'I know,' he said.

'Eleven weeks. Then we'll be together like this for the rest of our lives.' The wonder of it caught her breath. Then, because happiness and sadness are inseparable, she turned to him. 'Harry, you don't think there's going to be a war, do you?'

'A war? What ever makes you think that?'

'I overheard Dad and a salesman talking. Dad said the Germans are building up their Army and Navy to fight us. I've never heard him talk about it before. Do you think it's true?'

He ran a hand down her cheek. 'What if they are? It wouldn't last long. Everyone knows no one can beat our Navy. So why should they try?'

'Are you sure?'

'Of course I am. Ask anybody.'

With the resilience of youth, she dismissed the cloud from her mind. 'It does seem silly, doesn't it? I can't imagine why Dad should think such a thing.'

They lay back again. Above them leaves moved gently against the sky and sunbursts of light glowed and faded. The silence was cathedral-like and made their eyelids heavy. A butterfly landed on a clump of rosebay and reverently closed its wings.

The cry of a jackdaw awakened Mary. For a moment a slanting sunbeam dazzled her. Then she saw that Harry, resting on one elbow, was gazing at her. Her head lifted. 'What are you doing? I thought you were sleeping too.'

He smiled. 'No. I've just been looking at you.'

'All this time? What on earth for?'

'Because you're so beautiful,' he said. 'Because you're the most beautiful thing I've ever known.'

Something caught in her throat and she held out her arms to him. 'Oh, Harry, I love you. I love you so much.'

She never knew what he said in reply. They kissed as if their thirst could never be quenched. As the sun paused in its passage and she felt his heartbeats mingle with her own, some instinct in Mary Hardcastle told her that, if only because happiness is finite, life would never offer her a moment as golden and perfect as this again.

Chapter 12

They returned to the old couple's cottage three weeks before their wedding. The morning air was crisp now, the hedges gave a dry rustle when the wind stirred their leaves, and the flesh of the tilled fields was brown and naked beneath the autumn sky.

They went for a long walk on the Sunday morning, taking public footpaths that led along the fringes of private fields. As Harry helped the girl over a style, they heard the distant sound of a huntsman's horn. He gave a grimace. 'That'll be Chadwick's hunt. They must have found something to kill.'

'You don't like fox hunting, do you?' she said.

He glanced at her. 'Killing for sport? I hate it.'

She remembered the original reason for his quarrel with the squire's son. 'Does Michael take part in the hunt when he's home?'

'Of course he does. With his background I'd be surprised if he didn't.'

Although her mother did not believe it, he had never discussed his politics with her, so she had no real knowledge how much his father's beliefs had influenced him. At times she had thought the effect was minimal because she had been taught that all Socialists were atheists and she had long discovered Harry was deeply religious. He did not brandish his faith with pride as did Ethel; instead it was like rock beneath a house, almost out of sight and yet giving the entire structure strength against wind and tempest. Knowing her family were High Church, he had never suggested she accompany him to the simple Methodist chapel of his mother but lately, to the outrage and disgust of Ethel, she had gone with him and found the simple service more to her liking.

It was this deep faith of his that, in her ignorance of Socialism, had made her believe Ethel must be wrong. Yet occasionally, as now, his words or behaviour made her wonder. 'Surely not everyone of his class likes hunting animals, do they?' she said, watching him.

He shrugged. 'I don't know. I'd like to see the statistics.'

Knowing it was a reply that told her little, she followed him along a path that led to the crest of a shallow hill. As a scene of tilled fields opened out before them, he made an exclamation of disgust. 'I see they've made their kill.'

In the distance, alongside a clump of bushes to their left, a pack of hounds were leaping and tearing at some invisible object. Milling around them were twenty or more horsemen. The faint breeze brought them the barking of the excited dogs. Mary gave a shudder. 'They're not letting the dogs kill it, are they?'

He glanced at her. 'Of course. Those are the people we call gentlefolk.'

This time it seemed to her a committed answer. Protected until now by both parents from any contact with unorthodoxy her first thought was how her mother would react to it. Then excitement took over when she realised she was at last free to hear new ideas and different philosophies.

By the time they reached the foot of the hill the hunt

formalities were over. The brush had been recovered, a young rider had been bloodied, and the horsemen and the pack were returning home. As a horn sounded, two riders detached themselves and began galloping across the field towards the young couple.

Mary gave Harry an anxious look. 'What do they want?'

Harry's eyes fixed on the horsemen. As they disturbed a flock of grubbing starlings, he turned to her. 'One of them's Michael.'

'Michael Chadwick?' She showed concern when he nodded.

The leading rider reined back when only a few yards from them. Handsome in his scarlet coat, he gave a laugh as he addressed Harry. 'I thought it was you. I was told you were back at your grandfather's cottage.'

'Yes, I'm back. What do you want?'

Michael spurred his horse closer. 'You're trespassing again. Do you know that?'

'No I'm not. This is a public footpath.'

Michael grinned at his companion, a fresh-complexioned young man of his own age. 'Prove it.'

'I don't have to prove it. There's a signpost back there.'

Michael turned his gaze on Mary. 'Who's this? Your latest girlfriend?'

Harry's face set. 'Mind your own business.'

Michael lifted an eyebrow. 'I notice you're as rude as ever. Why don't you introduce me?'

'Because I don't wish to go. Go away.'

'Then I'll have to introduce myself, won't I?' Turning to the girl, Michael mockingly lifted his riding hat. 'I'm Michael Chadwick. Might I ask your name, ma'am?'

All the girl wanted to do at that moment was keep the situation under control. 'I'm Mary Hardcastle, Harry's

102

fiancée. And I don't think we are trespassing, Mr Chadwick. There is a signpost back in the lane.'

Michael touched his forehead with his riding crop. 'In that case I must accept your word, Miss Hardcastle. Will you please remove your hat?'

'My hat?'

'Yes. I want to take a good look at you.'

The girl did not know whether to take his words as a joke or whether to show anger. As she hesitated, Harry caught her arm. 'Come on. We're going back now.'

He turned to lead her back along the path but found Michael's horse obstructing him. His face lifted. 'Get out of my way, Chadwick.'

Michael lifted an eyebrow again. 'I see your boorish manners haven't improved with time. I'll let you go when your girlfriend removes her hat.'

'She's not going to remove her hat. Not for you or anybody else.'

Michael reined his horse closer. 'I think you're wrong, Harry Miles.' Before either of them could react, he leaned down and snatched the hat from the girl's head. As she gave a cry and Harry leapt forward, Michael spurred his horse away and handed the hat to his grinning friend. He then turned and gazed at Mary. 'Perhaps I'm wrong and our Socialist's son has some taste after all. You're quite a good looking filly, aren't you? What does your father do?'

'Give the hat back, Chadwick.' Harry said.

Michael glanced at his friend. 'What shall we do, Desmond? Give it back or make him beg for it?'

A high-pitched laugh answered him. 'Make him beg.'

With that Harry leapt forward to grab Michael's leg. Expecting the move, Michael spurred forward, driving the horse's shoulder at Harry and throwing him down. As Mary gave a scream, Michael snatched her hat from

103

his friend and threw it high into a nearby tree. He then turned to the distressed girl. 'You're making a bad mistake, Mary Hardcastle. He'll turn out like his father. A born failure. That's why they turn to Socialism. They want to drag the rest of us down to their level.'

With that he swung away. With mud flinging up behind them, the two horsemen galloped up the hill. The sobbing girl dropped on her knees beside Harry. 'Are you hurt, darling?'

Ignoring her question, he climbed to his feet and stood watching the horsemen. Trembling with shock, she clutched his arm. 'I wouldn't have believed a man in his position could behave that way. Are you sure you're all right?'

'Yes,' he said.

She shuddered. 'He hates you, Harry, doesn't he? After all these years. Why?'

He made no reply. Once again Harry Miles was being made to face the conflicting elements in his character that he did not understand. The man raised in boyhood to refute violence was wondering how another human being could behave with such spite and malice. The stranger in him that he neither recognised nor liked was gazing after the horsemen with a hard and impassioned anger.

The couple's marriage took place on the 10th October. The church chosen for the occasion was the Holy Trinity, dating back to the thirteenth century. In many ways it was an absurd choice but here Ethel would not be denied. If her younger daughter was to marry a nobody, then at least the fact should not be made obvious to all and sundry.

In this she met little opposition from William. While

he could be a trifle parsimonious over wages and household expenses, William tended to be over-generous on festive occasions and it had always been his intention to give Mary a day to remember. Accordingly, even if the attendance did look meagre under Holy Trinity's high vaulted roof, the music, colour and pageantry of the ceremony satisified Ethel, even if the bridegroom did not.

The reception that followed in the city's Assembly Rooms was equally bountiful. The food was excellent, the champagne flowed freely, and with Ethel receiving such comments as 'What a lovely wedding gown your daughter had' and 'Weren't the bridesmaids just gorgeous?' Ethel might have gone to bed that night feeling that in spite of everything else, the wedding had been a success.

It was, however, ruined for her (and for Mary) by one thoughtless remark from William. William, who beneath his Edwardian crust had a sentimental heart, had found the day something of an ordeal, for he was not only losing his favourite daughter but, as he believed at the time, his business partner too. It was true that Mary had agreed to continue working for him, but William took it for granted that once her first child arrived she would leave.

Faced with this prospect, William had drunk too much champagne by the time he rose to toast the bride and his blunder came towards the end of his speech. Leaning somewhat unsteadily towards Mary, he put an arm around her shoulders and at the same time waggled a finger at Harry.

'You know, lad, I'm giving you something more than a daughter. I'm giving you my right-hand man too. So you'd better be grateful and bring me in plenty of business.'

In the laughter and cheers that followed, no one noticed Mary's anxious glance at her mother or the way Ethel's cheeks paled at this confirmation of her beliefs. In later years, when seeking the time when her mother's jealousy had turned to active dislike, Mary would always look back to her wedding day.

With William, in spite of his generosity, allowing the couple only a week off work, they spent their honeymoon at Harry's grandparents' cottage. Although Mary had always enjoyed her weekends there, the affair with Michael Chadwick had upset her and it was only when Harry reminded her that Michael would now be back at university that she went with a clear mind.

In the event they had an idyllic week. The weather, with bright frosty days, allowed them to go for long walks every day. They took two train rides, one to the coast and the other to Buxton. For the rest of the time they did nothing but get to know one another in the way of lovers everywhere.

It was the nights Mary was to remember most of all. The old couple had insisted they used their own bedroom. It was full of heavy mahogany furniture, old prints, an ornate oil lamp, and a brass double bedstead with a huge feather mattress. Retiring soon after dark, they would light the lamp and sink down into a blissful cocoon of hot water bottles and billowing white clouds. There, safe in the silence of the countryside, Harry would take her into his arms while the old room, mellowed by the lamp light, told tales of other and older loves.

To her relief she discovered Harry was a patient and gentle lover. Her upbringing had made her self-conscious and shy and the first night was painful and embarrassing. But when no unwilling demands were made of her, her inhibitions began to disappear. It could not be said that by the end of the week (or even in the months ahead) that she became a passionate or erotic lover but with Harry limited in experience and their years of denial ended at last, neither could conceive greater joy than they experienced during those gentle, magical nights.

Their honeymoon over, they moved into a small house down a street only one block away from No. 57 and William's warehouse. William had found the house and offered them a down payment to hold it until their marriage. Both had liked it but with the same independence as his parents, Harry had at first resisted the offer. 'Let's begin the way we mean to go on, love. Let's pay our own way in everything.'

While appreciating his independence, Mary had her mother in mind. Without William's generous offer, they would have to live in a meaner suburb of the city which would further alienate Ethel's feelings towards Harry. 'It'll hurt Dad if we turn him down, darling. Can't we take it on the understanding we pay him back from our wages?'

For her sake Harry had agreed. In reward for the new business he had brought in, William had recently given him a pound a week rise and Harry felt that with Mary still at work they ought to be able to pay off the loan relatively quickly.

They soon found however that living close to No. 57 and the warehouse had both advantages and disadvantages. With Harry now a member of the family, William felt it right he should lunch with them on the days he was travelling locally. Acutely conscious how Ethel felt about this arrangement, it was not difficult for Mary, with her home so close, to suggest she and Harry have

107

lunch there, her excuse being a newly-wed wife's enjoyment in catering for her husband.

The debit side showed when William kept inviting them to dinner. Prior to the marriage William had tended to keep to the strict Edwardian demarcation lines of employer and employee which had given him little opportunity to learn more about Harry except that he was a bright and upright young man and an excellent salesman. Now, with kinship sweeping away the demarcation lines, he was surprised and gratified to find Harry was well-informed and had a wide range of interests.

The discovery was like a breath of fresh air to William. For twenty years and more his home had been dominated by women restricted by their education to domestic chit-chat and gossip and to find more enlightened conversation he had been forced out to his club. Now that he had a young man in his family to expound to, his invitations were genuine and frequent.

There was nothing that would have pleased Mary more than to accept these invitations, for in spite of her high regard for her father, he had until now treated her as a protected specie when it came to matters of the world and with Harry providing the opening she would have found deep satisfaction in talking to her father as an equal at last.

But the dangers were too great. Her mother knew that Harry's father had been a card-carrying Socialist and although Harry had been painfully careful never to discuss politics with the family, Ethel was clearly convinced he carried the same stigma. A wolf in sheep's clothing, he had penetrated her family by the seduction of her daughter. True to his kind he would enjoy their munificence as long as it suited him but would be only too ready to turn against them if and when the Red Call came. In short he was a hypocrite and a class enemy.

For Mary, with her love for Harry enriched even further by the intimacy of sex, it no longer mattered what his politics were. If all Socialists were as gentle and considerate as he, she felt her conversion could be painless. With his influence stimulating her mind and extending her tolerance, she had often wanted to discuss the subject with him but like most women of her time she had been taught that politics was a man's business and consequently had learned nothing about it. Afraid of making a fool of herself, she also remembered how irritated her father became when Ethel dabbled in masculine affairs. So, like millions more of her kind, she had thrust aside her curiosity and contented herself with her duties as a newly-wed wife.

But none of this solved the problem of a social evening with Ethel. In the past, during the brief occasions when Mary, Harry, and Ethel had met without William's presence, it had been relatively easy to keep the conversation on safe subjects, particularly as Ethel herself had kept the meetings as short and infrequent as possible. It was going to be an entirely different matter when the four of them spent an evening together and Ethel had the chance to probe and perhaps provoke. Even if Harry's political affiliations were not mentioned, Mary was only too aware that many of his ideas would either jar or shock her parents and she had no idea how he would respond if they were challenged.

On every count, then, it seemed only prudent to avoid social intercourse until some kind of an armistice was reached. In her heart Mary was hoping that armistice would come when she had a child.

None of this took into account William's feelings however. Ethel might show no great desire to entertain them but William was making it very clear that he missed Mary's company in the evenings and could not understand why the two of them kept refusing his invitations.

With William's birthday only a few days away, matters came to a head at the end of November. Mary mentioned it to Harry when they were having dinner.

'It's Dad's birthday on the fifth, darling. He wants us to have dinner with him. Can I tell him it's all right?'

He gazed at her, then sighed. 'I suppose we must?'

'I think we should, darling. For Dad's sake.'

He nodded, then changed the subject. 'I ran into Gareth today.'

'Gareth? He's the one you went to night school with, isn't he? The one you used to pub crawl with when you were a batchelor.'

He grinned. 'You don't forget much, do you?'

'I thought he'd gone to Wales with his sister.'

'He did. But from what I can gather he and his brother-in-law didn't get on. So he's come back to stay with an old aunt.'

'He's a Socialist, isn't he?' she said.

He laughed. 'More than that. He's a Welsh Socialist. And as bright as a button with it.'

She had always felt that if she could find out more about his political beliefs she could be better prepared for an evening with Ethel. With her limited knowledge she tried to draw him out. 'Is he like Lloyd George?'

He laughed again. 'Lloyd George is a Tory beside Gareth, love. Gareth wants to blow the world apart and start again. At least he did in the old days and I wouldn't think a spell in Wales has changed him.'

She thought how boyish he looked when he laughed, with his tousled curly hair and sensitive mouth. Afraid to ask the question outright, she tried it obliquely. 'What does he think of your views?'

'Mine? I'm not radical enough for him. But it's good to see him again. I said I'd have a drink with him tomor-

110

row night. You don't mind, do you, love? I think he's a bit lonely and looking forward to a talk.'

She felt an opportunity had been given her and she had let it slip. 'I don't mind. But don't let Mum or Dad know, will you? You know how they feel about pubs and drink?'

He raised a comical eyebrow. 'Your dad?'

She had to laugh. 'All right, then. Mum. She never breathes a word about it but one of her uncles ended up in goal because of drink.'

He stared at her. 'You're not serious.'

'It's true. He got three years for assault and battery. But don't ever mention it, for heaven's sake, or she'd kill me.'

He burst out laughing. 'A skeleton in your family cupboard. Tell me more.'

She pretended to throw the teapot cosy at him. 'There isn't any more.'

'No? What about that affair you had among the crates in the warehouse yard?'

'Oh, that. You mean with that awful little hooligan who was always fighting. I was too young to know what I was doing in those days.' Before he stopped laughing, she went on: 'Then I can tell Dad we'll go round for dinner on his birthday?'

His laughter ceased. 'Yes, all right. If it's Dad's birthday I suppose we must.'

Chapter 13

Fog was blanketing the city when Harry made his way to The Blue Boar on Hessle Road. It diffused the gas lamps and muffled the sound of traffic and the mournful hoot of ships. Figures materialised from it and disappeared as eerily. Men and women could be heard coughing as its miasma bit into undernourished lungs.

In patches it was dense and Harry stumbled off the pavement twice before the hazy lights of The Blue Boar appeared. Pushing open the door of the bar, he was halted a moment by the bright lights and the noise, and it was a few seconds before he caught sight of Gareth.

He was sitting at a table in the far corner. Wearing a soiled shirt and a pullover with ragged sleeves, he had a half-pint glass of beer before him and an unlit cigarette in his mouth. As always, in spite of his twenty-odd years, he looked like an undernourished street urchin. Catching sight of Harry, he let out a shout and waved him over.

'So you managed it, boyo. I thought your old lady might stop you.'

Harry dropped into the chair opposite him. He nodded down at the half-pint of beer. 'What's the idea? Are you going teetotal?'

Gareth scowled. 'Not from choice, boyo. The bastards gave me the sack last week.'

'What for? Redundancy?'

Pulling the wet Woodbine from his lips, Gareth spat out a shred of tobacco. 'Naw. The same as your dad. They caught me handing out copies of *The Dawn*.'

'What's *The Dawn*?'

Gareth grinned. 'You haven't heard of it? It's the latest revolutionary Socialist paper. Do you know what they're asking the workers to do?' When Harry shook his head: 'They're telling everyone to save threepence a week towards a revolver. They say it's the only way we'll ever get our rights.'

Harry frowned. 'That's plain stupid. Protest and strikes are one thing. Armed revolution's another.'

When Gareth was arguing his revolutionary case, his gaunt face resembled a predatory hawk more than an urchin. 'Don't you read the papers these days?'

'Of course I do.'

'Then you'll know about the labour troubles last year. Half the trade unions in the country were on strike in March. And what happened? The bastards put the Army in. Workers were shot and killed, boyo. So what are they supposed to do? Sit on their arses and take it?'

Harry had often wondered why he was never able to take Gareth's more militant threats seriously and felt the reason went back to their childhood days when Gareth had found a sick dog lying alongside the Marfleet canal. He had taken it home and Harry had hardly seen him for the next two weeks while he nursed it. Then came the proud day when he had appeared on Harry's doorstep with the ebullient dog straining on a piece of string.

The boy's joy had been short-lived. His sister had decided she could not afford to keep a young and healthy dog and that it must go. It had been put down and for

113

weeks Gareth had been broken-hearted. Militant revolutionaries, Harry knew from his studies, had emerged from lesser things but he could not see Gareth one of them. The shell seemed hard but the kernel was sentimental. Harry, whose fast-developing mind already had the ability to draw one hypothesis from another, wondered if that was not the paradoxical answer to all bloody revolutions. The leaders could not have a soft centre if they were to fight and without it they could dispense no more compassion than their enemy before them.

He shook his head. 'Shooting soldiers isn't going to make things any better.'

'Boyo, the people can't take much more. Work's just about stopped in the Potteries. That's nearly a quarter of a million men unemployed. And what do they get? Nothing but a meal of bread and soup from private charities. *The Dawn* says they've sold everything to the pawnbrokers: furniture, carpets, even their clothes to feed their kids. And what do our middle and upper classes care?'

'Can you believe these figures?' Harry asked.

'Yes. *The Dawn* has taken them from Roberts' report. Roberts is an independent industrial conciliator and he estimates that at least eight million workers are living on a family income of under a pound a week. Do you realise what this means? Thousands of people are starving to death.'

Harry's frown deepened. 'I know things are bad. But an armed revolution isn't the answer.'

'Maybe not to you, boyo. But what about those poor sodding dockers in London? *The Dawn* says one of its reporters found a mother begging a pawnbroker to give her two pennies for two glass vases. They were all she had left in the world and she needed the money to buy a couple of cod's heads to keep her kids alive a few days longer.' When Harry made no reply: 'Think of it, boyo. Eight million poor bastards starving while your class gets richer and richer.'

Harry's eyes lifted. 'My class?'

Gareth grinned at him. 'Yes. You're in the middle class now, aren't you? The sods who make profit out of our sweat and misery. You'll be one of the first to be shot when the revolution comes.'

'Thanks,' Harry said.

Gareth grinned again. 'Mind you, if you buy me a beer I'll ask 'em to shoot at your legs instead of your belly.'

Harry rose. 'You always were considerate.'

'Not considerate enough to buy you one back, boyo. I'm one of the starving millions now.'

Harry returned with two pints of beer. He laid a packet of Woodbines on the table alongside Gareth's glass. 'Peace offering in case you ever become a commissar.'

Gareth pulled out a cigarette and sucked in smoke greedily. At the far side of the bar a group of cloth-capped labourers and their womenfolk were singing the latest bawdy music-hall hit. At a nearby table a man in a grey muffler whispered a joke into a blousy woman's ear. As her ribald laughter shrilled out, Gareth gave a sardonic grin. 'I wonder what your mother-in-law would say if she saw you now?'

Harry, who had lit his pipe, exhaled smoke. 'She couldn't think much worse of me that she does already.'

Gareth eyed his face curiously. 'What about Mary? Does she know you're here?'

'Of course. She knows the two of us go back a long way.'

Gareth's grin showed his neglected teeth. 'Yes, but does she know I'm a bloodthirsty revolutionary?'

115

'Yes. It's a pity you don't talk to people like her for a change. You'd find out not everyone in the middle class wants to grind workers into the dust. Often it's nothing but ignorance. If they were told how bad things are, quite a number would help.'

'What's stopping them finding out?' Gareth challenged.

'Their environment. The books they're not given to read. The newspapers their parents don't buy. The people they're not allowed to talk to.'

'It's not their wealth they don't want to lose?'

'Not in every case, no. Some are the victims of it. They want knowledge but they're denied it.'

Although Gareth knew he was talking about Mary, he could not hide his contempt. 'You're saying that ignorance excuses them?'

'Yes. I think it does.'

'Then why doesn't ignorance of the law excuse a man if he breaks it.'

The quickness of the reply reminded Harry of the intelligent, self-educated mind behind the revolutionary mask. 'Perhaps it should,' he said. 'If the reasons are sound enough.'

Gareth's laugh jarred him. 'I think you're beginning to backslide, boyo. If you go on finding excuses for the bastards, you'll soon be on the other side of the barricades. And I don't think your father would have liked that.'

Harry's expression hardened at the comment. 'I'm what I always was. But I don't like this talk of violence. It would only make the Liberals believe what the Tories already believe: that we're nothing but mindless, stupid animals. And that would set reform back for decades.'

Engrossed in their argument, neither of them noticed the man and woman who entered the bar. Middle-aged,

116

expensively but flashily dressed, their expression suggested contempt for the company they found themselves in. As the man took the woman's arm to lead her outside, he caught sight of Harry in the far corner. Showing interest, he motioned at his table and said something that made the woman give a malicious laugh before they withdrew.

Gareth's thin cheeks hollowed as he sucked in smoke. 'You can afford to wait, boyo. Your belly gets filled every day. But what about those women with starving kids? You expect them to wait forever?'

Harry shook his head doggedly. 'I still don't believe violence is the answer. It's never solved anything.'

Gareth's Welsh voice mocked him. 'So you were alseep during those history lessons. What about those French aristocrats? It gave them a headache or two, didn't it?'

'And what happened afterwards? Weren't things worse?'

'For a time, boyo. Only for a time.' Gareth grinned again. 'What happened to the kid who once tried to knock Michael Chadwick's block off because he shot a couple of birds?'

Harry gave a start. 'Who told you about that?'

'Your grandad. Don't you remember taking me there for a weekend? Your grandad says you fought him in the ring too and put up a hell of a scrap.'

Harry shifted restlessly. 'That was different. I hadn't any choice.'

'And starving workers have?' When Harry frowned again, Gareth went on: 'You're a real mix up between your old man and your old lady, aren't you? You can't make up your mind who's right.'

Harry's eyes lifted. 'Since when did my old man get into fights?'

'Often, from what I've heard. Not picking 'em, I agree, but standing up for what he believed in.'

'That's different,' Harry muttered. 'You're talking about guns and revolution.'

Gareth shrugged. 'One's only a step from the other.' He eyed Harry a moment, then leaned forward. 'Tell me something, boyo. What would you do if this country went to war?'

Harry gave a faint start. 'War?'

'Yes. Since the Boer War we're the most hated country in Europe. Everyone hates us, for our national wealth, our Empire, and our arrogance. They'd all like a go at us but when it comes it'll be Germany. They've been preparing for it for ten years. All they need now is an excuse. What will you do, boyo? Join up or be a pacifist?'

Believing Gareth could be right about Germany, it was a question Harry had been asking himself in recent months. 'You know what I believe. Violence leads to more violence and settles nothing. All the same, isn't there a difference in defending your country and trying to overthrow its Government?'

'Is there?' Gareth demanded. 'To workers without food and jobs, the bastards who starve their kids are a damn sight more of an enemy than any foreign power. Even if you're not prepared to take up arms against them, why in hell should you take up arms for them?'

Harry knew he was avoiding the question. 'Does that mean you wouldn't fight for your country?'

'Me?' Gareth's mocking laugh made the woman at the next table turn and stare at him. 'There's only one reason I'd join up, boyo. To get a gun to turn against the bastards.'

118

Chapter 14

The 5th December turned out to be a cold, bleak day with a drizzle in the wind. With no possibility of avoiding her father's birthday party, Mary spent the day worrying about it and had a pounding headache when she arrived home. To make matters worse it was now raining heavily and Harry was an hour late. The bicycle on which he made his rounds had burst a tyre, leaving him no choice but to push it all the way home. He looked tired, was soaked to the skin, and like herself was apprehensive about the evening.

'It won't please your mother that we're late,' he told her as he struggled into dry clothes.

She did her best to appear sanguine but Ethel's appearance and voice did nothing to stifle their misgivings when she answered the door at No. 57 an hour later. 'So you're both here at last, are you? I thought you must have forgotten your father's birthday.'

Knowing she was usually more circumspect in front of William, Mary hastily ushered Harry through to the living room where William was already pouring out drinks for them. When he showed delight at his presents and made it clear how glad he was to have them round, the tension eased a little although the hostile glances

119

Ethel kept giving Harry both before and during dinner made Mary wonder if she harboured some new grievance against him. William's grunt halfway through the meal added to her misgivings. 'What's the matter with you tonight, Ethel? You're looking like a cat that's lost its tail.'

Ethel's glance was icy. 'You look after your own face, William, and I'll look after mine.'

In normal times William would have given as good or better than he got but tonight he was mellowed with bonhommie and whisky. Muttering something Mary could not catch, he turned to Harry. 'That was a good order you brought in yesterday, lad. Half a dozen casks of red cabbage – I had to set my men working overtime last night.'

While the conversation was on business, Mary felt able to relax. It was when the meal was over, Molly had been called in to clear the table, and the four of them were settled into their chairs in the living room, that Ethel made her move. Picking up the evening paper which was lying conveniently on a nearby table, she gave a sudden exclamation. 'I don't believe a word of it.'

About to light his pipe, William lowered the burning match. 'Don't believe what, love?'

Ethel glanced up. 'That scandal over the *Titanic* has blown up again. Sir Richard Earnshaw says his uncle was maliciously defamed at the Inquiry in June.'

'He was? Who by?'

'One of the survivors, a fireman called Marsden, claimed that the first- and second-class passengers were given priority in the lifeboats. He said they bribed the sailors.'

William frowned. 'Where does Earnshaw's uncle come into it?'

'This same man said he and his wife got away and

refused to allow their lifeboat to go back to pick up survivors in case they were caught in the suction. Even though their lifeboat was only half full.'

William sucked at his unlit pipe. 'Earnshaw, eh? I wouldn't have thought it of him.'

Ethel stared at him. 'You surely don't believe it? It's obvious Marsden was lying.' Her eyes switched across to Harry. 'Wouldn't you agree, Harry?'

Mary felt her muscles suddenly tighten. She broke in before Harry could answer. 'Why should the fireman lie, Mother? What would be the point?'

Ethel's scornful glance moved to her. 'Surely it's obvious. The man hates the upper class and saw a way of getting back at them. Ten to one he's a Socialist.'

Mary was convinced now that, birthday party or not, Ethel was hell bent for a confrontation with Harry. 'Mother, stop it, please. We've come to celebrate Dad's birthday, not to talk politics.'

Ignoring her, Ethel turned back to Harry. 'What do you think Harry? You're a Socialist too, aren't you?'

With the question asked in such an uncompromising fashion, Mary knew there was no turning back now. Breath held, she watched Harry give a quiet nod. 'Yes, Mrs Hardcastle. I'm a Socialist.'

In the tension of the admission, no one noticed the incongruity of Harry addressing his mother-in-law by her married name. Ethel's face lit up in triumph. 'I thought you were. Mary's always denied it but I was sure of it when she stopped going to church.'

Mary gave a start. 'What's the Church got to do with it?'

'Socialists don't believe in God, dear. They're all atheists.'

For a moment Mary believed this was the root cause of Ethel's attack. 'Don't be silly, Mother. Harry's more religious than any of us. Ask the minister at his chapel.'

Ethel gave a sniff of contempt. 'You call going to chapel being religious?'

'Yes, I do,' Mary said hotly. 'There are other ways of worship than burning incense and wearing your best clothes to impress people.'

'Is this what Harry has taught you?'

'Harry's taught me many things, Mother. Like having sympathy and tolerance.'

'Aye, I'm sure. Tolerance for revolutionaries and anarchists too, I'll be bound.'

'Revolutionaries? What are you talking about? Harry's no revolutionary.'

'Isn't he?' Two red spots were burning in Ethel's cheeks as she played her trump card. 'Then why did he spend last Thursday evening drinking with one in a public house?'

Mary's heart missed a beat. William, fuddled by whisky, sat upright. 'What are you talking about, Ethel?'

Ethel swung round. 'When did you last see Joe Turner, William?'

William frowned. 'Joe Turner? The last time I wanted oak casks, I suppose. September or October. Why?'

'Well I met his wife two days ago. And she couldn't tell me quick enough where she had seen your son-in-law. Laughing and drinking in The Blue Boar on Hessle Road with a Welshman called Gareth Evans. Do you know who Evans is?'

Out of his depth, William shook his head. 'I've never heard of him.'

'I'm not surprised but Elsie Turner has. She knows his whole family. His aunt told her Evans was up in Court last year for distributing a revolutionary magazine outside a Welsh fctory. And he's just lost his job here for doing the same thing here.'

Frowning heavily, William turned to Harry. 'Is this right, lad? Did you see him?'

Although his face was pale, Harry met his eyes without flinching. 'Yes, I did.'

'But why, lad? Why spend an evening with a fellow like that?'

'He's an old friend, Mr Hardcastle. That's why.'

'You hear that?' Ethel broke in. 'Those are the friends he mixes with. Men who want to overthrow our society. And now all our friends will know too.'

Mary knew that was the hard core of her mother's resentment. Her only surprise was that Ethel had been able to contain it until their visit. She made a desperate effort to repair the damage. 'People aren't going to take any notice of what Joe Turner and his wife say, Mother. They're both horrible people.'

Ethel's hard laugh betrayed her outrage. 'They'll listen all right. It's just the kind of scandal people love.'

With the friends Ethel had, Mary knew it was true. Before she could say more, William glanced back at Harry. 'What I was asking, lad, was whether you shared this chap's views?'

Harry rose sharply to his feet, behaviour that reminded Mary of his reaction as a boy when he had been unfairly accused of hooliganism. 'You've no right to ask me that, Mr Hardcastle. I don't ask you what your political views are.'

Ethel gave a laugh of triumph. 'There's your answer, William.'

Taking a deep breath, Harry glanced at Mary. 'I'm going home now. Are you coming or staying?'

She was already on her feet. 'I'm desperately sorry, Dad, particularly as it's your birthday. But you do understand why we have to go?'

He rose heavily from his armchair. 'Aye, I understand, lass, and I'm as sorry as you are. Wait and I'll see you to the door.'

Pausing on the front porch, he half-closed the door, then led them down the path. At the gate he turned to Harry. 'I want you to know this doesn't affect our relationship, lad. Not one bit.'

Harry's voice was bitter. 'Are you sure? I'll resign if you want me to.'

'Don't be daft, lad. You're my son-in-law.'

'I'm also a revolutionary according to your wife. So don't let our relationship stop you.'

William turned pleadingly to Mary. 'It's your mother's age, lass. Try to explain to him. You know how it affects some women.'

Suddenly touched by his efforts to excuse Ethel, she reached up and kissed his cheek. 'Don't you worry, Dad. But it'll be better if we don't come round in the evenings. Not for a while anyway.'

He sighed. 'Aye, I suppose so.'

She kissed him again. 'That doesn't mean you can't visit us, you know. Any time you feel like it.'

'Aye, I know that. Good night, then. See you both in the morning.'

Catching Harry's arm, she led him through the front gate and along the pavement. She glanced back before they reached the street corner and saw William was still watching them. Her eyes blurred as she gave him a wave.

Mary could not sleep that night. She tried not to toss and turn and keep Harry awake but when after an hour he turned to her, she knew he had not slept either. His question warned her how carefully she must tread. 'What's the matter? Have you the same fears as your mother?'

She winced in the darkness. 'Don't be silly. Of course I haven't.'

'Why not? I've taken you away from your church and I spend my evenings drinking with revolutionaries. I've been tried and convicted.'

She thought what a hindrance words were to love. 'You haven't taken me from anything, Harry.'

'Yes, I have. You go with me to chapel now. You wouldn't have made that change but for me.'

'No. I've made the change because I see the hypocracy of the rich going to show off their finery while millions starve in the slums. That's why I've changed.'

'And I've had nothing to do with it?'

She turned to him. 'I'm not denying it's you who has made me see the world in a different light. But the faults had to be there in the first place. So why are you blaming yourself.'

It was a few seconds before he answered her. 'I don't like coming between you and your parents.'

'Harry, you had a different family life. Mother and I have never been close like you and your parents were. She's always looked for reasons to attack me. If it hadn't been you it would have been someone else.'

He shifted restlessly. 'It's not just that. You've never asked me what my politics are. Why was that? Were you afraid what you'd hear?'

Unsure herself, it took her a moment to reply. 'In the beginning I hardly thought about it. When I did, I felt you'd tell me in your own time.'

'Then you have been curious?'

'Only recently. Women like us don't think about politics much, Harry. We take everything for granted.'

'Even when I go out with men like Gareth?'

'It didn't worry me. I knew you'd never take part in anything violent.'

125

'How could you know that?'

She laid her head against his shoulder. 'Because you're my husband and I've learned how gentle you are.' As he stirred restlessly: 'Oh, I'm not saying you wouldn't fight to defend somebody. But that's all you would fight for. There's too much of your mother in you.'

The perversity in him was not defeated yet. 'My mother was poorer when she died than when she was born. My father saw the unfairness of it but she never complained. Perhaps it's because of people like her that the world's never improved.'

She would not hear a word against his mother. 'Your mother was a lovely person. And she was right about fighting and violence. Dad always says that revolutions only make things worse for the people.'

About to reply harshly, he remembered her social education and his voice softened. 'You talk as if life and politics were separate things, love. They're not. One thing makes the other.'

'You know what I mean. You wouldn't take up arms against people just because they had different ideas to you. Or because they were ignorant of the social conditions of the poor. It's just not in you.'

Was she seeking reassurance, he thought with sudden humour. Then he remembered his discussion with Gareth about the rights and wrongs of ignorance and his mood changed again. 'You're quite right. I'm what Gareth would call a half-hearted Socialist.'

Recognising both bitterness and resignation in his voice, she snuggled closer to him. 'Then Gareth's wrong. You're a man who respects people. That's something I've always loved about you. If all Socialists were like you, I could become one. But not if they're like Gareth.'

'But it's people like Gareth who get things done, love. They take risks and I don't.'

126

'You change people by example,' she said. 'And that's the way to make it last.'

She loves my weaknesses, he thought. She doesn't realise that to win a political cause you must display total prejudice. Show no pity, no tolerance, no forgiveness. They are the sentiments of the loser.

He changed the subject. 'How worried are you about this quarrel tonight?'

She flinched. 'I hated it for Dad's sake and for yours. Dad's old fashioned but he's fair. Mother's a different person altogether.'

'You're afraid of her, aren't you?' he said.

'Yes, I suppose I am. I'm afraid of what she might do to us. She can be such a bitch, Harry. And yet she's very much in love with Dad. Sometimes I think it's because she sees in him things she hasn't got in herself.'

He nodded. 'The classic recipe of both love and hate.'

She was to remember his words later. 'All the same, we must stand up to her. She must learn she can't get away with her bullying.'

His only thought at that moment was to comfort her. 'You know, your dad could be right. It could be her age. Or perhaps she'll change when we give her a grandchild. Have you thought about that?'

'Yes, sometimes. I suppose it's possible.'

He drew her closer to him. His quirky humour that was never far below the surface made her blush. 'That's a thing we can do something about, love. Why don't we give it another try?'

Chapter 15

The following morning, which Mary had been viewing with some apprehension, came as a welcome anti-climax. Although William's mood was muted, his first act was to assure her that his feelings towards Harry had not changed by one jot, even if the same did not apply to his political views. He did however suggest that it might be prudent if they did not lunch at No. 57 that day. Although Mary had no such intention, William's mood made her curious and when Molly came over with their mid-morning flask of tea she buttonholed her at the foot of the steps.

'What happened after we left, Molly? Don't worry: my parents won't know you've told me.'

The event had clearly upset the girl. 'They'd a terrific quarrel, Miss Mary. I've never seen your dad so angry. He said he'd throw your mother out if she did anything like it again.'

Mary winced. 'What about my mother?'

'Oh, Miss Mary, she was in a dreadful state! She was still sobbing her heart out when I went to bed.'

Mary told Harry about the quarrel that evening. 'Dad's got a terrible temper. I almost feel sorry for Mother. But it does prove how fond he is of you. Did he say anything when you took your orders in?'

He nodded as he threw his scarf on the hallstand. 'He said much the same to me but he never mentioned a quarrel.' He frowned as he turned away. 'I seem to be tearing your family apart, don't I?'

She caught hold of his arm. 'Don't talk like that! Mother started it, not you. Anyway, who knows: it might be for the best. After all, Dad knows her better than anyone.'

In the weeks that followed it appeared she could be right. During their meetings with Ethel that sooner or later became inevitable, Ethel's behaviour was circumspection itself. She made no apology for her behaviour but then no one expected or desired one in case the entire affair blew up again. Nor could it be said she was friendly towards Harry or Mary but she was polite, she managed a smile now and then, and she was studiously careful to keep off any subject that had political overtones.

To Mary, who knew her mother better than Harry, it seemed more of an armistice than a capitulation and what worried her most were the unspoken terms of that armistice. Were they permanent on the condition Harry took no active part in politics or were they an enforced condition brought about by William's displeasure? When the girl remembered the dependence both she and Harry had on her family, a vague chill would run through her.

She discovered she was pregnant the following June. With Connie in Middlesbrough still childless and according to the doctors likely to remain so, William was delighted and began making all kinds of plans for the child. Ethel's response was more difficult to define because of her polite façade. At times Mary was certain she was pleased to have a prospective grandchild, at

129

others she felt Ethel was resentful that her first grand-child should come from what she believed to be an ill-conceived marriage.

It was not an easy pregnancy for Mary. She was sick throughout the months of August and September and in December she was ordered by her doctor to give up work. To help the couple out, William continued to pay her half wages, refused to take any more money off his house loan, and increased Harry's wage by ten shillings a week. Although grateful for his help, it made Mary realise their dependence on her family even more.

The child was born in March 1913. A healthy baby girl of over eight pounds, it gave the slim Mary a long and painful delivery.

In the fashion of the time it was born at home, a cheerful buxom Irishwoman being the midwife. At first Mary was disappointed at not having a son. She felt Harry would have preferred one and she was certain that William, plagued by women all his life, would have gone into raptures over a male grandchild who might one day carry on his business.

Her fears were soon put to rest. Harry, the first allowed into the room to see the child, assured her he had always wanted a daughter. And when ten minutes later the impatient Ethel and William were allowed inside, William was beaming as joyously as if the child were his own. However Mary's eyes were on Ethel as she went over to the cot.

The baby was crying lustily as the nurse picked her up. 'Here she is, the little darlin'.' She chucked the baby beneath the chin before offering her to Ethel. 'Sssh, my little beauty! You don't want to give your grandma a bad impression, do you?'

William peered over Ethel's shoulder. 'She's all right, is she, Nurse?'

'You mean has she got all her bits and pieces, sir? Aye, of course she has. She's a fine healthy lass.' The woman's eyes moved to Ethel. 'Mind you, I can see which side of the family she takes after.'

Ethel's frown was half haughty and half curious. 'Are you saying she takes after me?'

'To be sure I am. Look at her eyes and mouth and then take a look in a mirror. She's the splittin' image of you.'

Ethel took the child and gently drew the blanket back from its face. Immediately as if some strange symbiosis had taken place between them the child ceased crying and began to suck. The Irishwoman nodded wisely. 'There it is, m' dear. The family link. I've seen it happen a hundred times before.'

Ethel's features seemed to melt as she gazed down at the child. For the first time she gave Mary her attention. 'What are you going to call her? Have you decided yet?'

Mary glanced up at Harry who was standing alongside her. She knew it was appeasement but Harry had not objected to the gesture which she felt could only do good. 'We thought of Elizabeth Ethel. The names seem to go well together.'

She could not place the look in her mother's eyes. 'Well, whatever you call her, she's a beautiful baby. You can be very proud of her. Have you decided when you'll have her christened?'

Again Harry nodded at the glance she gave him. 'In a month or two. We thought we might use Holy Trinity for the service.'

Ethel's expression did not change but still cradling the baby as if loathe to put her down, she leaned forward and kissed Mary's forehead.

In her weakened state, the girl felt tears spring to her eyes. Was it possible that William had been right all the time? She had heard it said that the menopause could make women behave irrationally. Perhaps it was under-standing Ethel needed more than reproach.

Noticing her tears, Harry had bent over her in concern. 'What is it, love?'

She smiled up at him. 'Nothing. I'm just happy, that's all.'

Forgetting about the others, he kissed her on the lips. The act prevented either of them seeing the look Ethel gave him as she handed the baby back to the midwife. By the time Harry had straightened, she was turning away and ushering William from the room.

Chapter 16

The baby was crawling over the grass towards a pile of cushions. Reaching the pile she tried to climb over it but lost her balance and tumbled over on her back. Instead of crying, she tried again. This time she was successful although she rolled down the opposite side to the grass. As both her parents applauded her, her tiny face broke into a smile.

Harry grinned approvingly. 'She's a determined little devil: there's no doubt about that. Have you thought any more about your dad's suggestion?'

Mary hesitated. 'I wouldn't mind going back to work. It depends how you feel about leaving Elizabeth with Mother all day.'

The couple were sitting in deckchairs in their small back garden, enjoying the September sunlight. Before answering Harry leaned forward and waved a fly from the child's face. 'You know how I feel. I'd rather you stayed at home with her. We've managed all right so far.'

She felt certain William must have discussed the idea with Ethel first and wondered how much her argument was due to fear of breaking the armistice between them. 'Yes, but I'm wondering if it's fair to expect Dad to go on

133

paying me half wages. And you did say you'd like to get the loan paid off.'

His brows furrowed. 'There's no way we can manage that?'

'Not if I don't work full-time. We haven't paid anything off since December. Not that Dad wants the money back,' she went on as he was about to speak, 'it's you who wants to pay if off.'

Frowning, he plucked a stem of grass and put it between his lips. 'Do you think Elizabeth would be happy with your mother?'

'Oh, yes. She seems very fond of Mother. And it would only be for mornings and afternoons. I'd see her at lunchtime.'

He came to the thing she had been expecting. 'And how would your mother take it if we said no?'

Without knowing it, she winced. 'I suppose she might think we're paying her back for the things she said. I honestly don't know.'

For a moment he showed resentment. 'She couldn't be like any other grandmother and just take it you wanted to be with your own child?'

'She might. On the other hand she might just be hurt or disappointed. She has taken to Elizabeth far more than I dared hope.'

He drew the chewed grass from his mouth and examined it. 'You don't think she's taken to her a bit too much?'

'You mean all those presents she buys her?' When he nodded: 'Harry, you must remember Elizabeth's her first grandchild. And it is better she makes a fuss of her than ignores her, isn't it?'

'As we felt she might earlier on?' he said.

'Well, we did, didn't we?'

He threw the grass stem away. 'Aye, that's true

enough.' He gazed at the cooing baby for a moment, then turned back to her. 'Forget about the money for the moment. If we ran short perhaps I could get a few carpentry jobs in the evenings. You know your mother better than I do. Do you think it can do any harm if she looks after Elizabeth while you're at work?'

She was to remember his words later but at the time thought he was only talking about the child. 'Not really. I suppose Elizabeth will get a bit more attached to her but no more so than if we had a nannie looking after her.' Still shy with him, she felt her cheeks grow warm. 'After all, it won't be for very long, will it?'

He laughed. 'Do you mean until the next baby?'

Her eyes lowered to the garment she was knitting for Elizabeth. 'Yes. We are going to have more, aren't we?'

He reached out and squeezed her hand. 'I hope so. They say single kids get sulky and spoiled.' Then his tone changed. 'When does your dad want to know?'

'This weekend if possible. If I don't go back, he'll have to take someone on full-time. He can't go on sharing the work much longer: it's getting too much for him.'

He muttered something, then took a deep breath. 'All right. If you feel it'll work, we'll give it a try. Only make it clear to both of them it's only until we have our second baby.'

She wondered why she did not feel the relief she expected. 'Are you sure?' When he nodded, she dropped her knitting on the grass and rose. 'I'll run over and tell Dad now. I know he'll be delighted.'

Summer slipped by into autumn. With Ethel now acting as a nannie to Elizabeth five and sometimes six days a week, the truce between her and the young couple remained unbroken. It was true there were moments of

135

strain but as most of these were concerned over the right and wrong ways of bringing up Elizabeth, Mary made a careful point to be the spokesman for both herself and Harry. As a result, although the truce was sometimes severely tested, it did not snap.

Harry, with the forgiving nature of his mother, tended to the view that now she had a grandchild, Ethel's hostility to the marriage was dying away and in the fullness of time she would become an acceptable if not ideal mother-in-law. Mary, with a woman's sharper and more critical faculties, found she waxed hot and cold. After a sharp exchange with her mother she would return home convinced Ethel was merely wearing a mask and only biding her time to resume her attack on the marriage she detested. At other times she would feel shame at such suspicions. Ethel might not like her marriage but to believe she wanted to destroy it was pure melodrama. Ethel was her mother and, as Harry had once forecast, now they had given her a grandchild whom she clearly adored, she was coming to terms with her prejudices.

Nevertheless, even in her most sanguine moments, Mary had no intention of putting such optimism to the test and her most difficult problem during this time was to prevent any lengthy contact between Ethel and Harry. Some meetings between the two became inevitable as the weeks passed by but the strain on Mary's nerves as she weighed every remark they made to see if it contained any potential danger made a long encounter too painful to face.

To be fair to Ethel she did not make them any embarrassing invitations. Ironically William became the problem here. Obviously convinced Ethel was now under control, he tried again and again to entice the couple to spend another evening at No. 57. Finally running out of excuses, Mary decided to be honest with him.

'Dad, neither of us can face an evening like the last one. Please leave things as they are. It's better for us all.'

'But, lass, we can't go on like this. It's unnatural.'

'I know it's awful for you, Dad, but see it from our point of view. We'd be on tenterhooks all the time.'

'But she won't do it again, Mary. She's promised me. In any case, the baby's made a big difference. She's much calmer now.'

'I'm glad. But she's only been seeing Harry when you've been present or on the few occasions when he's collected Elizabeth. An entire evening's a different matter.'

'Why? I'll be there. And she's promised me not to talk about politics in front of you again. Or about religion if it comes to that.'

'How can she do that? When you've got a bee in your bonnet as she has, almost anything she says comes down to it sooner or later. Look what she made of the Titanic's Court of Inquiry.'

William's expression betrayed his own doubts but he denied them staunchly enough. 'I don't believe she'll do it again, lass. She won't risk your taking the child from her.'

Aware he had won a point there, she hesitated. 'Perhaps not but I can't risk it. She's got a tongue that runs away with her. I can't take the risk for Harry's sake.'

'But you couldn't have a more forgiving lad than Harry. That's one of the things I like about him. He hasn't a malicious bone in his body.'

It was a reply that renewed her determination. 'That's true. And it's the reason I try to keep him away from Mother as much as possible. It isn't a fair fight. He won't fight back for my sake.'

William's sigh was an admission of defeat. 'Then what

about Christmas? Surely we're going to celebrate that together?'

Christmas was like a jaggered rock in her mind, rising ahead from the turbulent sea they were somehow managing to negotiate. 'Perhaps the two of you could come round to us? Mother tends to behave differently outside her own home.'

William's frown was troubled. 'She wouldn't like it, lass. She's planning all kinds of surprises for Elizabeth as well as a big Christmas tree. She was talking about it only last night.'

'Why is she assuming we'll come for Christmas?' she asked. 'We didn't last year.'

William sighed. 'Aye, the first one we hadn't spent together since you were born. Don't let's make the same mistake again, love.'

Knowing how much the previous Christmas had hurt him, she felt her eyes sting. 'I know how you feel, Dad, but I'm married now and I have to think about Harry. You'd do just the same in my place.'

Suddenly he looked older and heavier. 'So you won't be coming?'

'Not to No. 57. But you'll be more than welcome here. You can come to dinner if Mother will agree to it.'

In the end, to everyone's relief, it was Connie in Middlesbrough who came to the rescue. Having learned from Ethel about her uneasy relationship with Mary and Harry, she wrote suggesting that Ethel and William spend Christmas with them. Although William privately winced at the invitation, he saw its advantages and urged Ethel to accept it.

Ethel, looking forward to overwhelming Elizabeth with presents, was at first hostile to the offer but when William made it clear there was no possibility of the child spending Christmas at their home she flew into a tantrum, declaring that if Mary didn't want to spend Christmas with her, then she would go where she was wanted.

Making no mention of this, William brought his and Ethel's presents to work on the eve of his departure to Middlesbrough. His subdued mood brought tears to Mary's eyes and she begged him again not to take the affair so much to heart.

Harry, who was a witness to the scene, showed an uncharacteristic bitterness when the two of them returned home. 'I was right, wasn't I? I've torn your family apart.'

Distress made her reply sharper than she intended. 'That's being ridiculous. Dad's just disappointed, that's all.'

'Of course he is. He's disappointed because I've taken his favourite daughter from him.'

She threw her arms around him. 'Don't you start now! He knows it's all my mother's fault. He's just a little sad about Christmas, that's all.'

'I don't wonder. He wants to spend it with his daughter and his grandchild.'

'Darling, we've given them the chance. It isn't our fault if go to Connie's.'

She managed to pull him round but that night she had a dream. She was a child again and her father was demonstrating the soluble quality of potassium permanganate by dropping a few crystals into a jar of clear water. At first only the adjacent water changed colour. Then, like the long legs of a spider, thin streaks of blue writhed out into totally unexpected directions until the entire jar was stained. She awoke feeling oddly chilled and frightened.

Chapter 17

1914 began peacefully and promisingly for Harry and Mary. With Northern tradition demanding the New Year be let in with some ceremony, it was William who performed the function for them. As sirens sounded at midnight, his huge figure, wrapped in a dark overcoat against the chill, appeared at their front door. He was carrying a piece of coal in one hand and a hunk of bread in the other, both of which he solemnly laid on the doorstep. 'May the New Year bless this house and all who live in it.' He then shook hands with Harry and embraced Mary.

Her eyes were wet as she hugged him. 'Thanks, Dad. Is Mother all right?'

'Aye, lass, she's waiting up for the New Year. I'm letting it in for her when I go back.' Fishing inside his pocket, William pulled out a hip flask. 'But let's have a quick drink first.'

When the glasses were filled, William lifted his. 'To 1914. May it be a peaceful and prosperous year for us all. And that includes that lovely child of yours.'

Mary's eyes shone back at him. 'Do you think it's going to be, Dad?'

William, who gave the impression of having had quite

a few drinks even before his visit, looked almost surprised at the question. 'No doubt about it, lass. Things haven't looked better for years.'

William was not alone in feeling confident about 1914. That very same New Year's Day in London, David Lloyd George, no mean prophet, made the statement: 'Never have the prospects for world peace seemed so bright. Never has the sky been more perfectly blue.' Sir Edward Grey, Britain's Foreign Secretary, was shortly to announce the setting up of an Anglo-American Committee to make 1914 'The Year of rejoicing for Peace.'

There was plenty of reason for this euphoria. Before 1914 there had hardly been a politician in Europe who did not believe that if a war were to break out among the Great Powers, it would begin in the Balkans, that festering sore of resentments and ambitions, and the uprisings against the Turks in 1912 and 1913 had seemed to many the beginning of the holocaust. Instead calm statesmanship had prevailed and trade was still flowing unmolested throughout the world. As a result men began to think the dangers of the Balkans had been greatly exaggerated.

It is true that the problem of Germany remained. A country that had made a cult of militarism, a country bursting with energy and pride, it had made it clear for years that it saw Britain as its major rival. To harass that rival it had poured arms into Ireland to encourage revolution, had attacked British foreign markets with enormous zest and at the same time made its demand for a greater share of African and other colonies even more strident.

The threat was well enough known. Nationalistic newspapers like the *Daily Express*, to which William was

141

a contributor, had been proclaiming it in various-sized headlines for nearly a decade. Alarmism however has a way of being counter productive if continued too long and by 1914, after the Balkan Wars had failed to drag in the Great Powers, the man in the street was either ignoring the warnings or seeing Germany in the role of the perpetual bogey man, a thing of shadow rather than of substance.

Politicians, financiers, and leaders of industry were even more sanguine. The longer the Great Powers could keep the peace, they argued, the more intertwined and interdependent their economies would become. Flushed with the success of Capitalism, politicians were beginning to believe international finance would soon make war impossible.

Not every one welcomed this new optimism. Some men, and they were not all young and irresponsible, regretted they were unlikely to taste the glamour and glory of war. Others, and Gareth Evans was among them, had regrets for different reasons. 'It's a pity, boyo. You get revolutions after wars. The poor sodding workers learn at last how valuable they are.'

In general however the mood in 1914 was buoyant and with an Old Age Pension and Insurance scheme starting (by courtesy of the Liberal Party) millions of half-starved workers in Britain and indeed in Europe too began to believe the millenium they had been promised for their children was coming into sight at last.

It was an optimism that permeated through all the layers of trade and industry even to small businesses like William's. Already Harry's hard work and popularity with customers had brought in fifty per cent more orders. To fulfil them William took on two extra ware-

142

housemen in February. In March, to quote Ethel's tart comment 'he went insane' and bought a motorcar, one of the new imported Ford models. Looking very pleased with himself, William led Harry and Mary into the stable to see it. 'I was thinking of getting a second traveller, lad. But this'll help you do your rounds quicker so you'll have more time to look for new custom. You'll be able to manage her, won't you?'

Harry was flushed with excitement as he examined the shiny black creation. 'Of course I'll manage her. When can I try her out?'

'As soon as you like, lad. Only I'd run her a couple of times round the yard first.'

William's self-satisfaction was not shared by Ethel. 'You've given him another ten shillings a week and also bought him a car. You spoil that young man to death.'

William frowned. 'I can hardly ask him to double his rounds without giving him a little extra, can I?'

'But a motor car? Do you realise what those contraptions cost to run?'

An astute business man, William had already done his sums. 'Have you thought what a second traveller would cost? Even if the Ford breaks down once a week I'll still be in profit.'

Ethel gave a sniff. 'I suppose you'll be getting rid of Prinny next?'

'No, delivery carts are still cheaper to run than motor lorries. Prinny can stay until she's put out to grass. Lorries might be a better proposition by then.'

Unable to argue further on the issue, Ethel found another objection. 'I hope you realise that once Harry's learned to drive he'll probably expect you to lend him the motor car for private use?'

William avoided the direct question. 'I thought we might all go out in it occasionally. Graham White's coming to Longfield in a couple of weeks. Wouldn't you like to see him?'

'Who's Graham White?'

'The aviator. He's giving a flying display. And taking up passengers.'

'You mean let Harry drive us there?'

'Why not? You don't think I intend learning at my time of life, do you?' Seeing Ethel was hesitating, William resorted to guile. 'What do you say, love? It's going to be quite an event. They say even the Mayor and his staff are going.'

'The Mayor? I don't believe it.'

'The evening paper says so. Graham White's a big celebrity.' William put an arm round Ethel's shoulders and gave her a squeeze. 'Come on, love. It isn't something we can see every day.'

When William was in his eager, youthful mood, Ethel had always found it difficult to resist him. 'Are you sure Harry will have learned to drive properly? And what about Elizabeth?'

'Of course Harry will. He can drive already. And Elizabeth can come with us. She'll love the sight of an aeroplane.' Seeing Ethel was almost there, William gave her another sly squeeze. 'Say yes, love. It'll do us all good to have a day out.'

Secretly curious both about the new motor car and Graham White's flying machine, Ethel feigned a sigh of resignation. 'Oh, all right. But make sure Harry knows what he's doing.'

To everyone's surprise, the trip proved a success. Although few of the roads outside the city were macadamised, the Ford behaved well and Elizabeth kept everyone in a good mood by chattering away and pointing excitedly at horses and cows which she recognised from her picture books.

Although there were plenty of carts on the country roads, they passed only five motor cars during the six miles to Longfield. In every case their occupants waved and called out to them. Motoring was an adventure and the enthusiasm so infectious that even Ethel laughed and waved back.

The lanes around Longfield however were packed with carts, traps, motor cars and charabancs. Flying was still in its infancy and few people had seen a real flying machine, still fewer one in flight. Every time Graham White's rickety machine took off and spluttered round the field there were loud oohs and aahs from the enrapt spectators. Seeing Harry's expression as the aeroplane passed directly over them, Mary laughed and hugged his arm. 'You'd like to go up in it, wouldn't you?'

His eyes were following the unsteady machine in fascination. 'It must be wonderful up there. Absolutely wonderful.'

An hour later they drove back to town. Although they had to stop once when, in the courtesy of the time, Harry halted to help a broken-down motorist change a wheel, Mary was feeling more relaxed with her mother than at any time since her marriage. With Elizabeth chattering away and Ethel laughing at the child and pointing out the animals in the fields, it seemed to Mary that the skins of her mother's resentment were peeling away at last.

It was the 4th of June when Mary learned she was pregnant again. With Ethel showing all the signs of a thaw, the girl was quite looking forward to telling her the news. After she and her father had lunch at home the following day, she told William not to wait for her: she would follow him back to the warehouse in a few minutes.

William left and Molly began clearing the table. Elizabeth, who loved story books, was urging Ethel to sit beside her on the settee and read to her. As the smiling Ethel obeyed, Mary made her announcement. 'Mother, I'm pregnant again.'

Ethel seemed to start but to Mary's concern she did not look up. 'When did you find out?'

'I've been sick the last few mornings. I went to Dr Armstrong's evening surgery last night and he confirmed it.'

'Have you told your father yet?'

'No. I thought I'd tell you first. I'll tell Dad this afternoon.'

Ethel's eyes were still on the book which the impatient child was urging her to read. 'So I suppose you'll be giving up work again soon?'

'Good heavens, no. I'm hoping to go on until Christmas. Maybe longer.'

At that Ethel glanced up and smiled. 'I'm sure your Dad will be as delighted as I am, dear. Congratulations.'

Believing she now understood Ethel's behaviour, Mary felt relief. 'I'm glad it's happened so quickly. There won't be too big an age gap between the children.'

Ethel nodded. 'That's true, dear.' She turned her smile on Elizabeth. 'Mind you, I don't think this little one is in too much of a hurry to have a playmate yet. I think she's quite happy playing games with her grannie, aren't you, darling?'

Anxious to appease her, Mary nodded. 'I'm sure she is. But all the same it's better she's not going to be an only child.' She glanced at her watch. 'I must get back to work now. We've a lot of orders to get out today.' Crossing over to the settee she bent over the child. 'Give me a kiss, darling. Mummy will pick you up later.'

Impatient for Ethel to begin reading, the child lifted up her face briefly for Mary to kiss, then reached for the book Ethel was holding and tried to turn a page over.

Ethel smiled. 'Be patient a moment more, dear. There's a good girl.'

Mary straightened. 'As we're so busy today, it might be six o'clock before I can collect her. Will that be all right?'

'Of course it will, dear. You know she's never any trouble to me.'

Mary turned at the door. 'Bye bye, then, darling. See you later.'

Peering impatiently over Ethel's arm at the book, Elizabeth did not answer. Ethel shook her gently. 'Say bye bye to Mummy, darling.'

The child's eyes stayed on the book. 'Bye bye, Mummy.'

Mary gazed at her for a moment. Then, annoyed at herself for being hurt by the child's thoughtlessness, she left the room and made for the warehouse.

Chapter 18

With both Harry and William delighted at the news of Mary's second pregnancy and William's business increasing its turnover almost weekly, the high summer of 1914 seemed to hold no shadows. The threat from Germany that had dominated the Press for so many years had given way to the possibility of outright civil war in Ireland but to the average man in the street that contingency meant nothing more than another unpleasant job for the regular army. And the recent assassination of the heir to the Austrian throne at Sarajevo in Bosnia – where was Bosnia? – seemed to pose an even smaller national threat, particularly after the anti-climax of the recent Balkan disturbances. Even the Press, ready as always to raise a scare if a scare could be found, had to devote itself more to crime, Court title-tattle, and entertainment to keep up its circulation ratings.

Not that entertainment failed the journalists in 1914. Seldom if ever had so many riches been on display in Britain in one year. The great Feodor Chaliapin and the incomparable Nellie Melba brought their glories to Drury Lane and Covent Garden. The young Thomas Beecham brought the dances of Stravinsky, Diaghliev and Nijinsky to a spell-bound London. And fans fluttered and cheeks coloured at His Majesty's Theatre when Bernard Shaw's new play *Pygmalion* was first produced and audiences heard for the first time the shocking word 'bloody' coming from the stage, and from the lips of a lady too!

Nor were the masses being denied entertainment. Wherever they went, George Robey, Little Tich, Elsie Janis, Nelson Keyes and Violet Loraine played to packed music halls. A new bioscope film, called *Harry Lauder among the Mormans*, had permanent queues outside the Kingsway Theatre. And if one could afford six shillings for a book, Marie Corelli's *The Innocent*, Baroness Orcy's *Unto Caesar* and Ethel M. Dell's *The Swindler*, were all available in the bookshops.

It was in many ways a golden year. Spring had come early and throughout June, July and August, Britain was swimming in a haze of sunshine. Among Harry's circle of friends and acquaintances, the only one who saw a portent in the assassination was Gareth Evans, and as Gareth's fertile Celtic mind was prone to see doom and gloom even at a child's christening, it was difficult to take his warnings seriously.

'This could be it at last, boyo. Think about it. Austria's been wanting to put Serbia in her place for years. Now she's got her chance. She's demanding conditions Serbia will never accept, like insisting Austrian police investigate the assassination. When Serbia refuses she'll take it as an admission of guilt and declare war.'

Harry was sceptical 'War? Isn't that a bit dramatic?'

'Why? She's been looking for an excuse for years and now she's got it. It couldn't have come at a better time for her. France is in a political mess over the Caillaux scandal; Russia, an autocracy herself, can hardly defend

Serbia when Serbia's under suspicion of plotting a Royal assassination; and we're up to our necks in the Irish troubles. It's the perfect opportunity for Austria to nip round the blind side of the scrum and slap Serbia down.'

Harry grinned at the analogy. In spite of his revolutionary aspirations, Gareth was a traditional Welshman in his love of rugby football.

'It all sounds a bit too complicated for me but suppose Austria does declare war? If Russia feels unable to help Serbia, how could the rest of us be drawn in?'

Gareth raised a portentous finger. 'Everyone's been spoiling for a scrap for years, boyo. If Austria and Serbia start to mix it, I'll lay you odds we'll all start mobilising.'

For once Gareth's Cassandra-like prophecies proved accurate. Austria declared war a few days later and the British and French Press suddenly woke up to realise how Austria was taking advantage of their political pre-occupations. Accusation followed accusation but with the Austrians still not moving into Serbian territory and the Kaiser announcing he was determined to do all in his power to maintain the peace of Europe, a war involving the Great Powers still seemed unlikely.

At least it seemed so to the vast majority of the British population, including William himself. In his way William followed international events with the same interest if not with the same motive as Gareth himself but his interpretations were tinted by the nationalistic and optimistic *Daily Express* instead of *The Dawn*. Also, because of William's more phlegmatic personality, his interpretation tended to be made after the event rather than before it.

'I don't think it'll come to 'out, lad. If it were Germany it'd be a different matter. But Austria and those Balkan States are all bits and pieces held together by string.

They'll each shoot a couple or so of one another and then say their honour's satisfied.'

But William and millions like him had not taken into account the inexorability of national fear. With mobilisation taking time and time being dependent on railway schedules, nations felt they should mobilise in case their rivals caught them napping. To their rivals however the act looked like a prelude to war and they in turn called their troops to the colours. Within weeks every Great Power in Europe and most of the lesser ones were mobilised and by that time there was no stopping the madness. On the 28th July, Germany joined Austria in declaring war on Serbia and sent an ultimatum to Russia and then one to France. A few days later she declared war on both of them. On the 4th she informed Belgium that for 'security purposes' her troops would cross its frontiers. In turn Britain gave an ultimatum for German troops to withdraw. When the ultimatum expired at midnight on the 4th August and the Germans had not complied, Britain issued a statement fifteen minutes later through its Foreign Office that Britain and Germany were at war.

There was no general dismay among any of the Great Powers. In Britain the next morning, when people heard the news, there was excitement and in many cases enthusiasm. Men shouted their approval and in the pubs and music halls that night they sang patriotic songs. Even William, no war-monger and sobered by the declaration, was sincere in his comments to Harry the next morning.

'It's a bad thing for the lads who have to go: there's no denying that. But we, the French, and the Russians against Germany and that tin-pot Austrian Empire? They'll go down like a pack of cards, lad. It'll all be over in two or three months.'

And so the world went to war in August 1914,

innocent in experience, guilty in national pride. Politicians told lies, military leaders struck postures, newspapers bragged and boasted. Women and children, caught in the mad fever, sang and cheered as if they were spectators at a football match. Their menfolk, crushed by years of grey drudgery, could barely conceal their envy as they watched their jubilant Army regulars marching off to France. There was no chance of sharing their glory: like William they were certain it would all be over before Christmas.

PART 3

PART 3

Chapter 19

William's expression was grim as he pushed the newspaper across the desk to Harry. 'You see this, lad? It's happened at last. They've dropped bombs on some towns in Cambridgeshire and Norfolk.'

The headlines screamed at Harry as he picked up the paper. *ZEPPELINS ATTACK. MANY CIVILIAN CASUALTIES FEARED.* He shook his head in disbelief. 'I never thought they'd do it. Not against civilians.'

William sank heavily back in his chair. 'God knows they've warned us long enough.'

Harry knew he was right. Since the first news of Count Graf Zeppelin's great 'Ships of the Air' had reached Britain around 1900, regular newspaper articles, encouraged no doubt by German propaganda, had issued dire warnings of the terrible damage they could do to the island if a war should come. Melodramatic stories of such attacks and the enduring or the forestalling of them had been the standard fare of the 'penny dreadfuls' Harry had read as a boy. As a result a deep-seated awareness of the Zeppelins had been planted in the minds of the British public and many had been surprised that a full scale attack, either to destroy military targets or to land invasion troops, had not been launched on the first night of the war.

It had come almost as an anti-climax when no such attack had taken place and for a few weeks the populace had relaxed. Then Zeppelins had raided the Belgium town of Antwerp and all the old misgivings had returned. Restrictions on London street lighting had come into force and civilians ordered to draw their blinds before lighting up their houses.

Yet when Christmas had come and gone without any attacks, the public mood had changed again. Perhaps the Zeppelins were too busy cruising about over the North Sea looking for the Grand Fleet? Or, better, perhaps the fickle English weather made the trip from Germany too hazardous.

But now, as William said, it had happened. And not against a military target but against two or three quiet country towns. After all the stories about the 'Hun's' atrocities in Belgium, was he about to do the same in Britain? The Zeppelin threat, illogical but implanted deep in the public mind, was sending its chill into a million homes that grey January morning.

Harry was looking troubled when he laid the paper back on William's desk. 'Do you think it's true?'

For the briefest moment William's voice turned gruff. 'It's the Government that releases the stories. You surely don't think they'd tell lies, do you?' Then his tone changed. 'You never could think badly of people, could you, lad?'

Harry changed the subject. 'It looks now as if the war could go on for a long time, doesn't it?'

William sighed. 'Aye, we were all wrong. They're going to take some shifting now they're dug in across Belgium and France. It's certain the French aren't going to do it on their own. And the BEF's too small to help them.'

With propaganda and national security hiding the

156

facts, William little knew how right he was. The British Expeditionary Force of 100,000 men, ironically to earn the title of the Old Contemptibles because of their valour, had been almost wiped out in the ferocious fighting of the previous year.

'So it's all up to Kitchener?' Harry said.

'That's how it seems to me. He's got to build up a volunteer army as fast as he can. Do you know young Johnson wants to join up?'

Harry gave a start. Johnson was one of the two extra men William had taken on the previous summer. 'But he's only eighteen.'

'I know that, lad. I've had a talk with him and he's agreed to wait a bit longer. But we'll lose him sooner or later: there's no doubt about that.'

Harry moved to the window and stared down at the wet warehouse yard where two men in oilskins were loading up the horse and dray. 'Have any of the others talked about joining up?'

'Barnes has mentioned it but I think it's only talk at the moment. I suppose the rest think themselves too old.'

Harry remained gazing down at the yard. 'I wonder how old too old will be before it's over? There's bound to be conscription sooner or later.'

William looked shocked at the suggestion. 'I didn't mean it would last that long. We'll never have conscription over here.'

'Why not? Every other country has it.'

'There'll be no need,' William argued. 'Kitchener will get all the volunteers he needs. More than enough from the way they're flocking in.'

Harry glanced at him. His laugh had a bitter ring. 'I'm not flocking in, Dad, am I?'

William suddenly looked uncomfortable. 'I'm glad you're not, lad. There are plenty of young tearaways who enjoy a scrap to go first. You're a married man with responsibilities, so you've nothing to feel ashamed about.' To save them both further embarrassment, William changed the subject. 'Is Mary coming in this afternoon?'

'Yes, I expect so.'

William frowned. 'I wish she wouldn't. She's too far gone at seven months to be climbing up and down these steps.'

Harry nodded. 'I know but I can't stop her. She knows if she doesn't come in it means extra work for you.'

'That's daft. Barlow's son's already promised to help out two or three days a week when her time comes. Leave it to me, lad. I'll have another go at her this afternoon.'

Nodding, Harry crossed the office and picked up a large leather bag. 'I'd better get started or I'll be late in picking up Elizabeth tonight.' He nodded at the newspaper on the desk. 'There's one thing, Dad. After those headlines we should do well with Phosferine.'

Always ready to latch on to the younger man's quirky humour and relieved at the lightening of his mood, William grinned. 'Or Eno's Fruit Salts, lad.' When Harry laughed, he went on: 'By the way, don't say anything to Ethel about these Zeppelin raids when you see her tonight. She's always had a fear of them.'

Harry, who could never imagine Ethel afraid of anything but William's temper, nodded as he shrugged on a mackintosh. 'No, I won't mention them if she doesn't.'

He left the office a minute later and crossed the wet warehouse yard to the stable where the Ford was garaged. He did not notice William watching him with troubled eyes from the upstairs office window.

Gareth lowered two pints of beer on the pub table and gave a faintly embarrassed grin as Harry lifted an

158

eyebrow. 'It's on the Kaiser, boyo.'

'The Kaiser?'

Gareth lit a Woodbine and blew out smoke. 'Yes. I've got a job making shell casings. They pay good money.'

'But I thought you'd no time for Capitalistic wars?'

Although Gareth grinned, Harry felt he was on the defensive. 'I've time for this one, boyo. I thought at first the Prussians were going to finish it quickly. But now it's going the way we hoped.'

'Which way's that?'

'Bogged down in the mud with nowhere to go. Men aren't going to put up with that for long. Sooner or later they'll throw away their guns, join up together, and the Big Day is here.'

'You mean international revolution?'

'That's the ticket, boyo.'

Harry shook his head. 'You think trained soldiers will disobey their orders? What are their officers doing during this time?'

Gareth grinned. 'Getting shot by their own men. It must happen now that the proletariat are getting guns at last.'

'And in the meantime you're busy making shells for our proletariat to kill their proletariat with?'

'It's their system, not mine,' Gareth argued. 'In any case the more shells the working man gets chucked at him, the sooner he's going to smash up the system.'

'You haven't thought about it the other way? Instead of getting fed up with the system, he gets more fed up with the working men on the other side and fights them all the harder?'

Gareth frowned. 'For a while, maybe. Until he's noticed the other chap's as miserable and fed up as himself. Then it's hands across No Man's Land and down with the common enemy, the King, the Kaiser, the

Czar, and all their bloody minions.'

Harry grinned. 'If it's going to happen that way, I don't see why you haven't joined up. You always said if war came it would be the chance to get your hands on a gun.'

Gareth's reply was half-defiant and half-triumphant. 'Who said I hadn't tried?'

Harry gave a start. 'You? When?'

'I went to Pryme Street six weeks ago. They said they'd too many volunteers to process and I had to report to the City Hall in April.'

Harry was looking amazed. 'You're actually going to join up? To fight for King and Country?'

Gareth's embarrassment lasted only for a moment before he gave a scornful laugh. 'Don't talk like a fool. I've told you what I'm in it for. I want to be there when it happens.' Seeing Harry's expression he swore, stubbed out his cigarette and lit another. 'If you don't believe me, sod you.'

Harry shook his head in disbelief. He took another sip of beer before addressing the discomforted Gareth again. 'What about these reports of German atrocities in Belgium? Do you believe them?'

Relieved at the change of subject, Gareth shrugged. 'I don't know. I suppose men can do things like that in wartime when they're licensed to kill.'

'What about the Zeppelin raids? Do you think they're aimed at civilians?'

'No, I wouldn't think so. They probably haven't found a way of dropping bombs accurately yet.'

'Then why don't they wait until they have?'

'Maybe they feel it's worthwhile to scare the public.' As Gareth studied Harry's expression, he saw a way of getting his own back. 'You're starting to hit the age-old problem, aren't you, boyo?'

'What problem?'

Gareth's grin was malicious. 'You find it easy to turn the other cheek for yourself but not so easy when you see innocent people getting a hammering. Aren't I right?'

It was Harry's turn to show resentment. 'Haven't you talked enough rubbish for one night?'

'Admit it, boyo. You'd the same problem when you were a kid. You said you hated fighting but I didn't notice you turning away when some smaller kid was getting bullied. Remember the time you helped me? Your mother's philosophy didn't allow for that, did it?'

Harry frowned. 'Leave my mother out of it.'

'Your mother was a real lady but she wasn't a man and couldn't understand a man's problems. Aren't I right?'

Harry drew in smoke without answering. Conscious he held the initiative now, Gareth went on: 'You're a sentimentalist, boyo, just like your dad was. If they plug much more propaganda at you, I'll lay a pound to a penny it won't be long before you're queuing up to fight those Jerries.'

'I'll still be behind you, won't I?' Harry said.

'It's not the volunteering, boyo. It's the reason.'

Harry rose to his feet. 'I don't believe your reason. I don't think you do either. In any case, you're wrong about me. I'm not volunteering to kill Germans or anybody else. I made up my mind a long time ago. Do you want another beer?'

Gareth grinned mockingly. 'Not when your customers make snide remarks to you? Not after some woman calls you a coward and hands you a white feather, perhaps in front of Mary? It's already happening, you know.'

Harry was looking resentful now. 'Can't we talk about something else? Do you want a beer or don't you?'

Gareth grinned at his victory. 'Yes, why not. I don't suppose you'll be able to buy me one when we're sloshing about in those Belgian trenches.'

161

Chapter 20

Mary felt the tearing sensation in her abdomen when she missed her footing and fell the last three steps of the office staircase. For a moment, as she clutched the banister for support, the pain seemed to subside. Then, as she tried to walk, agony exploded inside her. She did not hear her scream or see the shocked face of her father as he hurried out of his office. She found herself lying on the warehouse floor, helpless to move as a brown tide of unconsciousness swept over her.

She did not awake in the true sense of the word. She floated up through layers of consciousness, pausing for indeterminate periods in each. Once she thought she recognised the ceiling and walls of her old bedroom. Figures were moving silently about: she believed most ot them were men although more than once she recognised the hairstyle, the whalebone bodice and the bustle of her mother. She could hear no conversation. It was like watching a silent film, sepia-stained and out of focus. After a few seconds she sank again beneath the surface of consciousness.

At another time she heard voices but found her eyelids too heavy to open. She listened, trying to make sense of the voices but they were like waves on a seashore, washing over pebbles and then receding. Wearying of the effort, she allowed her heavy body to sink yet again into the warm and silent sea.

The third time she saw two shadows standing at the foot of her bed. She managed only a croak when she tried to speak to them but they disappeared immediately, only to reappear alongside her. A second later her mother's face, grotesquely out of focus, filled her vision. 'Hello, dear. Can you hear me?'

She managed a faint nod.

'How do you feel?'

Again she could only manage a nod. Then she felt a large hand seize her own and wrap round it tightly. A moment later her mother's face was replaced by William's.

'Hello, love! What's all this nonsense about? We can't have you sick like this, you know. We need you too much.'

His gruff, clumsy words filled her eyes with tears and she found her voice at last. 'What happened to my baby, Dad?' she whispered.

William's face spasmed with pain. 'Don't go worrying about that, love. Get yourself better first.'

She struggled to lift her head. 'My baby, Dad! What's happened?'

William tried to answer her but found no words. Instead his head bowed and she felt something warm splash on her face. Then there was a sharp exclamation and Ethel took William's place. 'I'm afraid you lost your baby, dear. You had a miscarriage. But Dr Armstrong says if you're sensible you'll be able to have others in the future. So try not to worry and get yourself well.'

Mary's eyes closed. She wanted to ask where Harry was but the wave of misery that swept over her left her no strength. She felt a hand lie on her forehead for a moment, then heard William's distressed voice. 'I think she's drifted off again. Why is she as weak as this?'

Ethel's impatient voice answered him. 'Didn't you hear Dr Armstrong? He said she had one of the worst haemorrhages he'd ever seen.'

'Then was it wise to tell her about the baby so soon?'

'She had to be told, William. In any case, she'd soon have guessed.'

William's sigh was profound. 'I begged her to stop coming. But she wouldn't listen.'

Ethel had never sounded more unforgiving. 'How could she? It was never her choice. It was that husband of hers, wanting the extra money. I gave him the length of my tongue yesterday, I can tell you.'

William sounded aghast. 'You didn't blame him?'

'Of course I did. She's our daughter, isn't she?'

'But Ethel, it wasn't Harry's fault. He's been trying to stop her too. She was doing it for me, not for him.'

Ethel laughed contemptuously. 'That's what he told you. What he told Mary to do behind your back is something else. You don't understand these people, William. You never have. They'll work their wives to death to make money.'

Mary made a last effort to cry out her protest. Instead the bed began to sway beneath her and a moment later she was spinning down again into a brown and bottomless vortex.

William paused at the back door of No. 57 and lowered his voice. 'I'll be dropping in to see Mary tonight, lad, before I go into town to see my friends. Is that all right?'

Harry shrugged. 'Of course. You know we're always glad to see you.'

'How is she managing with the bairn? She doesn't find

164

her too noisy and active in her condition, does she?'

Harry smiled. 'No, it's a change for her to have Elizabeth with her all day. Mind you, she says she misses the office too.'

It was a remark that clearly pleased William. 'I can't have her back quick enough once the doctor says she's fit.' He motioned down at the heavy leather bag Harry was carrying for him. 'Drop it in the sitting room and then get yourself home. We've both earned our suppers tonight.'

They entered the house. It was a Saturday afternoon in late April. Both men had been working late, Harry because of a backlog of orders and William because of Mary's absence. As William opened the rear door of the sitting room, they heard the sound of martial music on the road outside. Giving Harry a look of curiosity, William went out into the hall. As Harry followed him, he saw the front door was open and Ethel was standing in the porch. Hearing the men behind her, Ethel turned. Ignoring Harry, she motioned William forward. 'It's one of the Recruiting Lorries. Come and look.'

Harry moved up behind William and saw Molly was standing at the front gate gazing in fascination at a motor-driven lorry parked on the far side of the road. A large table rested on its flat top with a corporal and two soldiers seated around it. Recruitment forms and other War Office paraphenalia lay in boxes before them.

A huge moustached sergeant was standing alongside the table with a megaphone in his hand. Above him was a banner that ran the full length of the lorry. It read: *DO YOUR DUTY FOR KING AND COUNTRY*. Below it were posters of Lord Kitchener, War minister and hero of Khartoum and Omdurman. His stern handsome head was gazing out challengingly from the poster and beneath it was the caption *WANTS YOU*. To every

165

man in the crowds flocking the pavements it seemed the man was pointing an accusing finger at him alone.

William turned to Harry. 'Did you see what the *Express* claimed this morning? Kitchener's campaign's already pulled in over 1,000,000 volunteers. They think he'll double that figure before Christmas.'

When Harry made no comment, William glanced back at the tableau. To the right of the lorry a military band was waiting to play. Molly, who had run to the gate to make certain the soldiers noticed her, gave a giggle of excitement and glanced round at Ethel. 'Isn't it excitin', m'am? Don't they look luvely?'

Ethel motioned her to keep quiet as with a flourish the sergeant lifted his megaphone. His bellow made a distant horse rear against its traces. 'Now come along, lads. Show the ladies what you're made of. Take the King's shilling and join the lucky lads who're already fighting for King and Country.'

At a sign from him the band swung into the old Boer War favourite 'Soldiers of the Queen'. As the stirring martial music drowned the buzz of conversation, men felt the blood tingling in their veins. A woman began to sing. Others followed, some like Ethel, humming self-consciously, others opening their lungs. Soon even the shy and the haughty were caught up in the heady excitement.

> 'And when they say we've always won,
> and when they ask us how it's done,
> We proudly point to everyone of
> England's Soldiers of the Queen.'

William, who had moved on to the porch with Ethel, was singing as lustily as anyone now. The late April afternoon was full of colour, martial music and delirious patriotism. Unable to bear it any longer, a young man wearing a shabby cap and corduroy trousers tied round the ankles with string, ran forward and climbed on to the lorry. As cheers rose, the sergeant slapped him across the back and raised his megaphone triumphantly. 'Here's another brave lad. Who'll be the next?'

Harry was the only one at No. 57 who had not joined in the singing, a fact that had not gone unnoticed by Ethel who had taken a quick glance at him. His eyes were on a young couple standing just outside the front gate, the girl wearing an expensive fawn coat, the man in a top hat and fashionable high-waisted suit.

Both had joined in the singing. Now, as the bandsmen paused for breath, the girl turned her pretty, flushed face to the young man and said something. Laughing at her comment, the man gazed back at the lorry. When the girl's bright eyes remained on him, he laughed again, then ceremoniously removed his top hat and handed it to her. As she gave a cry of pleasure, he kissed her and then, to a great cheer, strode across the road. Helping him aboard the lorry, the sergeant saluted him before handing him over to his corporal. As another cheer rang out, the band broke into 'Tipperary'.

Two minutes later the procession moved down the road. Forgetting himself for a moment, William turned to Harry. 'It's getting 'em all in, lad. The rich and the poor. If this goes on a few more months, we'll have an army big enough to stop the Jerries on our own.'

Harry moved aside for Ethel and Molly to pass him. 'I doubt that, Dad. I still think it'll come to conscription before it's over.'

Ethel, about to enter the sitting room, paused. 'That won't please some people, will it?'

Harry stiffened but did not answer. Guessing Ethel's intention William did his best to sidetrack her. 'I hope it never comes to it, lass. It's never been the way we've fought wars in the past.'

Ethel was still too fired by the recent scene to guard her words. 'What's wrong with it? Why should only our best men go out and fight? If we had conscription, the cowards and the malingerers would have to do their share too.' Her eyes, hard and accusing, threw their challenge at the younger man. 'Don't you think so, Harry?'

William frowned. 'Not everyone's a coward who doesn't want to fight, Ethel. There're plenty of conscientious objectors in our own Church.'

'Cowards,' Ethel insisted. 'The Church of England's fully behind the war effort.' She glanced at Harry again. 'Isn't your Church or Chapel or whatever you call it?'

By this time the younger man's cheeks were pale. 'Yes, Mother, it is. Although I often wonder if it should be.'

'Should be? What on earth does that mean?'

'Isn't there something in the Bible about *Thou Shalt Not Kill*?'

Red spots appeared in Ethel's cheeks. 'I know there's a good deal about an eye for an eye and a tooth for a tooth. I go to church, Harry, and I believe what my minister tells me: that we're fighting a war against evil. Haven't you read about the Zeppelin raids and the atrocities in Belgium?'

'Yes, I've read about them.'

'Then don't you think it's the duty of every decent man to go out and stop them?' Incensed by the argument, Ethel forgot herself. 'Or don't you care about anything but yourself?'

That was enough for William. 'Hold your tongue, Ethel! Damn it, there isn't a more unselfish lad than Harry. Ask Mary, ask anybody. For the hundredth time,

168

keep your meddling fingers out of men's business!'

For once Ethel's resentment allowed her to stand up to William's anger. She drew herself up to her full height. 'I'm sorry, William, but I can't help having my own opinions. It seems all wrong to me that the best of our manhood go out to fight while the rest stay behind and profit from it.' With that and her characteristic sniff of contempt, she vanished into the sitting room.

Breathing hard, William turned to Harry to apologise. Instead he found the hall empty and the front door ajar.

William was bent over the *Daily Express* when Harry entered his office three days later. His shocked face lifted. 'Have you read this, lad? The Germans have used some kind of poison gas. Hundreds of our lads have been choked to death.'

Harry nodded. 'Yes. I heard about it at the City hall last night.'

'Poison gas,' William muttered. 'I never imagined things would go that far.' Then he gave a start. 'City Hall? What were you doing there?'

Harry crossed over to the window. It was a fine spring morning and blossom could be seen on the trees that flanked the lane. 'I've joined up, Dad. I've to report for a medical on the Seventh.

William sank back heavily. 'How has Mary taken it?'

'Like a million other women, I suppose. Do any of them want us to go?'

William winced. 'You shouldn't have done it, lad. There wasn't any need.'

Harry gave him a glance, then collected his order book. 'I might be a bit late tonight. I'm going out to Beverley and the local villages.'

William checked him. 'You shouldn't have taken any

169

notice of Ethel, lad. Half the time she doesn't know what she's saying.'

Harry picked up his bag. 'I don't agree. She was right. It is unfair for volunteers to take all the brunt.'

'That isn't what I meant, Harry. *You* shouldn't be going. 'You're not a . . .' Realising he didn't have the right word at his fingertips, William paused in embarrassment.

The younger man's voice turned cold. 'You mean I'm not a real man? Not the material they make good soldiers of?'

William flushed. 'Damn it, lad, don't take it out on me. I couldn't think more of you than if you were my own son.'

Harry's tone changed. 'I'm sorry, Dad. I didn't mean to get at you. It's just that . . . oh, it doesn't matter.'

As he turned for the door, William checked him. 'Just the same, son, I'm proud of you. I'd like you to know that.'

The younger man gave a bitter laugh. 'I wish I felt the same way, Dad. But thanks anyway. I'd better go now. See you tonight.'

Chapter 21

The brown envelope arrived on the 20th June – just two weeks after the city had experienced a Zeppelin raid that nearly destroyed the Holy Trinity Church – and Mary was at Harry's side when he opened it. He gave her a wry grin as he passed it over to her. 'It's like getting a dental appointment, isn't it? I've to be at Seaton Sluice next Thursday at three p.m.'

As she pressed against him without speaking, he ran a hand through her long golden hair. 'I know it's not going to be easy for you. Are you sure you'll be able to manage?'

With the die already cast, he knew it was a futile question. Aware they would not be able to keep up the house payments once he was called up, she had already asked William if she could return to work. With neither man feeling she was well enough yet, William had attempted to dissuade her by offering to make up Harry's pay.

She had not felt able to accept his offer. He was already paying Barlow's son to do her work and in addition had been forced to take on a salesman to step into Harry's shoes when his draft papers arrived. Good salesmen with a knowledge of the druggist trade and able to drive a motor car were not two a penny at that time and William had been forced to take on a middle-aged Londoner called Willis. In William's own words the man was too 'la-de-da' and sure of himself for his tastes but the circumstances left him no option. For the last two weeks Harry had been taking Willis round the city and the villages to introduce him to his customers.

Although the arrangement meant a shortfall in income – Mary's wage would not match Harry's – it seemed the only one that was fair to William. It had however one drawback that neither liked but could not avoid: it meant that once again Elizabeth would be spending her weekdays with Ethel.

Harry put a finger under the girl's chin when she did not speak and lifted her face. 'You didn't answer my question. Will you be all right?'

She brushed a sleeve impatiently across her eyes. 'I didn't answer because it's a stupid question. It's you who's going off to war, not me.'

He tried to lighten the moment. 'I'm not so sure about that. Your mother can fire some pretty big shells when she tries.'

Her attempt to smile was a failure. With a sob she threw her arms round him. 'Oh, Harry, why did you let her influence you? You didn't have to prove anything to me or anyone else who knows you. Why are you going?'

His hesitation and then his voice made her draw back to look at him. 'I wish I could tell you, love. But the truth is I don't know myself.'

The shadows that slanted across the warehouse yard were long the following Wednesday evening when the Ford drove through the gates but William was still at his desk. Knowing that Harry would have little time the following morning to say his goodbyes and that Mary would in any case want to spend those last moments with him, William had stayed on to say his own private farewell to his son-in-law.

There was another reason why William had chosen to stay. He knew how popular Harry was with his customers and felt certain they would want to say their goodbyes in the time-honoured way. If he, William, had gone home, Harry would have no option but to go round to the house, both to bring in his final orders and to say his goodbyes. If the customers had put out the boat the way William hoped they would, Ethel would be given yet another stick to beat over the younger man's back.

Below, a burly man in overalls had jumped from the driver's seat and was opening the passenger door. Waiting no longer, William hurried down the steps into the yard. The man, middle-aged and balding, turned to him. 'You Mr Hardcastle?'

William nodded. 'Who are you?'

'I'm Mr Clegg's vanman, guv'ner.' The man was wearing an amused grin. 'I've brought your young Mr Miles home.'

William pushed past him to see Harry, his hair dishevelled and his tie undone, struggling to climb out of the seat. William put a hand on his arm to steady him. 'Hello, lad. Has it been that kind of a day?'

Harry peered at him, his voice slurred. 'Is that you, Dad.'

'Yes, son. Let me get you out of there.'

'I'm all right, Dad. Jus' a bit wobbly that's all.'

'I know the feeling, lad.' William turned to the vanman. 'Let's get him into the warehouse.'

Between them they got Harry to the office steps. Pausing for breath, William gazed at the steps doubtfully. 'How do we get him up there?'

The vanman grinned. 'No trouble, guv'. Leave it to me.' Bending down, he heaved Harry over one shoulder like a sack of coke and carried him up into the office. 'Where now, guv'?'

William drew out a chair. 'Put him in there for a moment.'

The vanman dropped the protesting Harry onto the chair and straightened his legs. 'There you are, m'lad. You'll be all right in the mornin'.'

William fished into his trouser pocket and handed the man a half-sovereign. 'The lad's going off to war tomorrow. So I don't want news of this to get around. You understand?'

The man gazed in awe at the coin, then touched his forehead. 'They'll hear nothin' from me, guv. Or Mr Clegg. We like the lad.'

'Good. Then off you go. You can get the bus, can't you?'

'Aye, that's no problem. Good night, guv'nor, and thanks.'

William waited until the man had gone, then opened a cupboard door and pulled out a folded mattress. Laying it on the floor, he helped Harry from the chair and guided him to it. 'I want you to lie down there, lad, and go to sleep. When you wake up, we'll have a cup of coffee together. Come on.'

With Harry protesting and almost a dead weight on his arm, William was panting for breath when he finally eased him down. As he rose, a sudden pain fixed in his chest and ran down his left arm. Wincing, he was forced to sit down in the chair for a moment. When the pain eased he walked back to Harry. 'I'm going over now to tell Mary where you are. Don't try to get up and go anywhere unless it's to the toilet. I'll be back in fifteen minutes or so.'

There was no reply. Bending down William saw his words had been wasted: Harry was fast asleep. Tip-toeing out, he closed the office door and then walked round to see Mary. As he approached the house he felt the pain again but this time it was less severe and he dismissed it from his mind.

Mary met him at the door. 'What's happened? Where's Harry?'

'He's all right, love. It's just his customers have given him a drink here and a drink there and it's affected him a little. So I've put him in my office until it wears off.'

'Are you saying he's drunk?'

William frowned. 'Not exactly drunk, love. Just a bit over the top. Damn it, the lad's going off tomorrow. No one's going to blame him, are they?'

Mary was showing alarm. 'Mum will. You know how she feels about drink. She'll never let him forget it.'

William patted her shoulder. 'No, she won't, love. Just leave it to me. I'll stay with him until he feels better and then he'll come home.'

'You don't think I should come?'

William shook his head firmly. 'No. There are some things a man likes to keep from his wife. Leave things to me and everything will be fine.'

She flung her arms round his neck and hugged him fiercely. 'You're such a sport, Dad. I don't know what any of us would do without you.'

William kissed her, then went to the door. 'I'll try to get him back by first light. So get some sleep until then.'

His next stop was home. Like Mary, Ethel was quickly to the door. 'Where on earth have you been?'

William went to a closet and pulled out a large carrier bag. 'I'm snowed under with work, love, and it's not going to get any easier with Harry leaving tomorrow. So I'm going to work late tonight.'

Ethel watched him drop a bottle of whisky and a large thermos flask into the bag. As she opened her mouth, he turned to her. 'Get me three blankets, will you?'

'Blankets? What on earth for?'

'It'll be too late to come home when I'm finished. I'm going to sleep over there.'

Ethel's face was alive with suspicion now. 'Harry only got back half an hour ago, didn't he? Where is he now?'

William did not lie often but when he did he could look very innocent. 'Harry? He's gone home. Where else? The lad leaves for Seaton Sluice tomorrow.'

'I never saw him go past after parking the motor car.'

'Then you missed him, didn't you? Get me the blankets, love, please.'

Ethel returned with them two minutes later. 'You won't need the thermos,' she said. 'I'll bring you coffee over at ten o'clock.'

William folded the blankets over his arm, picked up the bag, then turned to her. 'No, Ethel, you won't come over. You won't come anywhere near the warehouse tonight. And you'll never speak a word about tonight again. Not to me, not to Harry, not to anyone. Is that quite clear?'

Her face turned pale. Her expression told William she had guessed everything but that did not matter. He had made the rules of the charade very clear to her and that she would break them only at her peril.

She gave a tight, resentful sniff. 'Very well. If you'd rather drink that dreadful whisky over there than here, that's your affair. Goodnight, then.'

Satisfied, William kissed her gently. 'Good night, love. See you in the morning.'

Harry was still asleep when he returned to the office. Covering him with two blankets, William brewed a pint of coffee on the gas ring and filled the thermos. Then he fetched a pail and a jug of water and placed them near the mattress. Lastly, leaving on the gaslight, he settled down in the chair with the bottle of whisky and wrapped the third blanket around him.

It was past two o'clock when Harry awoke. William was out of his chair immediately. 'What is it, lad? Do you feel sick?'

Harry's confused eyes were moving around the office. 'No, I'm thirsty.' He tried to rise. 'What am I doing here?'

William poured out a mug of water and held it to his lips. 'It's all right, son. You've just had a drop too much to drink, that's all.'

Harry gulped down the water, then gave a start. 'What about Mary? She'll think I've had an accident.'

William gently pressed him back. 'No, she won't. I've seen her and told her you'll be home around five o'clock.'

Harry sank back with a groan. Chuckling, William laid a hand on his hot forehead. 'Nasty feeling, isn't it, lad? I've had it a few times myself. Only don't ever tell Mother.'

Harry's bloodshot eyes stared up at him in dismay. 'Does she know? If she does she'll never let me forget it.'

William had never sounded more certain of anything. 'She'll say nothing to you, lad. Now or any time.'

Harry, still not fully sober, closed his eyes. He said something that William could not catch, then gave a laugh.

William bent over him again. 'What is it, lad?'

'It's funny, Dad, isn't it? It's funny how things work out.'

'What's on your mind, son? Tell me.'

'You remember Gareth Evans? The chap Mother didn't like?'

'The revolutionary chap? Aye, I remember. What about him?'

'He's joined up too. Two days before me.'

'He has? Well, I'm damned. Never mind, lad. He'll be company for you.'

There was a pause and from Harry's breathing William believed he had fallen asleep again. When his lips moved instead, William had to bend down to hear him. 'Do you know who else he saw, Dad?'

'No, son. Who?'

'He saw Michael Chadwick at the barracks. They've given him a commission.' The younger man's words were almost inaudible now. 'He'll be in my Company, Dad.'

William gave a sharp intake of breath. 'Are you sure about that?'

This time there was no reply. Pulling the blankets back over the sleeping Harry, William dropped into his chair, then reached for the bottle of whisky. He was feeling chilled.

Chapter 22

Harry and Mary did not take Elizabeth to the railway station the following morning. With no way of knowing if a troop train might be leaving, they felt the child too young to face the experience and left her with Ethel. In the event the station was relatively quiet with the train to Seaton Sluice steaming away gently on Platform Six.

Although Mary had been dreading the ordeal of parting, she had determined to be brave for Harry's sake and managed to confine her conversation to domestic matters and their future life together. It was only when she saw the guard jump down from the engine and begin walking along the platform that her good intentions faltered. The cry she gave was almost accusing as she turned towards Harry. 'Why did you do it, darling? It wasn't necessary.'

He could think of only one thing at that moment that might comfort her. 'They'll be bringing in conscription soon, love. So what difference does it make?'

She gave a short, bitter laugh. 'Only a few more months at home with me and Elizabeth. That's the difference!' When he did not answer, she went on: 'In any case, with your religious beliefs you could have been a conscientious objector.'

From his wry smile she knew he was thinking of Ethel's reaction to having a conscientious objector in the family. She leaned against him as he put an arm round her shoulders. 'Cheer up, love. I'm not going to France yet. We've months of training to do and the war might be over by then.'

She gave an eager start. 'Do you think it might?'

Nothing was less likely now, he thought. Even the newspapers admitted that on the Western Front the French and the British had hardly gained a yard of ground since the German advance had been checked, even though Allied losses had been enormous. The attempt to turn the southern flank of the Central Powers in the Dardanelles had also clearly failed. And on the Eastern Front where the Russians had lost entire armies, the situation appeared catastrophic. Yet the lie had to be told even if she did not believe it either. 'Yes, of course. Things can't go on like this much longer.'

Their conversation lightened after that. 'Will you get much leave?' she asked.

'I'm sure to get some. And you can bet I'll be on the first train home when I do.'

A whistle sounded. As people began to board the train he took her into his arms and kissed her. He half expected her shyness to inhibit her but she clung to him even after he released her. As he picked up his suitcase and turned for the train she followed him. 'Take care of yourself, darling. Don't do anything silly, will you?'

He knew now that William had not mentioned Chadwick and was grateful. 'No,' he smiled. 'I won't do anything silly.'

They met a moment later at an open carriage window. 'Give Elizabeth a big kiss for me,' he said. 'Tell her Daddy loves her.'

Her eyes filled with tears. 'I'll tell her. Look after

180

yourself, darling. Every day. Every minute. Promise?'

'I promise. And you do the same.'

There was a great hiss of steam, metal wheels clattered, and the train gave a jolt. She held his hand a moment longer, then drew back. As she stood watching him, one hand rose to her throat. A gesture of emotion, it was also one of unconscious grace and he thought he had never seen any woman as beautiful. Then steam drifted between them and when it cleared she was only one of many distant figures waving goodbye.

He waited until the train rounded a bend before drawing back. The civilian seated opposite him frowned at the open window and asked him to close it. He obeyed, then sank back onto his seat. He had no sensation of going to war. He felt numbed and slightly embarrassed by the civilian's stare.

When Mary arrived back at No. 57, Elizabeth was having her lunch. Ethel, who was feeding the child, glanced round as the girl removed her hat. 'Well, did he get off all right?'

'Yes. The train left on time.'

'Good.' Ethel nodded towards the kitchen. 'If you tell Molly you're back, she'll set out lunch for you. Dad's already had his. He has an early appointment this afternoon.'

Mary dropped wearily onto a chair, her hat on her knees. 'I don't want lunch. I'm not hungry.'

Ethel frowned. 'That's silly. He's not going to France today, you know. It'll be weeks and months before he finishes his training.'

'I know all that, Mother.' Since Harry's departure, the girl had felt as if she were living a bad dream and it was an effort to talk. Pulling herself together, she rose. 'I'd

181

better get over to Dad. Is the appointment in his office?'

'He didn't say but I think so.' As Mary leaned over Elizabeth's high chair to kiss the child, Ethel touched her arm. 'I want a word with you before you go, dear. It'll only take a minute.'

Wondering what was coming, Mary drew back. Ethel gave the child a bowl of custard before turning to her. 'I want to talk about your accommodation now that Harry's gone. Don't you think you ought to move back into your old room? It would be so much more convenient all round.'

Mary stared at her. 'You mean leave our house empty? Why would I do a thing like that?'

'My dear, it's going to be so lonely for you now. Haven't you thought about that?'

'Of course I've thought about it. But I'm going to be no worse off than a million other women.'

'Other women haven't got parents who can put them up as comfortably as we can. There are so many advantages if you come back home.'

'What advantages?'

'Well, for one thing you won't have to cart Elizabeth back and forth now that Harry's gone. For another you won't have to find the mortgage payments every month.'

Mary stared at her in disbelief. 'Are you suggesting I sell the house?'

'It'll only be until the war's over, dear. Then you can get another one. You're going to find it very difficult to make the payments without Harry's wages, you know.'

'Do you think Harry and I haven't considered that? I'm working full-time now and if I'm careful, we can manage.'

'You mean if you go without things, you can manage,' Ethel said. 'But there's no need for that. If you live with us, you'll have money to spend both on yourself and

Elizabeth. Neither Dad nor I would want any rent. And we could store your furniture here until you wanted it again.'

'Have you spoken to Dad about this,' the girl interrupted. 'Or to Harry?'

'No. I thought it best that we talked about it first. But Harry wouldn't object, I'm sure. Not if he knew it would be easier for you here.'

'Wouldn't object? How would it look to him if he had no sooner gone than I gave up his home? Or haven't you even stopped to think about that?'

Ethel's lips compressed. 'I'd have thought he'd be glad to know his wife and child wouldn't be living in penury. If he trusts you, he'd know you'd start up a new home as soon as the war's over.'

'Mother, this is the first home Harry and I have had. How can you think that I'd give it up?'

Seeing she was making no progress, Ethel changed her tack. 'Very well, then, consider your father. It worries him to think of you alone in that house at night. It could affect his health.'

'His health. What are you talking about?'

'Your father's not well, dear. He's had two bad turns this month. I want him to see a doctor but you know how stubborn he is.'

The girl forgot her hostility. 'What sort of turns?'

'He gets pains in his chest and sometimes it runs down his arm. I keep telling him to take things easier but you know how much the business means to him. And he will drink and Doctor Armstrong says he shouldn't.'

Mary turned abruptly and made for the door. 'I'll go and talk to him.'

Ethel checked her. 'No, don't do that. He made me promise not to tell you. He thinks you've enough on your mind with Harry going away.'

Her obvious concern for William killed the girl's suspicions. 'Then I'll talk to Doctor Armstrong about it and he'll find some excuse to examine Dad. We can't just leave him to get worse, can we?'

Ethel showed relief. 'That's a good idea. Only make him promise not to mention we're behind it. You know your father's temper.' When Mary nodded and opened the rear door, her tone changed. 'Keep in mind what I've said, dear. I know it would be a load off your father's mind.'

The girl turned back sharply. 'I'm not selling my home, Mother. And I don't believe Dad would expect me to. He'd understand how Harry would feel.'

'And how would Harry feel?' Ethel asked sarcastically. 'Upset because his wife and child were being well looked after while he was away?'

'You don't know Harry at all, do you, Mother? He'd be the first to agree if I asked him: he's that kind of a man. But I know it would make him feel he'd nothing to come home to.'

'What rubbish, girl. He'd still have you and Elizabeth and he could stay here when on leave.'

'And feel as uncomfortable as you've always made him feel?' For a moment the girl's voice was almost pitying. 'You've no imagination at all, have you, Mother? You can never put yourself in another person's shoes and feel what they feel.'

Ethel stiffened. 'I've enough imagination to know this, my girl. You might be only too glad to come back home before the war's over.'

Mary turned pale. 'What are you saying now? That Harry won't come back?'

Fearing William's anger if she went too far, Ethel modified her reply. 'No one's saying anything of the sort. I'm talking about the rumours there could be a food

184

shortage next year if the war isn't over. Three of us and Elizabeth could manage far better than if we're split into two households.' Seeing the look on the girl's face she flushed angrily. 'Ask your father if you don't believe me. He saw it in the newspaper this morning.'

Mary stood gazing at the discomfited woman for a long moment. Then, shaking her head, she turned and walked from the room.

Chapter 23

The parade ground was dusty, gritty, and stifling hot beneath the July sun. Squads of men, still in civilian clothes, marched, about-turned, and collided like bewildered marionettes. Instructors, many wearing bowler hats or cloth caps themselves, sorted out the entanglements, bawled more orders, and swore to heaven as confusion piled upon confusion. The process of pounding the newly-raised 16th Battalion of the East Yorks Regiment into a fighting unit was under way.

It was noon before a bugle blew and the footsore men were allowed to fall out and disperse to their huts. Gareth Evans dropped on to his bed with a grunt of disgust. 'Fred Karno's Army, boyo! – I bet the Kaiser's laughing his head off.'

Harry, sitting on the adjacent bed unlacing his dust-stained boots, gave him a grin. 'You think so? It is only our second day out there.'

Gareth, who was in one of his darker Celtic moods, threw him a cigarette, then waved a disparaging hand at the twin rows of beds where men were either lying back with closed eyes or exchanging cigarettes. 'First day, last day, what's the difference? They'll never make soldiers out of this lot. The stupid buggers don't know their left feet from their right.'

The two men had met three days ago on Harry's arrival at Seaton Sluice. Although originally given different billets, they were both in A Company, and it had taken only a packet of cigarettes to persuade the man in the next bed to Gareth to move over into Harry's hut.

Harry was laughing. 'Listen who's talking. Who about-turned instead of halted and tripped up half the squad?'

Gareth scowled. 'Don't blame me if I can't understand that hairy Scotsman. Where did he learn to talk anyway? In the bloody Congo? And why can't he give his orders on the correct foot? No wonder we keep falling over ourselves like a pack of schoolgirls.'

The object of Gareth's complaint was a stocky, bull-necked sergeant named Waddell who had been retired from the Army in 1908. Recalled for the present emergency, he tended to show his rustiness in badly-timed parade ground orders.

'At least he's had some active service,' Harry said.

Gareth refused to be comforted. 'Back in the Boer War? It's a different game of football in France, boyo. Its bullets and bayonets there, not prancing about on horses and charging with swords and lances.'

Harry grinned again. 'Aren't you getting your wars mixed up? They haven't charged with swords and lance since Omdurman. Anyway, what are you worried about? It's revolution you're after, isn't it, not killing Germans?'

Gareth scowled again and dragged off his sweat-soaked shirt. Like many of the recruits, evidence of an undernourished childhood showed in his thin white torso and skinny arms. 'I don't want to get myself killed before it happens, that's all. Look at the officers we've got. Nearly all of 'em kids from public schools. Like that chap Chadwick.' When Harry made no comment, Gareth went on curiously: 'He hasn't spoken to you yet, has he?'

'No.'

'Isn't that a bit odd? After all you've told me?'

Harry shrugged. 'Perhaps he's been too busy. Or more likely he's decided to forget it. After all, we're all in the same boat now.'

Gareth gave a sarcastic guffaw. 'In the same boat? With officers getting wine with their T-bone steaks while we get pig swill? He's probably waiting for the right moment, boyo. Like telling you to take a Jerry trench singlehanded.'

'Thanks,' Harry said.

Gareth grinned, then decided a little charity would not come amiss. 'Perhaps he'll just make you his batman. That wouldn't be bad, would it? Cleaning his boots and bringing him morning tea? And tucking him in bed at night?'

'Shut up,' Harry said. 'Don't talk anymore about him.'

Gareth dropped back, only for his body to come into contact with his wet, clammy shirt. Cursing, he jerked upright. 'When the hell are we going to get our uniforms? A couple more days of this and my shirt and pants will walk off without me.'

'Perhaps they won't bother to issue them,' Harry said. 'After all, they're calling it a Civilians' Army.'

Gareth grinned back wickedly. 'That would suit me, boyo. If we stay in civvies I could shoot our officers and get away with it.'

The confrontation between Harry and Michael Chadwick took place the following evening. Harry was

188

ordered by Sergeant Waddell to report to a small wooden building that the subalterns used as an office. When he knocked and entered, the room was only occupied by Chadwick who was sitting behind a desk.

Harry drew himself to attention and saluted. 'You wanted to see me, sir?'

Chadwick, who had grown a moustache since their last meeting, was looking exceedingly smart in his newly-purchased subaltern's uniform. He returned the salute, then leaned back in his chair and crossed his booted legs. 'Yes, Miles. I thought we'd have a quick chat while my fellow officers are in the Mess downing their pink gins.'

Harry's pulse was beating fast although his face was expressionless. 'Yes, sir. What do you want?'

The young officer's eyes moved over his erect figure. 'I want to talk about you, Miles. Stand at ease. Or sit down if you wish.'

'Thank you, sir. But I'd rather stand.'

Chadwick shrugged. 'As you wish. Then let's get down to business. Why have you joined up?'

Harry gave a faint start. 'I'm sorry, sir. I don't understand.'

'I think it's a straightforward enough question. If my memory serves me right, you were the boy who had been taught not to fight. It had something to do with religion, I believe. So what has changed your mind and turned you into a volunteer?'

Harry, who had remained at attention, stared at the wall behind the seated officer. 'I don't believe I have to give my reasons, sir.'

'That's quite true. Officially you don't. Unofficially I'm going to be one of your officers and I need to know I can trust the men I lead. You are asking me to believe that a lifetime pacifist has suddenly turned into a man

189

eager to kill his country's enemies? I feel that gives me a right to know your reason.'

Harry remained staring at the wall. As Chadwick eyed him, his voice changed in tone. 'I see in one respect you haven't changed: you're as obstinate and ill-mannered as ever. I'm asking you again, Miles. Why have you volunteered?' When Harry still did not answer, Chadwick leaned forward. 'It couldn't be because your wife has threatened to give you a white feather, could it?'

Harry's eyes lowered to the officer's handsome face. 'I'd rather leave my wife out of it, sir.'

Chadwick smiled and leaned back again. 'That's a pity. She's a very attractive girl. But you still haven't answered my question.'

'I've joined up to defend my country, sir. Apart from that, my reasons are my own business.'

Chadwick gazed at him for a full five seconds before pulling out a gold cigarette case. Clicking it open, he selected a cigarette and returned the case to his pocket. He held the cigarette between his fingers as if about to light it, then glanced at Harry again. 'No, Miles, your reasons are not your business. They are mine because you're going to be in my platoon. Some men join up not to fight but to avoid being called a coward. If you're one of those, you're not going to be very happy with me, Miles. Now you're in the army you're going to kill Germans and like it. That's my first warning. But it's not my last one.'

He paused to light his cigarette. In the momentary silence Harry heard an engine start up in the distant transport pool. He watched Chadwick draw in smoke, then lean forward again.

'It also hasn't slipped my attention that you've joined up with that friend of yours, Gareth Evans. From all I hear he's one of those revolutionary scum who cause

190

trouble wherever they go. So from now on we'll be keeping a very careful watch on you. One false move from either of you and you'll wish you'd never been born. Do I make myself clear?'

Harry gave a terse nod but made no reply. Chadwick eyed him, seemed about to say more, then gave an abrupt gesture of dismissal. 'All right. That's all I have to say at the moment. You can go now.'

Harry saluted and withdrew. Outside an evening wind was blowing across the parade ground. The chill on his back told him that his shirt was damp with sweat.

The forty men of No. 3 Platoon were sitting on felled logs or standing in small, whispering groups. Although most of them were now in uniform and carrying Lee Enfield rifles, a shortage of webbing and pouches meant they were carrying ammunition in their pockets or in small bags tied around their waists.

They were assembled in a pine wood. Ahead of them was a quarter mile swarth cut through the trees. About forty yards wide, it ended in a high bank of mud and sand. The bank had a dozen number-boards lined along it. Back from the range two firing points were indicated by red posts, one two hundred yards from the bank and the other four hundred yards away. A small, white-washed telephone box stood alongside the rear post where a dozen men were lying on waterproof sheets, their rifles resting beside them.

It was autumn now and the Battalion had moved on to firearms training. It was a grey chilly day and the breeze carried a hint of drizzle. Chadwick had led his platoon out at 07.00 hours and they had covered the five miles to the firing range in just over an hour. Every man had fired five rounds from the two-hundred yard firing point and while their results were being recorded, they had all moved back to the four hundred marker. Among the dozen men waiting to fire again were Harry and Gareth.

Gareth was keeping a wary eye on Chadwick who was checking with the Range Officer to find out if the targets were ready. As he saw Chadwick nod and lower the receiver, the Welshman turned to Harry who was lying alongside him. 'How did you learn to shoot like that? Did your grandfather teach you?'

He was referring to the score Harry had made from the two hundred yards marker. One bull and three inners was remarkable shooting for a novice and had not only surprised Harry himself but also Sergeant Waddell, the NCO in charge of the exercise.

Harry shook his head. 'I don't think the old man had a gun. And even if he had I'd never have been allowed to use it.'

'Then you must be a bloody natural,' Gareth said. 'Don't do well this time or Chadwick might start getting ideas about us. Like recommending us for snipers.'

Harry grinned. 'Us? You didn't get a bullet on the target, did you?'

'No, and I don't bloody mean to,' Gareth grunted. 'If Chadwick's got his eyes on us, the less conspicuous we are the better.'

Harry knew he could be right but as the targets rose into sight again and he began firing he found he could not take the Welshman's advice. Was it due to pride in a newly-discovered talent, he wondered. Or was it a perverse refusal to allow Chadwick's dislike to dictate his behaviour? When the last rifle shot rang out and the black discs rose from the pits to mark the scores, Gareth gave a low whistle of respect and concern. 'Three bulls and two inners? Christ, Waddell couldn't do better than that. Look, he's pointing it out to Chadwick.'

Harry saw the Welshman was right. Both men were staring in his direction and as the sergeant muttered something to the young officer, Chadwick pulled his shooting stick from the ground and moved nearer to Harry.

A whistle brought the riflemen's attention back to the butts. This time the targets that rose were 'figure' displays: targets whose upper half were painted white and whose lower half were sea green. Between them an indistinguishable effigy was painted. As another whistle sounded, there was a rattle of fire from the dozen men whose target was the grey smudge in the centre of the frame.

Harry was finding his confidence with the Lee Enfield growing with every shot he fired. As he emptied his clip and drew back the smoking breech of the rifle, a cultured voice made him start. 'That's excellent shooting, Miles. When have you fired a Lee Enfield before?'

Rolling on his side, Harry saw Chadwick and Waddell standing over him. 'I haven't, sir.'

The bow-legged Waddell let out a shout. 'Get on your feet when you speak to an officer, lad!'

Harry climbed to his feet. Chadwick was eyeing him with scepticism. 'Perhaps not a Lee Enfield then. But you have used guns before, haven't you?'

'No, sir. I've never fired one in my life.'

Chadwick glanced at Waddell who lifted his burly shoulders in disbelief. 'Then it seems we've got a natural marksman among us. Do you know how many Germans you've just killed?'

'Germans, sir?'

'Yes. Those grey effigies are supposed to be Germans. You've hit three out of five and all through the head. You're going to be an asset to us when we get to France, Miles. We'll have to find you a job worthy of your

193

talents.' When Harry made no reply, Chadwick turned to Waddell. 'All right, Sergeant. Call up the next batch and let's see if we've any more Buffalo Bills in the platoon.'

Waddell saluted and bawled out an order as the young officer moved away. As twelve men detached themselves from the murmuring groups behind the firing point, he glanced back at Harry who was folding up his waterproof cape. 'All the same, lad, don't let it gae to yer head. You've a long way tae go yet before you're a soldier.' His scowl turned ferocious as he rounded on Gareth. 'As for you, lad, I've seen your type before. A week of fatigues'll do wonders for yer eyesight.'

The dismayed Gareth watched the sergeant's bow-legged figure stride after Chadwick. 'The bastard,' he muttered. 'How could he know I was playing the old soldier?'

Harry had to laugh. 'You did overplay it a bit, didn't you?'

Gareth gave him a scowl. 'You think you did any better? Didn't you hear what Chadwick said? You'd better get in some lousy scores quickly or you could be in the shit when we get to France.'

In late November the Battalion moved down to Hampshire where A Company found themselves in a large manor house and surrounding outhouses. It was here that missing equipment began to filter through the ponderous Army sieve. First ammunition pouches arrived, then trench shovels and entrenching tools, and finally webbing. The shovels and entrenching tools proved necessary when the next stage of training began. Called Field Exercises, it consisted of learning how to read maps, to understand the clock code, to play war games, to dig a 'safe' trench and how to dig oneself in when under fire. Being life or death skills these digging activities took up most of the men's time. Boring, arduous and monotonous work, it went on day after day and week after week. With a wet autumn now fully established the work was universally hated and the heady burst of patriotism that had sent men thronging to the recruitment centres only a few months ago was now as thoroughly doused as the pathetic fires they tried to light for warmth on Hampshire's chalky hills.

In this mood the sudden rumour that A Company was to have four days' leave with pay and travel expenses provided was at first greeted with total scepticism. Then, when assurance came in tangible passes and travel warrants, men's spirits revived as if by magic. Who cared now what boredom awaited them on their return? Four days at home, no matter how humble that home, was like a door opening into paradise. The only regret men had was that their furlough would expire before Christmas.

Harry's excitement, however, was overshadowed by an order to report to Chadwick the day before his leave began. The subalterns shared a small makeshift office on the top floor of the house and Harry found two of them present when he marched up to the table where Chadwick was seated. 'Sergeant Waddell said you wanted to see me, sir.'

Chadwick returned his salute, then nodded at a sheet of paper on the table before him. 'Yes, I've got some news that will interest you, Miles. Two days ago I was appointed Machine Gun Officer for the Company, with orders to find twelve suitable men to serve under me. According to my instructions at least half of them should be men with higher than average ratings in marksmanship and so of course you came to my mind. How would you like to serve as a machine gunner?'

It was the last thing Harry expected and for the moment he could not hide his dismay. Even at this stage of the war it was well known that the fast-firing machine gun, with its ability to enfilade columns of advancing men, had brought a new dimension to slaughter.

He pulled himself together. 'I'd prefer not to, sir.'

Chadwick looked surprised. 'You wouldn't? But machine gunners are the élite, Miles. When they offered me the job, I volunteered in a flash.'

'You asked me a question, sir, and I gave you my answer. I'd rather not be a machine gunner.'

For a moment Harry believed the young officer was reasoning with him. 'Miles, you're a fine marksman. Think what a shame it would be to waste your talent.' When Harry made no reply, Chadwick cast a glance at the two subalterns before continuing. 'You can't imagine the struggle I've had with the colonel over this. When he saw your range scores he immediately suggested you were trained as a sniper but I felt you wouldn't like that. I mean, picking off unsuspecting men from cover is more a job for an assassin, don't you think?'

As one of the officers chuckled, Harry understood. They had been told about his pacifist tendencies and he was being baited before them. 'Are you telling me I have to choose between one or the other, sir?'

Chadwick gave a sigh of regret. 'I'm afraid that's the ticket, Miles.'

'You realise I don't know anything about machine guns.'

Chadwick's face brightened. 'That's no problem. I don't either. But there's a course starting when we get back from leave and they promise that within three weeks we'll be able to assemble a Vickers blindfold.' He

196

picked up a pencil. 'Then I can put your name down, can I? I'm sure you don't want to creep about killing Germans in cold blood.'

As Harry gave a tight, angry nod, Chadwick pretended to look puzzled. 'As a volunteer soldier you ought to be pleased, Miles. A rifle has its part to play but a machine gun can kill dozens, even hundreds of the enemy. The twelve of us will be the envy of the Company.'

Harry decided to bring an end to the cat and mouse game. 'Who else are you picking for the section, sir?'

Chadwick cast a glance at the two grinning subalterns. 'I've given this very careful thought. I've always believed it a good idea to keep friends together if possible and that friend of yours, Private Evans, has shown a marked improvement on the range recently. He's not in your league, of course, but then a machine gun loader doesn't need to be such an expert marksman. So he will be in your gun team.'

It was all very clear to Harry now. 'Do you want me to tell him, sir?'

'If you would, Miles. You'll get your orders when to report for training after your leave. That's all for now. You're dismissed.'

Chapter 24

It was five-thirty the following day before Harry arrived home. He had barely put a foot on the front step before the door was flung open and Mary was hugging him. 'Oh, darling, it's so good to see you! But why are you so late?'

In full uniform, with webbing, pack, gasmask and kitbag, he was finding it difficult to return her embrace. 'It's all these damn troop movements. My connection at Doncaster left early and I'd to wait another two hours for the next. That's why I told you not to meet me.'

She tried to help him with the kitbag but found it too heavy for her. As he swung it into the tiny hall he saw a diminutive figure in a clean white pinafore waiting timidly at the foot of the stairs. Mary caught her hand. 'Look who's here, darling! What do you say?'

The child made a brave effort to repeat her rehearsed lines. 'It's Dada. My dada. . . .'

Harry swung her off her feet. 'Hello, love. Give me a kiss.'

The child hesitated, then kissed him solemnly on the cheek. Mary laughed. 'You can do better than that, darling. Kiss Daddy properly.'

The girl's wide eyes surveyed Harry's face for a

moment before leaning forward and touching his lips. Then she buried her face shyly in his shoulder.

Harry put her down on the floor. 'I've got a present for you, love. Wait a minute.' Unstrapping his webbing, he pulled out a small teddybear from his pack. 'There. Do you like it?'

The child hesitated. Bending down, Mary took the toy and pressed it into her small hands. 'Isn't that a lovely teddy, darling? Say ta, Dada.'

'Ta, Dada. Tata.'

Harry laughed, kissed her again, then turned to Mary. 'I've a present for you too but it's at the bottom of my kitbag. Can I give it to you later?'

She lifted a hand to his face. 'I've got the only present I want. When do you have to go back?'

'Sunday. I have to be back at midnight so I'll have to catch the three-thirty train.'

'Sunday! So we've got two and a half days. Don't let's waste a minute of them.'

Harry approached Elizabeth's cot. 'What's the matter love? Why are you crying?'

The child gazed up at him through swimming eyes, cried out something, then began sobbing again. Seeing the small teddybear lying at the foot of the cot. Harry tried to press it into her arms. 'Here, love. Tell Teddy what's the matter.'

The girl's sobs became hysterical. One tiny hand seized the teddybear's arm and threw the toy away. Puzzled, Harry turned to Mary who had followed him into the room. 'What's the matter with her? She isn't in pain, is she?'

'No,' Mary said. 'It's not that.'

Something in her voice drew Harry's attention. 'Then

what is it? She's not frightened of me, is she?'

The girl winced. 'Don't be silly.'

'Then why is she sobbing like this?'

Mary knew there was no avoiding the answer. 'She wants her bed mate.'

'You mean another toy?'

'Yes.'

'Then why didn't you give it to her?'

The girl opened her mouth to speak, then walked across the small room to a cupboard. Toys spilled out on to the floor as she opened it. Among them was a pink teddybear almost as big as the child herself. Taking it to the cot she laid it alongside the sobbing child.

Her sobs ceased immediately as her chubby hands embraced the furry plaything. Tucking in the blankets, Mary turned to Harry with a strained smile. 'She'll be all right now.'

He followed her into the living room. Then he caught her arm and turned her to him. 'You didn't need to do that, love. I'm not that sensitive. Who bought it for her? You or your mother?'

She bit her lip and pressed against him. 'Mother. She spoils her to death, Harry. You should see the presents she's bought her. And there seems no way I can stop her.'

Mary lay listening to the rain pattering against the bedroom window. Beside her Harry's breathing told her he had fallen asleep. Half of her wanted to awaken him. If they only had until Sunday afternoon, the minutes were more precious than jewels and it seemed criminal to squander them away in sleep.

She no sooner had the thought than she quelled it. It was gone three o'clock and he had been travelling most

200

of the day. It was also his first night in a proper bed since his call-up. The miracle was that he had stayed awake so long and made love to her with such warmth and passion.

Her thoughts moved on to the morrow when they would have to go over and see her parents. As it was not yet the weekend, William would be at work and she knew Harry would rather see him on his own. Yet that would mean seeing Ethel alone too and without William present there was always the danger she might come up with some remark that would sour their few days together. Better see them both when they were together in the evening although the thought of losing one of her two precious evenings made the girl wince.

There was another danger in seeing Ethel alone, she thought. Within a few minutes of Harry's arrival she had noticed how the Army had changed him. He was not only sturdier in build but a trace more forceful and assertive. She did not dislike the change but wished now that she had lied and told him that she had bought the teddybear. If he were to complain to Ethel that she was over-indulging Elizabeth, the repercussions would be felt long after he returned to camp. She knew such thoughts were further evidence of her fear of Ethel but still made a note to caution Harry before they paid their visit.

Moving gently so as not to disturb him, she eased round in bed until his face was only a few inches from her own. Luxuriating in his closeness, with his breath stirring her hair, she lay that way for a while. Then, unsure whether her act was one of selfishness or impulsive love but still unable to resist it, she leaned forward and gently kissed his cheek.

He murmured something but did not awaken. She kissed him again, took one of his hands in her own, then lay back. With his steady breathing beside her and the pattering of the rain on the window she had a feeling of safety, that while they lay together in the small neat house no perils of the world outside could reach them. Her wish was that the night could last forever.

They paid their visit to No. 57 the following evening, and to Mary's relief all went well. Ethel's reception was cool and restrained but William's delight at seeing Harry again was enough in itself to make the evening a success. He asked Harry a hundred questions about the Army and the training he was getting and when he finally allowed the couple to tear themselves away, he insisted, to Ethel's disgust, that Harry took a couple of bottles of whisky with him to share with the men in his platoon. 'The lads deserved a bit of comfort, lass, when they're giving up so much for us.'

Although there was rain in the wind, he insisted in walking down the front path with them. 'Will you get another leave before you're shipped over to France, lad?'

Harry shook his head. 'I don't think so. Not that they ever tell us anything but I think we'll be moving out soon.'

There was an unsteadiness in William's bluff voice that Mary had never heard before as he held out his hand. 'In that case, lad, there won't be a day when we won't be praying for you.'

Harry's silence as the two of them walked back home told Mary he was equally affected. 'Dad misses you,' she told him. 'He thinks of you as a son.'

He turned to her. 'He doesn't look well. Has he had any more of those attacks?'

'Yes. Last week. The doctor's given him tablets to

202

take when he has them. Mother and I keep begging him to take it more quietly but he's worried about the business.' At his question, she shook her head. 'No. I think those early orders were just the Government buying up stocks wherever they could. Now they've had more time, they're ordering and buying direct from the drug manufacturers. It's making it difficult to get stocks and with so many men away and families having to live on Army pay, the shops have had to limit their buying.'

He frowned. 'Do you think Willis is pulling his weight?'

'No. Neither of us do. But Mother seems to like him and in any case who can Dad get in his place?'

She never knew what happened to the third day. It flashed past as if time itself was on the side of the war gods, impatient to place their sacrificial pawns on the battlefields. As it was Saturday, William had offered them use of the Ford and they took a drive out to Beverley where they walked with Elizabeth over the Westwood. Although the wind was cold, it was a clear, bright day and Elizabeth shrieked with joy when Harry offered to race her to the old windmill on the hilltop.

Afterwards, although they could not afford it, they had lunch in a café in the market place. She began to feel unreal as the hours slipped by. At one moment her heart would seem near bursting with the happiness of their reunion. In the next she would remember the morrow and her laughter would give way to a sense of loss and foreboding.

They went to bed early that night. Although they made love, it was his nearness that she wanted most of all. Love-making induced sleep and sleep was the great thief of time. She responded to him but her full contentment came when they were lying fulfilled and relaxed together.

She would not allow her eyes to close. His warmth, his assurance, would not be with her tomorrow. Perhaps if she tried she could cheat and slow down the clock of time. Eyes wide open, she gazed at the dark ceiling and concentrated while from beside her came the slow metronome of his breathing.

There was no rain tonight, only the lonely sound of the wind in the eaves. Perhaps she was succeeding, she thought. Perhaps her mind was lifting them all to a far-away place where men no longer fought and died and lovers could live forever.

It was the distant wail of a train that broke the spell. It came again, a sad, unconsolable cry from the night and she knew her safe haven was invaded. Her eyes were still open when the grey dawn that was to take Harry from her came stealing through the window.

Chapter 25

The Battalion remained in Hampshire over Christmas and the New Year and sailed for France the second week in January. Its first stop was the infamous 'Bullring' at Etaples. Until Etaples some men still cherished the illusion that the Army they had joined resembled a grim old Victorian father that wielded the rod not to punish the child but to save it. In other words that a heart beat somewhere beneath the hoary warlike chest.

At Etaples all such illusions were finally shattered. If a heart existed there, no man could yet claim to have found it. Instead there was discipline of a severity unknown in England and a course of training that made strong men wince. Undoubtedly one aim was to produce first class combat soldiers and in most cases this aim was achieved. Whether it was also intended to coarsen and brutalise men can only be open to surmise.

Bayonet practice alone had many a man fighting to hold down his stomach. The targets, transfixed by stakes, were grey-uniformed realistic figures with mock rifles in their hands. A man was trained to run at them with his comrades, to yell his hatred at the top of his voice and then vent it as savagely as possible on the enemy. A quick side step and a smash of the rifle butt into the groin or the jaw to cripple. Then the kill, an upward thrust through the stomach into the heart or a disembowling jab into the belly. Finally the twist of the rifle to rupture and rip the organs before jerking out the bayonet and go searching for another victim.

At less grisly times the Battalion were given more lectures on field tactics. Their instructors, however, were no longer the apple-cheeked officers they had known in England. Now they were grey-faced veterans, some missing an arm or a leg.

At first men listened in confusion. In England they had been taught to take cover from artillery in farmhouses, in plantations, behind embankments or any other prominent feature in the countryside. In Etaples they were taught the exact opposite. The enemy's artillerymen had their guns zeroed on every salient feature within range. A man's safest place was the middle of an open field which made it difficult for the enemy's rangefinders to gauge his position.

Men had also been taught to dig their trenches where they could see the enemy at long range. At Etaples it was pointed out the enemy would be able to see them too and blow them out of the ground. Whenever possible a trench should be dug on the *reverse* side of a hill. A field of fire of no more than two hundred yards was distance enough. Determined men could mow down attacking infantry from the face of the earth before they could be over-run.

But Etaples was never parsimonious with its horrors and soon gas warfare was on the agenda. To rub home the necessity of quick action during a gas attack, the Battalion were shown photographs of men who for one reason or another had not reacted quickly enough. There were pictures of men with their entire skin surface burned away and only their agonised eyes betraying they were still alive. There were pictures of men vomiting their lungs up from phosgene poisoning and men with their eyes burned out of their sockets by mustard gas. When the lessons had been driven home, orders were given to don gas masks and run round the parade ground.

The next step was to run up man-made hills in the masks. Men felt their lungs draining of oxygen; they choked and clutched at their throats, but all the time they knew that if they even twitched the rubber side of their masks to let in a breath of life-giving air, keen-eyed observers would report them for punishment.

Indeed crime and punishment came first and last on Etaples' agenda. Men were taught and taught again the grisly field reprisals they would suffer for active service offences and that an act of cowardice in the face of the enemy was a capital offence, either a bullet on the battlefield from one's own officer or a firing squad later. The ordeal at Etaples, while sobering Gareth, also reinforced his belief in imminent revolution. 'If Jerry puts his men through battle schools like this, boyo, and I suppose he must, then how long can it be before men chuck it up and raise the red flag? We'd all have to be crazy to fight under these terms. Christ, do you know what it's doing to me? It's making me more scared of my own lot that I am of Jerry.'

With many men of the Battalion feeling the same way, it is open to speculation whether that was another reason for Etaples' existence. Certainly it is true that a percentage of the soldiers who marched out of the 'Bullring' were changed in more than military knowledge from the young and eager men who had marched in.

The Battalion's next move was kept a military secret

from the ranks. Each man was handed two days' rations and then marched to a rail junction where fifty closed wagons were waiting. With a French legend on each wagon stating it was suitable for either eight horses or forty men and with ordure still present in some of them, men grumbled and cursed but discipline had a tight grip on them now and no one refused to enter his designated vehicle. The embarkation took a long time but at last the huge train lumbered out into the bleak, winter countryside.

With no man certain of his destination, rumours flew round the stinking wagons like birds trapped in a cage. Some believed they were going straight into action. Others thought they might be going to another Etaples and feared it more. But as the fifty wagons rattled along at a steady twenty miles an hour, speculation began to give way to boredom, and it was a relief to all when after six hours the wagons jolted to a halt, the doors were hauled back, and RTO NCOs poked in their heads to announce that hot water was available for tea making.

Thankfully clambering out to stretch their legs, men found themselves in a flat countryside dotted by irrigation ditches, gaunt farmhouses, and leafless trees. Gareth gave a grunt of disgust. 'La Belle France, boyo! Worse than Swansea on a Sunday afternoon!'

The train rattled for another three hours and then, for no apparent reason, came to a halt in another siding in the middle of a large featureless plain where men were told it would stay until the morning. Weary figures, they climbed out to relieve themselves, to obtain more hot water, and then, with rain drenching down, crawled back into their smelly trucks to spend a cold and comfortless night.

They were awakened around 04.00 hours by the train jolting forward again. It lumbered on until daybreak, to come to a final halt at a large siding where a row of horse-drawn carts were waiting. Men were told to deposit their blankets in the carts and then form up in sections along the road.

Thirty minutes later, with a fine rain falling from a uniformly grey sky, NCOs bawled out orders, and the Battalion began marching down the narrow French lanes. At first, in spite of the urgings of their NCOs and officers, men were mainly silent but as the rain ceased and a watery sun broke through, spirits revived and here and there whistling could be heard. The whistling grew and turned into singing. Soon the singing spread down the long column of troops and startled crows perched on leafless trees took fright and flapped away.

The road dipped into a shallow valley dotted with farmhouses. As the first section of men entered a hamlet, windows and doors burst open and women of all ages appeared at them. As they shouted and waved, young eyes that had been sobered by the experience at Etaples, began to brighten again. This was the war they had been led to believe in, with grateful women running out to them, kissing their cheeks and thrusting bottles of wine into their hands. As they swung along, their booted feet ringing proudly on the cobblestones, men felt once again the glory and indestructibility of youth.

Their mood was timely because by mid-afternoon there were signs they were nearing the Front. Occasional farmhouses showed the effect of bombs or gunfire and here and there shattered caissons lay overturned in ditches. Once the sinister cigar shape of a Zeppelin appeared on the horizon and shortly afterwards two Allied biplanes flew over them. But the thing that made men's hearts beat faster was the first sound of gunfire. It could not yet be described as a rumble – it was still too distant for that. Instead it was a noise more felt than

209

heard: a vibration that seemed to reach them through the ground rather than through the ears.

The Battalion reached its destination before the light faded, a gaunt industrial town built on and around a shallow hill on which stood an empty chateau. The officers and a number of NCOs were given billets in the chateau, the rest of the men were distributed among the townsfolk.

Harry and Gareth found themselves at the home of Madame Levrey. She was the wife of a doctor who, like the rest of the local men of military age, was away serving the Colours. Although the stone-built terraced house was no larger than its neighbours, suggesting the doctor's practice had been a small one, his wife spoke surprisingly good English, to the relief of Harry and Gareth whose French was non-existent.

Madame Levrey was a young woman in her middle or late twenties with a girl of five. Slightly taller than average, she was slimly-built with a long attractive face and large brown eyes. Although she wore her dark hair in a bun, it gave her face a grave rather than a severe expression. Her child, Michelle, was a pretty girl with braided fair hair that hung down to her waist.

The woman's reception of the two men was resigned rather than enthusiastic. As the tide of war had ebbed and flowed, Montoise had been occupied first by German Uhlans, then by the French, and now the British. While the inhabitants were glad to see their allies arriving in strength at last, it was perhaps too much to expect general enthusiasm for another influx of licentious soldiery into their homes. Harry and Gareth were taken upstairs to one of Madame Levrey's two bedrooms, shown the washroom and the earthern closet in the back garden, told when they could expect their food, and there their welcome ended.

210

That is until the woman found Harry giving chocolate to her daughter the following evening. When Gareth also produced a bar for the girl, the woman began to thaw. 'Do you both have families, messieurs? Wives and children?'

Shaking his head, Gareth pointed at Harry. 'He's the one who's hitched up. He's got a daughter, a couple of years younger than yours.'

The woman turned her brown eyes on Harry. 'Have you a photograph of them, m'sieur?'

Harry drew a photograph of Mary and Elizabeth from his wallet. Taking it from him, the woman gave a smile of pleasure. 'Your wife is very beautiful, m'sieur. And so is your little one. What are they called?'

'My wife's called Mary. The little girl is Elizabeth.'

'Mary and Elizabeth. They are pretty names.' The woman bent down to her little girl whose face was already smudged with chocolate. 'Have you thanked the kind gentlemen yet?' When the child gazed at her blankly, she repeated the question in French. This time the girl gazed up shyly at the two soldiers. '*Merci*, messieurs. *Merci bien.*'

When the two men laughed, the woman bent down again and kissed the child. 'I think we must ask the two gentlemen to teach you English, *ma petite*. But only if you promise not to eat any more of their chocolate.'

It was the breaking of the ice. That night there was a bottle of wine on the tray Madame Levrey brought up to their room. Although she gave Gareth a smile, it was Harry she spoke to. 'Perhaps tomorrow we can all eat together downstairs. Tonight two friends are having dinner with me.'

'Thank you.' Harry told her. 'We'd like that.'

She gave him another smile before leaving the room. Gareth, whose eyes had been moving over her slender body, turned to Harry with a chuckle. 'I think she fancies you boyo. That's only because you're married, mind. She thinks you've more experience.'

Harry pushed a glass of wine towards him. 'It's just the opposite. She's seen the look in your eyes and she feels safer with a married man.'

Gareth who had grumbled incessantly throughout the long march, grinned and tasted the wine appreciatively. 'They're the worst. Everyone knows that. Perhaps this isn't going to be such a bad war after all. Not with all these Frenchmen away at the Front. I wonder how long they'll let us stay here.'

'You watch yourself,' Harry warned. 'I don't want her throwing us out of here. That's all Chadwick needs.'

Before Gareth could reply a deep rumble made the flames of the paraffin lamp dip and lurch. Gareth looked startled. 'What the hell was that?'

Blowing out the lamp, Harry ran to the window and opened the wooden shutters. Beside him Gareth sucked in his breath. 'My God, look over there!'

Outside the darkness had long fallen and the town, under military orders, was showing hardly a glimmer of light. Because of the position of the house on the shallow hillside, however, most of the eastern horizon was visible and far to the north a huge red glow was hanging over it as if furnace doors had opened. Shouts from the road below told the watching men that both townspeople and soldiers were running out to see what had happened. As men watched, the glow slowly faded, to be replaced by red flashes around the original site. 'Artillery,' Harry said as a far-off rumble made the window rattle. 'Perhaps Jerry or ourselves are trying to break through over there.'

The shelling went on for over fifteen minutes, then began to die down. Gareth gave Harry an uneasy glance.

'What happens now? You don't think they'll rush us up to the line, do you?'

Slowly the horizon changed its mood. The red flashes ceased altogether and the dark line became overhung with an eerie phosphorescent glow among which nervous stars writhed upwards and slowly descended. Gareth watched for another minute, then turned back in relief to the darkened bedroom. 'Whatever it was, it seems to be over. Let's finish the bottle of wine, boyo, while we've got the chance.'

Chapter 26

An early morning parade the next day answered at least some of the Battalion's questions. Montoise, out of range of anything but German aircraft and long range artillery, was one of the many towns and villages chosen by the British Army as rest centres for its troops. The Battalion would stay there for a week, when the present infantry holding the line were due for rest. Then the exchange would be made, both in the billets and in the trenches.

In the meantime lectures would be given by experts on the latest enemy intelligence and on the latest artillery tactics. Inevitably as it was the Army, no mention whatever was made of the massive explosion the previous night and so one man's guess was as good as his neighbour's.

Nevertheless the news they were to stay in Montoise for a full week was received with great enthusiasm by the men. It was, after all, their first experience of France and the first thing a soldier learns is not to think about tomorrow but to live for today. Moreover, while they might still be novices in the art of war, they were hardly novices in the pursuit of pleasure and most of them had two targets when their daily route marches or fatigues were over: the *estaminets* where they could buy cheap wine and the brothels where they could find willing women. Officially the brothels were out of bounds but as the MPs who guarded them were usually tucked away safely in bed with some buxom prostitute well before the men arrived, they seldom had any problems in gaining entry. Not that all men found the need to go. As Gareth had suggested, some of the village women were only too happy to dispense other hospitality than food and shelter.

Yet as always there were men with different or quieter tastes. Some preferred to gamble the nights away with cards. Some preferred to read. Others, like Harry, spent much of their spare time writing letters, to Gareth's disgust.

'Christ, boyo, it's our last night. We're off to war tomorrow. And you must've written her a dozen letters since we've been here. Give yourself a treat and have a good time tonight.'

Harry shook his head. 'I don't feel like it. But I'm not stopping you going, am I?'

Gareth frowned. 'I don't like leaving you alone, kid. Not tonight.'

'Don't be so daft. You'll only be a nuisance if you hang around. Get along and enjoy yourself.'

Gareth hesitated, then shrugged on his greatcoat. 'Thank God I'm not married,' he muttered. 'You poor bastards get the worst of the war and miss out on the best of it.'

Harry picked up his pencil again as he heard the front door close. In the way of war, he had received a whole batch of letters from Mary that week. She was writing to him every two days: shy loving letters telling him how Elizabeth was growing, of the new words she was using, how they both missed him and how they both prayed for him every night. Like himself, she was not a good letter writer – both had the Northern restraint that made it difficult for them to express their feelings in cold print – but he understood her and the very simplicity and honesty of her words often brought a lump to his throat.

At the same time he knew she was telling him only the best of her news. There was never any mention of the childhood ailments Elizabeth must now be having or the clashes with Ethel that the older woman's temperament made almost inevitable. The only pensive lines in the entire batch of letters came in a postscript in the last one. 'Have you the time to write a few lines to Dad, darling? He misses you so much and he's lost weight recently. I do wish he would not work so hard.'

Conscious that letter writing could be at a premium from now on, Harry had decided to write to William as well that night. The task was not easy. With so many French coal mines destroyed or in enemy hands, fuel was strictly rationed and men were billeted on the understanding they would not be given or accept any of their host's ration. The result was that men spent most of their time when in their rooms wrapped in their greatcoats or their blankets.

Even greatcoats did not keep a man's fingers warm, however, and Harry was finding it difficult to keep his handwriting legible. As he paused and blew on his hands he heard the front door open and the chatter of a child. Knowing that Madame Levrey had taken the girl to a children's party that afternoon, he took no further notice and his mind registered only subconsciously their entry into the kitchen and the clatter of cutlery and plates.

He had finished his letter to William and was searching for another envelope when the woman brought the child upstairs to bed. Unable to find one, he slipped William's letter into Mary's and was just sealing the envelope when there was a soft tap on the door. 'Messieurs?'

Opening the door, he found Madame Levrey standing there. She was wearing a dress he had not seen before, long and emerald in colour with a high collar. She looked faintly embarrassed. 'Are you busy, m'sieur?'

'No; I've been writing letters but they're finished now. Why?'

She motioned at the other door on the tiny landing. 'I cannot light the lamp in our bedroom. I wondered if one of you would look at it for me.'

He spoke to the child who came to the door, then took the oil lamp into his own room. He found the wick had been turned down too far and was not engaging the teeth of the ratchet. Unscrewing the base, he fed the wick back and a minute later a comforting glow was spreading round the other small bedroom. Ruffling the child's hair, he was returning to his room when the woman's voice checked him. 'You look cold, m'sieur. There is a fire in the sitting room. Please take a glass of wine with me there.'

'There's no need for that,' he said.

'I know. But you are leaving tomorrow. I would like to drink to your safe return.'

He felt it would be unchivalrous to refuse. 'All right then. Thank you.'

She nodded. 'If you will go down and wait for me, I will only be a moment.'

Leaving her undressing the child, he descended the stairs and entered the sitting room. It was in darkness except for the small coal fire burning in the hearth. Crossing over to it, he stood with his back to the fireguard. As its warmth began to soak through his greatcoat, his eyes took in heavy mahogany furniture and the two photographs that stood on a desk. Seeing one was of a man in uniform he was about to take a closer look when her footsteps sounded on the stairs. Crossing the room, she closed the shutters, lit the lamp, then turned to him with a smile. 'Do sit down, m'sieur. In the chair by the fire.'

Feeling awkward in his greatcoat, he obeyed. She went to a cabinet and took out a bottle and two glasses. 'Your friend has gone out tonight, m'sieur?'

'Yes. An hour ago.'

'But you wanted to stay and write letters to your beautiful wife, *n'est ce pas*?'

He gave an embarrassed laugh. 'I thought it might be difficult to write up at the Front.'

She handed him a glass. 'A little cognac. To keep out the cold.' Crossing over to a chair on the other side of the hearth, she smiled at him. '*Santé*, To your good health and safe return.'

'Thank you.' He felt the spirit warming his stomach. He wanted to include her husband's safety in the toast but before he could think of the right words she laughed regretfully. 'Little Michelle is going to miss you both.'

'We'll miss her too,' he said. 'Did she enjoy her party this afternoon?'

'Oh, yes. They played games and were given toys. Not very good toys because of the war but still they all enjoyed themselves.'

Harry took another sip of cognac. He had not yet eaten the cold supper the woman had left them and he was feeling a slight headiness from the spirit. 'Your husband must miss Michelle,' he said.

'Pierre? Oh, yes. Like so many fathers miss their children.'

'Where is he, madame? Do you know?'

'Yes, I know. We have a little code between us. He is at Verdun.'

'Verdun? Where is that?'

'South of here.' She gave a faint shudder. 'Many Frenchmen are being sent there. They expect the Germans to attack any day and that it will be a long and fierce battle.

He did not know how to answer her. As if to quell her fears, she lifted her glass and drained it. Remembering the aloofness she had shown on their arrival he knew now it had only been a protective shell. With the firelight touching her dark hair and slender body, she looked both a vulnerable and attractive woman.

With an impatient exclamation she rose, picked up his glass, and went again to the cabinet. 'We must not talk about the war tonight. Tell me about your life in England and the work you do.'

At first, with no intention of discussing his personal problems, he talked only about William's business and his own part in it. But when the second cognac settled within him, he made mention of Ethel and from that moment Ethel seemed to dominate his conversation. The Frenchwoman was a good and intuitive listener and when he finished, his laugh was both wry and embarrassed. 'I'm sorry. I don't know why I've gone on like that. I've told you things I haven't even told Mary.'

She shrugged. 'Of course you have. One cannot tell a lover one's hopes and fears. One can only tell these things to strangers.'

He frowned. 'That doesn't seem right, does it? A husband and a wife should be able to share everything together.'

There was affection in her laugh. 'You are an idealist too. So is my husband. That is why we live here in Montoise. After we came back from England he could have shared a fashionable practice in Lyons. But not Pierre. He wanted to administer to the needy.' She

219

paused and smiled. 'The ones who cannot afford to pay their doctor's bills.'

'Do you mind?' he asked.

'I did at first. But not now. I realise it has kept Pierre the same man that I fell in love with. No, I have no regrets.'

'And now he is a doctor in the Army?'

A shadow crossed her face. 'Yes, but he should not be.'

'Because he is an idealist?'

She frowned. 'Not only that. Pierre is religious. He seldom talks about it but it runs deep inside him. And they say war can do terrible things to such men.'

He was watching her intently now. 'What kind of things?'

She made an uncertain gesture. 'I am not sure. But I'm afraid for him.'

'But he's a doctor, not a combatant soldier.'

'I know. But I am still afraid for him.' Before he could question her further, she went on quietly: 'You joined up because of this woman Ethel, did you not?'

He gave a start, then hesitated. 'I've never been sure what my reasons were. The Zeppelin raids and the atrocity stories might have had something to do with it. And I knew conscription wasn't far off. At the same time I knew she'd give Mary no peace if I didn't join up.'

She nodded at his honesty. 'You must be very careful of this woman. She is full of jealousies and acts on emotion, not reason. She could do great harm to you both if you are not careful.'

'I'm afraid of that too,' he said. 'But she's my wife's mother and we both work for her husband. So how can we keep away from her?'

'When the war is over you must. A woman like that can destroy anything, even love.'

220

In the silence that fell a heavy rumble rattled the window shutters. Her voice suddenly sounded very distant. 'When the war is over! How far away that seems tonight.'

He cleared his throat. 'Will you have to billet other men after we leave tomorrow?'

'Tomorrow or the day after. They will be the men you are replacing. They will be so tired they will want to do nothing for three days but eat and sleep. Then they will become boys again and start playing football or chasing girls.'

'Does that mean we might come back one day?' he asked.

Her brown eyes travelled over his face. 'If the Front remains stable, yes. Do you want me to ask for the two of you again or would you rather go elsewhere?'

'No, I want to come back here.' Then, afraid he sounded too eager, he went on: 'We'd both like it. I know I can speak for Gareth.'

She smiled. 'Then I will ask for you. By then it will probably be summer.'

He realised he was still wearing his greatcoat. Sitting there, with the firelight playing on her grave attractive face, with the savagery of war waiting on the morrow, England suddenly seemed a million miles away and so far back in time he could not remember the faces of Mary and Elizabeth. Confused and dismayed, he rose to his feet. 'I'd better go now, madame. Thank you for the brandy and for listening to me.'

She smiled again and rose with him. 'Please do not call me Madame. It makes me feel very old. My name is Nicole. And yours is Harry, *n'est ce pas*?'

He wondered why he should feel embarrassment again. She could not be more than two or three years older than himself. 'Yes.' He tried to make a joke of it.

'You say it very well. Don't most French people say "Arry"?'

She laughed. 'Yes, they do. So you do not think my English is too bad – 'Arry?'

He laughed back. 'I wish I could speak French half as well.'

At the door she caught his arm and turned him to face her. 'You will take care of yourself at the Front, won't you?'

She was standing very close to him and he felt his mouth suddenly turning dry. 'Yes. Of course I will.'

'You must. For the sake of Mary and Elizabeth.' Before he could reply she leaned forward and kissed him softly on the lips. As he stiffened, she drew back and smiled at him. 'My Pierre will not mind that, Harry. Nor I think will your Mary. The war has made us all lonely people. I hope some woman is making my Pierre feel less lonely tonight.'

He had never heard a woman speak that way before. As he took a step forward, she laid a gentle hand across his mouth. 'No, you would be sorry afterwards. Go to your room now and try to sleep. And may God take care of you tomorrow and keep you safe.'

He realised he had drunk too much brandy when he began to climb the stairs. She watched him until he was safely in his room, then withdrew.

He felt light-headed as he lay in bed. Near midnight Gareth returned, too drunk to remove anything but his boots and greatcoat but considerate enough not to light the lamp. Harry listened to his muttered curses as the Welshman found his bed and drew the blankets over himself. A few seconds later his snores filled the room.

A distant flurry of gunfire shook the window. Red lights glowed and faded on its shutters. Lying there, Harry had the disorientated sensation of being lost in an alien world. In a few hours he would be expected to kill when since his first memories he had been taught the sanctity of human life. Who was right? His mother, that gentle brave creature who had kept her beliefs and her faith to the end? Or the Government, the politicians, even the priests and parsons who blessed every soldier before he went out to kill his fellow men? As waves of doubt clashed in his mind, Harry found himself breaking into a cold sweat.

Nor did it end there. There was Nicole. If they had made love tonight, he suspected neither of them would have felt guilty even though they were both deeply in love with their partners. Nicole had even hinted she would not mind another woman sleeping with Pierre if it were done out of compassion. She understood the crying need of loneliness and tonight he had felt it himself.

Yet what would his mother, the Chapel she loved, or even Mary herself make of such tolerance? Was there, then, no absolute ideal, no perfect concept? Was morality dependent on circumstance? Lying there listening to the grumble of the guns, the frightened young Yorkshireman wondered what kind of a man he would become if he survived the war.

Chapter 27

The Battalion moved up to the Front just after noon the following day. The morning was spent preparing equipment, loading carts, and attending a religious service, an event that sobered the men and reminded Harry of his thoughts the previous night. His machine gun section's final act was to collect their heavy Vickers guns and ancillary equipment from the makeshift armoury, a stone barn on the chateau's estate, and load them on to a couple of mule-drawn carts.

Men were then allowed thirty minutes to eat the rations provided by their own cooks before forming into companies, platoons and sections. Fifteen minutes later bugles sounded, orders echoed through the narrow streets, and the steady tramp of booted feet rang out on the cobblestones.

There was not much emotion shown by the townspeople although here and there behind closed doors a few women silently wept. Some waved a handkerchief and blew a kiss, but in the main women and old men watched in silence. They had seen too many tall strong young soldiers march off towards the guns, to vanish forever or end up in fearful mutilation in base hospitals.

Harry did not see Nicole again after his breakfast farewell. The orders of his section were to stay with the mule-drawn carts and their route led them round the northern side of the town. The NCO in charge was Sergeant Wentworth, a man with previous experience in automatic weapons, and in turn he took his orders from Chadwick, the subaltern commanding the section.

Before the carts moved off, Chadwick had drawn Harry aside. Impeccably dressed in spite of the bitter cold, the young officer was looking both excited and eager at the nearness of action and his tone was almost affable. 'How have you enjoyed your week in Montoise, Miles?'

Harry had been very much on his guard. 'It's been a change from Etaples, sir.'

Chadwick laughed. 'Quite a change. Well, why not? The colonel's not a bad old stick and he doesn't see any point in pushing men too hard when they're on rest. But now it's down to business. How do you feel about it?'

Harry met his amused eyes. 'I don't know. I haven't been in action yet.'

Chadwick smiled. 'You'll be all right after you've heard the first bullets pass you and you've killed your first Hun. All the old sweats tell you that.'

'Do they, sir?'

Chadwick smiled again. 'I think you're in for a surprise when you get behind that Vickers gun, Miles. You're going to find it a lot more satisfying than shooting at targets on the range. All right, let's get back to work. We want to be settled in by tonight.'

Throughout the afternoon the long column of men and carts moved towards the Front, resting for ten minutes in every hour. By 16.00 hours the debris and destruction of war was growing around them. Stumps of trees stood in shell-pocked fields. Deserted villages began to appear, with jagged ruins and spires pointing up accusingly at the leaden sky. Shattered and over-turned carts littered the fields with putrescent mules still lying in their traces. Mixed with the smell of death came the acrid odour of high explosive. As a grey mist began to close in, deadening the sullen rumble ahead, it seemed to men that life had fled the land until Harry noticed a few splashes of colour on a bank alongside the road. He nudged Gareth's arm. 'Crocuses,' he told him. 'Spring's not far away.'

Gareth, whose bird-like face looked pinched beneath his tin helmet, was in no mood for comfort. He made a gesture of disgust at the desolate fields and thickening mist. 'Spring? What chance has spring got in this God-forsaken country?'

The road on which they were marching began to burst open like rotten skin as they neared the lines, exposing naked stretches of mud with ruts a foot deep. When the struggling mules could cope no longer, the order was given for the carts to be unloaded and the men to carry the supplies and equipment themselves.

In no time men were staggering under their burdens. Apart from their rifles, ammunition, packs, bayonets, gasmasks, waterbottles and entrenching tools, they were now expected to carry their share of Mills bombs, Hales grenades, smoke bombs, SOS rockets, Very ammu-nition, and a dozen other sundry items. Bowed beneath the weight, they began moving forward again. There was none of the cheerful marching into battle so lovingly described by the journalists in Britain. With backs aching, with sharp pieces of equipment jabbing into tender parts of bodies, men panted, cursed, and began wondering what madness had made them rush into the Army Recruitment Centres.

There was little activity ahead. The cold and mist seemed to have muted the guns and the only sights and sounds came from magnesium star shells and the occasional stutter of a nervous machine gun. Nevertheless the mist was worrying the MPs who were leading the Battalion to its sector of the line. Mist and gas were indistinguishable in the darkness and what air movement there was came from the east. Word went down the column for all personnel to have their gasmasks at the ready, an order greeted with dismay by the weary, panting men.

The path they were taking began to dip between two banks of clay: they were entering a communication trench. Pools were everywhere and booted feet sloshed through them or sank into glutinous mud. Winding like a snake, the path ran into huge spurs of sandbags every hundred yards or so that had to be painfully circumnavigated. Here and there, bridged by slippery planks, small streams ran across it. Occasional trenches, whose purpose was a mystery, ran both left or right but the column was led on until it came to a large junction of trenches where a muddied board read Piccadilly Circus. Speaking in low tones now, the MPs led the way down a trench nicknamed The Haymarket.

Soldiers became visible now, muddy figures sitting in igloo-like caves on either side of the trench. A few were still huddled in wet blankets but most were sipping tea and having breakfast. In the trenches normal life style was reversed. Men slept in the daylight hours and kept watch during the perilous nights.

Orders for total silence were now imposed. If the enemy knew a troop exchange was being made, he might well plan an attack before the new men were bloodied. Struggling, often unsuccessfully to keep their metal loads from clanking, the Battalion crept into the firing trench itself.

It was perhaps more spacious than most men had

227

expected, with tiny rooms, supported by timbers and planks, cut into the clay walls. It was lined with infantrymen but no one was sleeping here. With six days of withdrawal from the front line imminent, men urged the weary replacements to hurry into their positions with exhortations or with impatient curses.

Within an hour the transfer was made and with the same stealth of movement the replaced Battalion filed out. As always however the increased number of star shells rising from across No Man's Land made it obvious the enemy's listening posts had picked up the unusual movements and were investigating them. With the enemy reaction uncertain and the new Battalion fresh to combat, veteran observers from the replaced regiment remained behind to give advice if required.

During this time the machine gun section was being led to its posts. To help them carry the Vickers, its ammunition belts and boxes and its heavy tripod, Harry and Gareth were helped by a cheery young countryman, Jack White, and Freeman, two other members of the team. As they crept along the trench they kept encountering a sweet, sickening odour mixed with the stench of high explosives, cordite, and wet uniforms. With Sergeant Wentworth leading them, they eventually found themselves crawling through a low opening which widened out into a semi-circular gun-post slightly ahead of the main firing trench. The sickening smell was stronger here and made men glance at one another questioningly.

The gun-post's roof and sides were lined with steel plates which in turn were reinforced by sandbags, an indication of the extra venom enemy artillery felt for machine gun posts. There were loopholes for firing on both the left and right hand sides of the recess but none at the front. A Vickers gun rested on its mounting in the centre of the post. Two highly-impatient gunners, forbidden to withdraw their protective cover until their replacements arrived, glowered at the men who crawled in alongside them.

'What the 'ell's been keeping you.' The diffused light of a star shell, seeping through the embrasures, showed the speaker to be a stocky lance corporal with a flattened nose and an unlit cigarette stub in his mouth.

Wentworth frowned. 'We've had to find the bloody place first and no one seemed keen to show us.'

The corporal's eyes moved to Harry and his team who were struggling to drag their Vickers into the gun-post. 'You're a new lot, aren't yer?'

'Yes. Sixteenth Battalion, East Yorks. Why?'

The man grinned at his loader, a skinny youth with a muddy face and lank hair, and spat out his wet cigarette. 'You hear that, Woody. Thank Christ we're movin' out of here.'

Wentworth decided enough was enough. 'All right, Corporal. Cut out the funny stuff and give us some information. To begin with, what's the stink in here? Don't you people use the latrines?'

The corporal saw a chance of immediate revenge. 'That's not shit, Sarge.' Grinning at his loader, he leaned down and prised up a duckboard. As another star shell burst, a muddied bone could be seen in the eerie light. The corporal glanced up at Wentworth. 'They're everywhere, mate. Some still with flesh on 'em. The Jerries must've buried their dead here. We're dug in right across their bloomin' cemetery.'

Wentworth hastily replaced the duckboard. 'Your section leader said you'd a number of registered targets to fire at. I want to see them on the map.'

While Wentworth was being shown the co-ordinates, Harry and Gareth assembled their Vickers gun. As he nipped a finger, Gareth swore and motioned at the other gun still on its mounting. 'Why the hell had we to lug this bloody thing with us when there's one here already?'

Wentworth glanced back sharply. 'Shut your gob, Evans, or you'll bring their artillery on us. You brought it here because guns need servicing and this one's been in action for two weeks. Got it now?'

Changing the subject, Gareth glanced at the corporal's loader. 'What was that bloody great explosion we heard a couple of nights back?'

The sallow-faced youngster grinned. 'We think it was Jerry blowing his own arse off.' When the newcomers stared at him, he went on: 'Three or four miles along the line there's a bit of a salient and Jerry might've wanted to straighten it out. The boys think he was diggin' a sap and it blew up by accident.'

Gareth's eyes were huge in the fitful eerie light. 'Are you saying they dig under here?'

The loader winked at his gunner. 'All the time, mate. Jerry could have a sap under here now. If you hear picks and shovels and they suddenly stop, run like hell.'

Wentworth cursed. 'Stop talking bullshit.' He turned to his two men. 'Let's get these guns changed so these bloody Jeremiahs can piss off.'

Grinning somewhat sheepishly the corporal, aided by his loader, removed the Vickers gun and began expertly dismantling it while Harry and Gareth replaced it with their own. Before the corporal left the post, he glanced back maliciously. 'You know Jerry hates machine guns worse than the devil hates holy water, don't you? So don't forget to drop those shutters over the loopholes when he starts shelling you. And mind he doesn't take you prisoner. There's some nasty rumours about what he does to machine gunners before he shoots 'em.'

'Shoots them?' Gareth repeated.

230

'That's right, mate. We do the same to his. Everyone hates machine gunners.'

Wentworth moved towards him. 'You finished, Corporal?'

The man grinned. 'Yep. I'm away now, Sarge.'

Harry spoke for the first time as the man turned away. 'Do you know what part of the line we're in?'

The gunner shrugged. 'I haven't a clue, mate. Trenches all look alike to me. The district's called the Somme, that's all I know.' With six days of rest awaiting him, the corporal relented. 'I'll tell you this, mate. You're lucky. It's the quietest place I've been in yet. So mind you buggers don't stir things up and spoil it for us when we come back.'

Chapter 28

The sirens sounded when Mary was writing a letter to Harry, a rising banshee wail that made her heart contract and then begin hammering. Jumping from her chair, she ran to the front door and threw it open. The eerie sound was immediately louder and seemed to contain in its wail a hundred apocalyptic warnings.

The street was full of shocked noises. There were running footsteps, the hoarse shouts of men, the shrill cries of women. Although it was not the city's first Zeppelin alarm, public fear of the giant airships remained as acute as ever.

Mary had only one thought at that moment: the safety of Elizabeth. Slamming the door, she stood with her back to it for a moment as if to shut out the threat. Fighting back panic, she tried to remember the advice given in a magazine the previous week. If no stronger shelter existed, the cupboard beneath the staircase was usually the safest place. Wasting no more time, she ran up to the child's room.

A whistle was now sounding in the street below and a man's shout came through the wail of the siren. 'This is the police! Put out all your lights and stand clear of the windows. Put out all your lights immediately . . .'

Remembering the gas light in her sitting room, she flew downstairs and turned it off. Returning to the dark bedroom, she found Elizabeth still asleep. Picking her up gently and wrapping a blanket around her, she carried her downstairs and laid her gently on the settee. Opening the cupboard door, she dragged out two old suitcases and laid down cushions in their place. Then she lifted up the child and laid her gently on them.

Elizabeth awakened for a moment and murmured a word or two but her breathing quietened again when Mary soothed her and covered her with another blanket.

The sirens had ceased by this time, leaving a tense silence behind them. Approaching the front door, Mary peered out. Here and there lights momentarily glimmered but in the main the street was dark. Above, like a luminous sword, a single searchlight was quartering the sky. Clouds lit up and betrayed their secrets before fading into darkness again. In the distance the girl could hear the alarmed clang of street trams as they hurried to their sheds. From the docks a ship siren gave a hoot of warning. The entire city was girding itself up for attack.

Closing the door, she searched for a candle. Finding one in a kitchen drawer, she made certain all the curtains were closed before lighting it. She then returned to the staircase cupboard.

Elizabeth appeared comfortable and was sleeping soundly. Leaving the cupboard door open, Mary carried the candle to an armchair and sat down. She found she was trembling and her heart was beating abnormally fast. She wondered what would be heard first, the drone of the Zeppelins or the explosion of their bombs.

As the tense minutes passed an almost obsessional desire to be doing something came over her. She was about to try to finish her letter to Harry in spite of the candlelight when she heard hurried footsteps on the pavement outside, followed by the urgent ringing of her doorbell. As she gave a start, a familiar voice made her run to the door. 'Mary, lass! Let me in!'

She found a breathless William standing on the doorstep and pulled him inside. 'Dad! What on earth are you doing here?'

William was breathing heavily and his usually florid face was pale. 'I had to come, lass,' he panted. 'Your mother and I were worried about you.'

Concern for him made her voice sharp. 'That's ridiculous. You shouldn't be out in the streets with a raid on. Look at the state you're in. I'll get you a drink. I think we still have some whisky left.'

He caught her arm. 'No. Let's get back home before it starts.'

'I can't take Elizabeth outside,' she protested. 'The Zeppelins could be here any moment.'

William was looking distressed as well as anxious. 'Love, we must go. I can't leave your mum on her own.'

Her face set when she realised the trap she was in. 'Did she send you over?'

He avoided the direct answer. 'We were both worried about you, lass. We'd never forgive ourselves if something happened and you were on your own.'

Angry although she was, she knew she was left with no choice and hurried to find Elizabeth's pushchair. A few minutes later the three of them were hurrying up the darkened street. The disturbance and the cold air awakened Elizabeth and she began to cry.

The main road was almost deserted when they reached it and their footsteps sounded hollow on the pavements. Above, a second searchlight had joined the first and they were criss-crossing as if in combat. Halfway to No. 57 a policeman on a bicycle drew up and asked what they were doing outdoors with a child during an air-raid warning. With William struggling for breath, it was Mary who had to do the explaining.

When the policeman shook his head and rode off, Mary turned to William who was leaning against a lamp-post with one hand pressed to his chest. 'Have you got that pain again?'

He pushed his heavy body away from the lamp-post without answering her. 'Keep going, lass,' he panted. 'We're nearly there.'

Concern made her snap at him again. 'It's the daftest thing I've ever known, Dad. Don't ever do it again.'

Ethel, looking pale and frightened, met them at the front door. 'Oh, thank God you're here before it starts.'

Feeling remorse for her attack on William, Mary saw no reason to spare her mother. 'It was wrong of you to send Dad out like this, Mother. It's not just bad for him: it could have been dangerous for Elizabeth too.'

For once Ethel's indignation sounded justified. 'Why do you blame me? Your dad was just as worried about you. What a strange girl you are. Most daughters would be glad to know their parents cared about them.'

Before Mary could answer, a far-off crackle of gunfire brought Ethel's hand to her throat. 'They're coming! Oh, my God! They're coming!'

Her fear, genuine and undisguised, killed Mary's resentment. She was further disarmed by the way Ethel snatched the crying Elizabeth from the pushchair and tried to screen the child with her own body. She took the trembling woman's arm. 'Have you cleared the cupboard under the stairs?'

Ethel nodded jerkily. 'Yes. I've put in stools and blankets. We'd better go straight into it, hadn't we?'

The crackle of gunfire came again. It was followed by an explosion that was felt through the ground rather than heard. Ethel was pale to the lips now. 'That was a

235

bomb. Hurry, William. Spread out some blankets for Elizabeth.'

Although his own face was pale, William obeyed, then gallantly helped the two women and child into the shelter before squeezing in himself. His heavy breathing and the child's cries filled the dark recess.

With Ethel having taken it on herself to soothe Elizabeth, Mary was sitting next to the door and had her ears cocked for sounds outside. As the child's sobs died away, she opened the door a few inches but could hear nothing. 'I think it's over,' she said. 'The gunfire's stopped.'

Ethel's voice had the edginess of fear. 'Don't be silly. The all-clear hasn't sounded yet.'

'Perhaps it was a false alarm. Or perhaps they didn't break through. I'll go and take a look in the garden.'

William caught her arm. 'You can't hear them when their engines are cut off, lass. One could be overhead at this minute. Wait until the all-clear.'

Not wishing to put a further strain on him, she sank back. Five more long minutes passed, then the sirens sounded again and held a long sustained note.

Stiffly the three adults climbed out. Ethel, still looking shaken, turned to Mary. 'What shall we do with Elizabeth? You don't want to take her out in the cold again, do you? Wouldn't it be better if you both slept here tonight? I can lend you a nightdress and your bed's always ready.'

For the child's sake, Mary felt she had little choice. 'Yes, all right. But I want her in the room with me.'

'Of course, dear. Where else would she sleep?'

At that moment the front door bell began ringing excitedly. William, whose colour was beginning to return, gave a grunt and started forward. 'I'll bet that's old Ellis. After a shock like that he'll be wanting someone to talk to.'

236

While William was at the front door chatting to his agitated neighbour, Ethel helped Mary to lift Elizabeth and carry her upstairs. Although the child woke up momentarily, she soon fell asleep in the double bed that Mary was to use later. As the two women crept out, Ethel checked Mary at the door. 'You know that we're going to have more of these raids, don't you? All the newspapers say we're one of Germany's main targets.'

Certain she knew what was coming, Mary's voice was hostile. 'What if we are?'

'Dear, you can't allow your father to run round to your house every time. He's a sick man. It could do him harm.'

'Then he mustn't come. I'm perfectly all right on my own.'

'You try to tell him that, dear. He was quite frantic about you tonight.'

Mary's face set. 'Mother, I'm not selling my home. How often do I have to tell you that?'

'No one's asking you to sell, dear, if you don't want to. Just come and stay with us until this Zeppelin threat is over. If you won't do it for yourself, then do it for your dad. You saw the state he was in tonight. How often do you think he could do that without killing himself.'

At that moment Mary felt that even her father had betrayed her. 'I'll think about it. No, I'll ask Harry first and see what he says.' When Ethel opened her mouth, Mary walked past her and down the stairs. 'I'm not making a decision tonight, Mother. So please don't mention it again.'

Chapter 29

The call for the Battalion to stand by came at 04.45 hours. Men who were not already on fatigue duty or on periscopes, crawled out of their dug-outs and made for the firesteps. There was little conversation. Few had managed more than a couple of hours sleep since their long march and they were about to face their first dawn in the trenches. Fear of the unknown showed itself in pale, strained faces and nervous movements.

Their apprehension was shared by Harry and Gareth in their icy machine gun post. With a belt of ammunition to fire off into the darkness every hour, with the chance, however remote, that the Germans might launch a night attack to test the metal of the new Battalion, and with the possibility of Wentworth or Chadwick dropping in at any time to check their vigilance, neither had managed to sleep or even doze. In Harry's case there was an additional factor to keep him awake although Gareth's contempt for their orders brought him some comfort. 'They can't think we're killing anybody firing these bursts, can they? All Jerry'll do is keep an eye on his watch, move away when it's time, then give a belly laugh and walk back again. It's like the bloody sniping, a game the Top Brass play to stop both sides crawling out and making friends.'

In spite of their greatcoats, infantrymen shivered as they stood by on the firesteps. The pre-dawn air was cold and a cutting wind was edging along the trenches. It had carried away the mist and as a grey light appeared on the eastern horizon images began to appear before the curious men, the grey mud, the water-filled shell holes, a shattered tree with bare arms outstretched, the rime-covered barbed-wire in front of the enemy trenches. Remembering what they had been told at battle school – that this was the time, when grey merged with grey, that the enemy was most likely to attack – men felt their tight muscles aching with strain.

The slow minutes dragged past. A pink glow appeared in the lightening sky. Here and there, out of sight of officers or NCOs, men surreptitiously lit cigarettes and nervously gulped in smoke.

A thin red crescent appeared behind the enemy lines. As it grew in size it gave the mud a pinkish sheen. Company commanders glanced at their watches and gave the order to stand down. Released from tension, men joked and laughed as they jumped down from firing steps and drank the hot sweet tea brought round to them.

In B Company a man on periscope duty gave a loud laugh of disbelief and shouted at the men below him. Not believing him, men jumped back on the firing steps and two hundred yards away saw a dozen grey-uniformed figures stolidly repairing the barricade of a communication trench. One young soldier climbed on to a sandbag to gain a better view. As his head and shoulders appeared above the trench parapet, there was a distant crack and he tumbled like a broken doll into the trench below. Unable to understand, a friend bent over him and saw half his face was missing. The perilous dawn might have passed without incident but the snipers' day was only beginning.

Further along the line, Harry and Gareth were sipping tea and waiting for their relief crew to arrive. Gareth, eager for his breakfast, was telling Harry if the crew didn't come soon he was going to look for them when the blanket at the back of the post was drawn aside and Chadwick appeared. The young subaltern looked almost agreeable as he motioned the two men to continue drinking their tea. 'Sorry I didn't get the chance to see you chaps last night but the CO kept us all busy. How did you get on?'

'All right, sir,' Harry said.

'I've come to see you about your registered firing times. So far you've kept to the times given you by the previous gunners. I've decided to change that. Have you got the map of the German lay-out opposite you?'

Harry nodded and handed him a muddy map drawn up from aerial photographs. Chadwick studied it, then jabbed a finger at one of the registered targets. 'This road here: it must be one they bring their supply mules along. Tonight I want you to fire a belt at it half an hour before your scheduled time, then twenty minutes after. Reverse the procedure when the target comes round again. That'll keep Jerry on his toes.'

In his dismay Gareth could hardly have been more tactless. 'The chap we took over from last night said this was a quiet section of the line, sir. Won't this stir things up and spoil it for them?'

Until this moment, in his delight at reaching the Front at last, it seemed Chadwick had momentarily forgotten his animosity towards the two men. With Gareth's remark recalling it, his tone changed.

'That spineless crowd's philosophy suits you down to the ground, doesn't it, Evans? Don't provoke the other side and soon we'll have the joining of hands and the revolution you people want. That's not the war my section is going to fight. We're going to harass and kill the enemy wherever and however we can. The other gun-posts are being given the same instructions.'

Harry spoke for the first time. 'Has Colonel Wilson given these orders, sir?'

Chadwick's good-looking face flushed with anger. 'Are you questioning my order, Miles?'

'No, sir. I was just asking where it had come from.'

'That's none of your damned business. Your job is to carry it out to the letter. And you'd both better do that or you'll think a shell has dropped on you!'

Harry and Gareth came back on duty again that evening just as the light was beginning to fade. As he pushed aside the blanket, Jack White, the loader of the team being relieved, grinned at them and pointed at the left-hand embrasure. 'Take a look out there. We've started playing the same games as Jerry.'

The two men peered out. The forward position of the gun-post enabled them to see a party of soldiers repairing the wire and screw pickets in front of the British firing trench. As they stared at one another, White gave his infectious laugh. 'They're working under one of the last regiment's NCOs. The poor bastards looked scared to death when they first climbed out but no one's fired at 'em all afternoon.'

'Yet a sniper killed a man in B Company this morning,' Harry said.

'Yes, that's the crazy thing.' White jerked his head at his gunner, a lanky man named Wood with the inevitable nickname Timber. 'Timber here reckons they must have come to an understanding. You can pick men off when they're under cover but not out in the open.'

'Folks back home would never believe it,' Gareth said as White and his gunner went off for their meal. 'Maybe it's the start of the revolution, boyo. It if keeps up we'll all be singing "Auld Lang's Syne" out there and chasing our officers back into their funk holes.'

Harry drew back from the embrasure. 'One thing we can depend on. It'll all change once we strafe that road tonight.'

Gareth winced. 'That's true. Do we have to fire at the road? No one's going to notice if we lay off a few degrees left or right, are they?'

Harry threw him a cigarette. 'That's the first thing Chadwick will think of. Don't worry. He'll be here in time to check our sighting.'

'But even that doesn't make sense,' Gareth argued. 'If he's so keen to kill Jerries, why didn't he order us to fire on that work party of theirs?'

'That's why I asked where his orders came from. My guess is he doesn't want the last regiment's observers to see us break the truce. Which they're not so likely to do at night unless they keep a time check on us. In other words I don't think it's a general Battalion order to stir things up.'

Gareth scowled. 'We would get an eager beaver in charge, wouldn't we?' Striking a match, he leaned forward to offer it to Harry. At the same moment there was the eerie scream of a bullet ricochetting from one of the steel plates. Frozen for a moment, Gareth gaped at Harry. 'Christ, that came through the loophole, didn't it?'

Pushing him back, Harry dropped the steel shutter into place. 'It's the sniper. He's got our range.'

The horrified Gareth was fingering a tear in one of the sandbags. 'That's where it ended up.' The nearness of his escape brought an abrupt change in the Welshman's

242

philosophy. 'And we're worrying about killing Germans? The bastards don't seem to feel that way about us.'

'Our snipers do the same to them,' Harry pointed out.

At that moment the equities of retribution were far from the Welshman's mind. 'It's a bloody queer truce when a man can't strike a match without having his head blown off.'

Harry had to laugh at his indignation. 'It's still far quieter here than we expected.'

His escape was making Gareth talkative. 'Things must be bloody awful in some parts though. Timber Woods was telling me this morning about an old sweat he met in an *estaminet* in Montoise. He'd been up in Ypres earlier in the year and said things were so bad there men were firing bullets into their feet. When the MOs got wise to it, they tried something else. Earlier on, a couple of lads in the Company had caught syphilis and it had kept 'em out of action for two months. When the story got around, men started to look for the girls so they could get a dose too.'

'Had this old sweat done it?' Harry asked.

Gareth nodded. 'He'd done a stretch of jankers as punishment too but he seemed to think it was worth it. He reckoned some enterprising Mesdames keep these girls in special rooms for men who'd had a bellyful of fighting. Of course if the MPs catch 'em, the brothels are shut down but they soon spring up somewhere else.'

'Let's hope there weren't any in that brothel you visited at Montoise,' Harry said.

Gareth gave a shudder. 'Amen to that! From what I've heard about the treatment, it's enough to put a man off sex for the rest of his life.'

*   *   *

There was a sliver of moon that night when Chadwick ducked into the gun-post. 'Well, Miles. Are you ready?'

Mouth dry, Harry nodded. As he had expected the subaltern checked the Vicker's horizontal and vertical settings before glancing at his watch. 'Twenty-five minutes before they expect us. Off you go.'

Glancing at Gareth, who fed one end of a belt of ammunition into the breech, Harry settled down behind the gun. In his mind's eye he could see men and mules, weary after their long journey, queuing up at the German supply lines. As he hesitated, Chadwick's voice turned impatient. 'What are you waiting for, man? Fire.'

To Harry the Vickers seemed to open up of its own volition. Clattering deafeningly, jerking the ammunition belt through its breech, it hosed a stream of bullets over the German front lines and into the darkness beyond. Lying there, as if on a mental screen, Harry could see men and mules collapsing in a welter of flesh and blood. It seemed minutes to him before the belt ran out and the Vickers went silent.

In the confines of the gun-post the stink of cordite made all three men cough. When their ears recovered from the din, Chadwick gave a laugh. 'Well done, Miles. With any luck at all you'll have hit something back there. If it's done the damage I hope, you're already a good investment to the Army.'

When Harry did not reply, the young officer turned to the blanket that sealed off the gun-post. As he lifted it, he glanced back. 'At least it'll let the Jerries know we mean business. I'll see you both again in an hour.'

When the blanket fell back into place, Gareth turned to Harry. Seeing his expression, the Welshman made a clumsy effort to comfort. 'I'll bet we didn't hit a bloody thing, boyo. It's a hit and miss business, this night firing.'

Outside the German reaction seemed to belie his

words. Star shells were rising in clusters from their trenches, turning the night into day, and an enemy machine gun was already in action. As Harry was about to reply, the blanket was torn aside and a furious voice made both men spin round. 'What the hell do you two think you're doing? Who gave you permission to fire at this time?'

A major neither man had seen before was glaring at them. In the phosphorescent light his face was disfigured by anger. As he straightened within the post, they saw his faded and muddy uniform belonged to the regiment they had replaced. His voice struck at them again. 'Answer me, damn it! Why did you fire that gun just now?'

With his instinct of self-preservation alerted, Gareth was the first to speak. 'We were told to, sir.'

'Told to? By whom, damn it?'

'Our machine gun officer, sir. Second Lieutenant Chadwick.'

The major swung round on Harry. 'Is this true?'

Harry could see no way of avoiding the question. 'Yes, sir.'

The major cursed. 'Did he give a reason?'

As Harry hesitated, Gareth took over again. 'Yes, sir. He thought we'd be more likely to kill Germans if the firing time was changed.'

The man winced, then his jaw set in anger again. 'The bloody young fool! Where is he?'

'I don't know, sir, unless he's in the subalterns' dugout.'

The major snatched aside the curtain, then glanced back. 'You'll keep strictly to your firing times from now on no matter what other orders are given. Do you understand that?' As both men nodded, he went on: 'What are your names?'

'Private Miles and Private Evans, sir.'

'I may need you both as witnesses. So stay close by when you're relieved.'

The curtain swung back into place. Gareth gave a long whistle. 'It gets crazier by the minute. What are we in? A peace zone?'

Harry, who had been watching the major's expression, shook his head. 'I don't believe he'd behave that way just because we broke an unofficial truce. There's something we haven't been told.'

Chapter 30

Lieutenant-Colonel Wilson, a greatcoat hastily buttoned over his pyjamas, stared irritably at the flushed major. 'I'm not following you, man. What's all the fuss about?'

The major glanced round the spacious dug-out, his eyes moving from the bed with its thrown-back sheets and blankets to a telephone resting on an ammunition box. 'May I phone Brigade Headquarters, sir? Brigadier Ashton will explain.'

Wilson's tone modified in spite of himself. 'You're going to wake up the brigadier at this time of the night?'

'I must, sir. It's very important.'

Frowning, Wilson nodded at a young captain who was watching them curiously from a seat behind a trestle table. 'All right, Morrison. Get Brigade on and tell them Major Moore wants to speak to Brigadier Ashton.'

The young officer wound away at the telephone. Thirty seconds later he held out the receiver to the major. 'They're calling the brigadier now, sir.'

In the silence that fell, Wilson lit a cigarette. He was a tall thin man in his middle fifties, considerate to his men at most times but inclined to irritability in moments of stress. He had served in the Boer War like so many of his

247

contemporaries and been pensioned off at its conclusion. With the War Office, thinking like everybody else that the war would last a year at the most, he had not been called up until 1915 and so had missed the more mobile battles of 1914. This was a source of regret to him because he felt his African experience would have been far more suited to them than this damned static trench warfare which already seemed to operate under an entirely different set of rules. Was zeal in his young officers a fault, damn it! Weren't they supposed to kill Germans?

To his annoyance the major was now talking into the telephone in tones too low to be overheard. As Wilson inhaled smoke, the man straightened and held out the receiver. 'The brigadier would like to speak to you, sir.'

Instinctively stubbing out his cigarette, Wilson moved forward. 'Hello, sir. Wilson here.'

The irritability in the voice that sprang at him gave immediate warning that the brigadier was angry for more reasons than a disturbed night's sleep. 'What's the matter with you, Wilson? Can't you keep control of your junior officers?'

Wilson stiffened. 'I'm sorry, sir. I don't think I caught that.'

'Your officers, damn it. Major Moore tells me some damned fool ordered your heavy machine gunners to open fire out of season. Didn't I tell you I wanted your section of the line keeping quiet?'

'Yes, sir. But . . .'

'Don't "but" me, Wilson. It's damned important. Too important to discuss over the telephone. Major Moore, who's on my staff, will explain everything but it must go no further than you at the moment. Is that clear?'

Wilson understood now why Moore had remained behind when the main force had gone on rest. 'Yes, sir. But . . .'

248

'Do exactly as Major Moore tells you, Wilson. And if Jerry retaliates – and I'm surprised he hasn't already – you're to offer the minimum provocation necessary to hold your position. Do you understand?'

Wilson gave up. 'Yes, sir. I understand.' Returning the receiver to its hook, he turned to the waiting major. 'The brigadier tells me you'll explain everything. Have a cigarette and sit down if you want to, but for Christ's sake get on with it.'

Taking him at his word, Moore sank down on an ammunition box. 'It's really to do with the French, sir.'

'The French?'

'Yes. As you know Jerry's throwing everything he's got at them at Verdun. Foch is asking us to help out by drawing off his reserves, so Haig has decided on a major push in this sector.'

Wilson started. 'This sector?'

Moore widened his arms. 'In fact the entire Somme. It's going to be mostly a British affair and it's going to be big. They're already building up supplies and ammunition in the rear and soon they'll be bringing them up. Obviously we want to keep Jerry ignorant as long as possible. That's why it's been kept a secret from Front line troops in case any are captured.'

Wilson frowned. 'But aren't we likely to make him suspicious if we keep this sector of the Front too friendly?'

'Not really. It was quiet before this push was planned. It's manned by Saxons and they've always had a kind of affinity with British troops. What we're trying to avoid is antagonising them or having them stiffened up with Prussian regiments – Uhlans and soldiers of that kind.'

Wilson was beginning to understand. 'But surely an isolated incident like tonight isn't likely to change things?'

Moore shrugged. 'It could, sir. They'll already know we've brought in a new Battalion. That performance tonight might make them think it's brought a new policy with it. If they get that impression, there's no knowing what could happen.'

Wilson was in need of reassurance now. 'There's been no retaliation yet, has there?'

'No, sir. If there's none in the next twenty-four hours, we might have got away with it. But if there is, it could mean all kinds of trouble.'

The words had barely left Moore's mouth before there was an explosion that brought a shower of mud from the ceiling. A second one made the flame of the paraffin lamp dip crazily. Wilson rushed across to his bed and began dragging on his slacks, at the same time yelling somewhat unnecessarily at his startled aide. 'It's started, Morrison! Sound the general alarm!'

To Harry and Gareth in the forward gun-post, the German retaliation sounded as if the hounds of hell had broken loose and were baying all around them. Star shells were soaring up in clusters, shrapnel bursting overhead, and high explosive-shells hurling up great geysers of mud all along the phosphorescent Front. The earth kicked and heaved under their cringing bodies as if it were a creature in torment. The noise was appalling, even more terrifying than the steel splinters that sliced through the outer sandbags and screeched against the steel plates.

To make himself heard, Gareth had to put his mouth to Harry's ear. 'Close the shutters, for Christ's sake!'

The flashes of the bursting shells made their pale faces appear and disappear like a slow motion film. Harry grabbed Gareth's arm as the Welshman tried to close the shutters himself. 'No. Their infantry might come next.'

Gareth sank to the floor. The massive onslaught seemed to be unnerving him: he crouched with his helmeted head between his knees and his hands pressed against his ears. Half-stunned himself, Harry turned back to the embrasures. The great flashes and geysers of earth made it impossible to judge the extent of the bombardment. To Harry it seemed that the entire world was exploding.

His feelings were shared by the rest of the Battalion. Huddled in dug-outs, men were bewildered by the fury of the shelling. Their terrors were heightened by the frantic yells of NCOs reminding them that a gas attack could accompany the high-explosive horrors. In their worst nightmares the unbloodied young men of the 16th had never imagined an artillery barrage as frightening an experience as this.

In fact the shelling lasted only fifteen minutes. At first men held their breath, unable to believe it was over. Then, far-off in their stunned ears, they heard the yell of orders again. 'All men stand-by on the firesteps. Stand-by!' Fumbling for their rifles men crawled from their shelters into the smoke-filled, shell-damaged trenches. There, propped up on trembling legs, they stared out into the smoking desolation from which an infantry attack might come.

In the battered gun-post Harry was shaking his loader. 'Gareth, come on! They might attack at any time.'

For a long moment Gareth remained huddled on the floor. When he raised his head, Harry saw something dark trickling from one corner of his mouth. He bent forward in alarm. 'Are you hit?'

Gareth turned his head. In the light of a star shell, Harry saw his face was the colour of putty but the trickle from his mouth was only saliva. Relieved, he shook him again. 'Come on, Gareth. The shelling's stopped but we've got to be ready.'

A breeze, drifting in acrid smoke from the shell holes, started both men coughing. As Harry swung the Vickers round to cover the trenches, Gareth moved beside him, his voice hoarse and bewildered. 'That noise, boyo! It was like hell with the lid off.'

With the enemy trenches hidden by a luminous blanket of smoke, Harry dared not avert his eyes. 'We'll get used to it. Everyone seems to, sooner or later.'

The Welshman fumbled blindly into an ammunition box alongside him. 'That noise! My God. I didn't think it was going to be like this. Nobody told us, did they? Nobody warned us.'

Wilson's telephone rang just as a heavy shell brought down a shower of planks at the back of the dug-out. Coughing from the dust, he crawled to the phone and dragged the receiver down to the level of his mouth. 'Yes. Who's that?'

'Wilson! This is Ashton. What the hell's happening in your sector?'

Wilson thought it was obvious. 'We're being shelled, sir. Heavily.'

A ripe oath sounded through the din outside. 'That's buggered it. Now they'll be watching every move we make. Why the hell didn't you keep a tighter lid on your men, Wilson?'

Wilson felt a burn of resentment. 'We've only been in the line twenty-four hours, sir. I've hardly had time to unpack my kit.'

'But I told you to keep things quiet, didn't I? So what

the hell were your officers doing trying to win the war on their own?'

'It was only one officer, sir. And all he did was change the firing time of two machine guns.'

'All he did? He's alerted every Jerry right along the Somme. Have you spoken to him yet?'

It was perhaps fortunate for Wilson's future relationship with Brigade Headquarters that the line was cut at that moment. As a momentary lull came in the bombardment, Wilson lifted his dust-soiled face and glared at his equally shaken aide. 'As soon as this shindig's over, I want to see those two gunners.' His eyes moved to the major who to his secret annoyance was lying beside a couple of sandbags coolly smoking a cigarette. 'After that I want Lieutenant Chadwick brought to me.'

With their spell of duty over, Harry and Gareth were in their dug-out drinking tea when Chadwick appeared in the entrance. 'Private Miles. I want a word with you.'

Glancing at Gareth, Harry set his mug on the ground and ducked into the trench outside. Chadwick led him a few paces away from the dug-out before halting. 'Well, are you pleased with yourselves?'

Although Harry had been expecting the confrontation, he could feel his heart beating faster. 'I don't know what you mean by that, sir. We were ordered by the CO to explain why we changed the time of our firing. I don't see what else we could do but tell the truth.'

Chadwick's voice was richly sarcastic. 'And you hated doing that, didn't you?'

'We didn't enjoy it, sir. But what choice had we?'

'You had half a dozen choices, like saying you had misunderstood your orders or misread the firing times.

The most you'd have got would have been a telling off or a docking of pay.'

'But we'd already told the major you'd given us new instructions. How could we suddenly change our story?'

Chadwick's eyes, full of dislike, moved over Harry's face. 'I've often wondered why I've never liked you, Miles. Perhaps it's because every religious person I've known has been a hypocrite. All piety and forgive-thine-enemy on the surface and all tale-telling and malice underneath. Wouldn't you agree with that, Miles?'

Harry glanced round, saw they were not being over-heard, and took a deep breath. 'You know, sir, I don't give a damn that you don't like me. Perhaps that's because I don't like you either. The only change in you since you were a boy is you've put more polish on yourself. You've still got no more respect for people than you have for those birds and foxes you kill. My father had a name for your kind. He called you privi-leged bullies.'

For a moment the young officer's face tightened. Then he laughed. 'You're as big a revolutionary as your friend, aren't you? Only you keep quiet about it.'

Harry shook his head. 'Evans isn't a revolutionary. At least not in the way you mean. He still cares enough about his country to volunteer to fight for it.'

'The Irish volunteer too, Miles. And why? To get rifles for their cause. They're all traitors at heart and I like to believe they'll all get their deserts before the war's over.'

Harry did not miss the hidden threat. 'Evans isn't like that. He talks a lot but he's no traitor. I know him better than anyone.' Seeing Chadwick's expression, he went on: 'And he didn't give you away to the CO. I did all the talking.'

Chadwick smiled mockingly. 'Noble to the last. I

shouldn't worry, Miles. Time will put him to the test. Just as it will you. You know, I'm glad we've had this talk. I feel it's cleared up a lot of things between us.'

Harry could not hold back the bitter comment. 'Things have always been very clear to me, sir. Ever since you arranged to have us in your section.'

Chadwick lifted an eyebrow. 'They have? Good. Then we all know how we stand. Now you'd better get back to your tea or it'll be cold. I'll see you both tonight.'

To the relief of the shaken Battalion, there was no further retaliation that day. However, increased air activity over the sector, more persistent sniper fire, and a noticeable absence of enemy workmen made it clear that the Saxons both disapproved of and distrusted the replacements they now faced.

Although the English Battalion, acting under strict orders, made no more aggressive gestures in the next twenty-four hours, evidence of the Germans' misgivings came that night when Harry and Gareth were back on duty in their gun-post. Towards 01.00 hours Chadwick, heavily clothed against the cold, entered their gun-post. His eager manner and his low voice put both men immediately on the alert.

'Our listening posts have picked up a party of Jerries out in No Man's Land. They're either out there repairing wire or they're a raiding party trying to grab a prisoner or two to find out our intentions. We've all to stand by.'

Both men felt their pulses quicken. 'Which way are they?' Harry asked.

'A hundred yards or so to your left. Your post might even be their target. So keep your gun ready and your eyes open.'

All three men peered through the left-hand embrasure. It was a clear frosty night with an icy wind blowing from the east. A mile away the skyline was phosphorescent with star shells and an occasional red explosion but the ground in front of their sector was shadowy and ominously quiet. Gareth's hushed voice betrayed his apprehension. 'Why don't we light things up, sir?'

Chadwick's reply was full of contempt for the Battalion's orders. 'If they're only making repairs we have to leave them alone. We only illuminate them and open fire if they try to raid us.'

A long minute passed in which the only sounds were occasional distant explosions and the creak and rasp of barbed-wire shifting in the wind. Then the gun-post curtain was drawn back and a corporal muttered something urgently to Chadwick. The young officer spun round. 'They're moving this way. So it's probably a raiding party. Get ready!'

Heart hammering, Harry sank down behind the Vickers. In the darkness he could feel rather than see Gareth's apprehension as the Welshman crouched alongside him. Here and there new sections of barbed-wire could be seen in the starlight but in the shell-torn wasteland beyond the barricades the shadows were impenetrable. Through the sullen unrest further along the Front and the disturbances caused by the wind, Harry tried to isolate man-made sounds, knowing that a couple of hundred men poised on the firesteps were also straining their ears and holding their breath.

A faint metallic click was the warning, the sound of a wirecutter at work. Instantly a dozen star shells soared upwards and burst in the night sky. For a moment their brilliance dazzled Harry. Then he saw a party of grey-clad figures with blackened faces flattening themselves in the mud behind the barricades. The denseness of the wire made them difficult targets for the British infantry

256

but from the forward gun-post they were totally exposed.

Lying alongside Harry, Chadwick sounded exultant. 'It is a raiding party. You can open fire, Miles.'

Harry's throat felt parched and constricted. 'They'll retreat now they're spotted, sir.'

'Who the hell wants them to retreat? This time we've got permission to shoot. Open fire, man!'

Wiping his sweating eyes, Harry fired a three second burst. As small geysers of mud spurted to the left of the men, he was hoping they would run back to find shelter in shell holes but instead, paralysed by their exposure, they only shrank deeper into the false cover beneath the wire. As the hammering of the Vickers ceased, Chadwick cursed and turned to Harry. 'Damn you, Miles, shoot to kill! Shoot or I'll see you get a court martial!'

Across in the enemy trenches rifles and machine guns had opened up as the Germans tried to give the trapped men covering fire. For Harry time seemed to slow down as his sights shifted and settled on the doomed Germans. Even the hammering of the Vickers sounded slow and deliberate as its heavy bullets tore into the screaming men. Three jerked, twitched and appeared to die immediately. Five others leapt up and tried to reach a shell hole, only to be cut down by infantry fire. The last man tried to find cover by crawling beneath the barbed-wire barricade. Seeing him snagged there and trying to raise his arms in surrender, Harry ceased firing, only for Chadwick to curse and push him away from the machine gun. Sighting it, Chadwick fired a long and deliberate burst. In the brilliant, merciless light Harry saw the man's head shatter like an eggshell and almost disappear from his shoulders. The rest of his body slumped and lay across the lower strands of wire like a broken puppet.

For a moment Chadwick lay staring at his handiwork.

Then, with a laugh, he turned, his handsome face animated by an expression that the shocked Harry could not analyse. 'Well done, Miles. You're bloodied now. After this it'll get easier and easier.' Rising, he moved to the blanket and turned. 'I'm going off to make my report, so keep your eyes open. Jerry sounds angry enough to make a full scale attack.'

Smiling at Harry, he ducked beneath the blanket and disappeared. A retching sound made Harry turn. At the opposite side of the gun-post Gareth was bringing his stomach up.

Chapter 31

A relief crew came on at 04.00 hours that morning but there was no sleep for Harry. Try as he did, every time he closed his eyes he saw the shattered bodies of the men he had killed and the hideous figure hanging on the wire. The low moans from Gareth and his occasional twitching suggested he was having similar nightmares but at least he was asleep. Harry could come no nearer to sleep than moments of light-headiness when every sense became vulnerable. When the brutal vision came – and it came every time his defences were lowered – icy sweat broke out from every pore in his body.

Finding it less painful to stay wide awake, he lay watching the grey light of dawn seep into the dug-out which he and Gareth were sharing with two other men of their section. A small claustrophobic cave dug into the side of the trench, it was precariously supported by planks and timbers. With seepage from the winter rain covering the duckboards, the previous inhabitants had dragged in empty ammunition boxes and laid planks across them. The insecure footing made it almost impossible to undress and the half-frozen water below added to the bitter cold. All four men were lying fully clothed with their blankets wrapped around their greatcoats.

The dug-out stank of wet uniforms, unwashed bodies, cordite fumes, and the all pervading smell of the one-time German graveyard.

Harry lay listening to the sounds of war: the thud of distant explosions, the thin crackle of rifle fire, the squelsh of booted feet as men passed the dug-out entrance. Other sounds came from beneath him, the gnarling of sharp teeth and an occasional splash in the water seepage. The local rats, multiplied into hundreds of thousands by the readily-found food in No Man's Land, were everywhere, stealing men's biscuits and bully beef, even occasionally gnawing at unprotected faces and hands. Obscenely fat and a naked pink in colour, they were universally hated by the troops, some of whom believed they derived their colour from the human flesh they ate.

The sound of a mouth organ caught Harry's attention and the wistful strains of 'Annie Laurie' drifted towards him. Finding relief in the childhood memories it brought back, he strained his ears to listen. But in less than thirty seconds there was a loud shout, a curse, and the music ceased.

The vision of the German raid returned to him. He tried to suppress its more grisly details by remembering Chadwick's triumph after he had killed the German trying to surrender. There had been something almost orgiastic in his expression. There had also been shouts of triumph from the men on the firesteps after they had shot and killed the five fleeing Germans. Ordinary young men like himself who prior to today would have felt sick at drowning a litter of kittens. Had relief from danger caused their excitement and triumph? Or was there an element in man that found a dark and unexpected pleasure in killing his own kind?

Telling himself that his thoughts were feverish, Harry

tried to find sanity in the memory of Mary and Elizabeth. To his horror, every time he recalled the familiar sitting room at home and was waiting for Mary and the child to enter, the men he had killed took their place. Taught to believe that to kill a fellow human being was the ultimate crime and seeing no end to his part in it, it was easy for the young man to believe he was already in hell and every passing day would drive him deeper into its fires.

In spite of the slaughter of the German raiding party, there was no response this time from the enemy artillery, making the relieved men of the 16th wonder if raiding parties, like snipers, came outside the rules of the unspoken truce. Ironically, the first ascerbic response came from British Brigade Headquarters. 'Wilson? I'm told Jerry tried to raid you. And that he's also switched his own registered firing times. Is that right?'

Wilson who had just lost half a dozen mules and four men when bringing up supplies and ammunition, was glad the telephone hid his expression. 'Yes, sir. But he's made no other move since the raid.'

'I'm glad to hear it. But it's no thanks to that damned young subaltern of yours. Have you punished him yet?'

'I've reprimanded him, yes.'

'Is that all?'

'He's a keen young officer, sir. I don't want to kill his enthusiasm.'

Wilson could not decide whether the grunt at the other end of the line signified agreement or disapproval. 'Anyway, you know what's happening to all the Vickers teams, don't you?'

'No, sir. What?'

'They're all being brigaded to a special corps, the Machine Gun Corps. They'll be distributed from there

261

as they're needed. So you'll be losing this chap in any case.'

Wilson frowned. 'That's a pity, sir. I feel an aggressive officer like that could be an asset once he's learned to obey orders.'

'You mean you'd like to keep him?'

Wilson hesitated. 'Yes. But how can I when he's a trained machine gun officer?'

'There is a way and one that ought to suit his hot blood when we go on the offensive.'

'What way is that, sir?' After Ashton told him, Wilson's face cleared. 'That sounds a good idea. Of course it'll mean drawing him out of the line for a few weeks.'

'That's all right. We shan't be needing him yet. That's the way to handle hot heads, Wilson. They enjoy the action and the Army gets the benefit. Now let's get down to business. I want you and all Battalion commanders at my headquarters at 11.00 hours sharp tomorrow. We've a lot of talking and planning to do before the big day comes.'

Harry ducked into the subalterns' dug-out and saluted. 'You wanted to see me, sir?'

Alone in the dug-out, Chadwick was seated on an ammunition box smoking a cigarette. A mug of tea and an opened tin of condensed milk stood on a trestle table alongside him. He eyed Harry reflectively for a moment, then smiled. 'How did you sleep, Miles?'

'All right, sir,' Harry lied.

'You did? Good for you. I thought those Jerries you killed might have kept you awake. But it looks as if you might turn into a regular soldier after all.'

When Harry made no reply, Chadwick's tone

changed. 'Just the same, you'll be for the high jump if you ever turn your fire away again. Every dead German is one fewer to kill our own men. I don't suppose you've ever thought of it that way?'

Harry shook his head. 'No, I haven't.'

'You will when your own life's in danger. But that's not the only reason I wanted to see you. In three days' time you and Evans are going back to Montoise with me.'

Harry gave a start. 'Montoise?'

Chadwick nodded as he took a sip of tea. 'I've been given a new job. They've put me in charge of the Lewis gun section and I've decided to take half a dozen of my team with me. We'll be taking a course in Montoise on the Lewis gun and its tactical uses.'

For a moment Harry was puzzled. 'What's the reason for the transfer, sir?'

The sudden hardness of Chadwick's eyes gave him his answer. 'I'd have thought you'd have guessed that, Miles. The reason for your transfer is a little different. I wouldn't want to lose an excellent shot like you, would I?'

Harry saw it all now. 'No, sir. I'm sure you wouldn't.'

The subaltern's smile mocked him. 'When one thinks about it, Miles, you would be wasted in a Vickers team. Much of their time is spent giving the infantry covering fire. Whereas Lewis gunners go over in the first wave so they get plenty of action.'

Harry felt it was hopeless but the effort had to be made. 'Does Evans have to move too? Couldn't I be given another Number One?'

Chadwick raised an amused eyebrow. 'But Evans could be an asset to us. If he carries the revolutionary flag with him, it might stop Jerry shooting at us.' Noticing Harry's expression, he smiled again and made a gesture of dismissal with his cigarette. 'All right, Miles. You can go now and give Evans the good news. After all, you should both be delighted to have a few more weeks in Montoise.'

With the Saxons opposite still unsure about the intentions of their new adversaries, only one alternative was left after their small raiding party had failed to capture a prisoner. At 01.15 that night, flashes lit up the sky on a quarter-mile front and a fierce bombardment fell on the 16th Battalion, its object to blow a gap in its trench parapets so that selected teams of Germans could snatch men and take them back for interrogation.

The effect was stunning. Great trusses of barbed-wire were hurled into the air, some to drop back into the British trenches and entangle men unfortunate enough to be on observer duty. For fifteen minutes the air seethed with bullets, scything shrapnel, and torrents of mud. Then, at exactly 01.30 the bombardment ceased and the stunned recruits of the 16th were hauled out of their dug-outs to take their places on the firing steps.

To add to their misery rain was driving into their faces. As star shells and Very lights soared into the air, NCOs bellowed warnings into deafened ears and shook men back to life. Through yellow, drifting clouds of lyddite, grey-clad figures could be seen running towards them, some firing light machine guns, others hurling grenades.

The attack was being made to the right of Harry's gun-post. With both men half stunned from the blast of shells and with the attacking Germans fanning out towards them, there was no time to agonise now on the morality of killing. With the fixed bayonets of the shouting Germans making it clear it was a matter of kill or be killed, Harry's Vickers gun raked and re-raked the lines of advancing men. Men collapsed like dominoes under the enfilading fire, some with the looseness of limbs that told they were dead before they hit the ground, others to fall and then wave their arms in helpless agony.

The attack was within twenty yards of the shattered barricades before it began to melt away under the deadly machine gun fire. Shrill whistles were heard through the din and a red Very light arched overhead. Still firing, men began to fall back, taking cover in shell holes or even behind the dead bodies of their comrades. To give them cover, their artillery dropped a curtain of shells between them and the shocked infantry they had tried to overcome. At the same moment the British artillery opened up and No Man's Land became an inferno of bursting shells and geysers of mud in which the bodies of men just killed could be seen leaping into the air as if resurrected into a new and demoniacal existence. Hunks of flesh and bone, some black and rotting from the old graveyard and others fresh and raw with blood, showered down on the cringing young infantrymen of the 16th.

The shelling ceased when the last of the Germans reached their trenches although nervous star shells continued to rise from both sides. They showed a wilderness of drifting yellow smoke, desultory fires, and the grey mounds of men, some motionless, others lifting their arms and crying for help. In the Vickers gun-post, cordite and lyddite fumes were burning the eyes of the two men and hiding their responses from one another. Gareth, with his nervous system unable to endure shellfire, was retching again. Trembling, ice-cold with shock, he heard himself crying words that had no meaning. It was only after his hysteria had passed and Harry had not spoken that he conquered his shame and glanced round.

With the smoke still thick within the gun-post and no

movement from Harry, he believed at first that his friend was wounded or dead. Then, as he moved closer, he saw Harry was on his knees with his arms folded on the lid of an ammunition box and his face buried in them. It was the posture of a man in total despair, a man trying to hide from himself and the deed he had committed.

Chapter 32

The knock on the door came just before nine o'clock. With the street in darkness Nicole could make out only the outline of a soldier as she opened the door. *'Qui est-ce?'*

'Hello, Nicole. It's me, Harry.'

She gave a gasp of surprise and pleasure. 'Harry!' Then her voice turned anxious. 'What has happened? Have you been wounded?'

'No. I'm all right. Can I come in?'

'But of course.' She led him into the sitting room. 'It is such a surprise. I had not expected to see you for months.'

He glanced round the room that was illuminated by the oil lamp on the table. Its warmth and familiarity caught at his throat and made his voice uncertain. 'You don't mind my coming round to see you?'

She made an exclamation of impatience. 'What a silly question. Where is your friend, Gareth?'

'He's gone to an *estaminet* with some of the lads. But he asked to be remembered to you.'

She looked puzzled. 'But your Battalion has not come back, has it?'

'No. Just my section.'

She pushed him towards the fire. 'You can tell me about it later. Warm yourself while I pour us both a cognac.'

Before obeying he fished into his greatcoat pocket. 'Where's Michelle? In bed?'

'Of course. But you must see her before you go or she will never forgive me.'

He drew out a small cloth doll from his pocket. 'It isn't much I'm afraid but we haven't had a chance to go shopping since we got back. And children's toys are hard to get.'

There was a trace of moisture in her eyes as she took the doll from him. 'Thank you. You're very kind. Now sit by the fire and I'll get you that cognac.'

His eyes followed her slim figure as she crossed over to the cupboard and took out a bottle and glasses. 'How is Pierre? Have you heard?'

She kept her face averted. 'Yes, I get letters now and then. But the fighting at Verdun is very fierce now.'

'I know,' he muttered. 'We keep hearing about it.'

'How are your family, Harry? Mary and Elizabeth?'

'They seem all right. Except that Mary has moved in with her mother and father.'

She turned. 'Why is that?'

'Dad's not well and he worries about her during the air raids. I suppose it makes sense and in one way it's good to know she won't be alone . . .'

'But you do not like her going back to live with her mother, do you?'

He frowned. 'Not really. But there doesn't seem any alternative.'

She handed him a large glass of cognac, then drew the guard away from the hearth. 'You look cold. Pull your chair nearer.'

The glow from the fire lit up his face as he obeyed.

There were dark shadows beneath his eyes and his cheeks were pale and drawn. Sinking down on the settee opposite him, she raised her glass. 'It is good to see you again, Harry. *Santé.*'

He tried to smile. 'It's good to be back. Cheers.'

His return to Montoise and his unhealthy appearance were puzzling her. 'Where have they billeted you this time?'

'We're in a barn just outside the town. Gareth, myself, and the new section. It's not too bad. We can use the farmhouse to get water and to wash.' He paused. 'Do you mind if I smoke?'

She frowned. 'Of course not.'

He offered her a cigarette. When she shook her head, he lit one for himself. 'Is anyone billeted with you at the moment?'

'Yes. Two more soldiers.' She was watching a muscle flexing in his cheek as he drew on the cigarette. 'You still haven't told me why you've come back to Montoise so soon.'

He exhaled smoke, then told her about Chadwick and the night firing affair. 'He seems to think we ought to have taken the blame although I don't see how or why.'

'He is angry with you but still wants you to serve with him?'

He grimaced. 'Yes. It doesn't make a lot of sense, does it? In fact it never has. With his opinion of me you'd think I'd be the last man he'd want in his section.'

Her attractive face eyed him reflectively. 'Pierre once said that some men cannot leave alone those whom they envy. Perhaps that is the case here.'

A laugh broke from him. 'Envy me? Chadwick?'

'Why not? You care about life and try to protect it. He finds pleasure in destroying it. You have faith and perhaps he has not. You have a beautiful wife and child and

269

you say he is unmarried. There is a great deal for him to envy.'

He gave another self-disparaging laugh. 'That's rubbish, but even it were true, what would be the point of keeping me in his section?'

'To change you, Harry. What men cannot be themselves they like to drag down and destroy. He wants you to be an antilife man like himself.'

He gave a sudden violent start and his cheeks went the colour of putty. Startled herself, she leaned forward. 'What is it? What did I say?'

She saw he was breathing hard and there were tiny beads of sweat on his forehead. Jumping up, she took his hand and found it was ice cold. 'What's the matter, Harry? What have I said?'

He pulled himself together. 'Nothing,' he muttered. 'I was thinking about Gareth. It's damned unfair he's getting punished too.'

She pretended to believe him even though she did not. Picking up his glass she went to fill it. 'Perhaps that was inevitable. He is your friend and Chadwick knows you can be hurt through him. But you must not let that happen. You have enough worries of your own.'

When she returned he was staring into the glowing fire, his thoughts far away. Taking his icy hand, she put the glass into it. 'Drink this, Harry. Drink all of it.'

He stared up at her, then half-drained the glass. As he coughed, she said quietly. 'When did you last sleep, Harry?'

He gave a brittle laugh. 'I don't know. I don't seem to be sleeping very well these days.'

She nodded and motioned at the settee. 'Come over here. I want to talk to you.'

He glanced at the door as if looking for a way of escape. 'What for?' he muttered.

270

'Please do as I say, Harry. Come and sit over here.'

Again he glanced at the door. Then he crossed over to the settee and gave her a hostile stare. 'Well? What do you want?'

She took his hand between her own. 'A moment ago you looked as if you'd seen a ghost when I said Chadwick might be trying to change you. Is that what you're afraid of yourself?'

She heard the tremor of his breathing as he exhaled smoke. 'I don't know what you're talking about.'

She drew him round to face her. 'Yes, you do. We heard heavy gunfire from your lines a few days ago. Has it anything to do with that?'

She knew her guess was right when a shudder ran through him. 'It has, hasn't it? What happened, Harry?'

There was panic in the look he gave her. 'I can't talk about it. Don't ask me to.'

'You must. You must not keep it inside you. Did you have to kill men?' As he shuddered, she went on quickly: 'To protect yourself, I mean. That isn't a sin, Harry. Thousands of men are doing it every day.'

He was trembling now as if he had a fever. His laugh was harsh but the look in his eyes shocked her. 'Kill men? I'm a machine gunner. I killed dozens, perhaps hundreds. In the head, in the heart, in the belly. They kept on coming and I shot them.'

'But, if they were attacking you, what else could you do? You were saving the lives of your friends. I know how awful it is for you but you must not blame yourself. Blame the politicians, blame the generals, but not the soldier who is left to do the dirty work for them.'

His hoarse whisper made her eyes widen with shock. 'You don't understand. I didn't just kill them. I wanted to laugh and cheer when they fell. I found out I was no different to Chadwick. I enjoyed killing them, Nicole.'

271

She gazed at him, then drew his sweating head into her arms. 'You were attacked, Harry. It was relief at beating them off. It's natural to feel that way.'

'No, it isn't. It made Gareth sick. But I've felt that way before, when I was a child and fought Chadwick. We're alike, he and I. And I've only just realised it.'

She shook him fiercely. 'No! You are not like Chadwick. If you were, how could Mary love you? How could I care for you? You expect yourself to be a saint and when you find you are a man like other men, you turn against yourself.'

He was not listening. He was seeing again the grey-clad figures falling under his hail of fire and his sob made her wince. 'All those men, Nicole. Will they know it was I who killed them? Will they be waiting for me to take their revenge when I die?'

She crossed herself, then drew his face down to her breast. 'You must not talk that way, *chéri*. Any priest will tell you there is only forgiveness in heaven.'

'But what if there isn't? How do you face life not knowing?'

Her decision was no longer difficult to make. Easing him back until he was lying full length on the settee, she went to the door. 'Close your eyes and rest. I will be back in a moment.'

She returned five minutes later, wearing a dressing gown and carrying blankets. Slipping off the gown, she lay alongside him and pulled the blankets over them both. The settee was cold to her naked body and his uniform was rough against her skin. In the shadows his eyes were wide and full of conflict. As he muttered something and tried to rise, she pushed him gently back. 'No. Lie still and trust me.'

She waited until their bodies had warmed one another before she helped him undress. His movements were

272

clumsy and although his skin felt hot to her touch, his trembling told her his demons of remorse were tormenting him again. Drawing his head to her breasts, she whispered words of comfort.

His trembling ceased and in spite of his unsteady breathing she believed he had fallen asleep. Then, as he gave a spasmodic jerk, she knew his brief respite from guilt was over. Whispering, kissing him, she slid beneath him and ran her hands down his naked back. When she felt him stirring, she reached down and guided him into her.

For a moment his flanks moved slowly as if inhibitions were hindering him. Then, like a man who had suddenly found a way of escape from a nightmare, his movements began to quicken. As he cried something, her arms embraced him and her body gave aid to his bid for freedom.

The end came quickly. A loud cry broke from him and his body convulsed as if he were experiencing an exorcism. Holding him until his shuddering ceased, she allowed him to sink beside her and put a hand on his face. 'Oh, Harry, *mon pauvre chéri. Vous étes comme mon Pierre. Quelles terribles choses vous font-ils?*'

Although he did not understand her words, he reached forward and kissed her. Then the exhaustion of his flight proved too much in the peaceful void into which he was sinking. His head sank back and when his breathing quietened a few seconds later she knew he was asleep.

Chapter 33

William glanced at Mary again. Although pretending to write in a ledger, she was gazing blindly at the desk before her. William coughed loudly. When the girl did not respond, William decided he could bear her silence no longer. 'What is it, lass? What's troubling you?'

She looked at him blankly, then her eyes cleared. 'Sorry, Dad. I was far away.'

'You were, lass.' Rising, William crossed the office and put an arm round her shoulders. 'Where was it? France?'

'Yes.'

'Stop worrying, love. Harry's going to come back. I know he is.'

Feeling that even to doubt Harry's return was to doom him, she smiled up at William's ruddy, concerned face. 'I know that too, Dad. It just seems a long time since I saw him. And the war looks like going on forever.'

William showed an optimism he no longer felt. 'Nonsense, lass. When all those volunteers of Kitchener are trained and ready, it won't last two months. See if I'm not right.'

A shiver ran through her. 'Harry will be in that, won't he? The big push everyone's talking about?'

'You can't be sure of that. He's one of the earlier ones, so he might miss it. In any case didn't he say in his last letter he was soon due for leave?'

She nodded without speaking. Knowing his daughter well, William bent down and searched her face. 'What else is worrying you? Didn't he like you moving back with us?'

She knew better than to lie to him. 'He's not blaming anyone, Dad, and he's relieved to know I'm not alone during the raids. It's just that he's never had a real home of his own and ours means so much to him.'

'He's not losing it, lass. You can both move back there once the war's over.'

She shook her head. 'We can't let you go on paying the mortgage now the war's effecting business so badly.'

'But I'm not paying it on my own, lass. You pay half from your wages.'

For a moment the dimple appeared in her cheek. 'Come off it, Dad. I do your accounts, remember. There just isn't the work for me these days.'

William scowled. 'It's not just the war, lass. It's that damned playboy, Willis. He's not a quarter the salesman Harry was.'

'Then why don't you let me travel for you again? I could learn to drive.'

William's scowl deepened. 'I would if we hadn't to go so far afield these days to rake in orders. I don't want you spending even less time with Elizabeth.'

Did that mean he had noticed, she wondered. The hundreds of tiny subtle ploys her mother was using to steal the child's affections? 'You shouldn't be paying out money you can't afford,' she said again. 'I know why you keep me on and so does Mother.'

His gentle rebuke made her regret her innuendo. 'Your mum doesn't begrudge you a bit of help at a time like this, lass. It's just she finds it awkward to say so, that's all.'

Doesn't begrudge it, she thought. She resents every penny that helps Harry but you're too loyal to admit it. If anything happens to you, she'll punish Harry in every way she can. Pushing aside the fear that had been with her ever since William's first heart attack, she lay her head against his broadcloth jacket with its evocative smell of tobacco. 'Dad, let's face it. We'll have to think about selling the house. It's not fair to you to keep it on.'

If she had not known the seriousness of his financial affairs, she would have guessed it from his hesitation, and then his mock cheerfulness. 'No, lass, there's no call for that. But I'll tell you what. Why don't we let it while you're staying with us? The rent'll help pay off the mortgage and the two of you can move back when the war's over. How does that sound?'

Her eyes closed for a moment, then she glanced up at him and smiled. 'Yes, that's a good idea. Far better than losing it.'

From the way he cleared his throat, she knew a thought was embarrassing him. 'One thing you mustn't worry about. You won't lose any privacy when Harry comes on leave. I'll take care of that.'

She rose to her feet and hugged him. 'You think of everything, don't you, Dad.'

He kissed her, then frowned. 'I'm a bit worried about Harry, mind you. I wouldn't like the lad to think badly of me if we let the house.'

'Of course he won't think badly of you. I'll explain everything in my next letter.'

Looking relieved he patted her cheek, then began fumbling in his jacket pocket. She showed surprise when he pulled out his pipe and tobacco pouch. 'Are we finishing for the day then?'

276

He shrugged and grimaced. 'Aye, why not. I'm not waiting for Willis, not when he's probably chatting with some pretty shopgirl.'

She watched him pack his pipe. His behaviour convinced her he had something to say but was not finding it easy. 'What is it, Dad?'

He glanced at her. 'You reading my thoughts, lass?'

She smiled. 'They're not that difficult to read sometimes. What is it?'

He put a match to his pipe and pressed down a rising flake with a nicotine-stained forefinger. Puffing out a cloud of smoke, he frowned at the pipe before turning to her. 'It's about the business. At least about its future.'

'Its future?'

'Aye. I know things are bad at the moment but it's basically sound and should be all right once the war's over. Don't you agree?'

She was growing more and more puzzled. 'Yes. Of course.'

'Good lass. But it'll have to be in capable hands to get that way. That's what I want to talk about.'

'It will be in good hands,' she interrupted. 'Your hands.'

'I can't go on forever, love. There has to come a time when someone else takes over.'

Alarm was gripping her. 'For heaven's sake, you're still in your prime. So what are you talking about?'

He laughed at her concern. 'Things don't change because a man takes precautions. Everyone makes a will sooner or later.'

'A will? But you've got a will, haven't you?'

'Yes. That's what I want to talk about. But first you've got to promise me not to say a word about this to your mother. The last thing I want to do is hurt her. Do you promise.'

277

'Yes, if that's what you want. But what's this to do with your will?'

William puffed on his pipe before replying. 'It's this way, lass. In the past I always felt it right and proper that your mother should inherit the business. But lately I've been wondering if that's such a good idea. After all, folks can't be good at everything, can they? While your mum's grand at looking after the house and taking care of us all, I don't think we can say she's got the best of business heads, can we?'

Among other things, she now understood the cause of his embarrassment. 'Does that matter so much? After all, she can always get a good manager to look after things.'

The depth of William's scowl betrayed the love he had for his self-made industry. 'That's the last thing I want. I want this business to stay in the family as well as to prosper. That's the reason I'm changing my will and leaving it to you. Will you have it, love?'

Although by this time she had guessed as much, her first thought was the effect on Ethel. 'Dad, is it wise? You know how it'll upset Mother. And what about Connie?'

William sighed. 'Aye, I know the problems. But there are somethings a man can't bear to think of falling apart when he goes. If you and Harry take the business over, that won't happen.'

She threw her arms around him. 'Don't talk that way, Dad. I can't bear it.'

He kissed her golden hair. 'We all have to go sooner or later, lass, but we like to think we're leaving something permanent behind. You needn't worry about your mother or Connie. Mum will get the house and my life insurance and I want you to pay her and Connie a percentage of business profits. So they'll be looked after.'

'Are you sure about this, Dad?'

'Aye, I am.' Releasing her, William picked up a bunch of keys from his desk and walked over to the cupboard he always kept locked. Opening it, he showed her a long envelope. 'I finished this new will yesterday. As soon as old Ombler gets back from his daughter's wedding, I'll talk over a few points with him and he can draft out a proper one. Not that this wouldn't stand up in law, mind. It's properly signed and witnessed.' Replacing the envelope, William drew out a bottle of whisky and a couple of glasses. His eyes twinkled mischievously as he turned to her. 'Now that's settled I think we should have a drink on it. We can't very well celebrate at home, can we?'

She had to laugh at his expression. 'Are you sure about this, Dad? Really sure?'

He handed her a generous glass of whisky. 'Aye, lass, I am. And I'm a happier man now we've spoken about it.'

Ten minutes later they were walking down the lane that led to the house. Glancing up at the evening sky, William saw that it was clear and a full moon was rising over the trees. About to remark that it was good weather for Zeppelins, he checked himself. The girl had enough on her mind already. Instead William hugged her arm and quickened his pace. 'Let's see what Mum's got for supper tonight. That talk's given me an appetite.'

The air raid William had half-expected came two nights later. The sirens sounded just before ten-thirty in the evening and by the time their wailing ceased, the spanging of distant anti-aircraft guns could be heard. With the city having experienced a number of raids by this time, only Ethel wanted to take immediate cover in the cup-

279

board under the stairs. 'We can't be certain they're heading this way yet,' Mary pointed out. 'The gunfire isn't getting any louder.'

Ethel's voice betrayed her fear of Zeppelins. 'What else is there to bomb in these parts? At least let's get Elizabeth downstairs and under cover.'

To William's surprise, Mary shook her head. 'No, not yet. I don't want her to get too afraid of these raids.'

Ethel's pale face tautened. 'That's ridiculous. The more she realises the danger, the more care she'll take. I'm going upstairs to fetch her.'

Before Mary could stop her, the door burst open. Dressed in her nightgown and clutching a doll, Elizabeth was crying and half hysterical. 'Grannie! Grannie! It's the bang-bangs again. I'm frightened.'

Mary ran towards her. 'It's all right, darling. The bang-bangs won't hurt you. They're looking after you. Come over to the fire and I'll read you a story.'

To her dismay, the child ran past her and flung herself into Ethel's arms. 'You won't let the bang-bangs hurt me, will you, Grannie?'

With a glance at Mary, Ethel picked her up. 'Of course I won't, darling. I'll take you into the cupboard where they can't find you.'

Mary moved forward, then halted as Ethel laid the girl onto her makeshift bed beneath the stairs. As Ethel lit the oil lamp and settled down beside the child, Mary walked out into the hall. Pausing there a moment to regain her temper, she opened the front door.

It was a perfect April evening. The full moon was floating like a bubble among silver-lined clouds. Distant shouts and the popping of guns seemed to accentuate the silence. A voice at her elbow made the girl start. 'It's too good a night for war, isn't it, lass?'

She nodded jerkily. 'Yes, it is.'

William's tone changed. 'The bairn seems very frightened of the guns. I didn't notice it so much the last time.'

'It's Mother,' Mary said bitterly. 'She's always talking to her about air raids and about people getting killed. I've asked her to stop it but she takes no notice.'

'You don't think that's just because she's frightened herself, do you, lass?'

She was in no mood for excuses tonight. 'I don't care what it is. She should have more sense. I don't want Elizabeth made into a nervous child.'

The thud of a distant explosion drew their eyes back to the eastern horizon. Tiny sparks could be seen winking between a gap in the clouds. Mary pointed at them. 'That's where the Zeppelin must be!'

Half a dozen searchlights were now criss-crossing the sky. As the couple listened, a low throbbing drone could be heard through the gunfire. William touched Mary's arm. 'It's coming this way now, lass. Shouldn't we get into the shelter?'

Fascinated and excited by the spectacle, the girl ignored him. A searchlight, quartering the sky, suddenly paused. Giving a cry, Mary pointed at a silver, pencil-thin shape emerging from a cloud. 'There it is. Look! Isn't it beautiful?'

Another searchlight leapt up, transfixing the Zeppelin on two luminous spears. With their quarry visible at last, guns round the fringe of the city opened out in earnest. As sparks winked all around the silver shape, something long and diaphanous fell from it, to fade and disappear like a waterfall over a high cliff. At the same time the Zeppelin rose as if on an invisible lift, leaving the search-lights groping about blindly. Mary turned to William. 'What happened? Was it hit?'

'No, I don't think so. They say they carry water ballast

281

and if they're in danger, they release it and climb out of harm's way.'

As the gunfire momentarily ceased, the throbbing drone could still be heard. Hearing it was growing louder William gripped Mary's arm. 'That's enough, lass. It's just as dangerous, no matter how high it is. And it's definitely coming this way.'

Reluctantly she closed the door. 'They're brave men, Dad, aren't they?'

William, who had a no-nonsense attitude to his country's enemies, stared at her. 'Brave men? Coming over to kill women and children? They're bloody murderers, lass.'

'They're still brave men,' she said, following him. 'They must be, to fly up there among all that inflammable gas.'

He paused at the sitting room door before opening it. 'You'd better not let your mother hear you. Or she'll think you're dafter than you are.'

Smiling, she followed him into the room. The gunfire was heavy now, making the windows rattle. Ethel, who had managed to quieten Elizabeth, urged them frantically to take cover. As William pushed Mary forward, there was a loud clatter on the roof. Although pale himself, William shook his head at Ethel's cry. 'It's only shrapnel, love. From our own guns.'

Crouched in the small cupboard, they listened to the sounds of battle. As more shrapnel brought slates from the roof, they knew the Zeppelin must be closing in. The noise had awakened Elizabeth who began crying again. Before Mary could reach the child, Ethel snatched her up into her arms and began rocking her. 'There, there, darling. Grannie won't let the nasty bang-bangs hurt you.'

The all-pervading drone, punctuated by gunfire,

moved nearer until it seemed to pass right over the house. As William turned to Ethel, there were three heavy explosions that made the floor leap beneath their feet. A cry of terror broke from Ethel. 'Those were bombs. Oh, my God! Have they hit us?'

Two more explosions sounded. Then, as the drone and the gunfire moved away, Mary threw open the door and climbed out. 'It's all right now. It's passed over.'

Looking shaken, William joined her. As Mary reached for Elizabeth, the trembling Ethel shrank back. 'No. Leave her with me until the all-clear sounds!'

Unable to argue, Mary went to the back door where searchlights were now probing the western sky. As she turned to speak to William who had joined her, she saw a red glow was staining the sky behind the warehouse. Noticing it, William gave a gasp of horror. 'They haven't hit the warehouse, have they?'

She put a hand on his arm to steady him. 'No. It's on the far side. In one of the streets . . .' Her voice broke off as she realised what she had said. Turning, she ran for the front door, calling back as she went. 'Stay here with Mother and Elizabeth! I won't be long.'

Bells were clanging as she ran outside and she saw two fire engines swinging into the adjacent street. Heart in her mouth she ran after them. As she reached the street corner her heart gave an explosive thud, then seemed to stop. A hundred yards down the road half a block of houses had disintegrated into a mass of rubble and leaping flames.

For a few seconds she ran towards the fire engines that were now playing ineffective streams of water on the blazing rubble. Then she halted wearily. With her mind numbed by shock, it took William's breathless voice to pull her round. 'It's not your house, is it, lass? Oh, my God, it is!'

William's jacket was undone, his starched collar had broken loose, and he was panting as if he had run a marathon. She caught hold of him. 'Dad, why did you come? I said wait for me.'

His arms went round her, half-smothering her in his distress. 'Why had it to be you, love? In God's name, why?'

He was holding her so tightly she could feel the painful pounding of his heart. She kissed him, then eased herself away. 'Dad, don't go any closer, please. Let me take a look and then I'll come home. I promise.'

'But lass, maybe I can help.'

'No one can help,' she said. 'Everything's gone. You can see that from here. I just want to take a look by myself. Please, Dad, do as I ask.'

He opened his mouth, then brushed his eyes. 'You won't be long, will you, love? Please!'

She turned away to hide her expression. 'Only a few minutes, Dad. You go back to the house and stay with Mother.'

Mary returned to No. 57 twenty minutes later. She found her mother sitting alone in the lounge with a teapot and two cups on a table beside her. Seeing the soot stains on Mary's face and dress, Ethel gave a gasp and rose unsteadily to her feet. 'Was Dad right, dear? Has your house gone?'

The dullnes of her eyes told Mary she had not yet fully recovered from the raid. 'Yes. And three others beside it.'

'How dreadful. Was anyone killed?'

'Yes, the old couple at the far side. They think there might be others buried beneath the rubble.'

Ethel was unable to take in the full extent of the

tragedy. 'At least thank God you're safe. Let me get you a fresh cup of tea.'

Mary checked her as she started for the kitchen. 'Where are Dad and Elizabeth?'

'They're upstairs. Dad carried her to her room after she fell asleep.'

Mary's eyes were on the unused tea cup on the tray. 'When was this?'

'After Dad got back, dear. The poor child was tired out after all her crying.'

Mary backed to the door. 'That must have been over fifteen minutes ago. Why hasn't he come down? Didn't you tell him you'd made tea?'

'I called him, yes.'

'Didn't he answer you?'

Ethel's face puckered as she tried to remember. Then, as she saw Mary's expression, fear destroyed her apathy. 'Oh, my God! You don't think . . .'

Her voice broke off as Mary turned sharply. Running up the stairs to Elizabeth's room, the girl found the child fast asleep in her bed but there was no sign of William. Turning, she stumbled into Ethel who had followed her up the stairs. When she shook her head, Ethel ran across the landing to the opposite door. A moment later there was a piercing scream. Heart in her mouth, Mary ran into the bedroom.

William was lying on the floor at the foot of the bed. His head was turned and there was a large bubble of air resting grotesquely on one cheek. Ethel, panting with shock, had backed away to the fireplace. As she gave another scream, Mary tried to catch hold of her. 'No, Mother! Don't. Please!'

With eyes as wild as a hare, Ethel tore herself away and fell on her knees beside the body. As she caught Williams' face between her hands the bubble burst, bringing a cry of horror from her. Trembling with shock, Mary bent over her. 'Mother, please. Dad's dead. You go into my room while I call the doctor.'

To her dismay Ethel hammered the floor with her fists. 'You're lying. William can't be dead. He can't be, do you hear?'

Traumatised by her own grief, Mary could feel only pity for her. 'Mother, go to my room. Please. You're tearing yourself to pieces here.'

Ignoring her, Ethel threw herself over William's body. As Mary tried to pull her away, the frantic woman struck at her. Frightened by her agony, Mary backed to the door. 'I'll call the police too. They'll see Harry is told.'

Ethel's sobs ceased as if a switch had been thrown. 'Harry?'

'Yes. They sometimes get compassionate leave in cases like this.'

Ethel's stricken eyes lifted to her. 'Dad ran all the way to your house, didn't he?'

With the enormity of her own loss beginning to be felt, Mary had no idea what was coming. 'Yes. He shouldn't have done. I told him to stay with you.'

'And you believed he would? When you always were his favourite?'

The girl could not believe what she was hearing. 'Mother, you can't blame me for that. My house was hit: I had to go. I didn't know he was following me.'

A shudder of hatred ran through Ethel. 'I'm glad your house was hit. Harry made you buy it, didn't he? And because of it your father's dead.'

Mary began to think she was experiencing a nightmare. 'You're surely not blaming Harry? Mother, it was a Zeppelin that destroyed our house. Harry's over in France, fighting for us. Go and lie down while I call the doctor, please.'

The intensity of Ethel's passion made the girl's flesh creep. 'Your marriage has killed your father and the man who meant the world to me. I'll never forgive Harry for what he has done. Never, never, never!'

Chapter 34

A cold drizzle was falling from a grey sky when William was laid to rest five days later. As the last rites were being performed at the graveside, Mary could hear the cawing of rooks and the melancholy cry of distant ships. When the coffin was finally lowered into the ground, her mind suddenly rebelled and swept her like a frightened bird out of the graveyard and back to the security of childhood. At one moment she was lying alongside her sister, pretending to sleep as William crept in with two Christmas pillowcases of toys to hang on the foot of the bed. In the next she was a toddler sobbing over some childish mishap, to be swung up into his huge arms and comforted while her tearful face pressed against his shoulder. To the end of her life she knew she would always equate the smell of pipe tobacco with his gruff voice, his warmth and his kindness.

Gone now. Gone forever. The awful finality of death seemed to suck the very air from her lungs as the pall bearers released the ropes. She felt Harry's hand tighten on her arm and tried to smile, only for her eyes to burn and swell as if they would burst. Leaning against him for courage, she heard his whisper. 'Bear up, love. It'll soon be over.'

The church had been full to overflowing: William's warm-heartedness had not been confined to his family. With Ethel and Harry she had stood afterwards at the church doors and thanked everyone for their attendance but not a single face had registered on her mind, not even the slim young woman with swollen eyes who had emerged alone and slipped past them without speaking.

Harry, who had been given five days compassionate leave, had arrived the previous day and could only stay one more night. Mary had thought how much stronger and more self-assured he looked but her joy at seeing him again had been tempered by fears of Ethel's behaviour. In fact the enormity of Ethel's loss and her need to make the burial arrangements had left her no time or emotion to devote on Harry. Nevertheless the overpowering mixture of joy and fear and the all-pervading sense of loss had made a turmoil of the girl's mind. Did everyone feel this way when a loved parent died, she wondered. Then why was there so little mention of it in art and literature? Why did it not feature more in the chronicles of human suffering?

She was painfully aware that William's death had affected her re-union with Harry. Shocked in mind and body, with every act of pleasure seeming profane, she had found herself unable to give him the physical passion she felt was his due. Although blaming herself, she knew in her heart there were other factors too. Harry had also loved William and in his way was feeling his death as deeply. Then there was their residency at her parent's home. After Ethel's initial outburst against Harry, her hostility had taken second place to her grief and moreover she had needed the help Harry had given her. But the very knowledge she was sharing the house with them inhibited both their conversation and their love making.

289

The loss of their home was another factor. Although William's death had put it in perspective, it was still a tragedy for them. Knowing how much Ethel resented the help William had given them, they had under-insured the house contents in order to pay off a greater share of the mortgage. When the opportunity arrived to study their position, Mary knew it would preclude any possibility of their buying or even renting another house until the war was over. Which meant that she and Eliza-beth would have to continue living under Ethel's suzerainty.

It was true that if Harry survived the war and they inherited the business according to William's wishes, hard work could eventually restore their position. It was a thought that gave the girl little comfort at this point of time, however. If Ethel felt the way she did towards Harry now, what would her feelings be when she learned the terms of William's new will? With the solicitor arriv-ing to read it on the morrow it was a prospect the girl dreaded.

A whisper from Harry brought her back to the present. The minister was shaking holy water on the coffin and members of the family and friends were beginning to circle the grave. As Mary saw her mother, an erect but grief-stricken figure in deep black, pause there, she could feel nothing but pity. Whatever her faults, Ethel had worshipped William and his age should have guaranteed them another twenty years of life together. Ethel's expression as her gloved hand sprin-kled down soil was that of a woman throwing those empty years into the grave with him.

Connie, who had arrived with her husband the pre-vious day, went next and then it was Mary's turn. She felt rebellion again as the soil she dropped disfigured the oaken coffin and its fresh flowers. What cruel priest had deemed this ritual necessary? Were not the silent lips and the yawning grave enough a reminder of mortality? It took Harry's whisper and his urging hand to tear her away from her last sight of her father.

Although later the house was full of people and she had to help Ethel and Connie to attend to them as well as look after the chattering, curious Elizabeth, she remembered nothing about the ordeal. The camera of her mind seemed to function again only after she had put the child to sleep and was able to sink into bed alongside Harry. Allowed to be herself at last, she cried in his arms for minutes before drawing back in shame. 'Poor darling. What a leave you're having.'

He gave a wry smile. 'I hardly expected it to be a holiday.'

'It's still not fair to you. You should have had the chance to play with Elizabeth and relax a little.'

'I can do that on my regular leave,' he said.

She turned to him eagerly. 'Will you still get it? You don't think it'll be cancelled because of this offensive everyone's talking about?'

He found it ironical that while every effort was being made in France to keep news of the offensive from the Germans, in Britain the newspapers seemed full of little else. 'No,' he lied. 'I think I've got a good chance.'

Wanting to believe him, she did not question him further. She rested her head on his shoulder, her eyes watching his expression. 'How bad is it over there, Harry? Is it as bad as people say?'

His hesitation was her answer, not his words. 'Not too bad. We get our grub and our laughs. And our rum.'

'I hope you don't get drunk on it.'

Like herself, he needed the moment of humour. 'We would if we could. But they make us drink it in front of the officers; so we can't save it up and have a binge.'

She laughed with him, then memory came back. 'You were wonderful today, darling. I'd never have got through it without you.'

He frowned. 'I don't want thanking, love. He was like a father to me.'

'I know that. You'll miss him as much as any of us. Oh, Harry, why had he to die? He was such a warm and lovely man.'

For a moment there was a bitterness in his voice she had not heard before. 'I don't know,' he said. 'There are a lot of things I don't know any more.'

She thought she heard a noise in the adjacent bedroom and immediately her heart began racing. 'Harry,' she whispered. 'What's going to happen tomorrow?'

He turned to her. 'Nothing's going to happen. It wasn't you who changed the will, it was your father. She'll be upset – she might even throw a tantrum or two – but it'll pass over. In the long run she'll realise it's the only thing your father could have done.'

In the long run, she thought. How long is that? The question died on her lips. The last thing she wanted was to send him away with another worry on his mind. Hypersensitive to his perils in France, she imagined any distraction might mean life or death to him. 'You're right. I'm just being silly. She might even be relieved not to have the worry of the business.'

He knew she had as much faith in Ethel's forebearance as he did but that she needed the deception. 'It's quite possible. She'd still need you whatever happened. And it's not as if her income is going to stop. On a practical level she'll hardly notice the difference.'

Not notice the difference, she thought. That William had left his most precious possession to his child and not to her? She pushed the thought away before it could chill her. 'All this is assuming I can keep things going until you get back,' she said.

He drew her into his arms. 'Of course you can. Stop worrying about it.'

They made love a moment later. With both of them conscious of the adjacent bedroom, with the weight of the day heavy on them and with the morrow promising more pain and turmoil, it was an act of devotion rather than passion. After it she wept a little. 'I'm sorry, Harry, I don't know what's the matter with me. I love you so much but I feel so empty inside.'

He laid a finger on her lips. 'You've had a terrible shock, love, and you're tired out. Go to sleep now.'

'But you're going back tomorrow. It seems such a waste to sleep.'

'All the same, you must. Lie back and close your eyes.'

They lay in one another's arms after that, both pretending to sleep. With their breath on the other's cheeks, they could hardly have been closer and yet like the rest of mankind they remained islands apart in their thoughts and fears.

Chapter 35

Archibald Ombler, William's solicitor, arrived punctually at eleven-thirty the following morning. He was a small balding man in his early sixties with greying mutton chop whiskers. With his sober dress, high starched collar and precise voice, Mary had always seen him as a character straight from a Dickens' novel. This morning however her eyes were more on his leather briefcase than on the man himself.

At Ombler's request the family filed into the dining-room. Ethel, looking pale and tense, offered the man the chair at the head of the table, then motioned Connie and her husband to the far side. Connie, who had surprised everyone by becoming pregnant at last, was looking less distressed by the occasion than expectant as she pushed Ronald round the table. Ronald Arkwright, a somewhat sallow bank manager, had been seized on by Connie as a good catch and his behaviour since suggested he had never recovered from the experience.

Indicating Mary and Harry to sit opposite Connie, Ethel then went to the far end of the table where she sat facing the solicitor. As Ombler began his preamble in which he offered the family his condolences, animated sounds could be heard from the sitting-room where

Molly was keeping Elizabeth amused.

With his preamble over, Ombler turned and opened his briefcase. As he pulled out a large document, Mary felt her pulse quicken alarmingly. Unable to look at Ethel, she watched the solicitor draw a pair of rimless spectacles from his jacket and perch them on his nose.

The seconds seemed endless as the man scanned the document. Certain he was doing it for effect, Mary was grateful when Harry's hand crept beneath the table towards her. As she gripped it tightly, Ombler raised his head and glanced over his glasses at Ethel.

'If you will allow me, Mrs Hardcastle, I would like to dispose of the minor bequests before I come to the major ones. Do I have your permission?'

Ethel gave a terse nod although Connie looked far from pleased at the delay. Relaxing slightly, Mary listened to the beneficiaries of William's generosity. There was twenty pounds to Molly in recognition of her loyal service. Two life-long friends received token gifts of fifty pounds each. An old tramp who had often paid visits to the warehouse and in whose palm Mary had often seen William slip a half-crown, was to receive ten pounds. But it was the last bequest that made Ethel start and the two girls stare at one another. Two hundred pounds was to be given to a Mrs Edna Johnson of 20, Prospect Street. Ethel leaned forward. 'Who is Mrs Johnson, Mr Ombler?'

The solicitor gave a dry cough. 'A business acquaintance, I presume, Mrs Hardcastle.'

Ethel's curious eyes turned to Mary. 'Do you know of her?'

Mary was as surprised as anyone. 'No. But Dad did have business friends I never met.'

Harry broke in quickly. 'I think she's a buyer for a chain of chemist shops, Mother.'

Ethel's eyes rested on him for a moment before turning back to the solicitor. 'A woman buyer? Are there such persons, Mr Ombler?'

Expecting an enquiry, the solicitor was quick to accept Harry's explanation. 'Yes, I believe they do exist in certain trades, Mrs Hardcastle. And it is accepted business practice to reward them for their custom.'

Ethel was frowning. 'To the tune of two hundred pounds?'

Ombler gave his dry cough again. 'If this lady has given your late husband comparable orders, I would not think it unreasonable.'

About to speak, Ethel changed her mind. 'Very well. Carry on, please, Mr Ombler.'

As the solicitor glanced down at the will again, Mary gripped Harry's hand tightly. 'Now we come to the major bequests. The house at Fifty-seven Ellerby Road, being the deceased's sole domain, is left to his wife, Ethel Hardcastle. It is hers to keep or sell but on her death any profits that accrue or have accrued from its sale shall be divided equally between the deceased's two daughters, Mary and Connie. As to its contents they are also left to the deceased's wife except for the large sideboard in the sitting room which is left to Mary and the pair of bronze gladiators by the fireplace which is to go to Connie.'

For a moment Mary closed her eyes. William had not forgotten. Then as Ombler continued, her throat tightened.

'Now we come to the business trading under the registered title of William Hardcastle and Company. It is the deceased's wish that as long as the business continues trading and as long as he so wishes, Harry Miles shall remain its chief representative and, under the same conditions, his daughter Mary shall remain its accountant. The business itself is left to Ethel Hardcastle although it is the deceased's wish that the said Ethel Hardcastle gives full recognisance to her daughter and son-in-law's advice. It is also the wish of the deceased that the business continues to trade after his death and indeed to prosper. However, should it be sold at any time, twenty-five per cent of the return shall be given to each of the deceased's daughters, the remaining fifty per cent to be retained by his wife, Ethel. In the meantime, from the date of the reading of the will, three hundred pounds shall be taken from the deceased's private account and given to each daughter.'

There were a couple of codicils to follow but Mary was too bewildered to hear them. She heard Harry's low whisper. 'What's happened? Hasn't he seen the new will?'

'He can't have done,' she whispered back.

'Then you'd better tell him. It's bound to come out sooner or later.'

Knowing he was right, she suddenly realised the solicitor had ceased talking and all eyes were on her and Harry. Her mouth turned dry as the man addressed her. 'You have a comment, Mrs Miles?'

Not daring to look at Ethel, she braced herself. 'Yes. Have you looked through all my father's papers in his office?'

Ombler gave her a patient smile. 'Naturally, Mrs Miles. I and my colleagues are your father's executors.'

'But have you opened the cupboard behind my father's desk?'

'Of course. We have opened everything connected with your father's estate.'

'Then I don't understand. There was a letter in the cupboard addressed to you.' Mary took a deep breath. 'It concerned a new will.'

297

A gasp ran round the table. Ethel leaned forward. 'What did you say, girl?'

It took a physical effort for Mary to turn and face her. 'It was about a new will, Mother. Dad spoke to me about it last week. He was keeping the letter until Mr Ombler returned home from his daughter's wedding.'

'Then it wasn't a will?' the solicitor interrupted.

'I don't think it was in document form, if that's what you mean. But he said he'd signed it and had it witnessed.'

'Then it was a lawful document.'

'That's what Dad believed. From what he said, he certainly meant it to be.'

The solicitor frowned. 'You sound as if he discussed the contents with you, Mrs Miles. Did he?'

'Yes. He wanted my approval before he passed the letter over to you.'

Ethel stiffened. 'Your approval? What are you saying, girl?'

Bracing herself again, Mary turned to her. 'He had decided to leave the business to me and wanted to know if I'd accept it. He thought it a better arrangement for you.'

The violent reaction she expected did not come. Instead Ethel gave a laugh of incredulity. 'He thought it better for me? If you inherited the firm?'

'Yes. He felt if Harry and I ran it, it wouldn't be a worry and a burden to you. We were to pay you a percentage of profits.'

Before Ethel could reply, Connie broke in indignantly. 'What about me? Wasn't I considered?'

Mary turned to her sister. 'Of course you were. You were to have a share of the profits too. With Harry in charge of sales, Dad felt you'd all be better off.'

Ethel's voice was suddenly loaded with malice. 'With

Harry in charge? I'm beginning to understand now.'

Mary swung round on her. 'What does that mean?'

Recognising all the signs of a bitter family quarrel, Ombler hastily intervened. 'Before we discuss this any further, I would like Mrs Miles to take me over to the warehouse and show me exactly where she last saw this letter.' As Ethel rose to her feet, the solicitor smoothly checked her. 'With your permission, Mrs Hardcastle, just myself and your daughter. We will only be a few minutes. In the meantime I would suggest you do not discuss the matter between yourselves.'

That the matter had been discussed well and truly was obvious enough to Mary from Harry's expression when she returned twenty minutes later. No longer with the others, he was talking to Molly and Elizabeth. When she shook her head, he followed her and Ombler back into the dining-room. The babble of voices died as the three of them took their places at the table again. Ethel spoke first. 'Well, did you find this mysterious letter?'

'No,' Ombler told her. 'There is no sign of it in the cupboard or in his desk.'

Ethel gave a hard laugh. 'I never thought there would be, Mr Ombler.'

The solicitor glanced at her, frowned, and put on his glasses again. 'It is true that we have already made a careful search of all papers and documents relevant to your husband's estate, Mrs Hardcastle. I cannot think what can have happened to this letter.'

'You are assuming such a letter existed, Mr Ombler?'

The solicitor gave a start. 'Mrs Hardcastle, your daughter confirmed she saw it. You are surely not saying she has fabricated her story?'

'I'm asking how it could have existed when the cupboard was locked and only you opened it.'

The solicitor pursed his lips. 'The keys were in a

cubby-hole on the desk for at least a day before I was called in, Mrs Hardcastle. Anyone on the premises had access to the cupboard during that time.'

Red spots appeared in Ethel's pale cheeks. 'Are you suggesting that one of us took the letter?'

'I am inferring no such thing, madam. I am simply pointing out that for a day at least we were not the only persons who could open that cupboard.'

Ethel remained very stiff and indignant. 'That still means you believe someone took it. Who is that person?'

'I have no idea, madam. But as the letter was there and has now vanished, it must clearly have been taken by somebody.'

Ethel's small, ringed hand came down hard on the table. 'There never was a letter!' Her eyes, still swollen by grief, turned on Mary. 'You were told to say this, weren't you? Harry has wanted to take over the business ever since he married you and he thought this might be his chance. Why don't you admit it?'

Harry jumped to his feet, his chair falling against the wall with a clatter. For a moment he seemed about to reply to Ethel's attack. Instead he turned and walked from the room.

Forgetting everything in her anger, Mary also rose. 'That's a wicked thing to say. Harry wasn't even here when Dad told me about the letter. Anyway, what would be the point of my lying about it? If there never was a letter, how could the old will be changed?'

Before Ethel could reply, Ombler nodded. 'She's quite right, Mrs Hardcastle. That is why I believe a letter existed. I'm afraid I shall have to carry out a further search before I can implement the terms of this will.'

Ethel's lips pressed tightly together. 'Very well. Do another search if you want to waste your time.' Rising, she went to the door, then swung round. 'But please be quick about it. Until all these matters are settled, it's very distressing for us.'

As the solicitor nodded, Mary turned to him. 'I wouldn't waste your time, Mr Ombler. After listening to my mother, I'm quite certain you'll never find it.'

Her bitter words brought a cry of protest from Connie. At the door, Ethel gazed at Mary for a full five seconds. Then, saying something the girl could not hear, she turned away and disappeared.

The central railway station was in its usual wartime condition with servicemen in full kit jostling for space, women and children sobbing, and the hissing of steam a constant reminder that separation was only minutes away. Finding a spot on the platform between a pile of crates, Harry drew Mary and Elizabeth into it. The child, whom Mary had decided was now old enough to come and say goodbye to her father, was looking wide-eyed and bewildered by the noise. Noticing it, Harry picked her up and gave her a kiss. 'It's all right, love. Nobody's going to hurt you.'

As the child snuggled against his tunic, he turned to Mary. 'Isn't there any way you can get away from your mother? Couldn't you go and live with Connie for a while?'

The thought of a room in Connie's home made her smile. 'Darling, you keep on forgetting I've a job to do. With the house gone we're going to need all the money we can get if we're to start another home when you come back.'

His frustration at being unable to help her showed in his voice. 'To hell with the future. I'm thinking about your life at present. Your mother's never going to forgive you for suggesting she stole that letter.'

She knew she had somehow to make it easier for him. 'No, she won't go on about it – not when the others have gone home. How can she when she knows she stole it? There's another thing too. If she drives me out, she'll lose Elizabeth. And that's the last thing she wants.'

'You feel quite sure she is guilty?'

'Who else would gain by taking the letter?'

'What about Connie? She seemed jealous of you.'

'No. Connie didn't arrive until after Mr Ombler was given the keys. It was Mother all right. She's always been jealous of me since Dad called me his right-hand man. I think that's more her reason than a wish to take over the business. She'd have hated people to know Dad didn't trust her to run it properly.'

His mind was still on her living alone with Ethel. 'Couldn't you buy another house? You'll have enough for a deposit once the will's ratified.'

'You're forgetting Dad used to help us pay the mortgage. That'll stop now. And what about Elizabeth? I couldn't ask Mother to look after her if I walked out of the house. So how could I work?'

'You hate your mother looking after Elizabeth as much as I do. So give up work. We'll manage somehow.'

Keeping from him her longing to break free of her mother was more than difficult. 'Darling, how could I bring up Elizabeth on fourteen shillings a week and pay off a mortgage? There's another thing too. We don't want the business to fall apart before you get back. Jobs might be hard to get after the war.'

He gave a hard laugh. 'You don't think your mother's going to employ me, do you?'

'Yes, I do. Underneath everything else, Mother knows on which side her bread's buttered. She won't get rid of you when she knows you're the one person who

302

can pull the business round.'

She could read his thoughts, that Ethel would make his life a misery at the same time, but with the war filling both their horizons that was a problem that could be put aside for the moment. Instead she changed the subject. 'Harry, you said Edna Johnson is a buyer for a chemist chain. Why haven't I heard about her?'

At that moment Elizabeth plucked at a strap of Harry's webbing. 'What's this for, Daddy?'

Mary imagined she saw relief in Harry's eyes as he turned to the child. 'That's to hold up my pack and other things, darling.'

'What's in your pack, Daddy?'

'Oh, a blanket, food rations, all kinds of things. The next time Daddy comes home he'll show you.'

Seeing he was not going to answer her question, Mary laid a hand on his khaki-clad arm. 'Harry, Dad left her two hundred pounds. That's a lot of money. Surely he'd never leave all that to a buyer?'

'I don't see why not.'

'But I'd surely have heard of her.' When he did not answer, she went on: 'You said that to put Mother off, didn't you?'

He knew it was useless lying to her. 'Why not? I owe your dad a lot more than that.'

'But Dad . . .' She shook her head in confusion. 'I just can't believe it of him.'

He frowned. 'It doesn't change anything he did for us, does it?'

'No, of course not. But Mother won't let it rest. She'll want to know everything about that woman.'

He shrugged. 'If she wants to risk spoiling her memory of him, the more fool her. But don't you be so stupid. Your father loved you and he couldn't have been kinder to either of us. That's enough for me and it should be enough for you.'

'Then you do think he was having an affair,' she insisted.

'Frankly, I don't give a damn. If he was, he probably had his reasons. There's usually a reason for everything.'

'But Mother did love him, Harry. There's no doubt about that.'

'All right, if she loved him she won't go around looking for blemishes in him, will she? Isn't that what love means? Defending someone instead of attacking them?'

She had never heard him talk this way before and realised how the war was changing him. Before she could say more a whistle sounded above the hiss of steam and he turned to the child. 'Daddy has to go now, darling. But I'll be back soon.'

Mary managed a smile for the child whose bottom lip was beginning to quiver. 'What do you say to Daddy, darling?'

The child lisped her carefully-rehearsed speech. 'May God bring you safely back, Daddy.'

Beneath his cap, Mary saw Harry's face turn pale. Muttering something he kissed the child, set her down, and began re-fastening the cord of his kitbag. When he turned back to Mary, he had recovered. 'S'long, love. Try not to miss your dad too much. He wouldn't want that. I'll write as soon as I get back.'

She flung her arms round him. 'Come back safely, Harry. We love you so much.'

With couplings clanking and metal wheels screeching, the train drew out three minutes later, its heavy breath drifting over the sobbing women and children. With Elizabeth waving her tiny arms in farewell, Mary waited until it disappeared down the track. Then, with the child still in her arms, she joined in the queue for the barrier, able for the first time that day to admit her true feelings.

304

Of all the soldiers on the departing train, it is doubtful if any of them viewed his return to France with more apprehension than Mary Miles viewed her return to No. 57 and to Ethel.

PART 4

Chapter 36

Harry, who was ordered by the RTO to stay the night in Dover, crossed over to Boulogne the following morning in the *Victoria*. He found feverish activity in the French port. Cranes were swinging their loads from ships, NCOs and stevedores were bawling orders, engines were firing: the very air hammered with noise and urgency.

The reasons became clearer that afternoon as his train chugged slowly into the department of the Somme. Gangs of men, many of them Chinese, could be seen building new roads. Spurs from the rail track ran to newly-erected water pumping stations and hospitals. Transport parks packed with lorries could be seen half hidden among trees. As the Front drew nearer, the sinister camouflaged dumps of high-explosive shells could be seen everywhere. All the complicated infrastructure for a modern army's offensive was being prepared. As spring laid its pure green lace over trees and fields and ponds sparkled in the sunlight, men sweated, wrestled, and ruptured themselves in their preparations to kill.

Harry, who had bought himself a bottle of wine before embarking on the train, found his thoughts growing more fanciful as the bottle emptied. The immensity of the preparation and its indifference to human suffering shrank the human psyche, he thought. I am a khaki-coloured ant whose task is to destroy grey-coloured ants before they can destroy me. But why do we fight at all? My enemy eats, drinks, loves, suffers: in all but race we could be brothers. And yet we fight one another with this terrifying ferocity.

He thought of Gareth's explanation: that men were manipulated to hate and fight one another by the machinations of financiers and industralists. It was a possibility that he, Harry, had once conceded. But now that he had experienced the terrible lust of battle himself he believed it too simple an explanation. Wars had existed long before the capitalist system had evolved. For men to kill one another with such dedication, the will had first to be present, however much it was encouraged and manipulated afterwards.

He conceded it was nearer the surface in some men than in others, as with Chadwick and himself. But that it existed in both of them he could no longer deny. In all men there was a Cain as well as an Abel. Beneath the surface a Hyde crouched, only waiting his chance to leap out and destroy all that Jekyll created. What was worse, the dark side of Man seemed far more vigorous and single-minded of purpose than the light. It was a thought that Harry found infinitely depressing and made him drink more deeply of the wine that had encouraged it.

Then, in the way of alcohol, his mood changed. Because of his religious beliefs, Gareth had always accused him of being a simple idealist. But in the choice between Gareth's explanation of war and his own emerging belief that the evil lay in the dark and flawed structure of the human psyche, was it not the Welshman's ideas that seemed naive and simple?

310

Thinking of Gareth's indignation at such a summing up, Harry laughed aloud, then glanced in embarrassment at the two French soldiers sharing the compartment with him. Seeing them wink and grin at one another, he was relieved when a few minutes later a jerk and a hiss of steam announced the train had reached the end of its journey. Laying the empty wine bottle with exaggerated care on the wooden seat, he picked up his kit and followed the Frenchmen from the coach.

Harry's Battalion was in the reserve line when he finally reached the Front. After reporting to the Guardroom he made his way to his section's dug-out. It was empty except for Gareth who was lying on his bunk smoking a cigarette. The Welshman could not hide his pleasure at seeing him. 'So you're back, boyo. How did it go?'

Harry slung his kit on to his bunk. 'Not too bad. Mary's taking it hard, though.' Before Gareth could comment, he went on: 'How have things been here? Any more raids?'

Gareth grimaced. 'One, but it was further down the sector. They used Storm Troops this time and captured a couple of our chaps.'

'So now they know who we are?' Harry said.

'I reckon they've always known, boyo, just like they know most things. I don't know why they bother to take prisoners.

Harry sank down on an ammunition box. 'They're probably nervous about this offensive everyone's talking about. Have you heard anything yet?'

'Not directly. But young White said he overheard Chadwick telling Wentworth we'll be going into special training soon. That must mean we'll be in it.'

Knowing it was probably true, Harry changed the

311

subject by motioning at the dug-out floor. 'At least it's dry at last.'

Gareth shifted on his bunk. 'So what? If you don't rot in water in the winter, you're sent out to be shot in the summer. You pay your money and take your pick.'

Harry's eyes were beginning to adjust from the bright sunlight outside. Glad Gareth's mordant humour had returned, he was about to respond when he noticed how pale and drawn the Welshman looked. 'What's the matter? Don't you feel well?'

Gareth drew on his cigarette. 'I feel lousy, boyo. It came on two days ago.'

'What came on?'

'I keep having to go to the latrines but I can't pee. Can't pee properly, I mean. And it hurts like hell too.'

Harry gave a start. 'What did you do last time we were in Montoise? Go to one of the brothels?'

Gareth looked both defiant and ashamed. 'What if I did? Half the company went to 'em.'

'I know that. But did you go to one of the approved ones? Those that are medically inspected?'

Gareth hid his expression with another cloud of cigarette smoke. 'I suppose so. But I can't remember. I was pissed at the time.'

'Then you'd better report sick right away. If it's syphilis, the longer you leave it the worse it'll get.'

This time Gareth's attempt at humour was a failure. 'What are you afraid of, boyo? That it might drop off?'

'Get over to the MO,' Harry told him. 'If you tell the duty sergeant what the trouble is, you won't have to wait until sick parade tomorrow.'

Gareth, who had picked up trench slang quicker than Harry, doused his cigarette and climbed painfully to his feet. 'You don't think they'll send me to an SIW hospital, do you?'

An SIW hospital was a place where men with self-inflicted wounds were sent and rumour had it that conditions there bordered on the sadistic. 'I wouldn't think so,' Harry muttered. 'But why weren't you more careful? Didn't you wear anything?'

'I can't remember, boyo. I told you – I was pissed.'

'But didn't the woman make sure. I thought they were all supposed to.'

Gareth's sudden outburst betrayed the state of his nerves. 'For Christ's sake, why do you keep on about it? Either I've got it or I haven't. Why does it matter how?'

'It matters like hell if you're put on a charge,' Harry pointed out.

Gareth's expression changed. 'I suppose you're right. Then I'd better say I wore something, hadn't I?' When Harry nodded, he moved reluctantly to the dug-out entrance. 'You don't think I'm drawing it to their attention more this way than by going sick in the morning?'

'You can't leave it,' Harry said. 'Not if you're as bad as you say. Go and get it over with.'

Gareth, looking disturbed and shaken, returned twenty minutes later. 'Well,' Harry demanded as the Welshman flopped down on his bunk. 'What happened?'

'It's the pox all right,' Gareth muttered 'The MO gave me a hell of a blistering and said he was reporting me for criminal negligence. He's sending me back for treatment tomorrow.'

'Did he say how long the treatment will take?'

Gareth grimaced. 'No. But he did say I might be sent to one of the SIW hospitals. It depends on what the CO decides.'

Later that afternoon Harry was ordered to report to

Chadwick. As he made his way along the labyrinth of trenches, the effect of the belated spring could be seen everywhere. With the hated mud dried out at last, with wellington boots, greatcoats and woollens no longer needed, men could be heard joking with one another and whistling as they went about their fatigues. The irony did not escape Harry. Summer could soon be producing a grimmer harvest than the wild flowers that were springing up in No Man's Land.

He found Chadwick, as spruce as ever, exchanging words with another subaltern. 'You wanted to see me, sir?'

'That's right, Miles. How did your leave go?'

'Quite well, thank you, sir.'

'Were you able to salvage anything from your home?'

'No, sir.'

'I'm sorry about that, Miles.' For once Chadwick sounded sincere. 'It was a piece of filthy luck coming on top of your father-in-law's death.'

With no answer to give, Harry made no reply. Chadwick eyed him a moment, then his tone changed. 'You don't seem to have had any better luck on your return. I take it you've heard about your Number One, Private Evans?'

'I know he's not well, sir.'

Chadwick gave a short laugh. 'That's one way of putting it. The MO puts it another. He believes Evans has deliberately contracted syphilis to get out of the firing line. Or perhaps to dodge this summer offensive.'

Harry gave a start. Then, certain Chadwick had seen it, he did his best to repair the damage. 'I don't believe that, sir. He told me he was drunk when he visited the brothel.'

'And you think that's an excuse, Miles?'

'It means he didn't catch syphilis on purpose. Isn't that

314

the point you're making, sir?'

Chadwick's tone convinced Harry his contempt for Gareth's behaviour was genuine. 'The point I'm making is that the man's a scrounger and a coward and he's not getting away with it. The CO has asked my views and I'm recommending he gets his treatment in a SIW hospital where they'll make sure he never tries anything like it again. They might also do something about those revolutionary ideas of his.'

Harry felt the effort was futile but that he had to try. 'I don't believe he did this deliberately, sir. But it is true that his nerves won't stand the noise of shellfire. I don't see how he can be blamed for that.'

Chadwick leaned forward. 'Are you admitting he's a coward?'

Harry was sweating now. 'No, sir. He's done everything he's been asked to do. In fact he's a good Number One. But shell fire does affect him badly.'

'And it doesn't affect the rest of us?'

'No, sir. At least not in the same way.'

Chadwick's expression was a mixture of contempt and respect. 'I'll say this for you, Miles, you're loyal to your friends. But you're wasting it on Evans. He's no different from anyone else except he's not man enough to stand up to his nerves, like the rest of us do. But that's something the SIW people will put right.'

Harry could think of only one other card to play. 'Is it such a good idea with the summer offensive coming, sir? After all, it means I'm losing my Number One.'

Chadwick smiled and shook his head. 'Wrong, Miles. It'll be some time yet before we go into action and if he's as good a Number One as you say, we'll make sure he's back in time. And if he tries any funny business after that, I'll put him straight in front of a court-martial.'

Chapter 37

April moved into May. Letters began arriving from Mary, in the way of the Army in batches of three and four. They were always cheerful and gave Harry no indication how Ethel was behaving. The only hint he got of Mary's state of mind came in her occasional reference to William. Then, try as she would, her loss could not be disguised.

During this time the Somme Front was quiet, so quiet that the British began to send out night patrols to prevent the Germans becoming too suspicious. However, with rumours growing daily along the entire twenty-mile sector, the very air was charged with expectancy and the waiting enemy could not fail to sense it.

In the middle of May the cat was finally let out of the bag: a training programme reached all Company Commanders. A massive British offensive was to be launched in high summer and men were to spend six hours of every day training for their role in it.

In practice, with even men in reserve having to spend most of their nights on fatigues, it was an impracticable order, and the only real training the rank and file got was when they were withdrawn for rest. Instead of going to their regular billets, they were sent to camps specially set up for this purpose.

The 16th was one of these Battalions. For convenience it was split up into sections – Harry (now without Gareth) finding himself in the same light machine gun section as Chadwick – and each unit was first given an overall exposition of the battle plan and then briefed on its own specific role.

The offensive was to commence on the 24th June. From the 1,500,000 shells that had been stockpiled, the British artillery would begin battle by a heavy bombardment along the entire Somme sector. The objects of this bombardment were four-fold: to smash the parapets of the enemy trenches so that the British infantry could pass through; to kill or bury the infantrymen; to knock out enemy machine gun and artillery positions; and to deny the enemy the use of his supply roads.

This crushing bombardment would last five days. Then, at Z hour, it would lift and move forward, allowing the British infantry to run up their scaling ladders and cross No Man's Land. Before the enemy trenches were reached, the guns would be pounding the next line of resistance. This creeping barrage, gunnery officers assured the infantrymen, would assure them of an unmolested passage because not only would the enemy front line troops be killed but their reserves would also be put out of action before they could counter attack.

Because the majority of the British Battalions were made up of 'new' soldiers, their role was being kept as simple as possible. Divisions were to attack on fronts of one mile apiece, with two brigades going forward and one remaining in reserve. Broken down for the 16th, this meant its four companies would advance in four waves, each man two or three yards apart, and with fifty to a hundred yards between each wave. As Harry had half-expected, the light-machine gun units, each under its own NCO, would be distributed along the first wave of

317

infantry. For this purpose he was promoted to corporal.

It was a battle plan that gave confidence to all the Battalions taking part, not least the 16th. Having experienced barrage fire themselves, few men believed the enemy and his trenches could survive such a torrent of shelling for five days and nights. As a consequence little notice was taken of the grizzled French artillery officer who put up a hand at the end of the briefing and gave a warning in poor English. While he drank to the success of his Allies' offensive which would ease the pressure on his countrymen at Verdun, it might not be wise for the British infantry to loiter on their way to the enemy trenches. The Boche always built very deep, shell-proof dug-outs and if any machine gunners and their equipment were not buried, it would then be a race to reach the trench top. If the British were the first they could throw grenades into the dug-outs and all would be well. But if the Boche gunners reached their firing steps first . . . the old soldier paused and made an eloquent gesture.

There was silence for only a moment. Then the confident chatter returned. The British Army, at that time composed mostly of volunteers, had magnificent morale and defeat was unthinkable. This was going to be the Push that drove Jerry right back to where he belonged. This was to be the beginning of the end.

Like the rest of the Battalions that were to take part in the offensive, the 16th did a couple of weeks' intensive training and then were put on light duties. Knowing it was the prelude to battle, men found these days either too long or too short according to their temperaments. Some, the aggressive or the highly-strung, found the hours dragged by interminably. Some, of gentler temperament, counted every hour a bonus and found a new beauty in the drifting white clouds, the summer butter-flies, and the poppies that grew so profusely on the chalk downlands. Others, Harry among them, spent much of the time making out their wills and writing letters. Until now Harry had been inhibited by the knowledge Chad-wick was one of the officers censuring his mail but he had at last managed to obtain a green envelope. Green enve-lopes went out uncensored if the writer signed a declar-ation on their cover that they contained no military information, and although Harry was not an expressive writer, the letter he sealed inside this one was not only to bring tears to Mary's eyes but the suspicion he was on the eve of battle.

During this time horses and tractors were hauling up guns the entire length of the British Front. Every variant and calibre was there: 18 pounders, 60 pounders, 4.7 and 6-inch long range guns, 4.5 to 15-inch howitzers, and each piece had its own shells and target. By dawn on the 24th June all were in position, loaded and ready. At six-thirty a.m. precisely, artillery officers dropped their arms and every gun along the front opened up.

To the British infantry manning the Front Line that day it looked as if giants were suddenly lifting and slam-ming down the manholes of hell. As far as the eye could see fountains of earth, rock, wire and sandbags were being hurled into the morning sky. The noise was a physical thing, battering at the ears and deadening the brain. As even heavier shells sounded through the awesome thunder men winced and pitied the poor wretches trapped in the trenches opposite.

The thunder reached back to the combat Battalions waiting tensely in their camps behind the lines, shudder-ing the summer air and driving birds from trees. It even reached back to far-off Hampstead Heath in London

319

where men and women, taking their dogs for an early morning walk, paused to stare at one another. Its ferocity made the most timid soldier wonder if his fears were founded. This was only the first day. Four more would follow before he was asked to follow the shells across No Man's Land. How could anything, from beetle to man, survive such a holocaust?

The onslaught continued the next day but with a difference. While on the previous day nine-tenth of the shells had been filled with shrapnel, on the 25th the heavier batteries increased their firing rate. With their high-explosive shells crashing into the German trenches, dug-outs collapsed or were buried as the sides of trenches fell in. Other shells caused masses of earth to slide into the deeper dug-outs, sometimes to bury their occupants alive. By evening, parts of the German trench system were beginning to have the crated aspect of the moon.

On the 26th the British tried a new variant. Using projectors and the prevailing wind, they sent chlorine gas over with their shells. The gas, being heavier than air, crept down into the deeper German dug-outs, often before sprayers could destroy it. In the afternoon heavy mortars, fired from the British Front trenches, were used for the first time. With their shells falling almost perpendicularly they did further damage to the shattered trenches. But the most feared guns of all to the Germans were the heavy howitzers. Although there were few of them – a mistake that was to have the profoundest consequences – their massive shells that could hurl tons of rock and chalk into the air and leave craters twelve feet deep, made the deepest dug-outs unsafe. Earthern walls rocked like the sides of a ship and the concussion not only extinguished candles and acetylene lamps but also ruptured and burst men's lungs.

320

With the infantry scheduled to go over the top on the 29th, battalions had a church service in the morning and then prepared to move forward. At noon a tantalising order told them to stand down: the bombardment was to continue for two more days. The effect on tightly-strung nerves was unfortunate. Men found it difficult to sleep and if they succeeded their dreams were full of forebodings.

On the 30th, after another church service, the attack battalions began again to move into the line and this time the order was not recinded. From villages and camps where they had been billeted, they marched first along the roads and then into the communication trenches that reached back a mile from the firing line. Already loaded with 200 rounds of ammunition and two days' rations, they were given extra loads of screw pickets, sandbags and shovels to fortify any new positions they might take, signal rockets for communication, and Mills bombs for their attack. Some men were even handed pigeon baskets, for with radio in its infancy and telephone lines ending at the firing trenches, once men moved out into No Man's Land their officers would be out of communication with Staff Headquarters. By the time they were near their chosen sectors, some men were carrying eighty pounds of equipment. To add to their difficulties they had to pass the flow of men they were relieving. Colliding with one another in the dark trenches, stumbling, falling, bruising themselves, men were rewarded by curses from NCOs or officers who feared the noise they were making would alert enemy listening posts. After the mayhem of the last six days, with their ears deafened by British guns still hammering at the pulverised German lines although it was now past midnight, men took such admonishments as a natural part of the mad world in which they now lived.

One of the more heavily-burdened men was Harry who, along with Mills bombs, a Very pistol and rations, had his Lewis gun to carry. During his training he had repeatedly asked for a replacement for Gareth, only for Chadwick to announce that Gareth was not going to escape doing his duty and he would be sent back in time for the battle. As this now seemed unlikely, the tight-lipped Chadwick had given him the likeable young Jack White to carry his ammunition pans. Chadwick had further announced that Harry would be going over the top with him, a prospect that filled Harry with dismay.

With the columns of men having to stop at intervals to pick up their various equipment or to give way in the narrow trenches to the outcoming battalions, the journey seemed endless and when they finally reached their jumping-off places, men were sweat-stained and bone weary. Dropping their loose burdens to the trench floor, some men slumped down beside them and slept as they were, still festooned by ammunition pouches and grenades.

With the need to protect the delicate separation pins of the Lewis drums, Harry led the young infantryman to his dug-out. Seeing a candle burning behind the sacking that covered the entrance, he jerked the sacking aside and saw Gareth stretched out on a bunk with a cigarette in his mouth. The Welshman lifted his head, recognised Harry, and sat up. His greeting had a shamefaced quality. 'Hello, boyo. How's tricks?'

With battle imminent Harry could not decide whether he felt glad or sorry to see him. 'How long have you been here?'

'I got back yesterday afternoon. They told me to stay here and wait for the Battalion.'

Harry turned to White, a weary, dusty young figure loaded down with Lewis drums. 'Put the pans down and

322

get some sleep, Jack. We'll find out what to do with you in the morning.'

Tired though he was, the youngster managed a cheeky grin. 'If nobody wants me, you couldn't work me a couple of weeks in Montoise, could you, Corp? There's a widow there who thinks I'm Douglas Fairbanks.'

Harry grinned. 'She wouldn't think so now. You look like Little Tich playing a dustman. Get some sleep, you randy young devil.'

The weary youngster barely had the strength to climb into a bunk where he fell asleep almost before his head reached the sack of straw serving as a pillow. Turning back to Gareth, Harry saw how pale and peaky he looked. 'Did they send you to a SIW hospital?'

Gareth winced at the memory. 'Not half they didn't. Christ, they're all sadists in there, Harry. Not just the MPs. The doctors as well. They made the treatment bloody murder. I'd rather be shot than go through that again.'

'Isn't that the idea?' Harry said.

Glancing up at White, Gareth saw the youngster was asleep. 'You knew all along it wasn't an accident, didn't you?'

Harry fumbled in his tunic for cigarettes. 'I did feel it was too much of a coincidence.' Offering the pack to Gareth, he noticed the Welshman was smoking and took one himself. As he struck a match, the sound of the night guns made the flame tremble.

Gareth sank back on his bunk. 'Don't blame me, Harry. It's the noise I can't take. It screws me up tight inside. I even felt it yesterday and it was only our own guns.' His face, still full of pain from his punishment, lifted off his pillow. 'Christ, Harry, those poor bastards over there. Have you thought what they must be going through?'

Harry was wondering how to break the news to him. He glanced up at the sleeping youngster. 'Jack was to be my Number One tomorrow but now you're back, Chadwick's sure to make the switch. You realise that, don't you?'

'You mean that I'll be going over the top with you? Yes. I know that. What time are we down for?'

'We start laying smoke from seven-fifteen onwards. We're in the first wave, so we go out at seven-twenty-four.'

'What about the rest of the section?'

'They're all in the first wave,' Harry told him.

'What about Chadwick? Where will he be?'

Harry took a deep breath. 'He'll be with us.'

There was a low gasp from Gareth. 'Us?'

'Yes. He says he likes my gunnery and wants to direct it. At least that's the reason he gives.' As Gareth dropped back on his pillow, Harry went on quickly: 'There shouldn't be any problems, kid. We've been shelling Jerry for six days now. They say all we'll have to do is walk over and take what we want.'

He waited for Gareth to reply but only heard the sound of the Welshman inhaling smoke. Knowing it had to be said but resenting the need, he unbuckled his webbing and allowed his equipment to slide to the floor before turning back to the silent Gareth. 'We'll have to be a bit careful tomorrow, though. I think Chadwick took that SIW affair personally. You know, a slur against him as well as his section.'

The bitterness of Gareth's sudden laugh jarred him. 'What is it, boyo? Are you scared I'll panic and run?'

'No. I'm just saying we'll have to watch ourselves. He's got his eyes on both of us and if we make one wrong move he'll slap us straight in front of a court martial. And you know what that could mean.'

Gareth lifted both arms, squinted at the ceiling, and pretended to pull a trigger. 'Bang-bang! Is that what you're telling me?'

Unsure of his mood, Harry could only hope his warning did not rebound the wrong way. 'There'll be no problems if we both do our job. That's all I'm saying.' Suddenly his weariness overtook him. 'I'll have to get some shut-eye, Gareth. Don't worry about tomorrow. Everything's going to be all right.'

Chapter 38

There was a light rain falling through a morning mist when the weary men of the 16th were awakened by their equally weary sergeants. With little battle experience behind them, most men were apprehensive although their spirits were raised when a breakfast of bacon and fried bread was served to them. The unheard-of treat was due to a staff order that wherever possible men should be given a hot breakfast. Although in the main it achieved its morale-building purpose, there were inevitably the pessimists who muttered darkly about the condemned man's last privilege.

They were in the minority however, particularly after the British guns opened up in earnest again along the entire front at 06.25. With the 16th not yet having seen the bombardment at close quarters, men were encouraged to watch while having their breakfast. The fearful spectacle brought the colour back to many a pale cheek, and jokes, if only mordant ones, to the lips of the pessimists. To British and French airmen, who for days had been patrolling the sector to keep enemy aircraft and balloons from spotting the British guns, it was like looking down at a steaming lake from which was bubbling a thousand geysers. Surely nothing could remain alive in such an inferno.

Breakfast over, men began their final preparations. While other ranks strapped and hung on to themselves their multifarious loads, officers were being spruced up by their servants. Believing it was going to be a day of celebration rather than trial, many had decided to wear their best uniforms with shiny belts, epaulettes, and canes of blackthorn or ash. Some, believing it was their duty to lead and set an example rather than fight, did not carry revolvers although it was noticeable Chadwick was not one of them.

During all this nervous hustle and bustle, the bombardment came to a cresendo, like a satanic orchestra announcing the entrance of the Demon King. Every calibre of shell, from the eighteen-pounders to the fifteen-inch howitzers whined and rumbled overhead, further pulverising the trenches opposite and uprooting entire trees in the countryside behind them. The noise, earsplitting and awesome, affected the young soldiers in contrasting ways. On the one hand its brutality emphasised the frailty of their flesh and blood. On the other it gave greater credence to the assurance their passage across No Man's Land would not be contested.

During this final bombardment, Colonel Wilson came round on his final tour of inspection, trying to make his appeals to duty and patriotism heard above the din and mayhem. Immediately afterwards every man was given a large tot of rum. Gareth, burdened like a Christmas tree with Lewis magazines, gulped his down as if it were water. Harry, acutely aware how heavy shell-fire affected him, passed over his own tot. 'Go on, take it. The stuff doesn't agree with me.'

Gareth's attempt to grin was a brave one. 'What's the matter, boyo? Do you think I need it?'

'We all need it,' Harry said shortly. 'But the stuff gives me indigestion. Take it or I'll give it to someone else.'

It took Gareth both hands to hold the mug and lift it to his lips. Thanking Harry with his eyes, he leaned against the side of the trench. A few seconds later Chadwick approached the two men. In his impeccable uniform, with his handsome face radiating excitement and confidence, he looked every inch the young subaltern of romantic fiction. To his credit he did not add to Gareth's apprehension by making mention of his recent conduct although Harry noticed he avoided glancing at him. His shout came through the thunder of shells.

'As you know, Miles, we're in the first wave. We're not expecting much resistance but at the first sight of any, our job is to give covering fire. Don't wander off on your own: stick close alongside me. Don't waste your ammunition: remember we're not likely to get any more for a few hours. I think that's all for the moment. I'm off to see the other chaps now but I'll be back before the ref blows his whistle.'

Both men turned and watched his erect confident figure move on down the trench, pausing here and there to pass a word of encouragement to the burdened infantry. Gareth tried to spit, only to find his mouth was too dry. 'You hear that? The ref blows his whistle! It's a bloody game to him. They're all the same, those fox hunting bastards. It's a lovely day – let's go out and kill something.'

Always prone to introspection in moments of high drama, Harry felt sympathy for the Welshman's comment. At the same time he knew that he admired Chadwick's sang-froid. The man might have a strong element of spite in him but lack of courage was not one of his failings. He did not follow the popular myth that vindictiveness and cowardice went hand in hand. Indeed when those two characteristics were bonded together and set against his country's enemies, they perhaps

328

made him the ideal soldier, Harry thought.

The realisation how much he admired Chadwick's courage changed his mood. A man admires the characteristics he desires or shares. Then wasn't his admiration of Chadwick's *élan* further proof that they both possessed the same aggressive instincts?

Five minutes later Chadwick was at their side again. As he shouted something and pushed them towards a scaling ladder, a green Very light arched into the sky from the nearest traverse. It was followed by two more and then the urgent shrilling of whistles. As Harry, clinging to the Lewis gun, struggled up the ladder, he saw the mist had lifted and the sky was a perfect eggshell blue. A moment later he was standing erect in No Man's Land with a line of men springing into view on either side of him. The infantrymen's battle of the Somme had begun.

The 16th, like the rest of the battalions in the British 4th and 5th Armies, found its companies could not advance in regular lines. Although keen enough to reach their objectives, men burdened down by screw pickets and coils of barbed-wire could not run as fast as their more fortunate comrades. Moreover everyone had different obstacles to face. Some ran into shell-torn barbed-wire that snagged their puttees and entangled their feet. Others stumbled over chunks of masonry or had to surmount shell holes.

However at first there appeared no urgency. Although the barrage had now lifted and was pounding the enemy's rear positions, lyddite fumes and smoke shells were making a shifting grey wall ahead from which no counter fire was emerging. Platoon officers and their men began to relax in the belief that for once the Brass

Hats had got it right and enemy resistance had been shattered.

Had they only known the truth they would have strained nerves and muscles to snapping point to reach the German firing trenches. For the old French officer had been right. The Germans had very deep, reinforced dug-outs and the British had not used anything like enough heavy howitzers. As a result, although the enemy frontal defences no longer existed in their original form, the majority of their defenders were still alive. For a full week, living on iron rations, unshaven, stinking, and in constant peril of being entombed, the tough German infantry and its machine gunners had waited for the hellish din to cease, knowing that their lives and the battle itself depended on which side reached the entrance of their dug-outs first. The second the barrage had lifted and moved on, NCOs had dragged weary men to their feet, thrust their weapons into their hands, and sent them stumbling up to the surface.

They had not recognised the trenches they had left. All was rubble and devastation, a line of shell craters instead of a frontal defence. But shell craters can make an effective barricade when manned by desperate men and it was on the lips of these and on the remnants of their trenches that the Germans set up their machine guns.

They did not wait for the smoke to clear so they could sight the British attack. Knowing it was on its way, they set their Maxims to give enfilading fire. Still sobbing for breath from their exertions, gunners opened fire and a hail of lead ripped through the drifting smoke.

The effect was the more deadly because it came as a complete surprise, a surprise that was felt the entire length of the British front. In some cases the German defenders were in action before the British infantry left their trenches, as in the case of the Queen Victoria's Rifles although the riflemen still climbed out and faced the fire. Elsewhere, as in the case of the 10th West Yorks, the first wave actually won the race to the German trenches but believing it unmanned swept on to their next objective, a fatal error because when the enemy emerged they were able to turn their guns on the backs of the Yorkshiremen and annihilate them.

However it was the 16th's experience, caught halfway across No Man's Land, that was the most common. At one moment an unhurried line of burdened men were picking their way towards the drifting smoke. In the next they were collapsing as if being cut down by an invisible scythe. Quick to recognise the danger, Chadwick pushed Harry and Gareth into a deep shell crater. 'Covering fire!' he yelled into Harry's ear. 'Quickly!'

With all three men trembling from exertion and shock, it took longer than usual to prepare the Lewis gun and set it on its bipod. Helped by Chadwick, Harry clambered up the steep side of the crater and set the gun on its lip. Then, responding to the officer's urgent shout, he estimated the distance to the German defences and opened fire. As he hosed the bullets from left to right and the Lewis magazine jerked round on its spigot, he had the futile feeling of a man trying to stem a hurricane.

Gareth, a fresh magazine in his hand, was crouched beside him with his helmeted head below the lip of the crater. At first the Welshman had been too dazed by events to know what was happening, but now he saw the trap they were in. Not only were bullets clipping the long grass round the crater but the smoke protection before them was beginning to thin out as the British mortars ran out of smoke shells. In addition German artillery that had either escaped the British bombardment or been brought up during the night was now laying a counter barrage in a line that roughly bisected No Man's Land and put a barrier between A Company and B Company which had already left its firing trench. With the leading wave pinned down, its survivors had little hope of rescue unless the subsequent waves could break through and silence the murderous machine guns.

The Lewis gun ceased firing as its magazine ran out. Yanking the pan off, Harry grabbed a second one from Gareth. As Gareth fumbled to unhook a third one from his harness, it slipped from his hands and fell to the bottom of the steep crater where a shapeless black object lay half buried in a pool of dried mud.

An angry yell from Chadwick started Gareth edging after the magazine. Halfway down the slope his feet slipped and his heavy burden gave him no chance to recover. Half-sliding, half-falling, he landed almost on top of the mysterious object at the base of the crater. A moment later a cry, loud enough to be heard over the shell fire, made both Chadwick and Harry turn.

They saw Gareth on his knees, his head and upper body half hidden by a venomous cloud of bluebottles. Before him, relieved of its predators, the misshapen thing was revealed in its true colour and identity. Putrescent white, it was a naked, headless torso.

Brushing frantically at his face, Gareth stumbled to his feet. He gave the two men a wild glance, then began clawing his way up the opposite side of the crater. Seeing his intention, Chadwick let out a shout and slid down the crater after him. 'Evans! Get back to your post!'

Demented by horror, it is doubtful if Gareth heard him. As Chadwick shouted again and then began to unholster his revolver, Harry left the Lewis and slid down the crater side. 'No! Let me talk to him!'

Ignoring him, Chadwick drew out his revolver. 'Evans! This is your last chance. Get back to your post!'

332

Almost at the crater's rim, Gareth was scrabbling at the dusty soil to climb over it. As Chadwick lifted the revolver and took careful aim, Harry threw himself forward, hitting the subaltern with his shoulder. The impact sent the revolver flying and knocked Chadwick within two feet of the putrescent remains on which the bluebottles were settling again. As the officer rose to his feet, Gareth heaved himself over the crater edge and disappeared.

The revolver was lying beside a twisted piece of angle iron. Picking it up, Chadwick turned and aimed it at Harry, who was near enough to hear his words. 'I'm entitled to kill you for that, Miles. I hope you realise it.'

Harry stared into the dark muzzle of the Webley. As its hammer rose and the cylinder turned, he believed himself as good as dead. Time stood still for a moment, then Chadwick shook his head and pushed the revolver back into its holster. 'No. That's playing into Jerry's hands. I'll take care of you both later. Evans won't get far. If Jerry doesn't get him the Battle Police will.'

Harry knew he was right. The hated Battle Police, who were always positioned behind an infantry attack to turn back, arrest, or even shoot deserters, had been evident everywhere the previous day and in Gareth's state it seemed unlikely he would escape them.

Chadwick gripped his arm. 'Come on! Get back to that gun. We need all the firepower we can get.'

Although the smoke ahead of the shell crater had almost dispersed when they returned to the Lewis gun, the enemy counter barrage was making a backdrop of grey and yellow smoke behind it against which the advancing British infantry were silhouetted. All four waves appeared to be in action now but were hopelessly intermingled as the murderous machine gun fire smashed into the van and drove men into shellholes for protection. Here and there subalterns and NCOs could be seen leaping to their feet and urging their sections on, only to stagger and fall to the smoking ground. Wounded men, trying to crawl to safety, were hit again, to jerk spasmodically, then lie still. Half-demented by their seven-day ordeal, enemy gunners were firing at everything that moved.

Yet along the entire length of the British Front, men still drove themselves towards the enemy lines. The spirit of Kitchener's New Army was as magnificent as its battle plan had been defective. The flower of British manhood was being slaughtered in France that day.

Chadwick, risking death every time he lifted his head, was anxiously searching for the other gunners in his section and at one time was contemplating going out to look for them until Harry checked him. 'They'll either be in action or they'll be dead. In any case you'd never live to reach them.'

Fifty yards ahead enemy helmets kept appearing as infantrymen and gunners poured fire at the still advancing 16th. To their left, an enemy barbed-wire parapet had survived and half a dozen British soldiers were crawling along its base trying to find a way through. Although they were protected by the parapet from the enemy behind it, a flanking Maxim gun was raking the ground ahead of them and halting their progress. Nodding as Chadwick pointed a finger, Harry took sight of the Maxim post and the next time two helmets appeared he fired a long four second burst. As both helmets dropped from sight, Chadwick let out an exultant yell. 'I think you got them. Well done!'

A second later both he and Harry had to duck down as bullets raked the crater rim. Another enemy machine gunner, a hundred yards down the line, had spotted them. Realising the danger, Harry reached up to grab the Lewis but with an eerie scream of bullets it was snatched from his hands and hurled away. As it slid down the crater, Chadwick went down after it, to find its barrel and aluminium cooler twisted and bent. Throwing it down, he turned to Harry. 'We can't lie in here doing nothing. Let's try to get rifles from our casualties.'

Although every instinct told him it was suicide, Harry could only nod and follow him back up the crater. As Chadwick lifted himself to dive over it, the Maxim opened up again and a bullet caught the side of his helmet. Half-stunned, he would have fallen into the crater had Harry not grabbed him. 'It's useless,' Harry shouted. 'They know we're in here and they're waiting for us to crawl out. We'll have to wait a while, perhaps until it's dark.'

With his head still singing from the near miss and blood running down one cheek, Chadwick knew he was right. Fishing into his pocket, he pulled out a pack of cigarettes and took one. Hesitating, he then offered one to Harry. He nodded at Harry's water bottle as he flicked on a gold lighter. 'I hope that's full. You'll be needing it soon.'

For the first time that morning, Harry realised he was wet with sweat. The sun was now high in the cloudless sky and the drifting smoke and dust was trapping in the heat. By mutual accord the two men lay just beneath the crater rim, taking it in turns to give a quick glance over it to ensure the Germans were not making a counter attack. The response of the Maxim, lashing up powdered earth within an instant of them appearing, made it clear that any attempt to leave the shell hole would be fatal.

The scene around them was pure chaos. In an attempt to silence the deadly Maxims, the British artillery had begun trying to knock them out even at the risk of killing its own infantry. As a consequence shells were now bursting both in front of and behind the crater with the ever-present danger one would land inside it. The ground shook and the bright sky kept darkening as smoke drifted over it.

Half an hour passed and still men ran, crept or crawled towards the murderous guns. Both Chadwick and Harry turned as a British soldier appeared at the far side of the crafter. As he was about to leap into it for cover, a burst of Maxim fire sliced open his belly like a butcher's knife and hurled him back. With nails and boots scrabbling, he made for the crater again but just as Harry and Chadwick reached out and tried to help him down, his eyes rolled and his head went slack. 'His rifle,' Chadwick panted. 'Can you reach it?'

The rifle was only three yards from the crater but with the Maxim gunner waiting his chance it might as well have been a hundred. Crawling back to their forward positions, the two men sank down again. As a particularly noxious cloud of smoke entered the crater and started Chadwick coughing, Harry handed him his water bottle, 'It's tea,' he told him. 'With plenty of sugar in it.'

Nodding his thanks, Chadwick took a long drink before handing the canteen back. There is a bond growing between us, Harry thought. Not a lessening of dislike: that is an item outside the present terms of reference. But in this moment of danger we each need the other and Maxim bullets care little about rank and class.

The sun climbed higher. The bluebottles and flies, discovering they had other captive prey in the crater, began to plague the faces of the sweating men. As one crawled along Harry's lips he remembered where it had come from and gave a cry of revulsion. Ignoring Chadwick's curious glance, he dragged rag from his tunic

336

pocket, wet it with tea, and rubbed his mouth with it until he saw blood on the cloth.

Noon came and went and although the shell fire lessened, the crack of rifle fire, the hammering of machine guns, and the explosion of grenades and mortars were as fierce as ever. When the trapped men risked a glance over the crater, it was no longer Maxim fire that met them but a single rifle shot. It brought them no comfort: indeed they knew it increased their danger. The Maxim gunner had to share his attention among many targets; the sniper called in to take his place had only one and he would concentrate on it with the single-mindedness of the specialist.

The heat grew as the afternoon wore on. In the lulls between the firing, wounded men could be heard crying for water or their mothers. Listening to their agony, thinking about the men at the parapet with no hope of rescue, Harry found his thoughts becoming feverish. Men burned alive, blinded, mutilated beyond recognition, the very ground heaving in protest: surely this must be hell. And if it was, when had he entered it? Had he died when crossing No Man's Land, a death so instantaneous that his spirit had not noticed the severance? Or had hell always existed and Mary and Elizabeth were the fantasies men create to hold on to their sanity?'

He discovered he was not alone in his thoughts a moment later. Reaching for his canteen he found it empty. As Chadwick tapped his arm and offered his own, Harry saw his lips moving. Leaning forward he caught the subaltern's words. 'Tell me something, Miles. How is your faith holding up to all this?'

Harry stiffened. 'I don't know that you mean.'

Chadwick, whose handsome face was soiled by dust and lyddite fumes, waved a hand that embraced the

337

battlefield. 'All this mayhem and slaughter. How does it match up with your belief in a merciful God?'

For the moment Harry could not decide whether the question was mocking or serious. 'It's men who're killing one another, not God.'

'Of course it's men. But men aren't the only ones, are they? Everything on earth kills something else. Animals, insects, fish, even vegetation. The whole earth's a killing ground. And who's supposed to have made the earth, Miles?'

Gazing into the subaltern's soiled face, Harry saw only the scorn and not the hint of desperation. 'We've got the power of choice. We don't have to kill unless we choose to.'

Chadwick's laugh was derisive. 'Your kind like to think you're different, don't you? But you're not, Miles. You're a part of the world like the rest of us and you kill just as readily when the time comes. This war's proving that. It's only circumstances that makes men seem different.'

The dryness in Harry's mouth suddenly seemed to extend right down his throat and prevented him replying. A moment later a shell dropped only a few yards from the crater and showered them with earth. By the time Harry had taken a drink from the canteen and returned it, Chadwick's mood had changed. 'Stick it out, Miles. It won't be long now before it's dark.'

Sunset came two hours later behind the British lines. Golden rays reached upwards and turned a flocculus of cloud into smouldering embers. Arrowheads of birds winging home could be seen silhouetted against them. Here and there Germans as well as Britons watched the spectacle. Some saw it as a vision, a promise of salvation. Others saw it as a mockery and reviled it. Only ugliness makes hell bearable. Unattainable beauty merely adds to its torments.

The embers began to fade and the dusk deepened. Chadwick waited a further ten minutes, then nudged Harry's arm. Crossing the crater, they paused to compose themselves. Then, whispering for Harry to wait, Chadwick levered himself over the rim. When no bullet came, he motioned Harry to follow him and the two men began wriggling towards the British trenches.

In distance the journey was no more than a hundred yards and yet every obstacle modern war can provide seemed to litter their path: shell holes still hot and reeking, bodies chilled in death, coils of vicious wire, pieces of bricks and stone, wounded men crying for stretcher bearers and every few seconds the nervous star shells that made them flatten into the ground.

Nor was their danger over when they neared the British lines. After their massive casualties that day, the survivors of the 16th were on stand-by for a counter attack and firing at anything that aroused their suspicions. The first time Chadwick called the password, half a dozen shots were aimed in his direction. Lying flat, both men tried again and this time to their relief an authoritative voice told them to advance and identify themselves.

Feeling safe at last they rose to their feet and moved along the parapet to find a way through. Finding a gap, Chadwick turned to call Harry and at that moment a star shell burst above them, followed almost immediately by a burst of machine gun fire. Leaping down to the firing step, Chadwick shouted for Harry to drop flat and wait. Instead, with safety so near at hand, Harry ran towards the parapet and was only a few yards from it when there was a sound like a stick hitting a bag of wet sand. At the same time his left leg gave way and he fell forward into a truss of barbed-wire.

He lay half-stunned for a moment, then struggled to

339

free himself. A moment later he felt hands aiding him and heard Chadwick's voice. 'Take it easy, old chap. Where are you hit?'

'In the leg,' he muttered. 'I don't think I can stand.'

'You don't need to. Here we go.'

He felt himself being lifted bodily and a few seconds later being lowered down to men waiting on the firestep. From there he was passed down to the duckboards on the trench floor. As someone brought a shielded lamp, he heard Chadwick's voice. 'How bad is it?'

A homely Northern voice answered him. 'It's 'ard to say at the moment, sir. But he's bleeding bad.'

'All right. Get him off to the Regimental Aid Post immediately.' Dim in the starlight, Chadwick's face appeared in Harry's vision. 'You'll be all right, old chap. I'll come and see you as soon as I can.'

Harry tried to speak but the effort was too much. Chadwick's face seemed to grow huge, then to shrink into a pinpoint. A moment later the sky began to fall and bury him in darkness.

Chapter 39

So ended the first day of the Battle of the Somme. It had not been a complete failure. The 7th and 18th Divisions had taken some of their objectives, the 30th had taken all, while certain battalions of the 21st and 34th had secured the enemy trenches opposite their own. The French on the British right flank, more experienced and better trained and with much heavier artillery had taken all their first day objectives and might have gone on to take more had the overall plan been flexible enough to allow for such success.

Nevertheless the gains were pathetic when the casualties were taken into account. While the estimated German losses that first day numbered around 6,000, the British losses were nearly 60,000 of which 21,000 killed, and most of these losses had occurred within the first half hour of the attack. The plan had been badly flawed. The British troops had been poorly trained and their artillery, although numerous enough, had contained far too many nineteen-pounders and far too few of the heavy guns and howitzers that alone carried the explosive power to destroy the deep enemy dug-outs. Fearful of the effect on public opinion, the authorities re-routed train schedules so that the dozens of hospital trains making their way back to England arrived at their destinations at the dead of night. Even so, when the newspaper came out with their seemingly endless columns of casualties, an entire nation drew in its breath and went into mourning.

The one sustaining factor was the courage Kitchener's New Army had shown, although cruelly that courage had done it great harm. Had the second, third and fourth waves of men not gone forward against defences that were still resolutely manned, a half to three-quarters of the casualties might have been avoided. The question both civilians and politicians began to ask was why commanders had allowed such gallantry to immolate itself against the murderous guns.

The nation's sorrow was not lessened by the way Kitchener's Army had been structured. The well-meant but psychologically-flawed idea of appealing to friends and men of similar tastes and professions to enrol together in 'Pals' Battalions' had not only brought greater pain to men on the battlefield but now left great gaps in British society. The trauma of the Somme can be seen in a thousand war memorials in a thousand British villages to this day.

The 1st July was not the end of the battle. Like a disease flaring up and then remissing, it was to continue right through the summer and autumn, although by that time it was to become more of a battle of attrition than an offensive. In all, over 419,000 British soldiers were to become casualties on the Somme with nearly 200,000 of the French who fought alongside them.

Nor did their enemy fare much better. With no more exposed frontal attacks to mow down, with the British infantry learning its trade the hard way, the Germans found their losses mounting steadily. Although estimates vary according to different viewpoints, it is generally accepted that by the 18th November, when the battle on that sector was officially terminated, the casualties on both sides were around the 600,000 mark. Perhaps it was the Germans who coined the most appropriate name for the Battle of the Somme. They called it the Bath of Blood.

Long before November was reached, however, many of the battalions who sallied forth so bravely on the 1st July were replaced. Some, like the 16th East Yorks who had been so badly mauled that only a third of their number survived, were withdrawn from the line that same night. Exhausted, with some men in shock from the horrors they had witnessed, they were taken to rest centres to recuperate and await replacements.

Harry was also in transit that night. From the Regimental Aid Post where he received emergency treatment, he was sent to a Casualty Clearing Station where doctors sorted out the hopefuls from the hopeless. The latter were laid aside to die. Harry was passed on and taken by an ambulance train to a French hospital based in a large chateau. With the majority of British casualties shipped back to England, he was both puzzled and disappointed by the move and it was twelve days before he discovered the reason. An English nurse – the hospital was staffed by British medical personnel – approached his bedside and told him he had a visitor. Rising on his pillow and gazing down the long ward, Harry saw a British officer talking to the ward sister in the corridor outside. A minute later the man turned and approached him.

He was a tall, slender officer in his middle twenties, with fair hair and a wan and sensitive face. He walked with a pronounced limp and although he was clearly doing his best to hide it, Harry, who had become more

343

aware of leg injuries over the last fortnight, felt certain it was causing him discomfort if not downright pain. He gave Harry a smile as he reached his bedside. 'At ease, Corporal. You're still a casualty.' He pointed with his cane at a low stool beside the bed. 'Mind if I sit down?'

Unused to such civility, Harry found his curiosity growing.

'No, sir. Of course not.'

The young officer drew up the stool, sank down on it, and extended his lame leg with a sigh of relief. 'That's better. The damn thing's twinging today. It usually means the weather's changing.' He had a well-educated, pleasant voice.

'Where did you get it, sir?' Harry asked.

'At Loos. Six months ago. I'm afraid it's as good as it's ever going to be.' The officer's tone changed. 'My name's Shepherd, Corporal. I've been given the job of defending Private Evans at his court-martial.'

Harry's heart missed a beat. 'They've caught him, have they, sir?'

'Didn't you know?' When Harry shook his head: 'Yes, they caught him somewhere near Albert and I'm afraid they intend making an example of him.'

Harry winced. 'An example?'

'I'm afraid so. I understand he's a friend of yours, Corporal?'

'Yes, sir. I've known him since we were children.' Before Shepherd could comment, Harry went on: 'He shouldn't be punished, sir. His nerves just wouldn't stand up to it. A man can't be blamed for that.'

With an effort the officer rose, gave Harry a cigarette and a light, then sank back thankfully on the stool. He lit a cigarette for himself before replying. 'Between the two of us, I agree with you. Unfortunately his SIW record isn't helping him.'

344

When Harry did not answer, Shepherd frowned. 'It's particularly unfortunate because your CO didn't want to take it this far. Few battalion commanders do: it reflects on their regiment. But your section leader wouldn't withdraw his recommendation and so it had to be sent to Brigade HQ. And they won't be budged.'

Chadwick, Harry thought. Keeping his promise. He wondered if he would be the next once his wound healed. 'Has the CO appealed to Brigade, sir.'

'As a matter of fact, I think he has. But the Brigadier won't move an inch. So it's left to small fry like me to try to help him.'

It is doubtful if Wilson himself knew the reason for Ashton's adamancy. Frustrated by the failure of the 16th to gain an inch of ground, Ashton had convinced himself that the Battalion's truculent behaviour on entering the line had alerted the Saxons into deepening and strengthening their dug-outs. It was a false supposition: the dug-outs that had resisted the week-long bombardment had been constructed months earlier, but Ashton had made up his mind and in court martialling Gareth for cowardice he had seen a way of punishing the entire Battalion.

'So what happens now, sir?' Harry asked.

Shepherd frowned again. 'Frankly, it doesn't look good, Corporal. I can't go into court denying Evans ran in the face of the enemy; both you and Lieutenant Chadwick witnessed it. And of course the Battle Police will be giving evidence he was trying to escape when they captured him. My only hope is to plead a mental breakdown or something of that nature.'

'They aren't expecting me to witness against him, are they?'

Shepherd looked almost apologetic. 'I'm afraid they are, Corporal. That's why you weren't sent back to

345

England to recuperate. As you were the only other man to see him run away, you're a key witness for the Prosecution.'

Harry could feel sweat running down his back. 'How can I do that? I'm his friend.'

'I appreciate that. But human relationships don't count for much in war, do they?'

Harry was trying to understand. 'Then why are you here, sir? I thought you wanted me as a witness for his defence.'

Shepherd nodded, then changed the subject. 'How is your leg, Corporal?'

Harry started at him in surprise. 'It's not too bad. The bone wasn't broken, only chipped. They say I could be discharged in two or three weeks. I'm fit enough to witness for Evans, if that's what you mean,' he went on eagerly.

'That's not what I mean, Corporal. Are you exercising the leg?'

'Yes, I have to walk on it every day. Only a few yards but it's getting stronger. Let me witness for Evans, sir. I know how he suffered under shell fire.' Feeling he could trust the young officer, he went on: 'And let's face it, sir. No man deliberately catches syphilis unless he's desperate.'

Shepherd signed. 'I agree, but will they? I have thought of using you as a defence witness, Corporal. But the snag there is when you're cross-examined by the Prosecution you'll have to admit you saw Evans run away. On balance that almost certainly means you'd be more of a liability to him than an asset.'

'But won't the circumstances be taken into account? Hasn't Evans told you about the corpse and the bluebottles in the shellhole?'

Shepherd gave his war-weary smile. 'I'm afraid little

details like that don't count for much with Staff Officers, Miles. They expect us all to act like men, as they like to put it.'

Harry was growing more and more puzzled where the interview was taking them. 'But if I'm a key witness for the Prosecution, they're going to force me to give evidence, aren't they?'

Shepherd glanced round to see if any of the men in the nearby beds were listening. Satisfied they were not, he turned and lowered his voice. 'As you'll have gathered I don't like this affair any more than you. I've been in action myself and I know how shellfire can affect some men. Often very decent men whose nerves just can't stand it. So although officially I'm here to subpoena you as a defence witness, on the quiet I'm going to play it differently. The next time you exercise that leg I want you to fall down and say it hurts like hell.'

Harry was beginning to understand. 'But what happens when the Prosecution want to subpoena me?'

'Thats where your play acting comes in. They can't force you to leave hospital any more than I can without the Medical Superintendent's permission.' As Harry started to speak, Shepherd held up a hand. 'I know what you're going to say but wait. This is the hospital I was brought to and in four months here I got to know old Colonel Whitehead pretty well: in fact we used to play chess together. If you play your part I think I can talk him into declaring you unfit to attend the court-martial. After all it's only a week away.'

'But won't the Prosecution make me sign a statement or something like that?'

'Again that might depend on the MO's permission. Personally I think it's unlikely. If the other side got away with it, I could in turn get a statement from you about Evans' mental state and we could make it much more convincing on paper than you could make it in court when you're being bullied and told to shut up every few seconds by the Prosecution officer.'

Harry's first reaction was relief. 'Then you don't think I'll be involved and do him any harm?'

'I'm reasonably optimistic. Mind you, you'll almost certainly have a visit by the Prosecution. But if you play the wounded soldier well enough and give the MO the ammunition he needs, I think we can pull it off. Whitehead's a humane old boy and hates this punishment of frightened men as much as I do.' Wincing, the young officer rose from his stool and smiled down wryly at Harry. 'Only keep all this to yourself, for Christ's sake, or you'll have *me* in front of a court-martial.'

Harry nodded. 'Of course, sir. I appreciate all you're doing.' He paused, finding himself almost afraid to ask his question. 'What about Evans? Do you think they'll find him guilty?'

The young officer's smile faded. 'I can't anticipate the verdict, Corporal. Unfortunately on their terms he did show cowardice in the face of the enemy. But a court can reduce a sentence on the grounds of clemency and that's what I shall be trying for.'

'But what if they don't show clemency, sir?'

Shepherd opened his mouth to answer, then changed his mind. 'Let's just wait and see, Corporal. You can rely on me to let you know as soon as a verdict is reached.'

Chapter 40

Chadwick visited the hospital the following day. Impeccably dressed as usual with his Sam Browne belt, expensive tan riding boots and blackthorn cane, he drew the eyes of every nurse in the ward as he approached Harry's bed. He laid the small valise he was carrying on the nearby stool. 'Hello, Miles. How are you getting along?'

Conscious of his role, Harry played it with care. 'Not too bad, thank you, sir.'

'One of the nurses tells me you've already been up and about. Is that right?'

'Not really. I've tried a few steps but the leg keeps on buckling.'

'Does it? But the bone wasn't broken, was it?'

Realising Chadwick had been doing his homework, Harry decided ignorance was his best policy. 'I don't know what's wrong with it. It just doesn't seem to have any strength.'

Chadwick smiled. 'You don't want to be a witness at Evans' court-martial, do you?'

With the issue out in the open, Harry could see no harm in a blunt answer. 'No, sir, I don't.'

'Not even after the cowardly brute ran away and left

you stranded? You, his friend.'

'I'd have run myself if I'd fallen on top of that thing in the shell hole,' Harry said.

'No, you wouldn't. You're made of different stuff to Evans. I was right about him. He's a craven coward and never had any intention of fighting for his country.'

Harry shook his head. 'That's not true. He just didn't know what he was letting himself in for.'

'That's no excuse. You're facing up to it and so are the rest of the men.'

'Then why do you need to punish him? Hasn't he been punished enough already?'

'You're missing the point, Miles. One rotting apple in a barrel can affect the rest. That's why we have to make examples of his kind.'

'And that's your only reason?'

Chadwick frowned. 'Yes. What other reason could there be?'

To his surprise, Harry believed him. 'You people don't know much about rank-and-file soldiers, do you?'

Chadwick lifted an eyebrow. 'And you do, Corporal?'

'Yes. I'm one of them. You don't impress us when you shoot frightened men. You just disgust us and make us wonder what we're fighting for.'

Chadwick shrugged his beautifully-cut shoulders. 'Unfortunately our job isn't to be liked, Miles. It's to keep our men fighting until we win the war.'

'Even if they start disliking you more than the enemy?'

Chadwick shrugged again. 'By any means we have to. The end justifies the means. Don't blame me, Miles. These orders come from the top.'

Harry no longer cared what he said. 'No one from the top was in that shell hole to see Evans run away. Nor did it make a scrap of difference to us or to the offensive. But you still reported him and insisted he should be court-martialled.'

'Yes. That's all true. It was my duty as an officer. A duty I believe in, I should add.'

'I'm sure about that,' Harry said. 'I'm really sure about that.'

Chadwick studied him, then looked amused. 'From all this I gather you're not going to volunteer as a witness for the Prosecution.' At Harry's look, he smiled again. 'It doesn't matter. We'll simply subpoena you. You know what that means?'

'I know,' Harry said.

'Good. Then that's all settled. But before I go I want to say I thought you behaved very well that day. For that reason I've decided to forget what else happened.'

'Why do that?' Harry said. 'Why not kill two birds with one stone?'

Chadwick's laugh brought adoring glances from the nurses in the ward. 'You know, Miles, when you're not defending the indefensible, you're a very good soldier.' Picking up the valise, he opened it and slipped something beneath the bedclothes. 'I don't know if you're allowed this, so it might be an idea to keep it out of sight.' His voice rose. 'Cheerio, then, Miles. I'll look forward to seeing you sometime before the twenty-fifth.'

With a last nod at Harry, he turned and strode down the ward smiling at nurses and patients alike. When he disappeared, Harry felt beneath the bedclothes and pulled a bottle of five star cognac.

With Chadwick showing such confidence that he could force Harry to attend the court-martial, Harry found the week that followed a great strain, particularly as Shepherd's plan condemned him to bed. The only thing that helped take his mind off his fears were the half-dozen letters that arrived from Mary. Knowing how frantic she would be when news of the Somme disaster reached her, he had sent her a field postcard at his first opportunity and her letters were in answer to it.

In his weakened condition her letters moved him, on the one hand thanking God for his survival, on the other full of fear that he had minimised the seriousness of his wound and begging him for reassurance. With such concern for his health, she had little space for other news but he learned with relief that the Zeppelin raids had ceased and she and Elizabeth were well. Of her relations with Ethel she hardly spoke but it was not difficult for him to read between the lines and know that her life at home without William's moderating hand was anything but happy.

With the opportunity now to answer her letters in full, he wrote to her every day, although it was difficult to sound cheerful when he expected the subpoena to arrive at any time. It was not until the dawn of the 25th that he realised Shepherd's plan had worked.

It turned out to be a bright, warm July day. Harry, ignorant of the time the court-martial was convened, kept seeing in his mind's eye a pale-faced Gareth, flanked by MPs, facing his tribunal of class-conscious Staff Officers. With each man possessing a record of Gareth's SIW offence and his political leanings, with other tribunals having found men guilty with far less prejudicial backgrounds, Harry felt at times that the outcome was inevitable.

Then all that was civilised in him would recoil and protest. It was not the Middle Ages, nor was war an excuse to banish compassion. Gareth would be punished: that was necessary to balance the military ledger. But for punishment to be just, it must be commensurate with a man's strengths and weaknesses and doctors must already have established Gareth's lack of battle resilience. That would be the core of Shepherd's defence and when Harry remembered the young officer's success over the subpoena, he drew comfort from it.

It was in the mid afternoon that the ward sister, a stern-faced woman of the old nursing school, came to his bedside. 'That Lieutenant Shepherd is on the phone for you, Corporal. He mustn't do it again. It's most irregular to let other ranks use the telephone.'

Harry was already out of bed. 'Is the call on your office phone?'

The woman's frown grew. 'Yes. Wait. I'll get a wheelchair for you.'

Ignoring her, Harry limped down the ward and into the office. With his heart hammering with nervousness, it took him a moment to speak. 'Hello, sir. Corporal Miles here.'

'Hello, Corporal. I'm afraid I have bad news for you.'

Harry felt his heart stop and then his mouth turn dry. 'What is it, sir?'

'Then've sentenced Evans to death. By firing squad.'

The distant tinny voice suddenly seemed a thousand miles away. 'Corporal? Are you there?'

'Yes, sir. When will it be?'

'In three days' time. The twenty-eighth. At eight ack emma.'

'Can I see him, sir?'

'Is that wise, Corporal?'

'I must see him, sir. We're friends. And he has no one else. Please.'

There was silence, then a sigh. 'All right, Corporal. I'll talk to Colonel Whitehead and see what we can arrange. I'm sorry, Corporal. I did all I could.'

'Yes, sir. Thank you for letting me know.'

He put down the phone and remained bent over it. The ward sister was frowning suspiciously. 'I thought you couldn't walk on that leg!' Then she noticed his expression. 'What is it? Don't you feel well?'

He tried to speak but he was trembling as if struck by fever. The woman caught his arm. 'You'd better sit down. I'll call a doctor.'

He shook his head, pushed himself away from the desk and made for his bed. The bright rays of sunlight through the windows mocked him and the walk seemed like a hundred miles.

Chapter 41

Rising to her feet on hearing the car engine, Mary went to the office window. Seeing the Ford entering the warehouse yard, she glanced at her watch and saw it was 6.50. Ethel, who liked to have dinner no later than seven o'clock, would be growing impatient.

Willis entered the office five minutes later. In his middle forties, of medium height, he was a fleshy man with a fair moustache and sideboards. Although he was breathing somewhat heavily from his climb up the stairs, his self-confident voice with its London accent that William had disliked, echoed fruitily round the room. 'Hello, m'dear. Sorry I'm a bit late but I've had trouble with the car.'

She frowned. 'It seems to be causing a lot of trouble these days. What was it this time?'

He removed his hat and laid his leather bag on her desk. 'She began running on only three cylinders. The garage said it was plug trouble.'

'But didn't it have plug trouble only two weeks ago? And magneto trouble last week?'

His impatient expression betrayed his dislike at being asked such questions by a woman. 'Plugs and magnetos break down, m'dear. Don't you know that?'

'Every week or so?' she asked. She nearly added they hadn't when Harry had driven the car but checked herself in time.

He showed no embarrassment. 'It's the war, m'dear. Nothing's as good as it used to be. They're probably giving us throwouts from the factories.'

If he calls me 'm'dear' once more, she thought, I'll break the cash box over his head. She held out her hand. 'May I have your order book, please?' As he obeyed, she gave a start. 'Seven orders? Is that all you've got?'

He shrugged. 'I fear it's the war again. Shops aren't doing the sales and so they're cutting down on their orders. And I did have the car problem today.' Before she could reply, his eyes moved down to the tight-bodiced dress she was wearing. 'Is that a new dress, m'dear? It's very becoming.'

The intimacy of the question made her cheeks burn resentfully. She had noticed his glances before when he believed her attention elsewhere, moving reflectively over her breasts and travelling down her skirt. Her reply was curt. 'No, it's not new. About the car and these orders, Mr Willis. I think we'll have to . . .'

He went on as if she hadn't spoken. 'New or not, it looks delightful on you. You really should wear it more often.'

His belief that flattery could sidetrack her made her all the more determined to have matters out with him. 'I want you to get the car properly serviced, Mr Willis. These breakdowns are happening too often and taking up too much of your time. We can't survive on the orders you've been bringing in lately. I'll speak to Maynards – they seem the cheapest garage in town – and we'll arrange for the car to go in next week.'

He lifted an eyebrow. 'But I thought you were worried about lack of orders. You do realise, I hope, that a

356

thorough service will take all day?'

She smiled at him, enjoying her revenge. 'That's all right, Mr Willis. That day you can use the bicycle, as Harry used to do.'

He looked shocked. 'Bicycle? My dear young lady, I haven't ridden one since I was a boy.'

Her smile grew sweeter. 'Then it'll be your chance to practise again, won't it? Although I shouldn't worry. Like swimming, they say it's something you never forget.'

He eyed her speculatively, then, as if taking advantage of her lighter mood, changed the subject. 'Tell me something, m'dear. Do you ever to go the bioscope?'

She took immediate warning from the question. 'Not these days. I've no interest in films now Harry is away.' She glanced pointedly at the clock above the office door. 'I shall have to close up now, Mr Willis. My mother will be wondering why I'm so late.'

He made no move to leave. 'I've been wondering if you'd go with me one evening, m'dear. It would be a great pleasure for me to have your company and, of course, I would ensure you were home at a respectable time.'

Although his glances in the past had made his thoughts and desires clear enough, she had never believed he would dare to make them known and for the moment she was more surprised than angry. 'Mr Willis, you're forgetting that I'm a married woman with a husband at the Front. What sort of person do you take me for?'

He lifted a protesting hand. 'I mean you no harm, my dear young lady. It is just that as we are both lonely people, I thought we might find some pleasure in one another's company. Naturally I would treat you with the greatest respect.'

357

From the way his eyes had run over her bodice as she spoke she was certain his apologies were insincere. 'Respect, Mr Willis? You are a married man, aren't you? I heard you tell my father that you were.'

He sighed. 'Yes, but my wife and I do not live together. She is in London where, I believe, she shares a house with another man.'

She believed at first that her sudden rush of anger came from his effort to gain her sympathy, although for such a pathetic performance anger seemed an excessive emotion. 'That's your problem, not mine, Mr Willis. And it has nothing whatever to do with our relationship.'

'I realise that, m'dear. But surely we would be committing no wrong in enjoying one another's company for an evening?'

Snatching up the leather bag, she crossed to the office door and flung it open. 'You're making assumptions, Mr Willis. I wouldn't enjoy going out like that, not with you or anybody else while my husband's away. Now please go and don't make any more suggestions of that kind. You only embarrass us both and I know my mother would be angry if she found out.'

She spoke to Ethel about Willis over dinner that night. 'I'm certain he's up to something. I don't believe the car's always breaking down. That's just his excuse for getting few orders. I wonder if he's seeing a woman during working hours.'

Ethel, prim in a high-necked frock, looked shocked at the suggestion. 'Don't be silly, dear. He's much too well bred to be doing anything like that.'

'Well bred? He's just been to a fancy school, that's all. And we've only got his word for that. I feel like Dad did. I don't trust him an inch.'

358

Elizabeth, sitting between Ethel and Mary, was having difficulty in cutting up her slice of mutton. Before Mary could intervene, Ethel took the plate from the child and cut the meat into small squares before handing the plate back to her. 'There, darling. I know the meat's tough but it's the best we can get these days.' She glanced back at Mary. 'I wouldn't say too much to Mr Willis, dear. With all able-bodied men away, we'd never be able to get a replacement. And really I can't see a gentleman like him doing anything cheap or dishonest. Cars do break down, you know. That's why I never wanted William to buy one.'

It was on the tip of Mary's tongue to tell her about Willis's invitation but she felt it was not worth a major upset. The memory did bring back a return of her anger, however, and it was still with her when she retired to bed that night.

The reason puzzled her, for Willis's behaviour was hardly novel. From her friends' gossip, she knew that married women were being propositioned all the time while their husbands were away. And surely she was not a snob like her mother and resenting Willis's approach because he was an employee? Contempt he might deserve but this anger she felt seemed out of proportion to the offence he had committed.

The answer came when she heard the grandfather clock below striking midnight. The anger was with herself, not with Willis. Although she found the man unattractive with his soft body and suave ways, his invitation had reminded her how much she missed male attention, the feel of lips on her neck and breasts, the touch of strong hands moving down to intimate parts of her body.

It meant, she knew, that from now on, every time she saw Willis, she would be reminded of physical desires that Harry had awakened. She had no fear of actual infidelity. She knew her background and her love for Harry would take care of that. But to one of Mary's upbringing, to feel physical desire without her husband present to engender it seemed a kind of infidelity in itself and to expose a weakness in her. It was hours before she was able to sleep, unaware that millions of women all over Europe and beyond were sharing the same symptoms of deprivation.

Chapter 42

The sunset was a red strain on the horizon when Harry slid down painfully from the Crossley tender. Steadying himself with his stick, he glanced back at the driver. 'I'll be quite a time. What will you do? Come back?'

Knowing his mission, the driver shook his head sympathetically. 'That's all right, Corp. They said wait for you. You take your time. I can always kip down in the back if you're late.'

Harry gazed about him. Fifty yards to his left, across a muddy enclosure, was a dilapidated farmhouse with one wing shattered by shellfire. Miscellaneous outhouses stood around it. Ahead of him, just off the road, was a stone hut with an earthen roof: a one-time winter shelter for cattle. Seeing an MP outside, the driver pointed at it. 'That must be it, Corp. Just the kind of place they'd put the poor sod in for his last night.'

Thanking him, Harry made for the hut. Halting as the MP called his challenge, he held out a piece of paper. 'I'm Corporal Miles. I've a warrant to see the prisoner.'

The MP ordered him closer. With the last of the sunset staining him, Harry saw he was a stout corporal with a truculent expression. Knowing he was one of the Battle Police who never crossed the front lines themselves but

361

were always eager to pick up men who had, Harry took an instant dislike to him.

The man studied the warrant for a moment, then jerked a thumb at the farmhouse where shaded lights could be seen. 'They said you'd be comin'. You're a pal of the prisoner, aren't you?'

Harry nodded, then glanced at the farmhouse. 'Who's in there? Lieutenant Chadwick?'

'Not at the moment. But he was here earlier.' The MP grinned. 'He was checkin' to see his prisoner was safe. Johnnies like him don't like their men getting the wind up and running away. They think it gives 'em a bad name.'

Harry thought how true this was of Chadwick. 'Can I go in now?'

The MP looked him up and down. 'You're not carryin' any arms, are you?'

When Harry shook his head, the man drew out a key and unfastened a large padlock on the wooden door. 'I'll have to lock you in. Give me a yell when you've had enough. In you go.'

The stone shelter had a strong smell of ordure. It was lit by a small oil lamp resting on an ammunition box. In the centre of the cobbled floor two large crates pushed together served as a table. Standing on it were a Bible, a plate of half-eaten food, a mug, and a jug of water.

Gareth was sitting at the far side of the makeshift table. He was capless, his hair was dishevelled, and his tunic was open at the neck. Although he lifted his head at Harry's entry, he gave no sign of recognition.

Harry approached him. 'Hello, kid. How are you feeling?'

The Welshman's eyes, dulled by shock and fear, looked puzzled. 'Is that you, Harry?'

'Yes. They've let me out to see you.'

Gareth's brow furrowed. 'Where from?'

'The hospital. Hadn't you heard?'

Memory began seeping back to the Welshman. 'That's right. They said you'd caught one. How are you doing?'

'I'm all right. They'll probably throw me out in a week or two.'

'Will it get you to Blighty?' The yearning in the question brought Harry an irrelevant vision of an old man listening to the laughter and plans of young lovers.

'Not a chance,' he said quickly. 'How are you off for fags?'

Gareth's hand moved to his tunic pocket. 'You want one, boyo?'

'No. I've brought some for you. Here.'

Gareth watched him lay four packets on the table. Giving a laugh, he lifted his eyes. 'You think I'm going to live long enough to smoke that lot?'

Harry broke into a cold sweat at his mistake. Unable to think of a reply, he watched Gareth fumbling with one of the packets. As he drew out a cigarette, it fell from his fingers to the table. Instead of picking it up, he sat gazing at it as if the effort was too much. Pretending not to notice, Harry lit it for him and pushed it between his lips. While Gareth drew in smoke, he set the oil lamp on the floor and dragged the ammunition box to the table. Sinking down on it, he pulled out the flat bottle of cognac which he had hidden beneath his tunic. 'Do you feel like a drink, kid? I've got some of the real stuff here.'

When the Welshman made no reply, he reached for his tin mug and half-filled it. 'Here, Gareth. Have a swig.'

Lifting the mug, Gareth took a long drink. Then he spluttered and began coughing. Waving Harry back, he

363

wiped his eyes and gave a wide grin. 'Whew! That's potent stuff, boyo.'

Relieved, Harry sank back. 'The best. Usually reserved for officers and gentlemen.'

It was a mistake. Gareth's expression changed. 'Those bastards! I hate them, Harry. Every stinking one of them.'

Realising he had touched an agonised nerve, Harry tried clumsily to change the conversation. 'Have you heard they're drafting all Vickers machine gunners into a separate corps?'

Gareth did not hear his banality. 'I hate 'em and they know it. That's why they're going to put me beneath the sod, like all those other poor bastards they've starved and killed over the years.'

Feeling the explosion coming, Harry began to panic. Before he could think of anything to say, Gareth's tortured face turned to him. 'Didn't you know I'm going to die tomorrow? They're going to shoot me, Harry. My own mates from the Sixteenth. Just because I couldn't take all that noise.'

Harry could only bow his head as the man's agony poured out like a massive haemorrhage. 'I'm scared, Harry. I'm scared of the pain and what happens afterwards. Oh, Jesus Christ, I'm scared.'

Closing his eyes, Harry felt his teeth biting into his lower lip. The flickering oil lamp, the smell of ordure, the distant gunfire, the terror of a friend soon to have his body mutilated by his own comrades: surely this had to be a nightmare. At any moment it would all vanish in the light of a new day. The thought steadied him. 'Don't think about it, Gareth. Finish off that brandy and have another.'

To his relief Gareth obeyed. Half-filling the mug again, Harry handed it back to him. 'I wonder what the

CSM would say if he saw the two of us getting pissed on officers' brandy?'

'That old pissarse,' Gareth muttered. 'He'd slap us into jankers and then swipe what's left.'

Harry heard their laughter echoing round the stone walls. As the hysterical sound died away, Gareth lifted the mug and drank deeply again. When he lowered it Harry saw with relief that the neat spirit was taking its effect at last. His eyes were muzzy and his voice took on a maudlin solemnity. 'You know something, boyo? It's all shit those padres tell us . . . There's no God, Harry. Not here or anywhere else.'

Harry knew at all costs he must appease him. 'Isn't there, Gareth?'

Gareth hiccoughed. 'Naw. It's all part of the game. To make us so shit scared that we do what the bastard ruling class tell us. They're all in it together. You've got to hand it to them, Harry. They're as clever as hell.' His muzzy eyes peered into Harry's pale face. 'You hadn't thought of that, had you?'

'No, Gareth. I hadn't.'

Gareth hiccoughed again. 'It's true, Harry. You've seen swaddies blinded or crucified on barbed-wire. What sort of God would let that happen?'

First Chadwick and now you, Harry thought. He bowed his head without replying. Gareth muttered something, then turned to him again. 'Anyway, what's so wonderful about crucifixion. We're all getting crucified, out there or in here. And who cares, boyo? Who's going to build churches for us?'

There was the cartilaginous sound of his swallowing again. Then he gave a sob. Dreading what else was coming, Harry was afraid to look up. A second later the artery of the Welshman's torment ruptured again. 'But what about the morning, Harry? If there's no God and

365

no heaven, where will I go? Will it be hell? We all know *it's* there. Will I go there and burn forever?'

Sweat was bursting out from every pore in Harry's body now. 'Of course you won't. You'll be escaping from hell.'

The inadequacy of his words horrified him. Yet as if Gareth's emotions and beliefs were swinging on some grotesque pendulum, his hysteria died again. 'I believed in the rest of it, Harry. It's bloody stupid but I did.'

Harry lifted his head. 'Believed in what?'

'That talk about the brotherhood of man. That one day people like you and me all over the world would throw away their chains and live like one big family. But not any more, not after I've seen men killing one another the way they do here. We've got some sickness, Harry. Right through the human race.'

Harry was sitting as if turned to stone. With closed eyes he listened to the terror returning to Gareth's voice. 'But where does that leave me? I don't believe in God, I don't believe in heaven, I don't believe in people any more. Is that how I'm going to die? Shot by my mates and believing in nothing but the devil and hell?'

Harry was praying to find some words of comfort for him. 'There's friendship, Gareth. You can believe in that.'

'There's only been you, Harry. And even then it took the bloody war to bring us really close together.' As he remembered again his ordeal on the morrow, the veins stood out like cords on the Welshman's forehead. 'It's unreal, Harry. How can they kill a man in cold blood just because he's scared? Mock me, maybe. Laugh at me. But kill me?' Then his tone changed. 'Do you think it'll hurt, Harry?'

Harry cleared his throat. 'No. You're lucky there. The rest of us probably won't be so lucky.'

'Lucky,' Gareth muttered. 'That's funny, Harry. Don't you think it's funny?'

When Harry made no reply, the Welshman lifted the mug and drained it. Coughing, muttering something Harry could not catch, he slumped forward with his head on his arms. Praying he would sleep at last, Harry was about to take a drink himself to steady his nerves when the Welshman lifted his head. Seeing he was trying to say something, Harry put out an arm and steadied him. 'What is it, Gareth?'

At first Gareth's words were so slurred their meaning escaped him. Then, as if the Welshman's need was too great to be drowned by alcohol, his pleading became intelligible. 'Do something for me, Harry . . . Please, boyo! It's important . . .'

Harry's hand tightened on his arm. 'What is it? What do you want?'

Gareth's eyes, muzzy with fear and alcohol, tried to focus on his face. 'It's tomorrow, Harry . . . After it's over. Stay with me until they put me away . . . Please, Harry.'

For a moment the stone walls round Harry blurred dizzily. Horrified, he played the coward. 'Kid, I can't do that. They wouldn't let me. You know that.'

The Welshman's need seemed obsessional. 'Please, Harry. The others won't give a damn. But you're my friend . . . I'd feel better if you're the last one with me. Say you'll do it, Harry. Please.'

Not daring to think what he was promising, Harry gripped his arm tightly. 'All right, Gareth. I'll take care of it.'

His promise calmed the Welshman and allowed the brandy to take its effect. Gareth reached for a cigarette but the effort proved too much and his head fell on his arms again. A few seconds later his heavy breathing filled the shelter.

As Harry relaxed, he discovered he was drenched in sweat. He eased Gareth gently forward so that he could not fall, then picked up the bottle and saw over half its contents had gone. Feeling that amount of cognac must keep the terror of the morning from Gareth's dreams, he put the bottle to his lips and let the neat spirit slide down his throat.

He took a second drink and then a third, only to discover that instead of tranquillising his emotions, the alcohol seemed to aggravate them, at one moment increasing his aversion for Gareth's judges, in the next adding to his sorrow and personal despair.

Another half an hour passed. The brandy bottle was empty now and the cobblestones at Harry's feet were littered with half-smoked cigarettes. Although he knew his allotted time with the prisoner had long past and he believed Gareth unlikely to awaken for hours yet, loyalty to the Welshman and rebellion fed by alcohol determined him to stay by his side until he was driven away.

He reached for a cigarette only to find the packet empty. Leaning across the table for another packet, he saw the Welshman stir, then raise his head.

Dismayed, Harry drew back. 'I thought you were asleep.'

Gareth, with terror back in his eyes, did not hear him. The cry he gave contained such agony that the petrified Harry felt the stone walls of the shelter would retain it for ever. 'They're going to kill me, Harry! Because I was frightened! There's no pity left, is there? *Oh God, what have they done to us?*'

Chapter 43

Harry awoke to find himself being roughly shaken. 'Corporal! Get on your feet!'

As Harry's blurred eyes cleared, he saw the stout MP standing over him. A second, slighter figure at the far side of the table proved to be a young, pale-faced padre with a Bible in his hand. As Harry rose unsteadily, the MP gave another shout. 'Have you been giving brandy to the prisoner, Corporal?'

Glancing at the table, Harry saw Gareth was still sprawled out unconscious. As drunk as he had ever been, he turned to the glowering MP. 'What if I have?'

'It's against orders, that's what. He'd have been given a tot of rum after the padre's seen him.'

Ingoring the MP, Harry lurched round the table. 'Let him be, Padre. He's found a bit of peace at last. In any case, he doesn't believe in God any more.'

The young padre looked embarrassed. 'I must talk to him, Corporal. It's my duty.'

Lurching forward again, Harry drove a finger against the man's thin chest. 'I'll tell you where your duty is, Padre! It's to go to those murdering bastards who've condemned him to death. Who're shooting him because he'd the good sense to be scared of having his guts blown out. They're the ones who need your prayers because if there's a hell, as sure as God they're going there.'

There was an enraged shout behind him. 'Outside, Corporal! You're under arrest.'

Giving the MP a look, Harry prodded the padre's chest again. 'There's something else you and your lot ought to know.' He threw an arm out in the direction of the Front. 'Stop preaching to us before we go into battle and telling us God is on our side. Tell us instead we're a bunch of paid killers and if we go on killing one another we'll be damned in hellfire forever. Tell us that and you might start getting some recruits again.'

Cursing, the MP grabbed his shoulder and jerked him round. 'That's it, soldier! You're for the big drop. Outside!'

With a snarl, Harry snatched the man's bayonet from his scabbard and dug its point into his loose stomach. 'I kill better men than you every day of the week, you fat bastard! Take your hand off my shoulder or you go with them.'

The MP turned pale and backed away. Catching his eye, the padre shook his head, then turned back to Harry. 'I shan't be pressing charges, Corporal. I know the prisoner's your friend and you wouldn't be human if it didn't affect you. But I think you'd better go now.'

With a curse, Harry flung the bayonet to the cobblestones, took a last look at the sleeping Gareth, then limped out into the night. The sunset had long gone but as if in reproach to the star shells and crimson flashes on the horizon, a white moon was rising in the velvet sky.

The tender had been moved back and was now standing at the far side of a clump of trees. With no sign of the driver, with his stick forgotten and left in the shelter, Harry stumbled and fell twice as he made towards it. He was still drunk and his irrational desire to kill the MP had not abated. When he felt no shame, he remembered Gareth's last words and despair mingled with the outrage in his fevered mind.

As he limped from the moonlight into the shadow of the trees, he stumbled again. As he picked himself painfully up, the unearthy song of a nightingale broke out above him. For a moment he stood listening to it. Then he lifted his face and shouted curses at the bird that could sing with such beauty and with such indifference to the world of suffering that lay beneath it.

As he had promised, Harry was the last man to handle Gareth's body the next morning. In his last moments before his execution, the Welshman had affirmed again his wish to the padre and the man had kept his promise and arranged for Harry to be present when the body was carried from the execution post to its boxwood coffin.

Helped by two infantrymen, Harry lowered the body on to a brown blanket and then into the coffin. The Welshman's hand was still warm when he took it, although after the *coup de grâce* from the Presiding Officer's revolver, his features were barely recognisable. Harry kept hold of the hand until the last moment, then laid it gently down and covered it with the blanket. He stood and gazed at the brown mound until the coffin lid was safely nailed down. Only then did he limp away to a clump of trees where he was violently sick.

Across the large quarry where the execution had taken place, sections of the 16th Battalion were moving silently away. After dismissing his machine gun section, Chadwick walked over to Harry who, recovering from his sickness, was sitting on a boulder. Pulling out his cigarette case, he held it out. When Harry made no response, he said. 'You shouldn't have done that, Miles.

371

It wasn't necessary.'

Harry lifted his head. 'Wasn't necessary? It was his last wish.'

'All right, Miles, I respect you for it. It took a lot of courage.'

Harry said something and turned away. Chadwick eyed him and frowned. 'Look, Miles, you have to believe there was nothing personal in this. I would have done the same to any other man in my section if he'd behaved the same way. I'd even do it to a brother officer if necessary.'

Harry turned back to him. 'I know you would, Chadwick. You had all your compassion and humanity beaten out of you at that public school you went to, and you've been getting your own back ever since. In peacetime, when you pay starvation wages, you call it good business. In wartime, when you execute men, you call it doing your duty. To me you're a murderer either way and I hope you go to hell for it.'

Chadwick's handsome face paled slightly. 'You can't understand, Miles, because you've never carried the responsibility of leadership. Your view would change quickly enough if you were commissioned. If we're to win this war, there's no other way but to maintain discipline.'

Harry glanced at him, then spat into the red soil. 'Win the war? Both we and the Jerries lost it when we lost compassion and charity. Do you know what we're fighting for now, Chadwick? Do the Germans know? Damn your filthy war, Chadwick, and damn you to hell!'

Chadwick gazed at him, then took a deep breath. 'I'm forgetting you said that, Miles.'

'I don't want you to forget it,' Harry said. 'I want you to remember it for the rest of your life.'

'Nevertheless, I shall. We'll have another talk when the MO discharges you.'

This time Harry did not answer him. His eyes were on

372

the mule cart that was now carrying Gareth's coffin to the grave.

The following day when back in hospital, Harry awoke with a fever and his wounded leg was found to be inflamed. Unable to explain the reason, surgeons waited two days and then, when his condition worsened, they decided to re-open his wound. Finding a spot of infection had developed on the chipped femur, they removed a further small piece of bone and hoped septicaemia would not set in after the wound was closed.

To the relief of Harry's nurse, his fever disappeared after a few days but his weakened physical condition was to last throughout the rest of the summer and the autumn. Expecting to be transferred to England when ready to convalesce, which was the common practice, he was kept instead in the converted chateau. Puzzled at first, he made an application for a transfer. When he received no reply, he convinced himself he was one of the untidy items that had gone astray in the Army's massive recording machine.

He did not apply again. Since Gareth's execution an apathy had fallen on him. Part of him yearned to see Mary and Elizabeth again but another part of him feared a reunion. It would mean yet another separation and he wanted no more pain. He wanted nothing but to sit in the fading autumn sunlight and watch the russet leaves fluttering gently to the ground.

Although he did his best to hide his state of mind, it lay like a shadow on the letters he wrote to Mary. It brought back replies from her that grew more and more distraught but although he tried to reassure her, even that effort became too much to sustain. Soon he would be well enough to join Chadwick again and this time he would die. The thought did not frighten him: his apathy was too complete for that. Instead he thought of it like the approach of winter. An inevitable thing that would after all bring the end of pain.

In early November he had a surprise visitor. He was sitting on a balcony with a blanket round his legs, taking in a spell of autumn sunshine, when a pretty young WRAC nurse approached him. 'There's a Captain Chadwick to see you, Harry.'

Chadwick, Harry thought. There was a time when I would have spat on his grave. Now I feel nothing towards him. Rousing himself he turned to see the immaculate officer standing alongside his deckchair. 'Hello, Miles. How are you coming along?'

'I'm all right,' Harry muttered. 'What are you doing here?'

The blushing young nurse was offering Chadwick a chair opposite him. Thanking her in a way that made her blush deepen, Chadwick offered Harry a cigarette, took one himself, then sank elegantly down. 'I'm taking a few days' leave in Paris. This place is on the way so I thought I'd drop in to see you.'

Harry nodded at the three pips on his shoulders. 'I see you've got promotion.'

Chadwick dismissed his new rank with befitting modesty. 'They've been keeping us busy since you were wounded. In fact it's been go all the time.'

'How have the section got on?'

'Adams and Pearson have gone. Jackson got a Blighty but the rest are all right.'

He made it sound as if Adams and Pearson had just given up their jobs, Harry thought. Before he could comment, Chadwick leaned forward and tapped his arm. 'By the way, you'll be getting your third stripe soon. I put in for it last week. You've earned it and you'll

374

probably find the extra money useful.'

Harry shook his head. 'I don't want promotion.'

Chadwick frowned. 'Don't be stupid, man. Life gets easier when you're giving orders instead of taking them. You should get notice to put it up within a few days.'

About to protest again, Harry decided it mattered little either way. Feeling chilly, he drew the blanket higher over his legs, an act that made Chadwick take another look at him. 'Are you feeling all right?'

'Yes. Why?'

'I expected to see you looking more alive than this. I spoke to the colonel before I came up and he said they'd probably be releasing you in a couple of weeks.'

Harry felt no emotion. 'Did he? They never tell us anything. Where will I be going?'

'To a place called Gonnehem. They've decided our section's done its share for a while and we're going to have a spell as instructors. I made a protest but they wouldn't listen.' Chadwick smiled. 'So you won't be killing Germans for a couple of months. Aren't you glad?'

Once I would have thanked God, Harry thought. Now I feel nothing. Clearly puzzled by his behaviour Chadwick took another look at him, then crushed out his cigarette. 'Try to get a day or two in Paris if you can work it. A few drinks and a willing girl and you'll be on top of the world again.' Glancing at his watch, he rose. 'I'll have to go now. I've got three chaps down below in my car and they'll be getting restless. I'll see you in two weeks. All right?'

Harry nodded. 'Yes. Goodbye.'

He watched the man's elegant figure stride along the balcony, wave to a nurse, then disappear. Lighting a cigarette, he sat back. If he knew Chadwick, their spell at Gonnehem would be short-lived. The man's hunting instincts would not be long satisfied in teaching others

375

how to use weapons instead of using those weapons himself.

His eyes moved to a row of ornamental trees in the grounds below. In the bright sunlight, fallen leaves scattered around their feet were glowing like embers.

The illusion lasted only a few seconds. A sudden cloud crossed the sun and the leaves turned dead and brown. Feeling the chill of the wind that had sprung up. Harry drew on his cigarette and held the smoke in his lungs. Winter was very close now.

Before Harry was discharged, he had one more visitor. Entering the waiting-room downstairs, he saw a tall slim woman in a dark blue coat standing at the window. As he approached she turned, gave a cry of pleasure, and ran towards him. 'Harry! How good to see you again.'

His face cleared. 'Nicole,' he muttered. 'What are you doing here?'

She hugged him then kissed him. 'Your Battalion came back to Montoise. One of the men told me you had been wounded and I enquired about your hospital. Didn't you get my letter?'

He shook his head. 'When did you write?'

'Over a month ago. But why did you not write to me, Harry? I have been worried about you.'

He glanced round. 'Where's Michelle?'

'I left her with a friend. I had to go to Paris. Pierre is also in hospital.'

'He is? What happened?' Seeing tears suddenly spring into her eyes, he led her to a table in the sunlit window. 'Sit down and tell me about it.'

Obeying him, she dabbed at her eyes impatiently. 'I'm being foolish, Harry. It is all over now. But he was very ill for a time.'

'Where did it happen?' he asked. 'At Verdun?'

She nodded. 'He lost an arm, Harry.'

He drew in his breath. Unable to think of a suitable reply he heard a trapped fly buzzing against the sunlit glass. Then he glanced back at her. 'When was this?'

'Not long after we last met. As I say, he is much stronger now. He says he expects to be discharged in a few weeks and then will be coming home.'

'How has he taken it?'

She frowned slightly at the question. 'How does a surgeon take it when he knows he can never operate again? For a while he was unconsolable. But he has accepted it now. After all, even with only one arm he can still be a doctor.'

Harry nodded. 'And at least the war's over for him.'

Puzzled by his tone, she searched his face. 'Yes. I know he is luckier than some. But you have not spoken about yourself. Is your wound better?'

He shrugged. 'It never was very much. If it hadn't become infected I would have been out months ago.'

'As it is you will be getting some home leave, won't you? To see Mary and Elizabeth again?'

His behaviour was puzzling her. She watched his eyes fall away as he began fumbling in his tunic for cigarettes.

'I don't think it's likely,' he muttered.

'But why not? Don't all British soldiers get leave when they've been in hospital as long as you have?'

'Not all. And don't forget I was given leave when my father-in-law died.'

'But that was different.' Shaking her head as he offered her a cigarette, she went on: 'Surely you're going to try aren't you?'

When he did not answer her, she leaned forward in concern. 'Harry, what's the matter? What has happened to you?'

377

He frowned. 'Nothing's happened to me. I've had a slight wound, that's all.'

'No, it's not all. You've changed. Why don't you want to go home?'

He made a gesture of irritation. 'I never said I didn't want to go. I meant it wasn't likely I'll get the chance.'

It was then she remembered Gareth. 'Is it your friend? Has something happened to him?'

His wince told her she was right although she could not understand the sudden hostility of his glance. When he did not answer, she went on quietly: 'Do you want to talk about it? Or would you rather not?'

He shifted restlessly as if wanting to escape. 'I'd rather not,' he muttered. 'In any case it happened months ago.'

She did not know what to say to him. 'I'm sorry, Harry. I knew you were good friends.'

As he gave a terse nod, she had the feeling she was talking to a stranger. Driven into exchanging banalities with him, she was almost relieved when she noticed the time. 'I shall have to be going. The bus leaves in five minutes and if I don't catch the three o'clock train I won't get home tonight.'

He nodded and walked out with her to the stone stairway that led down to the chateau courtyard. 'Thanks for coming,' he muttered. 'Give my regards to Pierre the next time you come to see him.'

'Will you still be here?' she asked. 'I try to come every fortnight.'

'No,' he said. 'They're discharging me in a couple of days.'

'Then will you write to me now and then? To let me know you're safe?'

He hesitated, then nodded. 'I'll try to.'

She desperately wanted to help him but could not think of a way. Seeing he was not going to make the move

378

himself, she threw her arms around him. 'Harry, the war's not going to last forever. And you've got Mary and Elizabeth to think about. Are you listening to me?'

'Yes,' he said. 'I'm listening.'

'Then show more life, Harry. I'm worried about you. You look so . . .' She searched for the word. 'You look so resigned.'

He managed a smile for her. 'I'm all right. Give Michelle a kiss for me. Don't forget.'

Her eyes blurred with tears as she hugged him again. 'Oh, Harry. *Mon cher, cher ami. Il ne faut pas vous laisser abattre ainsi. Je me fais tant de soucis pour vous.*'

Although she knew he did not understand her words, she felt his arms tighten for a moment. Then he stood back. 'You'd better go or you'll miss your bus.'

She kissed him a last time. Then, turning sharply, she ran down the steps. Reaching the courtyard, she glanced back and saw he had not moved. Waving, she saw him lift a hand in reply. Something about the gesture, its weariness, its finality, sent a chill through her as she turned and climbed into the bus.

Chapter 44

The autumn wind, gusting out of the darkness, had a rawness that made Mary shiver as she pushed open the garden gate of No. 57. Starting towards the house, she gave a gasp of pain as she collided with a child's tricycle lying across the path. As she bent down to pick it up, a headache she had felt all day began pounding in her temples.

She carried the tricycle into the shed, then entered the house. Opening the sitting-room door, she saw Ethel was reading to Elizabeth on the settee. When the child did not glance up, Mary's voice was sharp. 'What's the matter with you. Elizabeth? Don't you say hello to your mother when she comes home from work?'

At a whisper from Ethel, the child glanced round. 'Hello, Mummy.' Without another word she tugged at Ethel's sleeve for the woman to continue reading.

Fighting her temper, Mary approached the settee. 'Do you know you left your tricycle down the garden? I nearly fell over it when I came in. Is that the way to look after your toys?'

'Sorry, Mummy,' the girl muttered.

Mary stood back. 'I want you to go upstairs for a moment. I'll call you when I'm ready.'

The child looked up sullenly. 'What for?'

'Never mind what for. Just go upstairs. It won't be for long.'

Pouting, Elizabeth glanced at Ethel. The woman, who was eyeing Mary curiously, nodded and closed the book. 'Do as your mother says, dear. I'll read to you again after dinner.'

The girl's sullenness grew. 'I don't want to go upstairs. I want to hear the end of the story.'

Mary caught hold of her arm and pulled her off the settee. 'I won't have you arguing with me like this. Go upstairs! This minute.'

The child stared at her, then burst out crying. 'You're horrible. I don't like you. Why did you come back from work?'

Mary took a step towards her. Elizabeth backed away, then turned and ran upstairs. A door slammed and in the silence that followed her hysterical sobbing could be heard.

Ethel, looking startled, was gazing up at Mary. 'What on earth is all this about? Why did you frighten her like that?'

Mary was breathing hard. 'I don't like the way she talks to me these days. Or the way she disobeys me.'

Ethel frowned. 'I don't know what you're talking about. The child was as good as gold until you came in.'

'Yes and why? Because she was getting what she wants. I don't like the way you're spoiling her, Mother. That tricycle you bought her cost money, and yet she's left it outside to rust. She doesn't value anything any more.'

Ethel laid the book down on the settee. 'You're in a fine temper tonight, aren't you? It's a pity you couldn't have left it back in the warehouse instead of bringing it here.' Then she noticed Mary's expression. 'What on earth's happened? Has the telephone broken down again?'

'No, Mother, it's not the telephone. It's Mr Willis again.'

Ethel gazed at her, then gave a resigned sigh. 'I see. What's the trouble this time?'

'The trouble this time, Mother, is that he's having an affair with one of our customers' daughters.'

This time Ethel gave a start. 'Who says so?'

'The customer says so. Mrs Tyson of Mersey Street. She came in specially today to lay her complaint. Her daughter and son-in-law have a house in a side street near her shop and she says every time Willis calls on her for an order, he drives round to her daughter's house. She became suspicious a few weeks ago and has been keeping an eye on him ever since. She says he sometimes stays as long as two hours. So now we know why he's picking up so few orders.'

Ethel was frowning. 'Has she spoken to her daughter about it?'

'Yes. Her daughter used to live in London and she claims they're just old friends and Willis only goes round for a cup of tea. But Mrs Tyson's certain they're having an affair. For one thing she's seen him going round to the house in the evenings.'

One of Ethel's hands was now tapping the arm of the settee. 'Is the daughter's husband in the Army?'

Mary's reply was bitter. 'Yes. And Willis is just the type to take advantage of it.'

Ethel was silent for a moment, then her eyes lifted to Mary again. 'I can't believe this of Mr Willis. What kind of woman is this Mrs Tyson?'

'A decent, hardworking woman. She's been running the shop ever since her husband died four years ago.'

'But she is working class?'

'Yes, I suppose you'd call her that. But what has that to do with Willis?'

Ethel's face was clearing. 'It's your explanation, dear. That kind of person can't live without gossip. They can't believe a man like Mr Willis could visit a woman friend without taking advantage of her.'

A laugh of scorn broke from Mary. 'Mother, what a snob you are. When are you going to realise there isn't a scrap of difference in the morals of the middle class. They're just a bit cleverer at handling things, that's all.'

Red spots appeared in Ethel's cheeks. 'We haven't all been influenced by the working class, my girl. And those of us who haven't know the differences only too well.'

Although she knew a quarrel was imminent, Mary was in no mood to avoid it. 'You believe that, do you? All right, now I'll tell you something about your wonderful Mr Willis. He's been ogling me ever since Dad took him on. And he keeps on asking me to go out with him. He pretends it's just for my company but from the way he looks at me, I know exactly what he's after.'

With Willis, in spite of his supposedly good education, still an employee, she had at least expected her mother to look shocked. Instead Ethel's expression was enigmatic.

'What have you said to him?'

'I've told him that if he goes on propositioning me, I'll report him to you.' Then, suddenly Mary understood. 'You wouldn't mind, would you? My God, you wouldn't mind!'

Ethel was sitting up very prim and erect on the settee. 'You'd come to no harm. He would see you were home in decent time. And a change would do you good.'

Mary's voice was hoarse. 'Has he spoken to you about this?'

'Of course he hasn't. How could you think such a thing?'

Mary took a deep breath. 'If I thought he had and you'd agreed, I'd walk out of this house and you'd never see me again. My God, I'm married to a man who's fighting for slimy toads like Willis. I feel unclean that he even thinks I might go out with him.'

Ethel frowned. 'Don't exaggerate, dear. Whatever else you might think of him, Mr Willis is a gentleman. He'd never do anything to you against your will.'

All Mary's disgust and anger exploded. 'You and your damned gentlemen! Willis wants only one thing. He'd give his right arm to get me into bed with him.'

Ethel gave a gasp of outrage. 'How dare you talk in such a disgusting way in front of your mother? If your father was alive, you wouldn't say such things.'

Mary was past caring what she said now. 'You're not that innocent, Mother. You know Willis is like any other man. But you wouldn't mind it if I had an affair with him, would you? Not if it ended with Harry and I separating.'

A sob broke from Ethel. 'I don't know what's happening to you. It all began when you married that wretched man, Harry. He's changed you into another person.'

'Yes, and I thank God he has. Otherwise I might have grown up like you – capable of doing anything to serve your own ends. I thank God every night that I met Harry.'

At that Ethel dropped her mask. 'You think he's so wonderful, don't you? If he is, why hasn't he come home on leave? Why hasn't he written to you like he used to?' Seeing Mary's expression, her voice rose triumphantly. 'We both know why, don't we? They say most of the common soldiers over there find themselves French girls or visit the brothels. While you're fretting about him and making such a fuss because Mr Willis invites you out, he's probably having relations with some French nurse or common prostitute. That would be a come-down for you, wouldn't it, my girl.'

There was horror in Mary's eyes as she stared at the woman. 'You bitch,' she said. 'You vicious bitch.'

384

Ethel gave a loud laugh. 'The truth hurts, doesn't it, my girl. And don't tell me you haven't had the same suspicions yourself. I haven't missed how you've been snapping at everyone around you these last few weeks.'

They were deadly enemies now, striking at one another with every weapon they could find. By this time Mary was white to the lips.

'That's it, Mother. It's the last time you're going to attack Harry. I'm giving up my job and leaving this house. Today.'

As lost in her temper as Mary was in hers, Ethel leapt to her feet. 'Then give it up! Give it up and find out how well your wonderful Harry can keep you when you've no wage coming in.'

Mary gave her a last look, then made for the staircase door. 'I'll go and pack Elizabeth's things. We'll leave first thing tomorrow morning.'

Ethel's defiant gaze followed her, then she gave a violent start. 'Wait a minute. You can't punish Elizabeth because of your temper. She needs a proper home to grow up in.'

Mary swung round. 'You don't expect me to leave her behind, do you? You've stolen enough of her affection already. And probably poisoned her mind against her father. No, Mother. She's my child and she's going wherever I go.'

There was apprehension as well as anger in Ethel's expression now. 'You can't be that selfish. Where do you think you're going to live? You won't be able to buy another house with no wage coming in. What right have you to punish Elizabeth too?'

Mary knew she had found Ethel's Achilles' heel at last. 'Dad left me enough to rent a couple of rooms and there must be thousands of women only too glad to let rooms while their husbands are away. We'll manage until Harry comes home.'

Ethel's face was a battlefield now. The stiffness of her words gave witness to their cost. 'It would break your father's heart to hear us quarrelling like this. If only for his sake, I think we should agree to forget and to forgive. I'm willing to do this if you are.'

Mary shook her head. 'I can't forget or forgive, Mother. I can't listen to you running down Harry any longer. I'm taking Elizabeth away and I don't want her to see you again.'

Ethel looked as if she had been struck across the face. 'That's cruel. You know how much I love her.'

'You know how much I love Harry but it doesn't stop you attacking him. You can't always have life on your own terms, Mother. This time you've gone too far.'

There was a second of silence, then Ethel braced herself. 'Then what do you want me to do? Apologise?'

'I don't want you to do anything. I just want to get out of this house and take Elizabeth with me.'

There was panic in Ethel's voice now. 'But I'd be all alone. You can't be that cruel.'

Mary felt no mercy at that moment. 'You should have thought of that before, shouldn't you?'

Ethel took an unsteady step forward. 'You mustn't take Elizabeth away, Mary. I couldn't live without her. Not with William gone. I couldn't bear it.'

It was the sound of her father's name again that brought compassion back to the girl. 'There's only one thing that could make me stay, Mother. That's your promise never to speak badly again about Harry while he's away. If you broke it by just one word, I'd walk out with Elizabeth and you'd never see either of us again.'

For a moment relief closed Ethel's eyes. 'Very well. I promise.'

'I want you to swear it, Mother. On Dad's grave.'

The woman's lips compressed but she nodded. 'I swear

it. Now will you let bygones be bygones and leave things as they are?'

Mary walked to the door, then turned. 'All right, for the moment we'll stay. But the next time you have one of your spasms of malice, you'd better remember your promise. If you don't, you'll find out quickly enough that I'll remember mine.'

She did not see the look in Ethel's eyes as she went upstairs to her bedroom. She found she was trembling with reaction and although Elizabeth was still sobbing, she was forced to throw herself down on the bed to calm her thoughts and nerves.

It was a full minute before her trembling ceased and she could estimate the extent of her victory. She had no illusions about Ethel: threats were hardly likely to diminish her dislike of Harry. But at least that dislike should now be contained within the woman and no longer blight her life or threaten Elizabeth's love for her father. If she, Mary, had not won the war, she had at least gained an armistice until Harry came home. After that, she told herself, everything would be all right. With a sob of relief, she ran over to Elizabeth and hugged her.

Chapter 45

Chadwick was wading along the dark trench, stopping every few yards to talk to the infantrymen crouched behind the sodden sandbags. The trench was little more than an irrigation ditch, with a foot of water covering the men's icy feet. Every man was festooned with grenades and ammunition pouches. As a star shell burst over the trench, it showed men and officers alike to have blackened hands and faces.

The young gunner crouched alongside Harry gave his arm a nudge. 'It's the captain, Sarge. Comin' to remind us we're fighting for King and Country.'

Harry, who was smoking a Woodbine, turned to watch Chadwick's approach. Although the officer's face faded as the star shell burned out, excitement and anticipation sounded in his every word as he addressed Harry's section.

'We take off in ten minutes, chaps. Do your best not to make a sound as you go out. It's imperative the Aussies get the wire cut and we're in position before Jerry gets wind of us. Keep close to Sergeant Miles and do everything he tells you.' His glance moved on to Harry. 'Don't forget your signals when you occupy your end of the redoubt, Sergeant. We must know when each section is

388

in position. But no giveaways until the position is taken. All right?'

As Harry nodded, the officer turned back to the silent men. 'I know this isn't going to be an easy job – Jerry's too well dug-in for that – but it's a necessary one if the rest of the Battalion are going to have an easier time than they had last July. So I want you all to do your best. If you do, I'm certain it'll all work out according to plan.'

Harry watched him wade back along the trench to his own section, reflecting how even in wading boots and battle order he managed to look elegant. His thoughts were interrupted by the young gunner again. 'You hear that, Sarge? It's going to go to plan! Which if I know the Army, means we're all going to have our arses shot off.'

The gunner was White, the young country lad. Reliable under fire, always cheerful, he was popular among the men and there had been no jealously in Harry's section when Harry had made him his No. 1. While he had come to rely on the youngster's dependability, he had also often wondered if his cheerfulness was not equally important to him, holding off as it sometimes did the darkness of his moods.

As Chadwick disappeared down the trench, Harry took a glance over the sandbags. Even in the darkness their objective could be seen: a cluster of bleached ruins that stood out starkly against the black horizon. Like old tombstones, Harry thought, each waiting for a second interment.

Rumour said it had once been a French brewery but three years of war had reduced it to shattered ruins and rat-filled cellars. A brewery whose name was unknown to the men who faced it and yet whose existence was a threat to them all. Some hundred yards in advance of the German Front Line, it had been turned into a strong-point by the enemy and to date had resisted every attack made on it. With its cellars reinforced, with pillboxes cemented to its thick stone walls, it had risen like a phoenix after every bombardment and with its forward position enabling its gunners to pour deadly enfilading fire to left and right, it had defied every infantry attempt to encircle it, as the hundreds of bodies rotting in the winter slime testified.

However, with an Allied offensive planned along the entire sector in a week's time, its capture or destruction was imperative. As brute force had failed to achieve this purpose, it had been decided that stealth and surprise should be tried instead and it had been the misfortune of A Company to be chosen for that role. Because it was believed the redoubt was manned by machine gunners and storm troopers only and because the more men that were used the greater the risk of detection, it had been decided an attack in company strength was adequate.

A Company were not alone however. During the war of attrition on the Somme Front, certain Allied units, in particular the Australians, had become specialists in night raiding. It was a form of warfare that took both nerve and a certain madness but the Australians had both in plenty and their fame had spread. Accordingly a crack unit of thirty men had been drafted in. Their task was to creep undetected across No Man's Land, cut gaps in the barbed-wire that protected the redoubt, and so open the way for A Company who would be guided by tapes to the entry points. After that it was hoped surprise would do the rest.

Chadwick and Harry, who was now the senior NCO in the unit, were to go out with the Australians, Chadwick on their left flank and Harry on their right. Their teams consisted of two Lewis guns apiece with three men to each gun, and their task was to attack and destroy the outer-most enemy gun-posts who could otherwise pour enfilading fire on the attacking force. Chadwick would have liked to take more firepower out with him but the four Vickers guns provided by the Machine Gun Corps had been ordered to stay back, both to provide support fire or covering fire if the attacking force was driven back.

As another star shell burst, Harry glanced at his watch. Although his heart was beating slightly faster than usual, he had nothing of the excitement and fear of his earlier days. He heard a whisper alongside him. 'How much longer, Sarge?'

'Two minutes,' he said.

White's whisper was full of admiration. 'How do you keep so cool, Sarge? I'm shaking like a bleeding jelly.'

The words were out before Harry could check them. 'You're lucky, lad.'

'Lucky? I'm peeing myself, Sarge. You call that lucky?'

Harry did not answer. With the star shell still burning, he took another glance over the sandbags. Black bundles that had once been men could be seen lying both in front of the redoubt and to either side of it. At least their presence would not be wasted, he thought as he sank back. Their numbers should adequately hide a hundred and fifty living men crawling among them.

The star shell dropped into the mud and fizzled out. As darkness returned, Harry heard a word being passed along the line of tense men. A hoarse whisper came from his No. 2, a thickset, ex-bricklayer named Freeman. 'The Aussies are on their way, Sarge!'

Although there was no moon and the sky was overcast, Harry could just see dark shapes slithering over the sandbags. He glanced round. 'Time to go! Stay right behind me and keep it quiet.'

Heaving up his Lewis gun, he dropped over the sandbags and waited until the rest of his party joined him. A moment later two half-frozen Royal Engineers, planted there earlier, guided him through a gap in the barbed-wire. Obeying their urgent whispers not to disturb the alarm tins dangling from its coils, the six-man party emerged a minute later into the evil-smelling expanse of mud and shell craters that reached out to their objective.

All the men had a feeling of nakedness now and, obeying orders, went down on all fours before moving forward. To their left they could just see the right flank of the Australian party. Every man carrying a weapon had a rag tied round its muzzle. The explosion of a .303 cartridge created a pressure of twenty tons to the square-inch. If a bullet were checked, even for a hundredth of a second by mud in the barrel, the withheld pressure could explode the breech and blow a man's head off.

Harry could feel a breeze on his cheek now. Although it carried the stench of the battlefield he knew the Austra-lians would welcome it. Blowing diagonally towards the German Lines it was fresh enough to make the enemy sentries believe it responsible for an occasional jangle of their alarm tins.

He had not crawled thirty yards before another star shell flowered above. As he flattened himself, he saw a shapeless black mound not ten feet away. Small creatures were crawling over it and as he lay motionless, one gave a squeak and ran over his outstretched arm. The smell was almost overpowering and he heard White gagging behind him. Whispering for him to keep quiet, he waited until the shell plopped out, then caught hold of his Lewis gun and began his painful crawl again.

To every man in the assault force, the sector seemed unnaturally still, the occasional, distant chatter of machine guns only serving to accentuate the silence. With their heavy equipment, the two hundred yards they had to crawl seemed endless. Nor was weariness their only problem. Rubble that cut and scratched unprotected limbs was everywhere: broken bricks, shards of shrapnel, vicious lengths of barbed-wire. By the time Harry was forty yards from the silent redoubt, he was soaked in sweat despite the cold wind. Reaching a shellhole, he motioned his section into it and whispered his instructions.

'We'll get our guns ready but no one fires until I give the order. Not a sound beforehand or those poor bastard Aussies will be murdered.' He turned to Dodson, the gunner of his second team. 'Take the shellhole next to this, Len. Then we won't both go west if they start to mortar us.'

Dodson chose one fifteen yards to Harry's left. With both shellholes full of water, men had no choice but to stand in it while the Lewis guns, supported on ammunition boxes, were rested on the rims of the craters. With their respective teams huddled alongside them with fresh ammunition pans ready, Harry and Dodson sank behind their guns and waited.

The southern end of the redoubt, where two pillboxes were known to dominate the surrounding area, was directly ahead of the two teams. The silence, broken only by an occasional bluster of wind that jangled the alarm tins on the German wire, seemed to grow as they listened. As the minutes slipped past, men began shivering as their wet clothes chilled in the wind.

The darkness appeared denser on their left, hiding from them the Australians who by this time should be cutting the wire. Harry was wondering where Chadwick had placed his section. If he had found suitable cover, he should be roughly a hundred and fifty yards to the left, ready to attack the pillboxes at the other end of the redoubt.

A further two minutes passed, drawing men's nerves to breaking point. Harry found the effort of trying to pierce

393

the darkness was making his eyes water. As he lifted a muddy hand to wipe them, three star shells burst almost simultaneously over the redoubt.

It was the signal for all hell to break loose. Shouts of alarm came from the redoubt, blood-curdling yells from the Australians, followed almost immediately by the explosions of grenades and mortar shells and the vicious chatter of machine guns. In the light of the starshells and the explosions, the Australians, with the element of surprise gone, could be seen as black silhouettes hurling themselves recklessly over the sandbagged parapets.

Harry could see his targets clearly now. Stabbing flames were jetting out from two embrasures almost directly ahead of him. The pillboxes, which were built into the ruins, were staggered, one at the corner nearest to him, the other at the opposite far side. A barricade of barbed-wire ran round the entire perimeter of the ruin.

Harry's team was not the target of the German gunners. They were hosing enfilading fire at the Australians and A Company, who were now pouring through the gaps cut in the wire. As men were seen stumbling and collapsing, Harry shouted his order to Dodson. 'Take the one on the left, Len! Make it quick.'

With star shells coming up in clusters now, neither man had problems in lining up his sights. Fixing his on the nearest embrasure, Harry fired a long but careful burst. As the flashes ceased, White, crouching alongside him, gave a yell of triumph. 'Great shooting, Sarge! You've got 'em.'

Hoping he was right, Harry turned his Lewis gun on the second embrasure that Dodson was already attacking. As he took sight on it the flashes lost their elongated pattern and became bright winking dots, a certain sign the enemy gunner had taken warning and had turned his fire on them.

The tables were turned now: behind his concrete pill-box the German gunner held every advantage. As splashes of mud came racing in their direction, both Harry and Dodson were forced to cease firing and duck down. Even so, Harry was not dissatisfied with the result. The enfilading fire that might have wiped out the entire right flank of the attacking force had been temporarily lifted and with luck men should now be pouring into the redoubt.

However, even if Chadwick were successful on the left flank – and Harry had little doubt that he would be – one machine gun was still enough to keep the redoubt from being over-run until the Germans launched a counter attack from their nearby trenches. With their usual thoroughness the Germans had sited the second gun to cover such an emergency and with Harry's two Lewis guns silenced, it was already resuming that role.

Finding their guns undamaged Harry and Dodson began firing at the stabbing flashes again but this time neither man had success. Either the angle of fire was wrong or the gunner had better protection: whatever the reason the Maxim continued to fire. Worse, as if he had realised he was safe from the Lewis guns, the enemy gunner was now giving his full attention to the attacking infantry. Seeing the bloody damage he was doing, Harry knew what his next move had to be and turned to Freeman. 'How far can you throw your smoke grenades, Les? Can you reach the wire?'

Freeman unclipped two grenades from his webbing. 'I think so, Sarge. Near enough, anyway.'

'All right, do what you can. Quickly!'

Throwing back a burly arm, Freeman threw in roundarm fashion. A black silhouette against the frantic sky, the grenade landed about five yards from the wire barricade, jumped as its fuse exploded, then began pouring out grey smoke. Grasping Harry's intention, Dodson called on his team to help. Thirty seconds later the pillbox disappeared in the drifting smoke.

Snatching up his Lewis gun, Harry turned to White and Freeman. 'Come on. We must get nearer that Maxim.'

Glancing at one another, the two men crawled from the shellhole and followed him. Fifteen yards to their left, Dodson was also urging his men forward, his No. 2 throwing smoke grenades as he went.

The smoke achieved its twin purpose of drawing the Maxim fire from the helpless infantry and giving cover to Harry's team. But machine guns are not like rifles: they can traverse and kill men they cannot see. Acutely conscious of his danger, the enemy gunner swung round his Maxim and hosed his fire from right to left.

It was the unfortunate Dodson and his team that ran first into the hail of steel. His No. 2 gave a grunt, then fell with the disjointedness of a man already dead before he hit the mud. His No. 1 gave a scream and fell like a cripple whose crutch has been kicked away. Dodson caught the bullets in his lower body and with his knees buckling fell on his face, his Lewis gun sticking into the soft mud like a spear.

The procession of fire, rapid though it was, gave Harry and his team just time to throw themselves down. As bullets swept over them, Harry gave a shout. 'Run for the wire!'

Running for their lives, slipping in the mud, they reached the barricade seconds before the enemy gunner began his backward traverse. With wire, a broken wall and the silenced pillbox between them and the German gunner, the three men knew now they were safe until they entered his field of fire again.

With no way of knowing whether he had wiped out the two machine gun teams or not, the enemy gunner commenced his enfilading fire again. Removing an ammunition drum, Harry turned to White for a new one. 'Stay here, both of you. I'm going to try to put that Maxim out of action. If I'm lucky, join me. If I'm not, get back to our lines as fast as you can.'

White caught his arm. 'Don't try it, Sarge. You haven't a chance.'

Aware of the youth's affection for him, Harry attempted a smile. 'I think I have. But no heroics if I'm unlucky. Get back home fast. That's an order.'

Looking distressed, the youngster opened his mouth to plead again, then turned away. Slapping his shoulder, Harry gripped the Lewis and began crawling along the foot of the wire.

The stabbing flashes of the Maxim came into his sight a few seconds later. Expecting it to swing round on him at any moment he squirmed gingerly forward, hoping no mines had been laid round the perimeter of the redoubt.

He was no more than fifteen yards from the pillbox when a green Very light, arcing up among the star shells, told him Chadwick had achieved his objective. He felt no surprise. Chadwick was indestructible.

Yet even Chadwick's success would count for nothing unless he could put this one deadly Maxim out of action. The evidence followed almost immediately after the thought. With the northern pillboxes silenced and their backs safe from attack, the British troops believed they could now move along the redoubt. As Harry paused for breath, half a dozen of them appeared, climbing over broken walls and peering into cellars for enemy survivors. As an NCO yelled for them to advance, the Maxim moved a few degrees and the men were tossed aside like broken dolls.

Harry knew that time was short: a German counter attack from their Front Line trenches could be only minutes away. He was very near the pillbox now but to fire into it he would need to leap to his feet to clear the wire barricade and reach the embrasure. In the end it would be decided by who had the faster reactions: he who had to swing up his Lewis and make certain his bullets entered the narrow embrasure or the German gunner who had only to redress his Maxim. Knowing he would only have time for one burst, Harry felt the odds were heavily in favour of the German.

The short but regular bursts from the Maxim told him the gunner was experienced. Needing to conserve ammunition until relief came, he was just doing enough to keep the assault force from advancing the full length of the redoubt, which would give his countrymen a foothold for their counter-attack.

Harry's first thought was that if the intervals between the bursts were regular enough – and gunners did develop such habits – he might be able to judge when to leap up and fire. Crawling forward until he was right beneath the embrasure, he waited. He had no idea whether he was beyond the vision of the gun crew or whether they had only to lean forward to see him. Putting the thought from his mind, he held the Lewis ready and began counting the seconds between each burst of fire.

The Maxim sounded deafening at such close quarters. A raking burst and then a pause – one . . . two . . . three . . . The gun muzzle moved a couple of inches and the jets of flame came again. Then the next pause – one . . . two . . . three . . . As tight as a coiled spring he lay counting. A third pause – one . . . two . . . As the Maxim hammered again he knew he could not rely on the time interval. His only option now was to wait until the Maxim was re-loaded and even that was something an experienced crew could do in seconds.

He felt the moment must come soon now. Cordite

fumes and high explosive fumes caught his throat and stung his eyes as he waited and counted. When a full minute of firing passed he began to believe the Maxim must already have been re-loaded.

Its hammering checked again. One . . . two . . . three . . . four . . . five . . . Not daring to think, Harry leapt to his feet, swung up the Lewis and fired.

He did not hit the embrasure immediately: he saw concrete chips flying from the cowl above and heard the eerie whine of bullets. Dragging down the muzzle in panic, he overcompensated for a split second and then, from the change of sound, knew that his bullets were richochetting around the inside of the pillbox.

He held down the trigger for a full five seconds before dragging the Lewis away. Weak from shock, he sank down in the mud. Hearing shouts, he lifted his head and saw White and Freeman running towards him. In the luminous, unreal light he could see the look of relief on the youth's blackened face.

Then the nightmare happened. There was a sudden roar like a passing express train and a long tongue of flame leapt out from behind one of the redoubt's shattered walls. It struck both running men head on and for a moment they vanished in a great cloud of oily black smoke. Then the roar ceased, the flame leapt back like a reptile's tongue, and the living torches that had once been men were revealed. One was screaming, a thin scream that pierced Harry's brain like a surgeon's probing needle.

Along with his flesh, Freeman had been left no eyes. Staggering forward, with arms waving, he collapsed into a shellhole. As his body sank into the water, a white cloud of steam arose.

White, however, could still see and, worse, could still think. Rolling over and over in the wet mud, he doused the flames, then struggled to his knees and began crawling towards Harry. He covered a few yards before his strength gave out and he collapsed.

Forgetting his own danger, Harry ran towards him. The smell of burnt flesh made him gag as he dropped to his knees. As he turned the youngster over, the buckles of his carbonised webbing burned his hand and brought him hideous imaginings of the agony imprisoned in the quivering body.

All the boy's hair had been burnt off and his glaring eyes were the only living things in a blackened lymphatic mask. As they pleaded with Harry and the shredded mouth shaped two words Harry gave a cry of horror and tried to pull away. 'No, lad! For Christ's sake, no!'

Two arms, hideously seared, clutched him with unnatural strength. With sweat running down his face, Harry would have welcomed a German bullet as an act of mercy. Instead the youth's head rose from the mud and his agonised eyes made their plea again. For a moment earth and sky darkened for Harry. Then, with a cry of pure despair, he snatched up the Lewis gun and fired a long downward burst. Then, with another cry that was not human, he turned and ran towards the redoubt.

He found the two *Flammenwerfer* operators disarmed and being covered by a beefy Australian corporal. One had dropped the nozzle that had projected the flame, the other was standing to one side of a large tank that contained the inflammable oil. When the Australian saw Harry's wild figure and his expression, he gave a shout. 'Go easy, mate! They've given themselves up.'

If Harry heard him, he took no notice. Seeing his intention, one German began pleading for mercy. The other showed desperate courage and drew himself erect. Before the Australian could grab him, Harry fired a long scything burst. When the Lewis gun ceased firing, both

400

men were dead and unrecognisable amongst the rubble.

It was only then that sanity returned to Harry. Dropping the Lewis gun he sank to his knees. Grenades were still exploding, shots were still being fired, but he heard nothing but the screaming of his mind. It took a familiar voice to make him lift his head, to see Chadwick standing over him. 'You shouldn't have done that, Miles. They were only doing their job.'

As Harry's head bowed again, Chadwick sounded perplexed. 'You're not praying, are you, Miles?'

Some untouched cell in Harry's mind saw the irony in the question. He did not recognise his voice. 'No, sir. I'm not praying.'

Chadwick sounded relieved. 'You're a rum character, Miles, but there's no denying you've done a wonderful job today. In fact I'm recommending you for the Military Medal.'

Before Harry could speak, Chadwick turned to the Australian soldier. 'This sergeant's action saved many of your men, Corporal.' He motioned at the two enemy dead. 'I want you to forget you ever saw this.'

The Australian shrugged. 'That's fine by me, sir. They were only Germans anyway.'

They were the last words Harry heard before a 5.9 shell, heralding the German counter-attack, burst among the barbed-wire close by. He felt no pain. There was simply a dazzling flash and then oblivion.

Chapter 46

The French major was talking to a young white-coated doctor on the terrace of the military hospital. He was a stocky man in his late thirties, of medium height and with a fine-boned, thoughtful face beneath his peaked cap. His empty left sleeve was pinned back. With his sound arm he was indicating a solitary British soldier sitting reading on a bench at the far side of a well-kept lawn. Although he had a slight French accent, his English was good. 'You say he keeps asking to go back into action, Captain?'

The doctor, ten years younger, nodded. 'Yes, sir. He keeps refusing home leave.'

'Doesn't he get letters from home?'

'Oh, yes. That's the embarrassing thing. They come almost daily from his wife, but although he reads them over and over, he won't answer them. One of the nurses writes to her occasionally but, of course, she can't convince the poor woman he's not seriously injured.'

'But can't he be made to take leave?'

The young doctor hesitated. 'I suppose so, but Colonel Whitehead doesn't think it would be wise yet.'

'Why is that?'

'It's not his wounds. Apart from concussion, he only had a few bad bruises and a cracked rib and they're all well healed by this time.' The doctor gave a helpless gesture. 'The trouble is in his mind.'

'Are you saying he might have brain damage?'

'It's possible, I suppose, but there's no sign of any. He seems rational enough when he makes the effort to talk. But something seems to have gone.'

'The will to live, perhaps, Captain?'

The young doctor looked uncomfortable. 'It does appear that way sometimes although I feel that's a bit melodramatic.'

'War is melodramatic, Captain. War is pure melodrama.'

The Englishman gave an embarrassed laugh. 'Yes, I suppose you're right. Did you say your wife knows him?'

'Yes. He was billeted in our house last year. She came to see him when he was in here before. He had suffered a shock then, had he not?'

'Yes. His friend was executed. That was why Colonel Whitehead arranged for him to be sent back here when he heard about his mental condition. He felt there might be a link with that earlier shock.'

The Frenchman's eyes turned again to the solitary figure. 'And yet he has fought for another six months and more before this breakdown. Does that not suggest there is something else?'

'You mean another mental shock? Yes, it's the only explanation we can think of. But we've given up all hope of him speaking about it.' The young doctor gave an embarrassed laugh. 'To be honest, he's becoming something of a problem. We don't like forcing him to take leave in case it worsens his condition yet equally we feel he's in no state to return to the Front. But if he goes on demanding it, they're certain to take him sooner or later.'

'I understand he has got the Military Medal? And been recommended for a commission?'

'Yes. But he won't wear the medal and he doesn't want the commission because that would mean at least six months training back in England.'

'So he is bent on self-destruction,' the Frenchman mused. 'Tell me one last thing. Has he ever asked to see a priest or a padre?'

The young doctor frowned. 'It's odd you should ask that. A padre came to see him after he'd been with us a week and he worked himself up into such a state the padre had to leave.'

'I see. Thank you, Captain. Might I go and see him now?'

The man hesitated. 'I suppose it's all right if you've got the colonel's permission. Only you will be careful what you say, won't you? He gets upset very easily.'

'I will be most careful, Captain. Thank you.' Nodding his appreciation, the Frenchman descended the steps and crossed the lawn. 'Good afternoon, Sergeant. Might I have a word with you?'

Harry lowered the letter he was reading. As he made a half-hearted attempt to rise, the Frenchman put a hand on his shoulder. 'No, please. Keep your seat.' He motioned wryly at his empty sleeve. 'Although I might still be wearing my uniform, I do not rate a salute. The war is over for me.' He sank down on the bench beside the Englishman. 'You know who I am, don't you?'

Harry nodded. 'I think so. You're Pierre Levrey, Nicole's husband.'

'Correct, my friend. Since you have not answered her letters and also because I am a doctor, she has asked me to visit you.'

'How is she?' Harry asked. 'And Michelle?'

'They are both well and send their love. Michelle wanted to come with me. She thinks you are a fine English gentleman.'

For a moment the Englishman's smile was wistful. 'She's a lovely kid. Give her a kiss for me when you go back.'

'I will. And what about your wife and daughter Nicole has told me about? Are they well?'

'Yes. They seem to be.'

'They must miss you, Harry. But I am told you will be seeing them soon. Colonel Whitehead says he can discharge you any day now.'

There was a sudden silence. Levrey pretended not to notice the Englishman's change of expression. 'That is true, isn't it, Harry? You can go home any day now, can you not?'

Harry glanced away. 'I don't want leave. I want to get back to my unit.'

'But you have done enough for your country, my friend.' The Frenchman gestured at his empty sleeve again. 'You and I are wastage now. Others must come forward and step into our shoes.'

There was hostility now in the Englishman's frown. 'You perhaps but not me. I'm as fit to fight as I ever was and that's what I intend doing.'

Gazing at his sullen face, Levrey knew the confidence between them was as frail as a cotton thread and that his next question could well break it. 'Why, Harry?' he asked quietly. 'Is it because of the men you have killed? Has it made you feel unworthy to be with your beautiful wife and daughter again?'

Harry gave a start. 'What gave you that idea?'

Levrey shrugged. 'Perhaps because I am a doctor and have seen it in others. Not very often, it is true, but there are men sensitive enough to feel that way.' His pleasant voice turned wry. 'Perhaps I have even felt it myself.'

Harry stared at him. 'You?'

'Yes. You do not know how I lost my arm, do you? It

405

happened when the enemy broke into our fort and began bayoneting my comrades. I went berserk, Harry. I picked up a revolver and emptied the chamber before they fired back and shattered my arm. I, a doctor who once swore the oath of Hippocrates, killed three men that day.'

Harry was giving Levrey his full attention now. 'How did you feel?'

'How did I feel? For a few seconds I was exultant. I had a feeling of power. I was wildly alive. God help me, I wanted to shout with triumph.'

Harry's voice was suddenly hoarse. 'So you have felt it too?'

Levrey nodded. 'Yes. I learned at that moment why men have wars. They like them because in battle they feel more alive than at any other moment in their lives.' Then humour quirked the Frenchman's mouth and changed his mood. 'Not that my battle ecstacy lasted long because the others were quick to shoot me. But I knew at that moment that man is the savagest animal on earth. Given the appropriate conditions, we all kill with pleasure.'

During his confession Levrey had imagined he saw relief in the Englishman's eyes but the bitter reply that followed seemed to deny it. 'Amen to that. That's why there's no hope for us.'

'No, Harry. You and I have felt shame. There must be thousands of others who feel the same. We can learn to handle the beast if we try. But first we must admit it exists in the meekest of us and structure our lives and society to contain it.'

For a moment Harry remembered his mother and her gentle philosophy. Then he gave a laugh of contempt. 'You believe we can do that? When we're in the middle of the greatest war in history? When men are slaughtering one another in thousands every day?'

'Yes, I do. And we must, Harry. If we do not, then

sooner or later, if not in this war then in another, we shall completely destroy ourselves. And in all likelihood we shall do it with the same sense of power and exultation that I felt when killing those three Germans.'

Harry stared at him, then turned away. 'You're an idealist. And idealism is dead. This war has killed it.'

The despair in his voice made Levrey wince. Knowing he had lost him again, he said quietly: 'Of course there are other things a man can lose in war than just the belief in his pacifism. Some men lose their faith, as one of my comrades did. In the early days he would kneel at his bunk every night and pray, no matter how the others mocked him. Then the killing began and I saw his faith wither before my eyes. Now he spits at every crucifix he sees. That man has lost more than an arm or leg, Harry.'

He did not miss the hoarseness that returned to the Englishman's voice. 'Where is he now?'

'Back at the Front. Like a drug addict he wants more of the drug that cost him his faith. He wants to go on fighting until he is killed. That is how drugs work, Harry. We believe we are damned and so we plunge with the desperation of the damned into the very acts that have given us that belief.'

There was dislike on Harry's face as he turned back to the Frenchman. 'He doesn't just believe he's damned. He is damned. He's become an unfeeling killing machine and he knows it.'

'But wait, Harry. Have you ever stopped to think what kind of people these are? They are not coarse or unfeeling men. On the contrary they are the poets among us. Men born with the cross of imagination that makes them carry the pain of others throughout their lives. They are the ones who question the mercy of their God when they see the sorrow and pain around them. Not only in the world of man, mark you, but in the animal world also. To some of

407

them that suffering makes the cross too heavy to bear. It is the insensitive or unimaginative men who find no fault in the Creation, Harry.'

Harry shook his head. 'No. They are the ones with faith.'

'True faith or blind faith, my friend? How can it be wrong to question cruelty, whether it is a cat playing with a bird or a man torturing his own kind?'

Suddenly, Harry believed he understood. 'You lost your faith too, didn't you?'

Levrey nodded. 'For a long time I thought I had. But then I began asking myself if I had not drawn my faith from the wrong places, like the stone temples that echo the word of man as well as God. Men have such a gift for using religion for their own purposes, Harry. Haven't you noticed that during this war?'

Harry gave another start. Then he frowned. 'But if you can't draw your faith from the Church, what else is left?'

Levrey made a Gallic gesture at the spring burgeoning around them. 'What else, Harry? The great mystery of life is left. The thing that stands behind everything. The mystery that awes and brings homage from the greatest of atheists.' As he paused, a jackdaw flew past them and landed on the bough of a chestnut tree. Smiling, Levrey motioned at the tree and its white candles that were quivering in the sunlight. 'Spring, Harry, with all its glories! How easy to worship for its sake alone.'

As Harry's eyes searched his face, Levrey felt hope for the first time. Then the sound of an engine caught his attention. At the far side of the lawn, a military ambulance was drawing up in the courtyard. As both men watched, four heavily-bandaged soldiers were lifted down and carried into the chateau. Hearing Harry make a comment, Levrey turned back and saw his earlier mood had returned. Although dismayed, he pretended not to notice. 'I must not forget the message Nicole gave me. She wants you to promise that one day you will bring your wife and daughter to France to visit us. Will you, Harry?'

The Englishman evaded the question. His eyes were distant again. 'Thank her for all she did. Tell her I'll always be grateful. And please give Michelle a kiss for me.'

Certain now that he had failed, Levrey sighed and rose to his feet. 'I'll give them your message.' As Harry rose with him, he held out his hand. 'Goodbye, my friend. *Puissiez vous trouver Dieu par vous méme.*'

Harry stood watching him cross the lawn. A second jackdaw appeared and joined its mate on the chestnut bough. A lark, disturbed by Levrey's footsteps, soared upwards and poured its liquid notes into the warm sunlight. The sound seemed to penetrate the womb of the watching man's mind and bring alive a hundred memories: his grandfather's cottage, a gently-flowing river, a dragonfly, a girl with long, golden hair. As a butterfly landed on a nearby bush, he saw Mary's white arms reaching upwards and the emptiness inside him turned into a sudden, terrible hunger. Like a man regaining his sight, he ran forward, his cry ringing across the lawn.

'Pierre, wait! Tell Nicole we will visit you one day. Tell her that I'm going home too!'